KNOW NOTHING

Also available in

SCRIBNER**SIGNATURE**EDITIONS

ON EXTENDED WINGS *by Diane Ackerman*

GROWING UP RICH *by Anne Bernays*

SOUTH STREET *by David Bradley*

THE TENNIS HANDSOME *by Barry Hannah*

WHAT I KNOW SO FAR *by Gordon Lish*

DEAR MR. CAPOTE *by Gordon Lish*

PERU *by Gordon Lish*

ELBOW ROOM *by James Alan McPherson*

THE MISFITS AND OTHER STORIES *by Arthur Miller*

VOICES AGAINST TYRANNY *edited by John Miller*

COOL HAND LUKE *by Donn Pearce*

PRIDE OF THE BIMBOS *by John Sayles*

BLOOD TIE *by Mary Lee Settle*

THE LOVE EATERS *by Mary Lee Settle*

THE KISS OF KIN *by Mary Lee Settle*

THE CLAM SHELL *by Mary Lee Settle*

PRISONS *by Mary Lee Settle*

O BEULAH LAND *by Mary Lee Settle*

THE SCAPEGOAT *by Mary Lee Settle*

THE KILLING GROUND *by Mary Lee Settle*

ALMOST JAPANESE *by Sarah Sheard*

20 UNDER 30 *edited by Debra Spark*

STATE OF GRACE *by Joy Williams*

MEDITATIONS IN GREEN *by Stephen Wright*

KNOW NOTHING

by

Mary Lee Settle

SCRIBNER **SIGNATURE** EDITION

CHARLES SCRIBNER'S SONS · NEW YORK
1988

Charles Scribner's Sons
Macmillan Publishing Company
866 Third Avenue, New York, NY 10022
Collier Macmillan Canada, Inc.

This is a work of fiction. Names, characters, places, and incidents either are the product of the author's imagination or are used fictitiously. Any resemblance to actual events or persons, living or dead, is entirely coincidental.

Library of Congress Cataloging-in-Publication Data

Settle, Mary Lee.
Know nothing / Mary Lee Settle.—1st Scribner signature ed.
p. cm. — (Scribner signature edition)
ISBN 0-684-18847-3 (pbk.)
1. United States—History—Civil War, 1861–1865—Fiction.
I. Title.
PS3569.E84K6 1988
813'.54—dc19
87-35930
CIP

First Scribner Signature Edition 1988
Originally published in hardcover by The Viking Press, 1960
Reprinted by arrangement with Farrar, Straus & Giroux

10 9 8 7 6 5 4 3 2 1

Printed in the United States of America

Cover artwork: Wet Fields and Twilight, *by James Winn; courtesy of the Struve Gallery, Chicago*

To U.J.B.

who lives compassion without speaking

who understands injustice as a weakness

CONTENTS

There is a time wherein one man ruleth over another to his own hurt.

—ECCLESIASTES 8:9

KNOW NOTHING

BOOK ONE

July 29–July 30, 1837

Chapter One

UNCLE TELEMACHUS told about water and women, how they sank a man, weak soft, tears and water, rot and win. He said so. He said, "Ifn the river don't git ye, a woman will. . . ."

He said, "A big catfish wait down in the dark, big ole nigger-belly layin in the mud coolin that ole slick hide, and a great big mouth open, Lord God almighty one-two feet across . . . open real wide, sick of black meat, the big nigger-belly, she like a little bit of white meat fer a change. So your paw's done put ye in the river this mornin. I do declare . . ."

By eleven o'clock the hot hard Virginia sun was blinding and heavy. Johnny sat under it, a tiny figure huddled in the stern of a crawling skiff on the Great Kanawha. His father sat in the bow, waiting, glancing over his nigger Jim's broad shiny black shoulder from time to time, willing him. His big-brimmed hat shadowed his face and made his eyes look sunk. Johnny could tell his father thought he wasn't anything but a little molly, the way he sat there and couldn't make up his mind. He made himself look again at the moving water.

His eyes were charmed by it as by a snake. One bright dragon-fly, graceful ghost, two dragons, one on top of the other, softly touched the shining surface. Toey had told Johnny, whispered what that meant, and he slapped her face for it but she didn't tell. The water held them up. The water was alive. He could see it breathe.

It held Jesus up, too, and the skiff. If it could hold them all, that live water, where the big nigger-belly was pushing it up from below and the current pulsed under the skiff floor, maybe he could race across it, safe to Minna, standing big and black and solid, far away on the shore under the willows. If only he had faith, it would happen. The skiff drifted, turned a little. He could hear the water suck and lap under the floor. Johnny clasped his naked arms and pinched hard for comfort.

"Johnny, it's time," his father called, impatient. "Ain't a thing to bother you. Just hold your nose, kick yourself up to the surface, and paddle for the shore."

Johnny whimpered once, like a dog; his hands stuck to the boat-side. He scrunched nearer and nearer the edge of the seat, his fingers white, biting into the safe wood.

"You don't want me to have to throw you in, do you?"

The water was all there was, no shore, no sun, just that moving darkness, waiting.

He waited for himself to move; his father's eyes waited near him. Jim waited with the oars up and dripping. The whole world seemed to stop and wait in the sun, listening to the water lap. An upriver cat's-paw brushed the surface, ruffled it. The distant trees turned the silver sides of their leaves, as if they were impatient to wait so long, then turned back, green and quiet again. The breeze made gooseflesh rise on his arms. He made himself lift his behind, and could feel the flesh unsticking from the seat. He didn't dare look back at his father again. He let himself fall forward because they all expected it.

It didn't hold him. The light disappeared upward; he slipped down, down through the heavy dark. Wet, heavy water-fear held his heart, hugged his chest. Cold black choked him, forced him downward. He could feel something flick past his stomach, and drew his legs up in a spasm. Another live thing was there, and he knew he was trapped, knew the big nigger-belly catfish was coming nearer, its whiskers floating in the darkness, ready to sting, to caress and cling to his body, its big ugly mouth with its thick smooth lips and its long mustache opening, its tendrils moving slowly, searching for white meat, a tender piece of white meat. Weeds slid over him seeking his ears, his nose, his eyes, his tender crotch, to wrap, to hold, to keep him in the wet dark. He fought at last, kicked at them, wilder and wilder, opened his mouth to scream for his pa and let the water into his head, kept on kicking it away, flailing with one arm while the other hand clutched at his nose, kicking the mud, weeds, fish, traps away from his body, his eyes tight shut, thrusting away the blackness, the weight, all animal now, fighting away the nigger-belly.

The surface freed his head, let him gulp the air. His hands pawed of their own will to keep him floating. He laid his head back and gasped at where the air and sun broke over him, paddled away from the deep darkness, not toward pa and the skiff, but toward the shore. He thrashed his way, fighting the river; the spray from his flying hands whipped into his eyes and down his throat.

But the water had stopped fighting him. The shore inched nearer. He could hear the skiff oars splash behind him. Now he had to get away from that, too; paddle fast, get away before the big lid floated over him, the big lid which was the skiff, his father's broad back.

His feet touched sandy bottom and he tried to run to where Minna was waiting on the shore. A sheet of water clung to his eyes, ran down his blind face as he stood up and waded, the water weighting his legs. Then he was free, wild, running on the warm sand, caught and held in Minna's big black safe arms. He hoped she knew it was the water and not tears that streamed down over his face and body.

He could hear her crooning over him. "Swum! Lil ole Johnny swum like a fish. Lil ole Johnny-Cake done licked the river. Hold still, let me wipe you. Hold yourself still."

He twisted in her dear warm arms and looked when he heard the skiff nosing in to the bank. His father stood up in the boat and stepped ashore, his face high in the trees, the river stretched behind him.

"Son," he told him, "you've licked the river." He sounded serious. Johnny didn't know why. He felt so safe; the sun and Minna's arms protected his shoulders, a dark tent.

"Come here, son." His father turned his back again and stood watching the river.

"Go on, mind your paw." Minna took away her arms, and all exposed again he trudged over and stood beside the tall figure. Neither watched the other, just watched the water where Jim was tying the skiff to a tree trunk.

In front of them, the wide band of the river spread, now almost motionless, except for its breathing, catching the sun in patches, and tiny swirls flirting against the sand. Near the upriver bend a side-wheeler was turning slowly, followed by a ribbon of cloudy flying water, a white toy against the green Alleghenies which seemed to touch at both ends of the long river-bend and make a protecting circle around the valley of Beulah. The boat moseyed, directionless, its wood lace decks like the summer house at Beulah, its red flags arrogant against the lush green of midsummer. Johnny could see a black barge at the opposite bank where small men moved around a deck swarming with hogs. Above the river flies and the delicate slap of water, he could hear a shote scream, giving pitch for the other shotes like Ma did in church, and they all took it up because Johnny Catlett, son of Mr. Peregrine Lacey Catlett of Beulah, little old Johnny-Cake, black Minna's sweet potato, Ma's mixed blessing, had licked the Great Kanawha, naked as a jaybird, with his small bare hands.

"Son," his father said again. Johnny looked up but his father didn't look back. He stood in judgment, his worried blue eyes sweeping from upriver down. "There's our lifeline. She can be mean, but she ain't a damn bit meaner than her mother nature, and she's a hellcat, God knows. We wait on her, we just wait on her, that's all."

He sounded almost mad when he said it. It wasn't anything new, what he told him. Johnny had waited, too, waited for the river boats to be released by the water's rise, when all of Beulah, black and white, would run down to the river at the sound of the first whistle of the year. He even prayed for water sometimes after daily prayers and self-questionings, please God, please let the water come. He fidgeted to get away but his father reached down and laid his hand on his sun-dried shoulder.

"When she's down we suffer; when she gets high and hungry . . ."

He could hardly believe it now, seeing the river there, calm and green, how furious and brown she'd been in the spring, when he sneaked off to see the flooded fields, a great sheet of brown water over the bottom-land, with dead sheep and cows caught in low branches, swollen twice their size. He'd seen what he thought was a new kind of boat, but it wasn't. It was a covered bridge floating downriver, that had cost the James and Kanawha Company eighteen thousand dollars. He liked it best when the Kanawha came right up and licked the porch of the mansion at Beulah and waited there, sucking the locust trees and the cedars of Lebanon. He and his brother Lewis found a hogshead barrel-lid and paddled around the porch until they got a licking.

Of course he didn't suffer when the river was down. He just forgot it. The grown people would tiptoe as if there were sickness in the house. "The river's down." He could hear it like a dirge. Sometimes he thought it was sick, the way it shrank and turned away, and wouldn't let the boats come. They talked about it in the same way, too. When he was sick, and Ma put her cool thin hand on his head, she said, "It's down a little now," or, with her voice shaking, "Minna, it's going up. Oh, my darling boy!"

That embarrassed him but at least she called him her darling, just like the baby.

"Are you listening, son?" his father asked.

"Yessir," Johnny told him.

"God in His Providence saw fit to give your family bottom-land along the river, and put our people under our care. . . ."

He liked the way Minna told him that better. She said, "Listen here, Marse Johnny, we owns this here valley. We owns the mose people, and the mose horses, and the mose cows, and the mose land. We ships the best salt and we got the mose plates and furniture. I knows, I done been a heap of places and seed. So don' you go actin like po whites ain't got nothin." That made him feel like the Knights of Old.

"Go on back to Minna. You ain't listening to a word." His father slapped his behind and laughed. "By God, there ain't a youngin of mine going to play around this river till they larn to swim. Now git.

"Jim," he called to the Negro standing patiently by the skiff. "Row me down to the west pasture. I want to see how bad the heifers have tramped the bank down." He climbed back into the skiff.

Johnny raced back to Minna. He wiggled and jumped while Minna put his pants on until she had to slap him, because he wanted so much to get back and tell somebody, anybody, that he had licked the river a year before Lewis had. Lewis hadn't done it until he was eight, and he'd had to be pushed.

On the same morning, the twenty-ninth of July, 1837, Brandon Lacey lounged on a rug overlooking the Great Kanawha, an hour's drive by carriage upriver from Beulah, ignoring his wife, Sally, who was twisting her rings around and around her frail little-girl fingers. If he thought about her, it was only an intruding wish, almost unconscious, that she stop the incessant twisting and make her servant Maria take her down to the water to wash the travel dust away and prepare herself. He stretched his long fine legs, looked out over the alien swift ungentle western river, and wanted for a second, after so long, to skip a stone, yawned, rejected that. Then his anger returned.

He took out his watch and noted that it was ten o'clock.

"What time is it?" Sally's weak, worried voice sounded far away.

"Ten o'clock," he muttered, trying to shut any more questions away by his tone. He wondered, bitterly, as he put the gold watch which had belonged to his Great-Grandfather Montague back into his fob pocket, if even that would have to go. Then he patted it and sought for the certainty that he had always had, had always prided himself on as a gentleman, what he called his "way of going." He could feel it permeating him, warming him like the July sun, and it left him relaxed to his bones with a sense of who, after all, he was. He was Brandon Lacey of Crawford's Landing. He was worth a million dollars in worked-out tidewater land and niggers. A ladybug crawled near his hand and he moved it over so she would jump on him for luck. He had always been rich, a word to be avoided; he had traveled; he knew as surely as he knew his step that certain things were his and always had been and always would be, as surely as the sun rose in the morning, as the world turned. The ladybug flew away.

But as the sun goes behind a cloud the surety left him and he knew, as he had known in moments of fear all the way across the terrible mountains from eastern Virginia, an excess of dead despair, panic so still he could not move for its weight. Panic. He blamed Jackson, he blamed Mr. Biddle of the United States Bank, he blamed his agent who had bought him stocks that weren't worth the paper they were written on; he even blamed the fate which had taught him to take the service of the world for granted. When he had run dry of blame, he prayed to God that Sally would not speak, for a minute, for just a minute.

Below him, beyond the trees, Napoleon, the coachman, was rubbing down the matched horses and watering them in the river. Even after the long trip across the Alleghenies, they looked sleek and sure with their whole finely bred bodies, standing pastern-deep in the water. Napoleon caressed rather than rubbed, concerned through his hands with their shadow-dappled rippling sensuous coats.

All the way to western Virginia the anger had grown as a new thing inside Brandon. He glanced at Sally, cousin, wife, still hearing her twittering voice, suppliant as he had been for the first time in their two satisfied, fully expected lives, heard it still, that gaiety with its sick edge of panic at Kregg's Crossing. . . .

"*They* won't let it happen," she had said, and patted his hand across the carriage; but they had let it happen.

High on the commanding cliffs of Albion above Kregg's Crossing where the Gloriana flowed into the upper James, they had sat with their Kregg kin behind the huge white columns of the mansion and looked down the great lawn. After the hundred-year-old English grace of the house at Crawford's Landing, Albion was, to Brandon, gross, republican, and rich, the grass groomed thick and heavy as the huge mansion with safe Kregg money. Where Lacey money danced and fluttered, Kregg money grew and matted, solid as the emerald turf. Even the Kregg boxwoods were fat and groomed, solemn and well fed, not a ragged branch allowed. At Kregg's Crossing across the Gloriana, through the virgin trees, the old Court House stood. Only its weather-beaten cupola with its faded clock, stopped long since, could be sighted through the carefully cut vista to show that there was any life for miles.

That was certainly no life at Albion, not what Brandon Lacey called life. Brandon Kregg, his cold-water-drinking cousin and brother-in-law, and his ugly wife, who was Sally's oldest sister, sat satisfied together, impregnable and sobering as the first foothills of the Alleghenies, pale blue bastions in the western distance. He wondered if it was the sternness of the mountains which made the people stern too. The farther west he traveled from the safe Tidewater, the soberer and more sinful the atmosphere. Brandon could have choked in sin. He also wanted a toddy like the very devil.

The Kregg kin sat preoccupied with pride, watching their one small son play solemnly on the lawn with his nurse. He heard his damned sister-in-law tell Sally again and again why she had the right as the eldest Crawford girl to use the name of Crawford for the brat, but when he tried to tell them what had happened, they paid so little attention to him after the *faux pas* of his admission that he still didn't believe that they had quite heard. At the tender touch of the word "money" they had both closed, protected as shellfish.

He had been so sure, and so had Sally, that they wouldn't let it happen, for pride if not for affection. Sally's sister was triumphantly kind and under the hopeless coldness of her unhelpful sympathy Sally dimmed and shrank.

They had left Albion five days before, Sally in tears as soon as the carriage drove away, and he too disheartened to give her the comfort she begged from him like a dog.

"Damn cold-water rock-ribbed Presbyterians," Brandon had muttered.

Sally stopped moaning long enough to say, "Hush that, Brandon. They're kin."

The Peaks of Otter seemed to loom in judgment above their frail carriage as the shadow of its wheels danced gaily along the pale dust of the turnpike.

At the Natural Bridge he watched Sally, knowing he could not keep her from saying it. He didn't.

"There isn't anything in all of Europe to compare with this natural wonder!" Brandon thought of the dark calm Borghese Gardens he would never see again, and made himself look down the gorge. Three hundred feet below, the water roared and flung itself, wild along the rocks. He wondered when it was that his pride in Sally's demanding innocence had turned to boredom, and that into new twinges of dislike. He watched her in her expected attitude, frail, pale, being lovely and awed at the edge of the cliff, one hand clutching a gnarled root of a huge dying tree, the wind whipping her Paris skirt. Pity, sick pity, chased the moment of dislike so that he muttered, "My dear, be careful," wrenching the words out of his obsessed thinking and making her smile gratefully.

Brandon had begun to loathe the endless rejecting barrier of the mountains, mile upon insane mile of winding wild roads past a few dismal log farms, the only relief from the desolation of the great woods. Sometimes he thought the only time they saw the sun at all was in the bleak groves of deadened trees, left to fall as he had been left to fall, his own sap source cut, his taproot of the past dying. They drove on and on down the always shadow-covered road, Sally making efforts from time to time to enjoy it, because she thought she ought to.

Once, when they were resting, some sort of cat screamed in the dark woods and released Sally's panic so that she sobbed like some weak animal herself, comforted after what seemed hours by Maria's sal volatile.

At the Spa at Egeria Springs in Dunkard's Valley they had a day of respite with the kind of people they had always known. During the evening stroll Brandon heard Sally across the meadow agreeing shrilly with the ladies about the magnificence of . . . When had the shrillness crept into her well-ordered pretty voice? Magnificent—mountains, mountains—magnificent. In his new bleak world the easy attitudes did not answer any more and, with nothing to replace them, he turned away in disgust, wanting to rage at nature and defeat as King Lear had raged. Sally, glancing up, had read the familiar petulance of his face and dropped her voice shyly, knowing he was annoyed.

Now, in the valley by the river, Brandon put his hand up to his already closed eyes as if to shade them. In the past he had thought her silliness so dear that she had cultivated it as carefully as her blond curls.

Sally couldn't keep still any longer. "Brandon." She touched his arm across the rug. Her timid insistence made him open his eyes. "What happened?" She didn't know how many times she'd whined the vague question.

"I've told you what happened. It wasn't *my* fault, Sally." He rolled away from her and readjusted his fawn trousers.

"I just can't take it in." She threatened to cry again but loose words tumbled instead of tears. "Everybody thought we were the luckiest . . ."

"Luckiest!" He had to laugh at the blackmail of her blaming disappointment.

Sally mistook the laughter for relief. "Oh, Brandon." She giggled, pleased and relaxed into familiarity again. "Won't Aunt Mamie Catlett be surprised? She hasn't seen me since Ma and Pa used to send me out to her because I was frail." She patted her lap gently.

Brandon smiled hopefully and said, "Peregrine's a good fellow, a true gentleman of the old—"

"Oh, *he's* a good fellow, but dear Lord knows who he married. None of us know Miss Leah. I hear she's from even farther West. Ohio! My mother always told me that people who didn't have any family had to get their names out of the Bible."

They made a little moan of pleasure together, because they had to, surrounded by the mountains and the fear; for a little while they had to be secure in the kind of judgment they were used to.

Sally looked sweetly sorry. "Of course they're plainer people than we are, and haven't had our advantages, but they're very kind."

Brandon laughed again, now at instead of with her. He could see her easy childish optimism rise as it always did, making her face vapid with hope. He got up and stretched. "I'm sure your backwoods Catlett kin are very kind," he teased, and walked away up the rugged slope to the carriage.

"They're not like that. They are Virginians even if they are transmontane, and they're your kin, too," Sally defended, mostly because Brandon had forgotten to help her to her feet. He wasn't listening. "At least they haven't let themselves be ruined," she muttered hopelessly to the back of his fine jacket. She, who had made the most dashing match of all the five Crawford sisters, struggled up, stepping on her wide skirt, began to twist her rings again, and tried to keep from crying.

"Maria," she called, annoyed, to the mulatto woman who sat on a stone near the water, watching Napoleon lead the now rested clean horses past her, and holding on to a tiny child to keep her from darting into their path.

She didn't hear.

"Maria!" Sally's voice sharpened. "Come and help me freshen up. Marse Brandon will watch Sara in the carriage."

Maria sighed.

Half an hour later the horses were harnessed, the carriage dusted, and Napoleon, so high and mighty that the lowest leaves of the trees brushed his Byronic cap, cast his whip with a prodigal, happy gesture along the square rumps of his beloved pair. They flung up their heads, wheeled, thundered in a new direction down the rutted dirt road of the western valley. Then he drew them back to a patient walk, saving them for their last proud charge into Beulah. No one inside the carriage noticed the change of pace; they shifted their positions a little and lapsed again into the timeless drowsiness of too long a journey.

Sally had thought so much that she was sure she could never think again. She yawned a little, looked out of the narrow carriage window, her face a small mask as her eyes sighted without focus through the forest trees which covered the rocky slopes so near her face that she could have reached out and touched the rocks next to the road. Even when the road ran under an overhanging ledge so wide that it seemed like a tunnel, she did not change her staring in the dimness. She ignored the others: the child Sara, who lay already asleep again with her head on Maria's lap; Brandon, who sat opposite, staring in much the same way, only at the floor. No one said a word within the carriage.

Maria still sweated, remembering the precipices of the maniac mountain road which Marse Brandon had insisted on whirling by, laughing at the two scared women, as if that would help his new anger. Maria, who had grown up with him, still couldn't believe he could be that way, but she was beginning to remember how he was when he was little, before he became such a fine young man and went all the way to Europe and even met royalty once without having to pay. She watched, out of the other window, the wide, calm river.

But Sally couldn't keep from thinking. She found her handkerchief in her sleeve and held it against her eyes to shut out the incessant marching trees. Brandon leaned forward and touched her lap as if he were gently prodding a sick pup. He said lightly, "It will be all right."

There was no answer. The words hung in the carriage for a long time, like a haze of dust.

So the Laceys from Crawford's Landing in eastern Virginia were carried on toward Beulah on the Great Kanawha to visit the last hope they were related to, what Brandon had called their backwoods Catlett kin.

Chapter Two

When Leah Catlett had plenty to do, her old alien hurt among the strangers receded and became a tiny gnat in her brain instead of possessing it. The piles of harsh cloth for the Negroes' clothes, the constant knocking at any door she sat behind, the impelling sense of daily crisis, sore throats, cuts, things dropped, broken, stolen, duties not done, evasions, confusion, the blacks who suddenly would be like strangers, all of this slipping out of her attempts at control, even with her constant wakeful tight awareness.

But the satisfaction of trying kept her listening to the busy swish of her skirts as she moved quietly from room to room of the big new house, or, grabbing her wide leghorn when all else failed, charged with her thin body against the rose garden, to catch and groom the malicious lovely plants, winning by the force of her fingers, caught and bloody from the briars, a pretty formal garden. Too taut and tired to enjoy it in the evening, she would watch from the observatory through shining waves of painful light from an incipient sick headache while Cousin Annie and Mrs. Catlett rolled slowly up the straight crossed paths in their full heavy skirts, too far away for her to hear them talking about the Savior.

All that cleansed daily what her husband jokingly called her Martha soul. But even now, right in the middle of the busy morning, the gnat returned, grew bigger. She hesitated, running up the stairs at Beulah, her warm cheeks faintly flushed from hurrying, her frail fingers drumming on the banisters as if they could not pause so quickly. The wide hall stretched below her, dim and silent. She took a shaky breath and sighed, almost knelt on the stairs to look into the nearly dark parlor. She could just make out the clock at a quarter past eleven. Its tick, insistent, quiet, was the only sound she heard, until, rising, her skirts rustled, shutting it out.

But she went more slowly up the stairs, paused at the landing to run her finger over the frame of a picture of a woman with loose hair, bending faintly across a tomb with a carved funeral urn under a cyprus tree. It was called *Sorrow*. She looked at her dusty fingertip, annoyed, went faster up the last stairs to the second floor, and flung open the door of her own chamber.

Her eyes lost their disciplined focus on household chores. She wandered to one of the front windows, blindly watched the trees, and finally let the homesickness at the back of her mind take over her body and tighten it, let the high loud whine of the locusts enter her head. She closed her eyes, shut out the morning, and let flow back her own always waiting town with its excitement of German and Irish voices, the noisy quays, the cloying blood smell of the Cincinnati yards where the hogs were slaughtered, screaming until there were times when the sound buffeted the town like waves.

She could still see her father, standing on the quay, his emaciated beloved saint's face stern with a sorrow Mr. Catlett didn't even notice.

"Remember"—her father had touched her arm—"you have certain beliefs, my daughter. What else can I say?" he finished almost in a wail. He spoke like the Bible where the spiritual half of his life was lived; the rest was lived at the stockyards. But then the lilt of the German violins for her wedding, singing in her excited nerves, drowned out that voice. She heard instead, shamed with impatience, the calls of the dockers, the easy sure voice of her new husband ordering his Negro Jim to find their room on the boat.

It was then that her father fell on his knees on the dock and called out loudly enough to hush all the voices. "Oh merciful God who hast vouchsafed to lead Thy servant Leah to forsake her old father and go into the land of slavery, keep Thou her heart and mind free of the evil snares. Watch over her, a stranger in the land of Egypt. Let her be a light in that wilderness, a warning to the heathen. Keep Thy stern hand upon her and the iron in her soul."

She had lifted him up, crying.

"Holy Jasus, thim Methodists," one of the Irish dock-workers said and laughed. She heard someone answer, "Hold your tongue, sir." It was Mr. Catlett who had said it, and now took her arm to lead her onto the riverboat. She tried to turn back once, but his hand tightened and she let herself be led on, dumbly. She looked back, though, to see her father standing watching Mr. Catlett with what, if she did not know his saintliness, she would have thought was hatred.

Slowly, full of fear, she was carried up the wide Ohio, past the groomed and ordered German farms in the flat valley. But with all Mr. Catlett's gentleness, she did cry from time to time, surprised, embarrassed to be in love, which made her shy and faint, but guilty, an ungrateful child. Mr. Catlett had brought a woman to look after her, Minna, whose watchful brown face frightened her. But she was used to doing things for herself, and persevered; in three days she had gone so far as to jerk the brush from Minna's hand when she tried to groom her hair. It seemed sinful not to brush her own hair, which had been always one hundred times a bounden duty, every day.

Then, with Mr. Catlett at her shoulder, she had stood at the frilly wood railing of the *Texas* deck and looked from that height over the whole turn as they made a wide, easy sweep into the mouth of the Great Kanawha. He put his hand over hers and said, "My dear, you are in Virginia."

Virginia! After the order of the Ohio fields, the country beyond the first straggling town looked unkempt, illusive, weedy, the hills already gentle swells, lush with disorder. Like the laughter, it could not quite be caught, cleaned up. Then awareness, not even noticed at first, of the slow-moving presence of a few black field hands permeated her mind, as she saw, and hardly believed she saw, human slaves. For the first time she knew, not with her mind, but with a heart which she felt physically as it sank, what she had done.

"That's good quail country," Mr. Catlett said proudly, pointing toward the rises.

"Ragweed," she stated, more firmly than she meant to, and stumbled a little as she turned from the railing and saw the way he was looking at her, amused, not caring.

Now, leaning against the chamber window, she let two tears seep from her closed eyes. It had taken so long to accept that look which she had first felt as a vague warning there on the towering deck. That was the way they watched, all of them, that glance, then the light attractive bullying. They bullied the way they shot birds, consciously, easily, coolly. They allowed you to love them, then used their instinctive comprehension to hurt your own once confiding soul, but not ever letting you see into theirs. Even after she had allowed, through duty, conception in the dark, and borne him four children in pain and suffering, Mr. Catlett still looked at her like that, and made her ashamed, as a married woman, with all it had to mean, though he was always courteous and careful of her. Once he had cried in the night and she didn't know why. Under the lamplight he would never have cried. She knew him that well.

She brushed away the tears, dreamed again, let her new river form for her as she had first seen it. It was by its side, still standing on the *Texas* deck, that she had seen that first encampment of blacks, some washing by the river bank, a few sitting under the trees. They looked tiny from where she stood; a tiny white man with them carried a long gun.

"They're so slow," she thought aloud.

Mr. Catlett took it for granted that she was speaking to him, and smiled. "God's laziest children," he said. "No decent man is in that kind of trade. We deplore as Virginians—"

"Mr. Catlett, they're going to be sold, aren't they?" she asked him shyly, not daring to believe it, so taken for granted after what she had been taught, the prayers, the terrible whispered stories of the manacles, the whips. "Aren't they?" She wanted to force him to say it.

He turned away and she murmured, panicked, "Oh, Mr. Catlett, have you no religion?"

"None to brag of." He still watched the water, not the bank. When she saw his sad face, she felt curiously ashamed for a second of her own father, but rejected that wickedness.

When he spoke again he said, "Don't—" and didn't go on.

She expected him to say, "Don't question me," but instead he repeated, "Don't," as if it were hard to say, and then, "see only what you are looking for. If you do I can't help you." He walked away down the deck as if he had shut a door in the air between them and left her there feeling shrunken with loneliness.

They pushed on slowly up the river for another day, struggling past the wing dams on the shoals, where the current itself seemed trying to push her back, and the ropes on the nigger-head winches screamed and groaned, pulling the boat on through the swift channel, through miles of iridescent water whose oily smell clung to her nostrils. She had heard the boatmen call the Great Kanawha "Old Greasy," and she imagined herself spending all her years with the taste of filthy oil in her mouth. But after the blackened desolate treeless valley of the Salines, the river cleared again, and the green deep water let them go on to Beulah, through the narrowing valley corridor between the ever higher hills. Beulah itself, as the boat slid around the river-bend, looked like a huge hand, lying between the hills. She saw, far away on a rise, the small clapboard house, smoke from the salt furnace by the river, and wide fields separated by snake fences, like children's pencil drawings in the distance. That was all she could remember. She was too dumb with fear.

Beulah jetty was built of huge logs, rubble-filled, the whole landing swarming with strange faces, grinning, yelling at the boat; black, brown, yellow, white, they had all come down, a wall of curiosity, to see her. She shivered. Then, with one of those gestures of incredible tenderness which these people could have, Mr. Catlett, in front of them all, almost lifted her small body close in his arms.

"Ma will fall in love with you too," he whispered in her hair.

His mother was not there among the people who milled around her, but Mr. Catlett had said she couldn't get around much. He'd told her that, so it was no use scanning the faces for her. She couldn't get around. That was it. An old Negro woman was hugging him.

"Darling, this is Loady," he said, smiling at the Negro with that same careless tenderness, loving everybody a little and nobody enough. "How is Ma?" he asked her quietly.

"She been cryin for two days," Loady whispered, but Leah heard anyway and her face set.

Twelve years ago it hadn't been the new Mansion but the clapboard-covered log house he took her to. It had a wide porch with columns to the roof, and a pretty hall she could see had been made from a dog-run. It seemed to have grown, room by room, sprouting wings and outbuildings, all white, huddled under the glaring summer sun.

At the steps Mr. Catlett scooped her up in his arms, joining the following crowd of Negroes in their gusting laughter, as they clambered about them, shutting her in with their fearful, strange bodies. He carried her over the threshold and up the stairs, kicked upon a door at the top, lifted her in, and shut the door with his back. Then he kissed her, still in his arms and hoping never to get down to face anything. The room was as still as the moment after a sigh, as dim and cool as a cave, a raftered vault under the eaves.

"Darling, this is your kingdom." He pointed out her place in the new world softly, his breath against her hair, and kissed her again, put her down in a rocking chair, and went out quickly, shutting the door behind him, to prepare his mother.

It was then that she looked around at the room. It was like a monk's cell, masculine, plain, a prison. She jumped up from the rocker in a spurt of fury at Mr. Catlett's words, and ran to the mean cabin window under the eaves. Beulah valley stretched out below her. One of the Negroes in the yard saw her and yelled out, "Dar Miss Leah. Miss Leah!" Caught, she hid behind the sloping wall, out of sight.

"I am not a brood-mare," she said aloud to the room, and vowed then and there, her fists clenched, to find a place for herself, to make those lazy ragweed people feel the weight of her usefulness, her sense, the iron core behind her small pale face.

Leah, having had her rest, almost a nap, opened her eyes at a whine of wheels from the distant road, and was surprised to find that her fists were clenched again, remembering, after that long.

"At least I know," she said irrelevantly, to the fine big sixteen-paned window, with its wide carved sill, of her new chamber twelve years later, "the difference between right and wrong," and brushed away intruding dreams for present duties.

Far across the hall, through the closed door, she could hear Cousin Annie call, weakly but imperiously, "Leah!" She made a tiny shrug of impatience, rejected the voice, and went on scanning the horse field, which lay blanketed with thick grass, hiding the legs of the colts to their fetlocks. Her eyes followed, not registering, back and forth, as one of the spring colts ran to and fro along the rail fence, still snickering sadly after its lost dam. Behind it the new harness colt stood munching grass, its sleek hide rippling, its lovely tail whisking, curling along its back, seeking flies.

"Leah!" Cousin Annie commanded from the room opposite.

Leah jerked open the bedroom door and ran out.

Even with her flat body thrown across the bed, her eyes closed, the straight thin ridge of her nose shining, and her long buttoned shoes sticking out in Leah's face like a dead man's feet, Cousin Annie was formidable. Leah tried not to speak first. There was a tiny war of stillness. She knew that if she did speak, Cousin Annie would put her on her defenses at once. She always did, by habit, even when, as they all said, Cousin Annie had become as fiercely devoted to her as to the rest of the family. Leah stood, watching her, trying to wait.

Cousin Annie didn't move, or open her eyes. She seemed to be pointing Leah with her shoes, as concentrated as a setter dog.

"How are you feeling now?" Leah finally fluttered, giving in.

Cousin Annie opened her eyes and raised up on one elbow. The great bun of her auburn hair had slipped from the top of her head toward one ear, so that she looked drunk. She squinted at the dim light filtering through the closed shutters.

"Somebody slammed a door." She spoke weakly.

Leah wanted to say, You have agate eyes like a wildcat, like a caged wildcat. Don't look at me, Annie. I can't stand it today.

Instead she said, "I'm sorry. It slipped in my hand. Can I get you anything?"

Annie fell back again. "No," she murmured. "I took some opium. Have you seen Melinda? I've tried and tried to find her. This is all her fault."

Leah put her hand to the door to be ready to get out.

"I can't do a thing with her, Leah. You know I'm fiercely devoted to the child."

"She's just out playing," Leah reassured.

"Listen to me." Annie sprang up from the bed and sat rigid with anger. "I can speak plainly to you."

Dear God, you always have, as plain as a knife. Leah wished she would say that, then laugh at Cousin Annie's long mean boy's body, laugh at it, pound it, tease it. She brought herself back to the complaint.

"I know what it is not to have a home." Annie had got to that part of it. "I've done everything I could for Melinda so she wouldn't feel the same way."

"Annie, don't keep going over this. You just worry yourself every time you do it." Leah swam through the reassurance to Annie's headache talk almost unconsciously, she had done it so often. "Melinda's a cousin. She's not alone in the world."

"She's only a second cousin. I'm a first cousin," Annie snapped. She put one large long hand to the tight-stretched skin of her forehead and began to rub it. "I've thought and prayed and whipped until I can't do any more. Orphans have to be better behaved than the more fortunate of God's children. I told her that. Made her face facts. Death. Hell. Everything. Hardened her." Annie's voice never rose in pitch. It grew stronger, pounding.

Leah broke in. "Annie, let the child alone. The child is all right. She's just mischievous."

"Let her alone! That's all the thanks I get!"

"Oh Annie, you do so well." Leah tried quickly to shore up the break and, bored and caught, couldn't help watching Annie's shoes as they rose and fell, the light catching the buttons.

Annie was talking again. "She wouldn't have a soul in the world. I've told her that. I took her in my arms the day she came, poor little thing. I told her she could be my little girl. For three years now I've given her the best that was in me. Just took her up when she was nothing to me. She runs away and it makes me sick. Don't give a thought to anybody but her own self."

"I'll get you some tea. That helps sometimes." Leah could smell the kind of sickness in the room that an animal leaves, penned up too long.

"Oh let me alone." Annie lay back again. "There don't anybody care." She drew her well-formed heavy lips back in a smile of pain. Leah could see her beautiful, frightening, small white teeth, all the same size.

"I'm only trying," Leah muttered.

"Just go on and let me alone." Annie, having emptied her mind for the moment at Leah, closed her eyes, much to Leah's relief. Then, as if Leah weren't poised in the door, she said, "I do the best I can. It was all taken for granted when I first came here. Don't take anything for granted. Take. You've got to take in this world."

Leah slipped out of the door before she heard any more of the old story which came to her from time to time in whispers, in remarks, in sad smiles or headache talk from the women, how Cousin Annie Brandon had come there, eighteen years old, to visit for a while, how it had been taken for granted that someday Mr. Catlett would marry her, how beautiful she had been for such a tall woman, just like a willow tree, how she'd stayed on bravely even after disappointment and humiliation, visiting forever because she had no place to go, with her strong religion to sustain her.

Fourteen years later Annie looked strong and bitter, a weathered board, not a willow tree. Leah smiled to herself for the first time that morning, forgetting her ugly memories of such a short time before. She put both her hands to her tiny waist and stroked herself gently.

"Take everything for granted!" She giggled, and then benignly whispered to the huge linen cupboard, "Poor Cousin Annie." That reminded her and she started to count the sheets, to check if Aunt Tilly had brought the flat washing up.

She had not been conscious of the sound of Mrs. Catlett's rocking chair until she heard it stop outside on the observatory, and heard the old woman's strong voice call, "Come out here, Leah."

"I'm at everybody's beck and call," she whispered again to the sheets, and went dutifully out onto the observatory, where, sun or rain, her mother-in-law sat for an hour before dinner. Stamp the butter and sit on the veranda; that was all that was left of duty, but

Leah had not seen the rod of iron slip from her gnarled, tree-root hands—not yet.

Mrs. Catlett sat under a canopy in her favorite place, where she could see the property as far as her weak eyes would allow, over the trees down the gently rolling bottom, over the carriage road, the horse field, the turnpike winding across Beulah where the old buffalo trace had been. Beyond it a cluster of buildings seemed set in a sea of now blue-green tall corn; yellow hayfields and green pasture checkered the bottom-land downriver. From time to time the hot breeze lifted the leaves of the trees near the river and where they had been thinned around the salt derrick she could see flickers of green water.

"What's that boat?" Mrs. Catlett squinted into the distance.

Leah leaned over the balustrade and strained her eyes for the shape. "I do believe it's the *Pride of the Kanawha.*"

"Why ain't everybody down there?"

"It can't land. They ought to have known downriver it couldn't land this late in the year."

Now that Mrs. Catlett had drawn Leah onto the porch, she sat back. Her movement changed her relation to the sun, which peeped under the canopy and tried to find her. Her servant, Loady, adjusted it without either of the women's being conscious of her movement.

"Last night," Mrs. Catlett began comfortably, "I drempt—"

"Cousin Annie's ailing," Leah broke in with a panicked whisper.

"I know. She has a headache. I'm a little tired of Cousin Annie's headaches."

"She has nerves," Leah whispered again, and then, "She'll hear you."

Mrs. Catlett went on with her opinion. "Oh nerves! Weakness of the Brandon blood. I conquered mine. I'm more Kregg by the mercy of Providence."

Mrs. Catlett always scared Leah when she divided the credit for her health equally and fairly between herself and God. She missed nothing. Her ears had grown so sharp with age and curiosity that Leah was nervous of even hiding away to think or cry. Sometimes, as now, Mrs. Catlett would eye her coolly, judging, Leah was sure, her chest depth, wind, and sturdiness, as if she were a nigger breeder up for sale.

"You're fidgeting." Mrs. Catlett stated a simple fact.

"I'm worried sick." She turned and leaned against the railing, the sun heavy on her hair, making it glimmer where she had pulled it to a tight knot at the crown of her head, not letting an errant tendril escape her neatness. "Mr. Catlett has Johnny on the river. He says it's time to make him swim."

"Of course it is. You ought to know that. But you weren't reared with boys. Put your bonnet on, Leah. You'll make your skin even darker complected. Have you been forgetting your buttermilk?"

Leah's hands clutched at the railing until the veins stood out. "I can't stay plastered in buttermilk," she said softly, desperately. "I don't like the smell. It stays in my hair." That reminded her that all morning her senses had been too keen, much too keen. She could smell the freshness of Mrs. Catlett's clean ironed white dress, even her old skin sweating under it. She feared a headache and tightened her eyes against the drilling sun. Even with her back turned, she could sense the beads of sweat on Mrs. Catlett's slight mustache. With the heat such things unnerved her, made her voice rise, if she didn't control it, to a dry nagging pitch.

Mrs. Catlett pretended not to hear. "A half a crushed cucumber. You ought to fix a mixture of cucumber with the buttermilk. *Our* education wasn't neglected about those little things, no, not Virginny gals. I recollect a yellow wench once belonged to the Brandons. She put it on until she almost passed for white. She run away. Only nigger that side of the family ever run away. She must have had bad blood. Said she didn't like her Christmas gift. Said pink wasn't her color. Imagine." Mrs. Catlett chuckled.

They both grew still, staring up and down the Beulah road, pastime for a July day, the minutes gently slipping by as they both watched without hope that someone, anyone, would come up the turnpike from somewhere outside the confining hills of Beulah, turn in, and wake them all from the weeks of days when nothing ever happened, and all the great force of life had to be concentrated on details too small to hold it, or on the delicate subtle clash of women's habits.

"They never did catch her." Mrs. Catlett waited for a reply and, not getting it, went on. "Anyway, my brother Stuart Brandon, you never met with him, that's Annie's pa, ran through with ever' last thing. The Brandons never did have money sense. Plenty of people ruined this year too. This is a bad year. The worst I've ever witnessed." She rocked easily, slowly. "Thus are the mighty struck down."

"I've got to . . ." Leah didn't finish, but switched around as if she had been called from inside the house.

"Don't just run away. Kiss me, Leah. I feel old this morning." Mrs. Catlett smiled up at her, and Leah wondered at the blank expectant eyes of the very old and the very young. She leaned down and softly kissed the ruddy cheek. "I've got to catch up. I'm sorry," she murmured, fleeing into the upstairs hall.

"God bless you, my child," Mrs. Catlett called after her, disappointed; then, left alone with Loady, she began to tell her dream anyway. Loady was as old as Mrs. Catlett, almost to the day, and had been her dark shadow since she was a child. Now, her ears gone dim, Loady squatted nodding in the sun, half hearing the voice which was sometimes like another voice of her own in her mind.

"I drempt"—Mrs. Catlett rocked harder, interested—"that I saw with my own eyes the awful day, the Day of Judgment." The chair raced faster. "There they stood before the terrible majesty, sorry too late; there they all stood, oh it was an awful sight, the card-players trying to hide their cards, the dancers still drawing in their breath from dancing, caught, all caught, some men with licker on their breath. I stood there and I waited for the Lord in His majesty to find me out. He came nearer, around a great circle of anxious moaning sinners, all waiting before the awesome assizes."

Mrs. Catlett's voice had risen; the chair hammered the board porch. Annie, her thin body relaxing at last after her dose of opium, woke up and thrashed over on her quilt and moaned. Then she opened her eyes and had to listen to Mrs. Catlett's voice, just outside her window, but far from its peace and shade and sweet drowsiness.

"Lord God, they shivered as if it was cold, as if it was the cold light of an everlasting dawn, caught with their sins heavy on their heads. . . ."

"She never had that dream. It's from a tract. I read it myself," Cousin Annie informed the bedroom wall. Now awake, she began to dream a different dream. Her rigid listening body relaxed; she sighed with relief and put her arms up, resting her head on her hands, felt the pleasure of her breasts pushing against her dress, flexed the strong muscles of her legs, lifted her knees, and sighed a contented sigh of pleasure, sigh after sigh, breathing deep. Mrs. Catlett's story faded, but she could still hear it through the private peace.

"Then He came nearer and I was blinded, I tell you I was blinded by His awful majesty in judgment. He's about to touch me on the shoulder to show me I was saved, oh blessed moment, saved—when Johnny's pups started up that whining they do in the morning, and I woke up."

"Did He git round to me? Did He touch me?" Loady begged, scared.

"I disremember right now." Mrs. Catlett closed her eyes for a nice morning nap.

Inside the bedroom, Annie went rigid again. Mrs. Catlett's vision had poisoned hers with fear. She lay straight as she had been before, staring at the ceiling, her thin face tight with pain, her heavy hair damp and tangled from her hands, remembering with loathing the terrible sin which lay like the beating summer sun, breathless, demanding, upon her bruised shoulders.

Chapter Three

As Johnny reached the turnpike the sound of hammers away through the trees at the salt well sent even the river out of his mind.

"Don't tag after me. Quit tagging. Tagalong!" He twisted and sprang out of reach of Minna's black hand.

"You come right back hyar, come back, Marse Johnny! I gone tell your mammy on you."

"You my mammy. Quit following me. I'm too big for a nigger mammy. You go home!" Johnny by now was running under the dappling trees.

It was too hot, too half-dead hot, for fat Minna to follow him. She called as he turned down the Irish road, "Marse Johnny, you go down playin with thim black Irish whelps I gone tell your pappy horsewhup you!"

Her voice wailed for nothing. Johnny had already gone too far down the forbidden beckoning way which led to the dock and the salt furnace, past the fascinating Irish houses.

Minna wanted to cry, but it was too hot even for that. "Here it is dog days, bringing down Irish sickness on us all," she muttered to herself, sounding like Miss Leah. She slowed down when she heard herself saying Miss Leah's words, and sadly trudged toward trouble. Ahead of her she could see the entrance to the carriage road from the turnpike, and, through its bordering trees, the Mansion like a huge trap.

She was so intent on it that she didn't hear the carriage until it was nearly over her. She jumped back against the fence at the yell of the coachman, looked up into the faces of the fine horses rampant above her a second; then the carriage streamed past her. When she saw what she saw, the grace, the speed, the fine paintwork, the glistening brass even under its layer of traveling dust, she too forgot river and trouble, dog days and heat, just settled back on her heels and gaped as that splendor turned in toward Beulah, appearing and disappearing between the locust trees.

Johnny ran on down the dirt track and, seeing only the empty road, began to jump from rut to rut, over stones, happily kicking as hard as he could to raise the dust. The trees met over him, making a cool tunnel to run through. Now, having had the first taste of his freedom, his movements slowed as if he meant to savor it, make it last, like some sweet fruit he did not need to share. He nearly stopped, put out his tongue, licked the salt sweat from around his lips thoughtfully, and began to saunter casually, taking big steps, watching the patterns his feet made, dragging through the dust.

"By God, you cain't catch me," he bragged to nobody; then to a tree he said boldly, "Goddam hellfar, Ise borned mean and reared up rugged," as he'd heard a man say at the inn once. He glanced behind him, hearing his own voice say the taboo cusswords.

Through the trees to his left he could see the inn which Mr. McKarkle ran for his father, but he glanced away again, paying no attention. It had become so empty in the last months. He heard people say it was the panic. It didn't look like any panic to him. It just looked dead, from the long shed where the men slept to the benches in front of the bar, which sat blank and deserted in the shade of the porch, the only movement the swimming shadows from the trees on their polished wood.

There, only a short while before, big wagons had been thick in the dirt yard by evening, and the strange children who were going over into the West played in the fiery patches of setting sun around the wheels, squinting at him through it but paying no real mind because he wasn't going to the West; he wasn't going anywhere.

Some day he was going to the West, though. He was planning to go on the biggest and fastest and meanest horse his father had.

He and Lewis had gone to watch and yearn until his bull bitch Prance got into a fight and threw a yellow foxy feist over her shoulder like torn paper and broke its neck. They were forbidden to go back any more after that. It didn't matter, though. The wagons no longer came. Oh, one or two came, sorry-looking things held together with rope, spit, and hope, with sorrier families, real cornfield tackies, drooping to the West, not like it once was even last year; not what his father called a steady stream.

A steady stream made him see wagons, carts, and here and there, bobbing among them, a coach, float by on wheels of connected water. He couldn't remember much Pa said to him, except once when he was watching, Pa stopped beside him. Johnny thought he was going to be sent home, but instead his father told him while he stared at his shadow, stretching and bouncing on the sides of the passing wagons, "Son, there goes our life's blood, flowing over into Ohio, the life's blood of our old state, Virginia, bleeding down the Kanawha turnpike, over into Ohio, over into Ohio, gone West. What for, goddammit to hell?"

He had stalked off then toward the inn, going away from Johnny that evening without even remembering to tell him to get on home. When the dog bled in the road, he could see its blood mingling with the dusty watery bloody stream, flowing West. He could still almost hear the wail of the boy who owned the feist, who had come up, covered with tears and snot, looking like he had fallen into water, all bedraggled with sorrow, and tried blindly through his tears to feel toward Johnny and whip him, but Lewis whipped the boy instead and they took Prance home. He would have been sorrier about the feist, sorry as he was about the lifeblood of the Old Dominion, if the boy hadn't tried to whip him. That made him mad instead.

Far away ahead of him down the road the fence began to break into hanging, ragged gates where the Irish houses were. They were really his father's houses. Everything was his father's.

He hated the boys down there, but something made him want to play with them, beyond the boring safety of Lewis and the blacks, and darling Liddy Boo who he had to remember was only a baby; only a little crybaby tagalong was Liddy Boo, the darling girl. Sometimes Cousin Melinda, whom he called Coonface because of her dark, sunk eyes, was all right to play with, better, although he hated to admit it, than the others. But once in a while, like the gingerbread man, he had to run as fast as he could, be eaten, be damned, and see the big world of the hated wild Irish.

Beyond the last of the trees he could see beside the road, like a thing alight, the scarlet musk mallow, taller than a grown person's head, and the scarlet patch under it where the vivid saucer blossoms drifted into the dirt. A face peeped from the other side of the musk mallow, a dim face beside all that color. It retreated, warned like an animal, and there were suddenly two faces, then three, then four. The O'Neills had seen him coming and were waiting for him, strung along the fence.

Johnny couldn't help looking behind him just once more, and seeing no one to help, no Lewis, no Minna, tightened his mouth and stumped on, his heart pounding. After all, even the road was his father's. He had a perfect right to walk down the road if he wanted to. No O'Neills could stop him. His father sometimes didn't even know their black Irish names, and would laugh about it. But when he was with the men down at the salt furnace, he would call them by their first names and put his hand on their backs. Anyway, he had the whole time Harrison was running for president, but Old Kinderhook had won instead and the Irish got the last laugh there, even if most of them didn't own a damn thing and couldn't vote like his father.

A rock landed near him and he jumped by instinct under the shelter of the musk mallow close to the fence, a burning bush away from the Irish. He waited. Nobody seemed to want to throw any more rocks.

"Git offn our road," he heard from behind the bush. It was Little Dan O'Neill's sniffly harsh voice, which he never kept below a yell. He was only Little Dan because his father was Big Dan. He didn't seem little at all most of the time; maybe to Lewis he did, but by God not to Johnny.

"It ain't your road. It's my pa's," Johnny said to the field across the road, not bothering to look at the Irish. He folded his arms, leaned back against the fence rails, and spat into the dust. A blossom seemed to bless his head, it fell so softly. He brushed it away, annoyed.

"We hate you, Johnny Catlett, ye dirty spalpeen," the voice grated at him again.

"I hate you too." Johnny scuffed at a rock. "You ain't nothing but field-tackies."

Dan O'Neill seemed to take that for granted. He didn't say anything.

"I swum the river this morning," Johnny told the fence.

"That ain't nothin." Dan spoke for the rest.

"It is too," Johnny said calmly.

There was a long silence.

"The whul river?" Dan O'Neill asked.

Johnny held his breath. He crossed as many of his fingers as he could so he wouldn't go to hell. He crossed his legs. He even crossed his eyes.

"Yup," he said, and spat to make double sure.

"Then what air you aspittin fer?"

"I had a bad taste in my mouth." Johnny uncrossed everything and wandered around the musk mallow, flicking with great concentration at the pool of scarlet blossoms. He looked at them for a long time, feeling eyes on his head; then he looked up.

The three O'Neills hung on the fence in a row, staring down at him with their Paddy blue eyes under judging brows. Johnny looked only at Little Dan. The sisters didn't matter. Little Dan's mouth looked angry, thin and red in his pale, dirty face, his lips curled back to show his snaggled teeth. Standing up on the first rung of the fence, his proud head reared back, he was giant-like to Johnny; it was like being too close to a colt you couldn't trust.

"We hate you." One of the wild sisters piped her tune, unmindful that the boys had long since passed that stage of their meeting.

"Git on in the house," Dan told them without moving his head.

"We don't have to," the sister said.

"Git, Molly, I *told* you!" Little Dan hollered, and doubled his fist to swing it. The small girls clambered down from the rails and ran into the whitewashed cabin, their wails tuning up.

"Come in hyar, Dan!" a woman called dimly from inside the one shade-darkened room.

But Little Dan had already climbed the fence, spurning the gate next to him. He dropped into the road, and he and Johnny, matching strides, ran down it.

"I'll whup ye," the woman yelled without passion or spirit to the empty fence, but the boys were already gone.

"Where are we agoing?" Johnny was trying hard to keep step with Little Dan's longer strides.

"I got to go down to the furnace," Little Dan told him busily.

"I cain't go." It was out before Johnny thought. He slowed down and dropped behind Little Dan. "I ain't allowed. . . ." He stood, not knowing what to do, watching the bigger boy strut on down the road.

"Won't your nigger mammy let you?" Little Dan grinned back at him, making him feel the full condescension of his eleven years.

"I ain't got no nigger mammy," Johnny muttered.

"My paw says the only difference atween him and a gintleman is a heap o' niggers." Little Dan offered this information as a new subject when he had taunted Johnny into walking again slowly toward him. "We're gonna have some too. I hate niggers."

Johnny was completely silent, sadly watching his feet toil down the road. His father called the O'Neills nigger-hating trash; his mother would fold her mouth when he said it and look someplace else. Only for a second, he didn't even want to be with Little Dan.

High above them, topping the trees like a watchtower against the pale blue heat haze of the sky, was the log derrick of the Beulah salt well. They could hear the blowing of a mule on the treadwheel behind the trees, and away in the air, an imprisoned bird, the singing of the grass rope on its heavy wooden winch. A barrel lay on a trestle at the top of the derrick, as if it had been forgotten there.

Johnny wanted to go and see, just stand and watch the old blind mule go round and round and round in the sun, but Little Dan had already turned left, down through the trees toward the furnace. Johnny figured quickly, yearning both ways. Minna wouldn't dare come down. She never did. She was scared. His ma wouldn't. She was always too busy to do anything. He could hear again Pa say he was going to the lower field to see the heifers. Lewis . . . Lewis always told on him but he hadn't seen Lewis all morning, and besides if he told on him that would mean he was there, and he wasn't allowed any more than Johnny was.

"Wait for me," he called after Dan, and the older boy stopped with studied patience for tagalong to catch up with him.

"My paw was a gintleman too when he was in old Ireland. He was the son of kings." He went on with his own thought, telling it to the road. "Fortune niver favored him." He wandered along at an easy gait until Johnny caught up with him.

There were times when Johnny envied Little Dan more than anyone in the world, and here, down the forbidden road, with the steam from the log pipes whispering, sighing, beckoning him to come, was one of the times he did more than any other. Nothing was forbidden the tall thin boy; he, wild-eyed and watchful, could do anything in the world.

Little Dan turned, caught Johnny's look at him, and read it, dog-worship. He spat and began to brag. "They wouldn't let no nigger do what my paw does." He let Johnny fall into step beside him.

"They would too." Johnny found himself, surprised, fighting back, defending himself through the niggers, for Dan O'Neill wasn't the biggest pebble on the beach.

"Huh! My paw would fight 'em off. He'd throw 'em in the grainers and let 'em bile if they took his job."

Johnny had, finally, heard this so often that he found himself wishing Dan would just shut up.

They turned behind the trees and hit a wall of shimmering heat.

The long graining shed was veiled in steam. Through it Johnny could hear the easy swing and scrape of the lifters. He could taste the salt in the humid air; the smell of it, the hot wet hemp, the tallow, clung to his nostrils. As he got more used to the steam, he could see figures moving, like Shadrach, Meshach, and Abednego in the fiery furnace, hovering easily over the long troughs of boiling brine.

Little Dan listened for one voice above the other noises—the scraping, the murmuring, the yelling from far inside the shed. Then he found it, singing in a surprisingly graceful high tenor, and knew at once that his father was in a good humor. The bitter song floated out through the white vapor. He had got to the words he always sang loudest: "When he in a rage did cry, I said you are a paddy, and no Irish need apply. . . ."

Little Dan grinned. When his father sang that song, his Irish up, none of the blacks ever came near him, but worked far up on the other end of the shed, for he held his moods in a body as strong as a rock jug. On Saturday nights if he got to singing that, and pounding on the table with his huge scarred fist, all alone there with no one to drink with, his mother would crawl up into the loft with the children and pray and whisper to Little Dan, "Oh Gawd, Danny, don't tell him I'm hyar"—then, "Jasus help me, Jasus help me, Jasus look down on a poor sister, Jasus . . . uh . . . Jasus . . . uh . . . Jasus save us . . . uh . . ." She would keep up the grunting rhythm until she rocked herself to sleep across the pallet, still on her knees, smelling sweet of the blackstrap herself.

"Paw!" Dan called from the road to show off to Johnny. He could hear a copper shovel drop with a ring, and it made his heart turn for fear that he might have misjudged.

A huge figure seemed to detach itself from the steam and float out toward them. Big Dan O'Neill, king of the valley, the finest lifter of those aristocrats of the furnace, who worked in a wet hell, shoveling the salt crystals up from the brine, stood teetering on the edge of the platform above their heads, blinking into the sun. When Johnny saw that brawn, the muscles of his shoulders wet and dark with heat and sun, he couldn't have told him from a black except for his roofed and penetrating eyes, pure deep blue, and his black hair curled from the heat into soft ringlets almost to his shoulders, ridiculous for such a big man.

Big Dan wiped a wet wad of kerchie across his heavy mouth, and without speaking threw his arm up in an impatient gesture, pointing toward the big barrel under the tree across the road. Little

Dan ran over, dipped the molasses water up in a gourd, and carefully balanced it in both hands as he came back and stood below his father. Big Dan took the handle from him, stooping, and in one movement drank, letting the water fall around his mouth, down his chest where Johnny watched, fascinated, as it ran through sweat and thick matted hair.

"Now git the hell to your home," Big Dan said quietly, and threw the gourd at his son. He was just turning away toward the steam again when Johnny felt his ear grasped in plier-like fingers.

He twisted as much as he could, his face creased with sharp, mean pain.

That old devil Telemachus had caught him.

"You git yourself home, Marse Johnny, Ise gone tell on you. Fall in one of them grainers and git yourself biled alive, your skin come off like a biled apple. Ain't nobody gone pull you out. Ain't nobody gone be bothered with bad chillun. Now git!" He started to turn Johnny's ear again, his angry old talon of a black hand squeezing.

Johnny managed to pull away. He meant to say something, but Big and Little Dan were already laughing. Their laughter gusted over him worse than the hot steam.

"Go find your mammy, nigger-sucker, nigger-sucker!" Little Dan chanted.

"Quit that talkin dirty to Marse Johnny," Telemachus roared out of the laughter back at the boy; then, whining, "Ise sorry, Mista O'Neill, Ise mighty sorry to of spoke sharp to your boy." Telemachus backed away, his apology floating in the now still air.

Johnny ran. He didn't care where he was running, just away, as fast as he could get away from it. He couldn't help crying, he couldn't help it, right in front of all of them.

He bolted down behind the furnace beyond the boilers, where it was suddenly quiet and he was by himself. He leaned his hot head against the huge log wall, where river and salt had preserved the wood so that it was soft and mossy and scented like dried roses. Tiny, huddled against the huge virgin logs, the boy released his tears and they fell into the briny sweet wood and down where the sea itself once had flowed and covered it all, the hills, the valleys, leaving what his father called gifts of God.

Telemachus, having soft-spoken himself safely away from the Irish, looked down and saw him there. His face, now gray with age and runneled with years of stern judgment, tightened even more when he saw what the boy was up to.

"You come right hyar to me, Marse Johnny. Ise gone tote you home. Quit that cryin like a little molly. Ever'body gone dress you up in skirts and make you come down show off in front of thim O'Neills."

Johnny made himself draw away from the protection of the bins and the shade and climb up slowly into the sun, which blinded his tear-stung eyes so that he scrunched them up and only felt Telemachus take his hand and lead him up the road again. Little Dan was gone. Big Dan had disappeared back into his mist kingdom. The ride home in the gently groaning wagon, back up the creek track, cool and dim in the willow grove, was slow and peaceful, and gave him time to consider carefully how, when he grew up, he wouldn't let Dan O'Neill even live at Beulah, just Telemachus and Aunt Minna and the blacks and his own family. This thought comforted him so that he forgot the ear-pinching and stole a hand onto Telemachus's knee, naked and bony, sharply sticking out of a hole in his nigger-cloth jeans.

"I swum this morning," he told him, "and there warn't no nigger-belly."

"Was you skeered?" the old Negro asked him.

"No," Johnny said. "I just swum. It was easy."

Telemachus let the mare find her own way up the track, her small hoofs making a pretty hollow clatter on the loose stones. Johnny listened for a while and dreamed. The willows slipped by them and touched their faces. Johnny began to hope that in the stillness Telemachus would listen to the creek and forget to tell on him. At the same time he knew he wouldn't.

Telemachus never did forget. Once he had even told on Big Dan for being drunk at the furnace, and Big Dan had come charging up the brick walk of the big house and shouted to Johnny's father, to the whole house really, that he was quitting to go West, that it was devil enough to have the need so great he had to get blear-eyed without some dirty black whickering about it. Then he said he'd kill the nigger if he got his hands around his black neck, by God. Johnny remembered his father's voice, quiet, cool as a knife-blade, saying, "You lay a hand on one of my niggers, Dan O'Neill, I'll have you hung."

That voice, so still after all that hollering, made Big Dan go quiet, and he had just stood and looked at Johnny's father for a long time, then turned and walked away. When he got to the end of the walk, he swung around once and muttered so they could hardly hear him from the porch, a faint cry far away.

"By Jasus, you was not born with the glamour . . ."

Big Dan had gone away then, for three weeks, and Cousin Annie had looked after his pale dim wife. Cousin Annie, whipping her skirts through that cave of a room where the O'Neills lived, while Johnny peeked from the road, had washed everything, even the children, even Little Dan. She moved and talked about Christian charity at the same time for three weeks, but she said she loathed the memory of Big Dan with her whole soul, and that didn't sound like Christian charity. She said she could feel the disgust stir strong in her body as she touched his ragged clothes and his bed, but she conquered it with prayer and went on doing her duty. He never heard Mrs. O'Neill mumble three words in what time he watched Cousin Annie there, but Mrs. O'Neill was always sick anyway; everybody said she was just wasting away.

At the end of three weeks Big Dan came back, thinner than Johnny had ever seen him, quieter too. His father said he'd let bygones be bygones. He told his grandmother, with Big Dan standing there, that something got into a man, and his grandmother nodded with comfortable understanding and said she'd seen it happen to horses. Big Dan looked away beyond their heads and didn't say a word. He seemed to be listening, patiently, to something they couldn't hear.

In a few days Big Dan was back in his proud stride, stronger, harder than ever, a singing man of defiance, rising through the salty steam. His father smiled when he saw him and said, going home, his hand on Johnny's head, but talking mostly to himself, that it was as if the roots, all the way back to County Clare in old Ireland, which kept him alive, could only stretch so far without breaking. The root had stretched all the way across the Atlantic, down the new railroad beds, some of the way marked with Big Dan's sweat ("We owe them a lot," his father said). Now, at Beulah, across the Virginia mountains, the root had stretched far enough. Except for his escaping soul, Dan had settled, married, put down suckers for his weaker relations who whined across the water and rooted under his shadow, making a little colony under the trees near the salt well, in and out of their dirty cabins, spawning, complaining.

Johnny knew how Dan would shake them off, go and talk, sing, and brag with the men from the caravans and the drovers when they stopped at the inn. But beyond the one flight down to Cincinnati which for those few weeks took something from him and made him look dry and shrunken when he got back, he had not gone again, but had just stayed in the valley, worked like a driven giant, and cursed the Catletts. Johnny had heard him lots of times, but not in front of his father.

All this Johnny knew; he felt a gorge of anger when his father talked about the Irish most of the time as if they were some kind of animal not worth catching, and made him ashamed of himself for liking them. Telemachus knew it too, knew he could bait Big Dan just so far, as you bait a bear, jump away, see him simmer, knowing that his father's cool, protecting voice would always lay down the law. They took it all as for granted as the rocks they heard flick in the roadbed.

"When I was a little nigger . . ." he heard Telemachus say way up above the top of his head.

"Nigger . . ." Johnny picked up the word to help him, as he often had to, to stir grownups to go on with what they were going to say. They always stopped in the middle.

"Well, over that side"—the old man pointed to the other bank where it rose in a long grove of new trees and underbrush toward the upriver bend of the turnpike—"they wasn't no little trees; they was a big flax field, and a ole pile of logs whar the Injun fort was oncet."

"Did it look like a fort? Did it have gunholes?" Johnny had asked the question at least a hundred times, but Telemachus always disappointed him.

"Naw, I done tole you, it was ole pile of burned logs. Folks jest said it was the fort. I don' believe it was atall." Telemachus dropped the reins and pointed to the creek sternly, where the shallow slow water combed the wet maidenhair weeds as they floated darkly below the surface in long hanks, swinging downstream.

"Afore the horse mill went in they was plenty water all the time and they was a swimmin hole up by the big house under a Lord God biggest sycamore tree you ever seen. That's whar they found your great-grandpaw when the Injuns throwed him in. Leastways that's what my mammy tole me."

"Tell me about your mammy," Johnny interrupted. He'd heard so often about his great-grandpa, and it scared him, especially in the mornings when the creek was misty, and Telemachus said he had been seen any number of times, rising through the mist in what Telemachus called his towering grief, without any head at all. "They done cut off his whole head," Telemachus always told him.

"My mammy Lyddy?" Telemachus asked, pleased. "She belong to the Brandons; then your other great-grandpappy bought her."

"That's some of my kin anyhow," Johnny reassured him, to show Telemachus his mammy wasn't altogether out of the family when she belonged to the Brandons. The forgotten horse stumbled a little and Telemachus automatically jerked at the reins. He didn't answer and Johnny tried again to make him talk some more.

"What was your pappy's name?" That was one question he never could make Telemachus answer, so he never ceased asking.

"I done sprung from mighty noble loins," Telemachus told the road, as his mother had told him. He could still hear the voice of the drunken old stranger saying, "Brother, brother, take my goddamned shoes off, little brother," and hear his single short grunting laugh over his head as he knelt.

"Now quit sashaying aroun. Ise gone tell you 'bout that tree." He drew his attention back to his half great-great-nephew, the little master waiting at his side.

"Now that fell in the crick in a big storm. I hyared it way up on the hill, woke up and hyared it."

"Why did it fall if it was so big?" Johnny interrupted, impatient with the old man, who caught the note in his voice and went on mournfully.

"Caze it got too ole and wore out, jest like po ole Telemachus hyar."

"How much are you worth?" Johnny interrupted again, beginning to wiggle on the seat.

"Ise worth a mighty sight less'n I war." Telemachus laughed. "Oncet I'd of fotched 'long 'bout ten thousand dollars, but in this hyar panic I reckon I ain't worth over 'bout five thousand dollars."

"You ain't." Johnny stated that peacefully. "Ain't no nigger worth nothing like that even in good times, and these ain't good times."

Telemachus got mad. He stared at Johnny, his own face slotted up and down with angry wrinkles. Then he decided what to say, and looked sad again.

"You needn't to talk to po ole Telemachus thataway. You ain't gone git much more chance."

"Why?"

"Caze Ise gone die right soon and you gone be sorry. Ise gone leave you all by youself with nobody and go to a better place prepared fer me."

"Why?" Johnny asked again calmly, playing the why game without listening to much Telemachus was saying, only catching the stopping of his voice to put in his word.

"Caze things ain't like they was." Telemachus sighed.

"Why?"

"They jest ain't like they was, and it gits me so melancholy sometimes I jes don' know nothin to do but lay myself out and die. These hyar salt works. Bad's gone come of them. That ain't nothin fer a gintleman to do." His creased face puckered up even more, and he shook his head back and forth, no, no, no, and wouldn't stop.

"Why?" Johnny picked up the reins, hoping Telemachus was too sad to notice, and he could hold them a while.

But the old man saw the movement and took the reins back, still shaking his head. "Gintlemen jest raises things like corn and horses and some tobacco, little nigger-head, little lady's twist fer the folks. They don' do no dirty diggin, and they don' har no whites, that's why. What he want with whites when he got a heap of niggers? Quit askin me why ever' time I shet my mouth." Telemachus stopped shaking his head at last and clicked his tongue at the mare, which started a little, but only speeded up her walk.

They had had this conversation, or one like it, so many times since Johnny could talk, since he would sit on Telemachus's lap and try to rub the light tan color off with his damp baby hands, then look wonderingly at his palms, disappointed, while Telemachus laughed. So neither of them paid much attention to it any more, just let it go out of hearing, die down, let the mare plod on, her head hanging, so that if Johnny's father had seen the way he was driving her he would have spoken to Telemachus; just rode, sleepy and contented, hauling the Jersey wagon full of cattle salt up to the barn, forgetting for a moment Johnny's future inevitable whipping.

The barn rose in the distance, its steep shake roof dwarfing the creek trees ahead of them. They didn't even look up, just let the creek go on combing its maidenhair, let go and moseyed along, moving slower and slower through the warm, blank minutes of the everyday morning.

Chapter Four

THE CREEK no longer charged down the valley, wiping out the ford of the buffalo trace every year in its spring anger. Upstream behind the Mansion a moss-softened log dam controlled its flow and backed its water into a millpond which soaked most of a little patch of bottom-meadow at the mouth of the hollow. Ducks wallowed and waded at the edge, hunting in the spongy grass. There was a damp, cool smell about the millpond, even in the heat of July, partly because, in the narrowing hollow, the big wooden mill itself took the place in the sun and cast a shadowed reflection over it for most of the day. Its glass windows shone in the water, breathed when the ducks dived. Its wheel turned and groaned, dragging always its dark damp passengers of moss. Inside the mill the growling of the huge stones, the flour-covered old Negro miller, Uncle Cuffee, made the children avoid it, made ghost stories in the Mansion attic begin or end there.

Beside the tiny path which climbed the steep hollow, beyond hearing of the mill, the creek flung itself freely from the mountain, protected still by the untamed woods, carrying trout in clear rock pools and shallows. A few huge virgin trees stood almost in it, their thick roots naked, holding the rocks in place like strong arms as the water rushed by. Even where the rocks were big, the channels almost fissures, there were pools reflecting the sky and the branches, seemingly motionless for a few feet until the water tumbled over the next clean rock and made tiny waterfalls.

Melinda hushed Toey with a quick nervous flutter of her hand.

The whole mountain world of the trees was quiet as the perpetual breeze paused. Melinda fell on both knees on a flat rock, and leaned far down, listening to the music of the creek. With her hand raised to keep Toey from speaking (or even breathing too loudly), she waited. At first she heard one single rushing note. Then she began to sense the different sounds: high, light sighing where the water trippled; a strong roar where a channel tunneled between the bigger rocks; below it all a beckoning base whisper, which could have been the movement of the small stones, even the sand shifting, complaining at the ceaseless onslaught of the water.

Without a word Melinda reached back and pulled at Toey's cotton shift to make her kneel and listen too. But when she obeyed they forgot to listen and watched the pool instead as Toey's face appeared, slightly wavering beside Melinda's own. They watched with the objective contemplation of women at a mirror, coolly judging their reflections in the water. In such concentration they could have been two images of the same spirit except that Melinda's big black eyes controlled a thin, pale face, almost scowling in its watchfulness, made whiter by a tangle of black hair which fell and tumbled around it as wild as the creek. Toey's eyes were black too, but they protruded from a brown sad patient face; her hair in thirty tiny woolly braids stood straight up on her head.

Melinda, quickly tired of staring, reached into the water and ruffled the faces so that they jumped and disintegrated into flickering parts, then disappeared altogether as she stood up, lifted her wide white skirt and tatted petticoats, and stepped barefooted into the water, as gracefully as she could, lost in a dream of her own.

She was tall for her age, as thin as a weed. She was a head taller than Toey, who was eight too, but standing in the creek she had to look up at her as the Negro child sat back on her heels and, finding her mouth with her thumb, looked over it calmly to watch Melinda. They stared at each other, wondering for a bleak pause what to do, now that they had run away forever.

All of their belongings lay safe on a dry table-rock under the big tree. Melinda's pile contained a broken doll, like a little invalid lady; her china face, scarred where once Melinda had given her smallpox so she could nurse her back to life, gazed blankly at the sky, her cloth arms flung out, one ending in sawdust, the other in a useless china hand. The hand lay on the dull iron serrated handle of a pistol Melinda had found in the grass. Piled together were a summer cotton dress, wound like a bundle of rags and showing a little edge of Cousin Annie's stern ugly tatting; an empty medicine bottle of deep green; her catechism, which she planned to learn on the road West; a shining gold comb; and a miniature, with its glass broken, of an old bearded man in what looked like some sort of uniform. He too gazed blindly up at the tree, like the doll. Against them, very carefully, Melinda had set her best buttoned shoes and her red striped stockings. Against the tree, as if on guard over the little pile, leaned a large black umbrella.

Toey, on the other hand, had brought only two apples. They lay apart, a windfall bruise on both their red shiny surfaces. Toey knew there wasn't any use bringing anything else. She knew she would have to tote Miss Melinda's bundle when they got to the woods. She always had done it when they ran away, and since they always went back when Miss Melinda got over her streak of wildness, she didn't see the sense in bringing anything. Besides she didn't have anything but a corncob doll which was really hers.

Melinda could feel the tug of the water on her bare legs; she threw up her head, lifted her skirts higher, and began a trudging prance against the current, her bare feet finding smooth places for themselves.

"I am the queen of far Araby"—she spoke gently, making her game into words "—and this here is my golden skirt afloating around my feet." She tried to dance a little, the water dragging against her. "It feels so heavy it's just agoing to drag me down. I am the queen and the princess of far Araby." She swung her hair defiantly at Toey and the trees.

"Who am I?" Toey, trapped by Melinda's watching her as she crouched on the rock, asked in a reedlike wail.

"You ain't nothing but my minion, arrant knave." Then, relenting: "I am so rich you got golden clothes on too, and golden shoes."

Toey looked down at her bare brown dusty feet and was glad she had on golden shoes.

"Ain't I nice to you?" Melinda asked.

"Yassum," Toey told her.

"You got to do my bidding or I'll put you in durance vile." Melinda turned to clamber up the next rock, feel the next pool around her feet. She sat down across the creek from Toey and held her legs to a small waterfall, watching it splash.

"When we goin' home?" Toey finally ventured. "Ise gittin hungry."

"We ain't never going home. P'like we're poor wanderers on the face of the earth. P'like we ain't got no place to go," Melinda went on, almost to herself, not bothering to call over the water noise. Her eyes were bleak; she was hungry too.

"I want to go home." Toey's face wrinkled to cry.

"Don't you be a crybaby!" Now she did call out, impatient with Toey's thin whine. "I ain't got time to fool with you. You ain't no fun atall. I'm sick and tired of not playing with nobody but you."

Toey's face was mute with patience. "You gits to play with the boys sometimes."

"I don't care." Melinda put her chin on her fist and turned her head upstream to a new pool, hypnotized. "If we'd aboughten a pole we could live on fish."

"Let's eat thim apples," Toey suggested mildly.

"All right."

Toey scrambled up and reached for the apples, but her hand knocked at one of them, and it rolled off the rock into the weeds.

"Miss Melinda, I dropped one," Toey wailed.

"Well go get it," Melinda didn't raise her head.

Toey started to cry. "Ise skeered to. Ise skeered of snakes."

"I ain't skeered of nothing," Melinda told her proudly, and waded across the pool. She climbed up beside Toey, jerking at her skirt, annoyed as it caught on a jagged edge of the rock, freed herself, and knelt to feel for the hidden apple. When she clutched it, she jumped away so fast she stood up, lost her footing, and tripped into the pool.

"Oh Gawd, Miss Melinda, you gone git horsewhupped," Toey moaned, but couldn't move to help her.

Melinda sat in the water, too scared to get up. Then she giggled. "It feels good. It feels *good.*" She began to turn and wiggle, writhe and splash, putting her whole self, hair, head, arms under the water. She could feel it take her hair and softly comb it downstream. As suddenly she sat up, quiet again.

"I am Ophelia." She tried to float, face up in the shallow water, but her bottom was still on the sand.

"Who that?" Toey asked.

"Oh she died. You ain't never heard of her." Melinda patted the water in rhythm, making bigger and bigger splashes as she chanted, "There *is* a *wil*low *grows* a*slant* a *brook* . . ."

"What you want to be her fer?"

"Poo!" Melinda stood up, dripping. "I don't. I want to be a boy. I hate little old prissy girls."

"Right now you better git right out of thar and dry youself."

Melinda crawled to the rock again and sat pouring with water beside Toey. She looked around her, smiling, and wiped her face with a perpetually scratched hand, its fingernails bitten to the quick. Then she sat straight, crossing her legs primly.

"P'like I'm a lady. I'm a bride and you're my servant. You got to get me all dressed for my wedding day."

"Less see. First you git that wet thing off 'fore you catch your death," Toey said, imitating Minna. "Skin a rabbit."

Melinda lifted her seat enough to free her clothes, then obediently let Toey pull them over her head.

Toey tried to wring them out, and then flick them as Aunt Tilly did in the laundry. Then she spread them carefully where the sun caught a patch of sand.

"Oh Lawd, Miss Melinda, you done tore your clothes. I declare I don' know what Ise gone do with you." She fussed importantly. She looked around wide-eyed when she heard Melinda sob.

Melinda's face was hidden by wet, bedraggled hair which stuck to her naked shaking shoulders. She had huddled down, cold and tiny on the big rock. Toey grabbed the first thing she could, Melinda's Sunday dress, and knelt behind her to dry her hair, crooning to her.

"Now what you want to act like that fer?" It was a whisper, a sweet whisper, comforting.

"Ain't nobody cares what happens to me," Melinda muttered.

"I'm just a good-for-nothing. I'm sick and tard of being whipped all the time. It don't do no good."

"We'll tell somethin. We'll jest make up somethin," Toey told her hair as she shook it out. "Now let's you tell me somethin nice. You tell me 'bout that funeral. That's nice." She always suggested this when Melinda cried. It cheered her up quicker than anything else.

"I want my grandpa." Melinda started to wail, adding another sound to blend with the rushing water. "Nobody don't pay no 'tention to me but Cousin Annie. I'm just wore out being Cousin Annie's duty." She stopped crying with a shaky sigh, defeated. "She cain't do a thing with me. I'm too bad for her Christian spirit. She don't even like me."

Toey combed carefully, her brown hands caressing as she combed.

"She pulls my hair when she combs it. She cain't even tame that."

"You got the prettiest hair," Toey told her.

"Horsetail!" Melinda jerked impatiently. "I don't care." She whipped around so fast that her hair switched into Toey's face.

"Ouch," Toey hollered. "What you do that fer?" She hid her eyes and sat back.

"I didn't mean to," Melinda said, frightened. "You're my best friend."

"I don' want to be no best friend somebody always slappin me with her hair," Toey said from behind her hands.

"I only did it once," Melinda explained. "Now quit that and I'll tell you about the funeral."

"Then kin we go home?" Toey still refused to take her hands down.

"Yes." Melinda was contrite. "Please look at me."

"Promise?"

"Cross my heart hope to die. Please." Melinda put her hands over Toey's. Toey let her pull them down and grinned, putting her thumb squarely into the middle of the grin. Melinda bounced to her feet, happy, and waded into the pool. She bent down.

"Here's your apple. I dropped it in the creek."

Toey wound herself around and reached for the other one, where she had let it fall.

"Hyar's your apple too," she said.

They exchanged apples, as sedate as ladies, and sat together, chewing them noisily. Melinda stretched her long bare legs out in front of her and arched her naked stomach to the leaf-veiled sun.

"Now I'll tell you about the funeral," she said through the apple. "Once upon a time . . ."

"This wasn't no story. This was real," Toey broke in.

"You just shut your mouth. Whose funeral was this anyhow?"

Toey shut up. She was afraid Melinda wouldn't tell.

"Once upon a time, there was this great Injun fighter and glorious hero of the Revolution," Melinda went on comfortably. "He lived in a big palace in the West with his dear little granddaughter, who he loved more than life itself."

"You forgot the daddy," Toey reminded her.

"He died a hero's death."

"Who was the dear little granddaughter?" Toey prompted on.

Melinda put her arm around Toey. It still felt wet and cold.

"That was me," she yearned, making up details as she went along. "We all lived in this palace with a heap of niggers. Then Ma died and we was left all alone. So Grandpa decided to come back home to die. He hadn't never been here since he was a boy. So we rode a long ways in a coach and I sat on his lap. Except when he was drunk, then I sat on a lady's lap. She had bony legs and smelled like camphor. We come about ten thousand miles. Then we got here and Grandpa told them he come home to die." Her voice took on an edge of belligerent pride. "It was *his* home after all. He had a right here same as they did. Everybody was real glad to see him. First place they thought he was already dead. He was a legend on account of his great exploits. He was an American hero and patriot."

"So he died." Toey pushed her on to the funeral part.

"So he died. The hand of God struck him down just before the glorious Fourth. He went to sleep in Jesus. We all went downriver in a boat and there was a band playing on Canona docks, only we got there too soon and had to wait for the band to come. They took and put Grandpa's coffin on a cannon, but they couldn't hardly get the mules to pull it and lots of men had to hold it on anyhow. There was fireworks. One was a Catherine wheel that rained red and golden stars. There was a heap of flags, and the boys from the Academy and the militia and the Sunday schools, they all marched to the meeting ground on the riverbank. And there was speeches. They told how famous Grandpa was and they drank a toast to Colonel Peregrine Lacey, patriot. They had a funeral oration but I didn't like it. They didn't hardly talk about Grandpa; it was just about who was going to be President, Mr. Van Buren or Mr. Harrison. Two men got in a fight. I took myself a little nap. When I woke up a boy was reciting the Declaration of Independence."

Melinda pounded the rock. " 'We hold these truths to be self-evident,' " she called to the creek, " 'that all men are created equal . . .' "

"What about ladies?" Toey asked.

"It don't say nothing about ladies. I don't 'spect so." She brushed the Declaration of Independence aside.

"And then . . ." Toey helped.

"And then I had to be excused. Cousin Annie took me way up behind the trees. She told me to hurry up but I couldn't hurry up any faster than I did. Way back there you could still hear the glorious Fourth and the cannon. It skeered me. It smelled bad. The militia all shot in the air and it made the ground bounce. Then a preacher prayed for the longest time I ever heard."

"And then . . ." Toey slipped her by the prayer. Sometimes she said it all, and it wasn't any fun, just scary.

"And then they run that mule team up the hill behind Canona and they had a grave dug and they wrapped Grandpa's coffin up in the American flag and lowered him in. I cried and a man who was drunk told me I was a brave gal and Cousin Annie ordered him away in no uncertain terms. Then there was more shooting and they had a big picnic."

By this time Melinda was lying on her back looking up at the trees. Toey nestled down beside her and ran her brown arm under Melinda's neck to draw her closer.

"Didn't nobody say no poem?" she prompted on, a question close to Melinda's ear.

"Yes. A boy said one." Melinda flung both arms up as if she were reaching for the branches. She closed her eyes and groaned. "Horror!"

Toey pulled away and sat up.

"The reptile strikes his tooth deep in my heart so crushed and sad." Melinda struck her bare chest with one fist. She sat up and shouted to the patch of sky, "Ah laugh, ye fiends; I feel the truth: your task is done; I'm *mad*. I'm *mad!*"

"Is that all you remembers?" Toey asked after a silence.

"There ain't no more."

Toey loved the end of the funeral best, because every time Melinda got to the poem part she said something different. This time it was part of a poem from Lewis's reader that he was trying to learn to declaim. Melinda got it right, at least the part she remembered, and she was powerful at remembering. She got the gestures right, too, better than Lewis and he was going on twelve.

"Oh." Melinda fetched a big sigh. "Why do we have to go home?"

Toey, who wanted to, was on her feet before she had finished speaking, and was feeling her dress.

"It ain't dry yet," she wailed.

"I'll put it on anyhow." Melinda's voice was muffled. She was deep in thought, her head bent against her knees. "I need something sharp," she commanded. "Toey, I *got* to do something."

"I ain't got nothin sharp." Toey's high thin voice was annoyed.

Melinda was already on her stomach, searching with both hands in the pool, her hair almost touching the water. Irritated, she flicked one bird's wing of hair back to see better. "I felt one with my foot," she said to herself. Then, finding a small sharply pointed stone, she stood up, satisfied.

"Come here, Toey," she said solemnly to Toey, who was already close beside her. She held her fist out and they both studied it, smooth and ready.

"P'like a snake *did* bite me and I ran in the creek to get away. P'like we sucked it and saved my life." She closed her eyes, lifted the sharp stone above the back of her hand, and jabbed it as hard as she could twice without flinching. Then she opened her eyes and looked. She had managed to break her skin enough for two tiny scratches to show. She sucked hard until the back of her hand was red around it and she had drawn two small rubies of blood. It did look something like a snakebite. "There, ain't that good?" she asked Toey.

"Yessum," Toey answered sadly.

"What's the matter?"

"You tell a lie you gone to hell, Miss Melinda." She held Melinda's dress up for her.

"What do I care? I won't get a whipping anyhow." Melinda let the Negro child slip it over her head and gentle her hair down her back.

"Anyhow I have a feeling," Melinda said, "that I'm agoing to die young."

"Me too," Toey agreed, pleased. "Here, lemme hike up your petticoat."

They gathered their belongings to trudge home, both stepping daintily under the huge umbrella so the sun wouldn't injure their delicate skin. Toey carried most of the load, but Melinda clutched her only inheritance, her grandfather's picture. She always carried it when she ran away. Something at least of Colonel Peregrine Lacey, Indian fighter, stayed on at Beulah, having had no place but the hated valley to go to die. His stern old face now lay hidden in his granddaughter's tight eight-year-old fist.

As they broke out of the woods into the sunny mill-road, they drew closer to each other and held hands in a conscious effort to be frightened. Slowly, making their own darkness in the hot sun, they neared the high blank wall of the mill. It seemed to bear down on them, and they edged by, suppressing nervous laughter.

The dusty air still hung over the road, survival of a lately ridden horse; old Cuffee, the miller, paced up and down the mill, still excited at what he had heard, but, in his solitary job, having nobody to tell.

Seeing the little girls in the road, he came to the wide mill door and called out, "Miss Melindy, lemme tell you somethin. Company! How you like that?"

He teetered above them, grinning, with the halo of flour which always clung to him and made him as near a ghost as could be found at Beulah. He had, in time, become almost a hermit, driven by Gothic chilly pleasures which crept from the attic to the house Negroes, haunted the field-hands' children, left him, flour-covered old man, alone, principal in legends he never knew existed.

Melinda pulled at Toey's hand. "He's agoing to git us. He's coming to git us."

They balanced their umbrella and their "things" and stepped awkwardly toward a run.

"Miss Melindy, I got somethin tell you," the old Negro cried. "Nigger come git mo flour for the Mansion."

The girls broke and scattered down the road, whiffs of giggles floating behind them. Old Cuffee watched, malicious with disappointment, from the loading platform. It was then he saw the golden comb, shining in the dull dry dirt.

Chapter Five

As soon as she had recovered her breath, Minna began to follow after the resplendent carriage, waddling in its dust in an excited surge of movement to be the first one to tell the news, but the carriage cut away up the drive too fast for her.

She had started to whisper to herself, "Company coming . . ." when she slowed and resumed her tired walk, disheartened almost to tears, cursing her fat. She had seen ahead of her that yellow goblin of Marse Johnny's, Tig, jump down from the gatepost where he had been squatting with all the concentrated patience of his seven years, watching for them to come back from the river. She spoke again. "I ought to alet him come to the river. I jest din want to be bothered with him for oncet."

His shinny down from the gate precipitated action. Upstairs a curtain flicked. On the observatory old Mrs. Catlett stood up, her rocker rocking on its own behind her. She turned to push Loady out of her path, and Minna could barely hear her fine whine quaking with excitement: "Leah, Leah! Company!"

A Negro ran across the yard to the smokehouse, another dashed into the front door, now yawning open, nearly colliding with Miss Leah, who was running out, tentatively smoothing her dress.

Mrs. Catlett leaned over the railing. "Leah, who is it?" she called. "I can't see."

"Aunt Mamie, it's me! It's Cousin Sally." A new voice, light and airy as a carefully rung bell came from behind the carriage.

The Negroes scuttled like bugs in a rain-barrel. Cousin Annie's shutter was flung open and clattered against the brick. The Mansion at Beulah changed focus, no longer lay upon the landscape in its isolated slumber under the slim blue cedars. Like the Sleeping Beauty, its people pushed aside their boredom and their drowsing, Cousin Annie her headache, the Negroes their evasion, Leah her preoccupation, Mrs. Catlett her redemption in the warm sun. They woke, swept together, and flowed with welcome toward Cousin Sally who had, by coming, broken the ever-present lonely spell.

Aunt Minna sped to a near run, so that she, nearest the carriage, got there first to bob and grin her best welcome.

"Well, I declare ifn it ain't Miss Sally! Dear Lord, ain't you the prettiest thing?"

Sally Lacey ignored her, swept past the rest, and threw herself at Mrs. Catlett as she appeared in the door, calling into her white hair and cap, "Oh Aunt Mamie, I just can't believe I'm here. It's just the nicest moment of my life."

Behind her Brandon Lacey stood, at ease as always, waiting for the formal birdlike sounds of affection between the women to end, so that he could step, poised and sure, toward his kin. Inside the carriage, the mulatto woman impatiently shook the sleeping blond child who had been placed in her lap, whispering, "Wake up, Miss Sara. Come on, Miss Sara. You got to wake up. You just squashing me flat, you heavy thing."

Sara opened her big blue eyes. (She could open them very wide ever since her father had teased her about her big blue eyes and her mother said, Don't spoil the child.) She flirted with the mulatto.

"I ain't too heavy. I'm as light as a little fairy, ain't I?" Maria was too busy peering out of the window to answer her. Philosophically, Sara stretched, twisted a curl, and said, "I know I'm a sight."

"Give that baby here to me." A tall woman opened the carriage door, which had swung shut with no one noticing it. She put her head into the dim, dusty interior. "I'm your Cousin Annie," she said, her voice crackling with special child-talk. "You come be *my* little cousin."

Sara quite sweetly put out her hands. She liked the thinness of the woman, her attention when the others on the walk were dogging her mother, all talking at once, with their backs to the carriage.

Cousin Annie lifted her into her arms, smelled the warm sweat in her soft hair, held her close, feeling against her dry cheek the healthy alive moisture of Sara's mouth. "We'll get along, won't we, you and me?" she whispered, and carried her up the walk after the others, conscious of being huge and lonely, noting the silk dress of her doll-like cousin.

Sally clung to Mrs. Catlett's waist and tipped her head nearly to her shoulder, and Leah walked beside them, an embarrassed attendant with no train to carry.

"We were at the Spa and I told Brandon it would break my heart if I didn't lay eyes on Aunt Mamie just once. The lovely times we used to have in your woodland retreat! It was like a sylvan bower to me." She turned her head, and explained prettily to Leah over her shoulder, letting the sun caress her blond curls, arranged so carefully to escape from her bonnet. Leah, at the gesture, reached up and touched her own hair to see if it was smooth.

Suddenly, Cousin Sally stopped in the shadow of the porch and, thrusting Mrs. Catlett away from her, took on surprise as a garment, and clasped her hands.

"My stars, I was so excited I didn't even notice!" Her musical voice was almost a screech.

The new white-painted brick house rose three stories above her. She tipped her head back slowly, so that her bonnet gradually slipped down to her neck. "It's the most elegant thing I ever saw! An observatory! And beautiful wood shutters! And sweet little columns! Oh my stars!"

She darted through the front door, turned around to admire its fine glass fanlight, its heavy brass lock, ran out of words, gasped; rushed to the door of the parlor and tipped in so daintily that her skirts flipped up behind her like a wagging tail.

"Brandon! Lookee here!" She turned great eyes to find him and caught his glance. Those tired eyes and hers rested within each other's understanding for a pause, quite coolly, and Brandon came forward through a space parted by the proud women.

The parlor had not waked with the rest of the house. Shrouded against the destroying sun, smelling of the summer damp caught in its velvet hangings, it looked forlorn. Its large red plush sofa loomed in the shadows; beside it the shape of a table was covered with a velvet cloth which touched the floor and let its burnished fringe lie gracefully abandoned on the flowered rug, like a woman's skirts. The only sound was the ticking of the gilded clock on the carved wood mantel.

Leah slipped by them, her dress shivering through the dimness, and flung open one shutter proudly, her hand high on it. With a hostess gesture of prodigality, she welcomed the wearing sun into the room to light the dim purple into red, the flocked wallpaper, the red velvet of the hangings over the bookcase, the horsehair master chair: it caught the gilt filigree of the clock, lit the Empire carving of the huge gold mirror on the far wall. The red flowers on the pale rug leapt up into brightness.

Sally breathed a great sigh. "Oh Brandon!" she said, and took his arm. *"Le dernier cri!* They've got flock paper! Why can't we have it? All the latest thing. That darling clock." She walked into the room. *"All* the latest thing—oh, our little old furniture we've just had for generations!"

Leah, still at the window, arrested her hand on the second shutter, let it slide down, pushed the outer shutter as if it were heavier, and slowly turned back, her eyes cold.

Sally didn't see her. She was watching the dignity of her own movements in the long mirror. She sailed slowly past and let herself settle into the sofa, untying the ribbons of her bonnet and letting it fall to the floor behind the reading table.

Mrs. Catlett said kindly, "This is Leah's room. She bought it all new from Cincinnati last year. *Our* old things are in the library. Leah, come here." Mrs. Catlett put out her arm to draw her into the circle and claim her.

But Leah had slipped quietly from the room. The last she heard as she paused in the front hall at the sound of her name, was Mrs.

Catlett's voice going on. "Leah was a Cutwright. Her people were Virginians. They went over into Ohio when Cincinnati was just a place of logs." Delicately she added, "They stand for something in Cincinnati."

"I never thought Peregrine would marry." Sally Lacey giggled.

Mrs. Catlett sighed, pleased. "Of course I always wanted him to—sometime."

Leah couldn't hear what Brandon answered, but Mrs. Catlett laughed, so she must have been talking to him. From the sound of the laughter, which Sally counterpointed with another light giggle, he had said something which brushed Ohio out of the red parlor.

Leah slipped through the door of the dining room and closed it behind her, already counting, her fingers thrumming against her palm, how many there were for the table.

In the dining room, Melinda had stopped too, just in the act of slipping in from the kitchen passage. One of Aunt Christie's girls was polishing the milk cups, placing them in a shining silver circle around the milk bowl in the center of the table, her black face reflecting company pride in each one as she held it up. When Melinda saw Miss Leah, she stepped backward away from her.

But Leah only said, "You look all draggle-tail, child. Go and tell Minna to clean you up. We've got company." She slapped her out of the way gently and went on into the kitchen.

"Company!" Melinda yelled, wanting to dance, or run, or jump.

"Hush up, Miss Melindy. Go git washed," the girl ordered her, still looking at the silver mugs.

Melinda ran out into the hall, tiptoed by the voices in the parlor, slipped up the front stairs, and huddled by the landing post, listening, peeking.

The most beautiful tiny lady Melinda had ever seen was leaning back on the red sofa, her deep blue summer traveling dress like a pool around her, her hair a blond silk pillow high on her head, her short curls forward on her thin cheeks, her voice murmuring, "Then we went to Rome and saw the ruins. I will show you my sketch book." She adjusted a curl and leaned her head against the sofa-back, as if she were tired.

Melinda could feel herself lulled in her blue lap, rocked against her small bosom, her head on the lovely pulsing place at her throat, listening to her, living, close, warm. Charmed, she could not move a muscle, stooped on the stairs, hardly breathing.

"Ah Rome! Firenze!" The woman sighed.

Somebody grabbed Melinda's arm roughly. It was Cousin Annie, towering above her. "Come up here at once, you little ragamuffin!"

Behind her, respectfully, stood a delicate child as pretty as the lady. Melinda looked from her kid slippers to her blond curls, now damp and sausage-shaped with Cousin Annie's brushing. She could almost see Cousin Annie's harsh fingers in each curl.

"This is your Cousin Melinda." Cousin Annie softened as she pulled her on up the stairs. "You run down, Sara, and stay with your mother."

Sara pulled away from them as they came close to her. "She's awfully dirty." She made a simple statement of interest.

The queen of far Araby hung her head to hide her eyes from the girl. Cousin Annie's hand tightened on her arm, and the damp, cold clothes clung drably to her body.

The nursery was so full of familiar people that Melinda didn't notice them. The murmuring of the two Negro women who were bending over Liddy Boo, the sound of Liddy Boo's faltering speech, which had only a few real words and then would lapse into a private language of her own, interrupted by her biting at her neck penny from time to time; the vague, always present smell of urine because Toey forgot the slops in the nursery until the heat of the day had made it permeate the bed covers; the row of beds in a barracks line along the wall with their patchwork quilts laddered by the summer shadows from the half-closed shutters; ages of broken toys piled on the bottom shelf of the open cupboard: all were so much a part of the room that she stood isolated, alone in the midst of it, feeling only the cloying heat after the cool mountain stream. She wanted to escape like a scared colt back to the safety of the woods, but she didn't dare.

Instead she kept watching Liddy Boo's doll on the floor, a nigger doll of cloth which she was always having slapped out of her inquiring mouth. It had fallen under a rung of the now neglected cradle where Little Sister had lain, shrunken and blue, dead of the croup. She could still hear the rock of Cousin Leah's chair in the dark while she cuddled the baby whose life seemed to be fading from its little gray face as they all watched, unable to call it back. She had been rocking with it there all night, oblivious to the other children, her intentness on its face, no longer tender but terrible, willing the baby coldly to live with a force that scared Melinda into trying to run out of the room.

But Cousin Leah had looked up then and called after her, "Girl, girl, you too will come to this." She looked like a wild woman, a field-hand called Till whom they had to keep locked up.

Cousin Annie had dragged Melinda back to make her go on watching because she said she had to strengthen her soul on sorrow. She saw the light fade from the baby's eyes. Even after it was cold and dead, Cousin Leah went on holding it, rocking and sobbing.

Melinda was remembering so hard she was surprised when the inevitable voice of Cousin Annie began to fuss over her again. Now she knew her punishment was coming, and froze. Cousin Annie didn't even seem to notice. She bit hard at her words, hurrying.

"Where is your Sunday dress? I can't find it. Minna."

Minna raised up from Liddy Boo's bed, lifting her with her, and waited patiently.

"Yassum?" she muttered, taking the penny from Liddy Boo's mouth at the same time. Liddy Boo began to yell.

"Is the wash up yet?" Cousin Annie yelled louder.

"No, ma'am." Minna concentrated hard on the baby, who, at two, kicked against being held, and wanted to walk. She hit ineffectively at Minna's black face. The laundry had come up, and Minna had put it away, but she knew by instinct, without even thinking, to avoid any responsibility for it.

Melinda's Sunday dress was hidden with the rest of her bundle behind the milk-house in a hiding place she and Toey had had for some time, covered with a rock until they could sneak it into the wash. Only the two of them, and Johnny and his nigger, knew where the hiding place was.

Nobody said a word.

Cousin Annie gave up, frustrated on all sides by children and niggers.

"That trifling Tilly never ironed it. Here." She tore open a drawer of the big chest, which had "Ezekiel Catlett" carved on it, and the date 1790. It had traveled in its time from the cabin parlor to a corner of the nursery. She found Melinda's last summer's dress.

Melinda ran behind the nearest bed. "I won't," she screamed. "It's too short." Loud enough, hard enough—that would keep huge Cousin Annie from making her ugly, making her foolish. She could see the angry spite shine in the woman's eyes.

Ignoring the noise, the mulatto Maria, who had come in the carriage, complained in the corner to Minna, "I ain't got the heart to do nothin. Way out hyar in the West. Don' nobody keer ifn things is right. I likes Eastern Virginny."

"Thim folks sells niggers to pay fer a fiddle-player," Minna informed her. "We-uns carries the Tidewater on our backs." She had heard Marse Peregrine say this and was pleased at remembering it to tell the upstart, who wore a bonnet like a white woman and didn't even have manners enough to take it off in the house.

Maria, remembering, too, the conversation which had struggled on by worried fits and tearful starts all the way across the mountains, said nothing.

"Maria!" A strident voice called from the hall.

"Now I got to go clean her up." Maria looked sullenly toward the door. "Ain't even my name. My name Rachel. She done change it when we went across the ocean." Over there was too far away for Minna to think about. She had only once been out of Beulah valley to fetch Miss Leah. She waited stolidly as the woman went slowly out, and then turned to see what was making Liddy Boo squall.

Cousin Annie's stern eyes won at last. Melinda crept toward her, beginning to cry softly, "I don't want to see any old company." Cousin Annie grabbed her, as she sometimes did chickens to wring their necks when the blacks weren't quick enough or turned chasing them into a game.

"I've had just about enough," she told the child's head by habit. "You're wet as water."

"They all gits so riled up when they's company," Minna said complacently, comforting Liddy Boo.

Muffled against Cousin Annie's skirts so she couldn't get away, Melinda sobbed her excuse lamely. "I got bit by a snake, and I fell in the creek, and I had to suck it."

Minna heard her and laughed, crowing at the baby's curly hair.

"Don't you tell me any of your lies. I just ain't got the time to listen." Cousin Annie dressed her with strong hands, watching herself in the dresser mirror, reminding herself to wear her gold comb to dinner because her hair was her best feature. "I'll settle with that later. I won't forget."

Melinda, having failed with her story, was too defeated to pursue it. She stood quietly while Cousin Annie rubbed the heavy washrag over her face, working faster and faster, grabbed a comb and began pulling it through the stubborn tangles. Melinda bit her lip, hard. She wouldn't cry again, not if Cousin Annie pulled her hair out. She could feel the fingers then, winding, winding, trying for impossible respectable curls. She could hear, down the well of the stairs, the whirr and chime of the first stroke of noon. It made Cousin Annie pull harder.

"Not even your hair will mind."

At the door, polished at last, Melinda balked once more in a faint hope.

"I don't want to," she begged dumbly, trying to pull her dress long enough with one hand. "I don't like company."

Peregrine Catlett rode slowly across his fields, slack in the saddle, obeying the noon call of the Mansion. The dry faces of the women, the constant questions of the children which were to come, even his own nagging daily questions—the drought, the niggers, money—receded from him as he bowed under the sun in his only sure moment of peace for the day. The relieving pause showed on his unguarded face. He looked younger, more tender than the legion of women and children, the blacks, the men at the salt well ever saw, except in glimpses which made them wonder what kind of man he was behind his easy, offhand authority.

A covey of quail flushed ahead of his horse. He reined in as he heard the whurtle of their wings, watched the birds, free in the air, fly toward the woods. He forgot to spur his horse on, the stillness reviving him.

Somebody called from the road, "Marse Peregrine!"

As if the yell were a spur, his heels dug at his horse's sides. He had one pure reaction, flight, away. A boy alive, pretending not to hear, he took the fence in an easy jump, free as the quail for one short gallop. Then, guiltily, he reined in again and set his horse toward the house, hoping to have at least a julep by himself before he faced the large white dinner table, once more in the armor of lord and master, receiver of the thousand pinpricks of demand. He thought of how lonely God must be sometimes, with the judgments demanded of Him, but with no one to turn to to be judged.

Even the sight of the carriage did not break his mood. He only wondered what trouble, of all the troubles of the panicked, ruinous year, had crossed into Beulah to assail his stolen secret peace of mind.

Leah came back into the front hall in time to meet Mr. Catlett at the door. He had scooped Sally Lacey up in his arms and was kissing her and saying, "Sally, my darling gal!"

"Oh, Peregrine!" She was giggling, struggling playfully to get down.

I'm his wife and I still call him Mr. Catlett, but of course I'm not a cousin!—Leah yelled this without making a sound as she looked at Brandon Lacey who was noticing her at last, bending forward with a small bow.

Mr. Catlett let Sally go and turned to his cousin Brandon to grasp his arm. "By God, Brandon, this is a pleasure, sir! You've met my wife?"

"The gals in Virginia will never forgive you." Brandon Lacey already teased. He and Mr. Catlett looked at each other and laughed, and Mr. Catlett put his arm over Cousin Brandon's shoulder to lead him into the library for a toddy, away from the women.

"Oh, Ma." He paused and looked back at the old woman over Leah's head. "The boy did it. Johnny swum."

"I knew he would." Mrs. Catlett smiled fondly.

Leah faded into the corner by the piano. As the women's talk rose she didn't listen.

"He didn't even tell me first. Told his mother first." She didn't realize she had muttered the thought aloud until she heard Mrs. Catlett say, "What did you say, Leah?"

"Nothing. I was counting."

Mrs. Catlett went on with what she had been saying. "We haven't seen each other . . . Let's see . . ."

Sally leaned forward in her chair, excited. "Fifteen years! I was the ugliest thing."

"Now you never was," Mrs. Catlett broke in. "The beaux you had . . . We got a letter that you and Brandon were married."

"Six years," Sally told her, surprised. "That's been *six* years." She clasped her hands in a single fist, hit her lap, and leaned back again.

"Fifteen years. By damn." Mr. Catlett's voice came back as the men disappeared into the library.

Leah looked after them, worried, shaken at their closeness of memories behind the banality of their talk, and settled herself to try to be caught in the inevitable family fetters of small shared events.

"We Kreggs," Mrs. Catlett was saying, contented. "Let's see. We're kin to the Crawfords two ways. Through Brandon Kregg marrying a Crawford—"

"Only one son," Sally interrupted seriously. "He's eight now. They call him Crawford after our side."

"What a shame. All that money." Mrs. Catlett got straight to the point.

"Money," Sally said bitterly, and covered it by adding, "That's not everything."

"It's everything to that side of the family." Mrs. Catlett crowed with pleasure.

Leah stopped trying to follow them. She was listening to quick footsteps running up the walk. She waited, aware, excited on the piano stool. When she saw who it was, her chin lifted. She called, loud enough to stop the women.

"Lewis!"

A boy of eleven stood barefooted in the doorway, hiding something behind him. His shyness before the strange woman made him watch the floor angrily, a spot just before his feet. His square dark face, so thin it made his eyes jut, looked almost fierce in its attention to the floor. Something had happened to a sleeve of his short jacket. It fell open in a long tear, exposing a skinny arm. Leah caressed his bent head with her eyes, the child most like her side, most understanding, her ally among the besetting sins she fought in these strange people, who would listen when she told him secretly the teachings of her father, which she felt compelled to pass on to one of them, like passing on the immortality of her own misunderstood righteous soul. At least, with silent Lewis she could whisper her bounden duty.

"This is Lewis, my oldest son. He favors *my* father," she told Cousin Sally proudly; then, concerned, "What happened to your jacket? Did you hurt yourself?"

"Got caught in a fence," the boy mumbled.

"Mind your manners, Lewis," his grandmother called sharply from across the room, slapping her hand down, once, on the chair arm.

"Hi do, ma'am," he whispered painfully, and fled, managing to shift what he was hiding to his chest as he ran.

"Go wash yourself, dear," he heard his mother call after him. Her voice dropped, but he could still hear her. "Lewis is the religious one"—a note of pride which made him slam the back-hall door.

"Where's Johnny?" he said sharply to Tig, the yellow goblin who, having given the great news about company, now felt neglected and sat in the dirt just off the slate paving of the back porch, idly wriggling a stick in snaky patterns.

"What are you adoing?" Lewis came closer.

"Writin."

"You cain't write. Niggers cain't write."

"Telemachy kin."

"He cain't. He just lets on to. Go find Johnny. Git!"

The Negro boy didn't move. "He ain't hyar."

"Git I said." Lewis aimed a kick which the boy avoided calmly, rolling and finding his feet to run. He only had to go as far as the back of the kitchen wing when he saw Johnny sneaking up the back path, trying to slip in without being caught.

Tig simply turned around without speaking and jogged along beside Johnny, who meandered, elaborately unconcerned, toward Lewis, to see what he was holding behind his back.

"I got something," Lewis said, as he brought his treasure forward to bait Johnny. It was a withered jack-in-the-pulpit, its root hanging dirty from the stalk.

"I dare you," Lewis told Johnny.

"You do it." Johnny inspected the bulb. They stood for a little while, contemplating the earthy bulb as a masculine problem. Johnny walked away and leaned importantly against a small square porch column. Finally he pronounced his judgment. "I cain't think of nobody," he said.

"Let's do it on Aunt Minna. She ain't got no teeth," Lewis suggested casually as if he had just thought of it.

Johnny whinnied with glee at the picture. He could see Minna already, biting on it. Besides, he was mad at her, really mad, full of strength now that he had been in the river and with Little Dan, too, all in the same morning. Anyhow, she would probably tell on him for running off from her. But a doubt rose when he looked at Lewis's face. The older boy was watching him as if he were trying to will him into it. Johnny, used to the look, was stubborn.

"You go on and do it." He stood with his back to Lewis, examining the grape arbor where the leaves made a huge pattern of lace shadows, moving a little on the ground. He forgot Lewis for a second and searched the still green hard bunches of grapes hoping to find the first ripe one. Some were already blushing, but none were even soft yet.

"Aw, go on, Johnny. Be a sport," Lewis wheedled. "You're a molly, you are. Molly, molly, molly."

The trap fell without Johnny's even knowing it. "I ain't." He turned on Lewis, mad; his lip trembled and he sucked it in.

"Y'are too." Lewis grinned, showing his two new grown-up teeth. Tig giggled. Johnny made himself giggle too. They all began to holler, outdoing one another. Johnny laughed hardest, beating his stomach.

"Wait! You just wait," he screamed.

At that minute, Minna's heavy tentative tread was heard, coming down the outside back steps from the upper porch. She hardly noticed them. She had obviously forgotten Johnny's disobedience in the excitement.

"Hyar, you youngins." She slapped at them. "Git cleaned up. We got company all the way from eastern Virginny. Great big carriage. Real folks."

Johnny and Lewis both subsided under her glance, Lewis through impatience to put the joke into action, Johnny out of surprise and pleasure at the news. He forgot Lewis and wondered what kind of presents the company had brought. He nestled his hand in Minna's big, hard black fingers, and squeezed.

"Now you come on." She squeezed back, pleased, and began to herd them up the stairs.

Lewis looked at Johnny and tried to make him catch the giggling again. Johnny, remembering the dare, the fun they were going to have, part of all the fun of the day, kept on looking at Lewis for strength so he wouldn't feel a traitor.

Minna grinned widely enough at the boy to show her toothless gums. "Lil ole onion," she crooned. This sent Lewis into a wilder fit of giggles. "Run off from ole Minna like that. Neb mind. You jest full of spit and vinegar. Your mammy know."

The chant, "Nigger mammy, nigger mammy," filled Johnny's memory; he could see Little Dan's dirty jeering face. He pulled his hand away from Minna's and hung behind her on the stairs. She, now intent on pushing Lewis, called back, "Come on, balky," and, hearing him clump heavily after her, was satisfied.

It was even worse when she treated him like a baby and sang, "Shoe the gray horse, shoe the gray mare," as she put on his Sunday shoes. Lewis never took his eyes off him.

"Let the lil colty go bare." She spanked his behind tenderly as she drew him up from the chair, and led him over to wash his face.

Over the basin she talked, her words fading as she scrunched the washrag into Johnny's ears. She conjured up the brass of the carriage, the fine clothes, the purple seats, the spanking, fat-rumped matched pair of horses, the sensuality of their sleek coats.

"Don't scwunch your face. I cain't wash thim cracks." She punctuated the story several times with this remark.

Lewis, having torn off the stalk of the jack-in-the-pulpit and thrown it into a corner, forced the root into Johnny's hand and quietly submitted to being washed.

"Johnny's got something for you," he finally interrupted, tired of waiting.

"Ain't that nice?" Minna, preoccupied, went on scrubbing.

Lewis prodded Johnny, hard.

"Lookee." Johnny finally held out the root.

"Now ain't that nice?" Minna paid no attention. She inspected them, standing there together, clean and neat, a pair of youngins to be proud of.

"It's mighty good eating," Johnny pleaded, wiggling the root in her face. He and Lewis were in an ecstasy; it was like landing a fish.

Johnny looked so disappointed that Minna decided to pleasure him, just for a minute, now that they looked so pretty.

"Wild onion," Lewis broke in, and nudged Johnny.

"It's powerful good!" Johnny squealed, persuading.

Minna hesitated. "I don' want to smell like no onion with company."

"We done brought it all the way for you." Johnny sounded so let down that she couldn't resist him.

"All right, honey." She took it from him and made a party gesture, solemnly dipping it into the water bowl. "You real good to think of po ole Minna."

Then, watching Johnny's fascinated face, she bit politely, as hard as she could without teeth, into the root.

Lewis howled and slapped his legs, but Johnny saw her pleased smile disintegrate, her look of mild surprise; then a stab of pain creased her fat cheeks, and the tears started from her eyes. She spat the burning root against the wash pitcher as she buried her whole face into the nearest water in the basin, sucking up the dirty, soapy mess with her mouth, gulping, sucking, spitting, sucking again, all the time trying to wipe the tears from her eyes.

Johnny couldn't move when Lewis ran. He could hear his feet pounding down the back stairs, but he could only stare at Minna, frozen at what he had done to her.

Minna stood erect and wiped her face and eyes with her apron. She turned to him, bland and calm.

"What you want to do a mean thing like that fer, Marse Johnny? Ain't I done ever'thing fer you 'cept borned you?"

They watched each other, masks of new distrust.

Johnny sobbed. He ran against her, pushing his head to her huge breasts where he had once fed. "I never meant to," he kept sobbing. "I never. I never."

She tucked him into her arms and backed into the rocking chair.

"Neb mind," she whispered over and over, kissing his hair as they rocked. He could feel her tears on his head.

"I never meant to." He gasped for breath.

"Neb mind," she whispered, and went on rocking until the dinner-bell clanged, and she had to tip him out of her lap and run the washrag over his face again.

When Cicero called them into the dining room, Peregrine was still remembering the flight of the birds. The hot smell of food, the crowd of familiar strangers, caught at him to take command.

Mrs. Catlett sat down. When the chairs stopped scraping, Peregrine sighed and hoped no one heard him. At his mother's formal nod, obediently he began, "We will bow our heads in prayer. . . ."

Even the peacock feathers of Cicero's fly-switch hesitated devoutly above the table, letting the flies settle on the ham, the platter of chicken, the mound of corn, the milk foam in the silver bowl.

"Almighty and most merciful God, who has vouchsafed to gather us together for Thy bountiful mercies, we thank Thee for Thy manifold blessings, and ask . . ."

A fly buzzed angrily, swimming in the milk.

". . . Thy mercy on us and on our people in the travail of the day. Keep us from sin . . ."

The fly droned, filling the close food-hot room with noise. Peregrine glanced up, annoyed. Cousin Annie, without lifting her head, flicked her hand over the bowl. He went on, softly, ". . . temptation and iniquity in our hearts. Bless this food for our intended use, and us to Thy loving service. Amen."

The "Amen," murmured around the table, brought them all alive. Peregrine sat down. The fly-whisk began its easy sway over the table, brushing the heat haze from the food. Leah sprang forward and leaned over Melinda's head to extricate the fly from the milk.

"How many times do I have to tell you to keep the fly-whisk going during prayers?" Mrs. Catlett rapped at Cicero. His mask face never moved. He went on waving the great feather wand in the air.

Peregrine leaned forward to catch Johnny's eye and make him stop whispering with Melinda, but Mrs. Catlett had heard them with that discerning ear of the censoring deaf.

"Children!" She ordered silence with the word from her end of the table. They shut up and sat straighter on their books at the rap of her authority.

At least when he was serving, Peregrine could escape answering the taken-for-granted conversation, the opinions babbled politely around the table. He stuck the silver fork in the mound of ham.

He had already resolved to treat his Cousin Brandon delicately when he finally approached the subject of his visit. He watched him as he concentrated gallantly on Mrs. Catlett. Beyond the fine cut of his English jacket and his high stock, his casual politeness, the worried sadness and the controlled anger of his face had not left him even when he laughed, ever since Peregrine had walked into the house. Over their toddies in the library, Peregrine had wondered once what would happen to the whole formal order of the day, and to the safe cloak of expected opinions, which were no more cut by Brandon than his jacket was, although he wore them with the same ease, if he had said to him, I know what you came for. You didn't come over the mountains for nothing. I haven't a red cent.

A red cent. Who did have in Virginia, with that damned upstart Jackson taking his Tennessee backwoods money-hate out on the whole country, destroying Mr. Biddle's bank, dissolving solid money so that the country was drowning in paper shin-plasters printed by any fool who wanted to turn his dry-goods store into a bank? Paper! Paper money, paper politicians, paper notes—the word as ephemeral as what it stood for; he could hear Cousin Brandon as clearly as if he'd already said it: I'm on too many people's paper.

Why in the hell hadn't he stayed home and looked after his interests instead of gallivanting all over Europe? Why had he succumbed like a damned fool to that bounden duty of the Virginia gentleman to sign notes for any senseless reason a blood relation could give? Peregrine wasn't going to have it, that blackmail of trouble and foreclosure. It was hard enough to keep his own people afloat without having to sell some of them at such a time. He felt that even his one salt well pulsed with his own heart's blood. There was honor enough to be faced, the honor of keeping things going, any way, until the paper disease was over, the temperature of the country down, the crisis passed, when convalescent Virginia would need calm men who had survived.

Would he have carried the yellow-jack to his family from Cousin Brandon? He wished to God the man hadn't come to harass his soul with hard decision.

"Peregrine, you know I don't like ham. It gives me the gas," his mother complained; then she turned heavily toward Cousin Brandon, having put all her children in their places. "When I was young we suffered from a certain lack of discipline engendered by revolutionary feelings. The men gambled somewhat heavily. Let the Lees be a lesson to us all. Profligacy!" She said it as a sin. "My handsomest gown weighed one pound, shoes and all. There was a great need for religion, and with things as they are . . ." She sighed and clapped her lips. "Children should be seen and not heard." She looked hard at Cousin Annie. "Religion is a great solace. The *right kind* of religion."

She settled back and tucked her napkin under her chin. Sally Lacey took hers from her glass and placed it delicately in her lap. Cousin Annie glanced up, looked surprised, and did the same.

Peregrine made himself concentrate on poor involved Cousin

Sally. "As I was saying," Mrs. Catlett called down the table to interrupt them and go on with the inevitable conversation which had started in the parlor before the men escaped. "The Catletts now"—Mrs. Catlett attacked her chicken, a mound of corn, and the butter almost at the same minute—"were French. Norman French knights. Their name was really de Chatelet, which means castle. They laid claim to Beulah with a ruby ring and a silver riding crop. It shows what fine folks they were to have such things." She pushed her gnarled hand under Brandon's eyes. "The head of the house. Lookee. Ever since." The smooth, egg-shaped ruby, confined in thick gold, caught the summer light.

Having heard his mother begin her favorite subject and her food, Peregrine shut away from the group as neatly as if he had closed a shutter between himself and them. He found himself tenderly watching his daughter, Liddy Boo, whom Leah had begun to feed, shushing her at the same time, and keeping the spoon aloft from her grasping little fingers. He wondered how she could ever grow from the dear little round elf she was into as pretty, troubled a woman as Cousin Sally. For that sweet, valued reason, if for no other, he knew what he had to do.

"They came over to England with William the Conqueror. They were knights," Mrs. Catlett still went on. "The first Catlett came to Virginia because of religious persecution. My sister-in-law's niece found all this out. Let me see who she married. Sometimes I forget. . . ."

"Not often." Peregrine caught Leah's mutter, but knew his mother hadn't heard. Leah slapped Liddy Boo's hand away from her milk in a tiny fit of anger, then stuffed her mouth with pickle when she began to cry.

Mrs. Catlett remembered. "She married a Mr. Carver, a minister of the Gospel. She went to sleep in Jesus ten years ago. Once she went all the way to Europe. That's where she found out. She had a growth."

"The Kreggs descended from the Scottish kings," Cousin Annie called down the table from the other side of Peregrine.

"We all know that," Mrs. Catlett called back.

"The Cutwrights is kin to Pocahontas," Lewis said quietly through a mouthful of corn. His mother smiled at him.

Mrs. Catlett had heard. She turned to include Leah. "Leah here is a regular princess, right down from Pocahontas on the Cutwright side."

Beside Peregrine, Cousin Sally was making a philosophical remark about manners; he dragged some attention to her as he went on serving the mound of chicken, startled when he heard the end of what she was saying, as if she had read his mind.

"Of course we was asked of the panic in Europe." She giggled a little. "I had to hint we never talked of such things in Virginia." The silence was so deep she had to breach it with anything except the obsession she was so ashamed of and compelled to mention. "In Rome," she went on, more shrilly than she meant to, "we went to see Saint Peter's. The arches in front were . . . beautiful." Her voice limped on. She couldn't stop throwing her chattering pebbles into the gulf of silence she had made.

"I made a sketch." She foundered in the abyss of sudden disapproval rising around her.

Melinda, transfixed by her view through the glass and silver of the cruet which made a princely jewel in front of lovely Cousin Sally's bosom, spoke up to help. "Grandpa said the Catletts was just—"

Mrs. Catlett interrupted, "Melinda's grandpa was addled in his age."

"He just came and sat down," Cousin Annie said. "He was such a notionate old man you couldn't tell him a thing." Her laughter was left with her as Mrs. Catlett went on.

"He came to lay claim to Beulah or some such, something about his mother's right. She was married to a Lacey. You know, Brandon, that was your, let me see, Great-Grandfather Jonathan. The property came down through my mother-in-law. She died when Daniel was a child from childbirth, so we never knew much about that branch of the family. All we have is Johnny's name. He was killed in the war with England, wasn't he, Peregrine, wasn't he killed in the war with the English?"

Peregrine came back from his silent retreat at the other end of the table, "I believe so," he said, but didn't care. "Uncle Perry couldn't tell us much about him." He deftly finished the subject of the unknown Jonathan Lacey. It didn't stop Mrs. Catlett. She went on in full spate.

"Now my father-in-law reared the children. That was Ezekiel. He ruled with a rod of iron. He built the place up from nothing, bought most of the servants. After his wife died all in the world he cared about was money. Daniel always told me that."

The room had deadened. Time crawled under the garrulity of remembrance and pride. Peregrine tried to draw Cousin Sally away from her nervous twisting of her napkin. She hadn't eaten anything.

"Still a frail gal," he noticed to make her feel better. She looked up as grateful as a comforted child.

Through his words, Mrs. Catlett leaned quietly toward Melinda so she wouldn't interrupt the conversation, and almost whispered, "Melinda, you may leave the table."

"Why?" Melinda looked up, her face red with surprise.

"Because I tell you. You talk too much for a child."

Without another word, Melinda slid down from her book and ran out of the room.

"Little colts should be well broke," she heard Mrs. Catlett say as she ran, and the strange man laughed. She hid in the parlor where she was going to cry, but she couldn't. Her body was hot and cold by turns with fury. She could only watch the door and listen to the soft murmur of voices down the hall.

Inside the dining room, no one else noticed her going.

"Such a mistake, I do believe, the war with the English." Cousin Annie was being awkwardly sprightly with Cousin Brandon.

"We only exchanged one tyranny for another." Brandon made a safe answer and smiled by habit. Cousin Annie shot a glance of triumph at Peregrine.

"Sir?" Peregrine said very softly.

"At the North," Brandon murmured, staring at him, "they mean to bleed us to death."

Peregrine watched the stupid stubbornness, almost a hurt-boy look, spread across Brandon's handsome face, and couldn't help smiling. "I cannot think they wish to kill the goose that lays the golden eggs. I see us all in this trouble together."

"Look at their tariff!" Brandon's voice rose. "Look at their underhanded attempts to make our niggers rise and slaughter us all—"

"We had risings before the abolitionists and you are well aware of it, sir," Peregrine warned, bored already with having to state his case to the man. "I stand pat for a protective tariff, Western improvement, and the United States Bank. In matters of this import, sir, I believe in making myself clear. A Whig, sir, by inclination and interest."

"I am at your table, sir." Brandon bowed a slight bob, without rising.

Mrs. Catlett did not tolerate politics at the dinner table. "The Catholic Church is the Whore of Babylon mentioned in the Revelation of Saint John the Divine," she stated loudly, shutting them both up. "Sally, my dear, I'm ashamed of you, entering the very portals of Popery in Rome." She safely steered the conversation back to Sally's *faux pas*.

"Oh, it was only the architectural magnificence," Sally apologized, "not Popery. If you could imagine the hold it has—"

"They fully intend to take over this country, lock, stock, and barrel." Leah turned away from Liddy Boo. "I saw the immigrants in Cincinnati, all paid by the Pope to take over the West from the Americans."

"It's the filthy Irish, mark my words," Mrs. Catlett expounded comfortably. "They aim to take over for the Pope of Rome. . . ."

Having safely agreed through the perils of Popery and the *Awful Disclosures* of Maria Monk, they arrived at last, as Peregrine knew they would, at the question of the Institution.

"We just seem to live on a powder keg, a heap of pesky blacks." Sally groaned prettily, then leaned forward, ignoring Cicero, who had moved the peacock feathers nearer her because she was lady company.

Over thick cake, desultory murmurs came in unwelcome waves about Peregrine's head. He felt all his forty-three years trapped in the master chair, unable to leave the table to keep from having to hear yet again the formal progression of stories.

Picking at the fear as one of the children would at a scab until it bled again, they talked Nat Turner, Nat Turner, the nigger who could read, the preacher who struck in God's name and kept slavery from being abolished in Virginia, the name and the fear seeping on and on around the table.

Cousin Brandon began the story of the man in Westmoreland County who asked his own body servant if he would have joined Nat Turner and killed his white family, and the nigger, who had nursed at the same woman, had said, "Yes, Marse Robert, I ain't never lied to you."

"Miss Katy Smith was poisoned by her own half-brother who was her butler because she said her will freed him and he didn't want to wait. He said he'd already waited fifty-seven years," Mrs. Catlett told Cousin Brandon and they had to laugh.

Peregrine watched Leah, poor little stranger, sitting straight as a perpetual visitor, the secretive girl who had charmed him because she was one of the few women he hadn't known all his life—always a stranger, disapproving of them all with her stiff blind will.

"No answer," Peregrine wanted to yell at her. "I know of no answer."

Like bindweed the subject seemed to throttle him with a constant debilitating sense of a problem unsolved, a duty not a sane man in Virginia wanted, the military boredom of watching and waiting, with no move ever made; each path closed by contemplation and responsibility and forever demanding family needs.

By the time the slow scrape of Johnny's fork over his empty pudding plate made him look up, frown, and shake his head, Peregrine was so sleepy from the heat and the food, and the anger turned inward at the indecisive interview to come with Brandon, that he felt his head grow heavy. The few minutes before they left the table crawled like hours.

The house slept. No sound, no movement came from the women's rooms. Heavy with hot food, caught in the atmosphere of rest, they napped, or lay inert, lulled by the heat.

The children slept too, watched sternly by Minna, who sat in her rocker at the end of the line of nursery beds, quieting the giggling, counting them one by one as their noise faded into peace, and finally nodding herself. The only sound at all was the faint hum of men's voices which floated through the open door of the nursery, the house so still that it carried from all the way behind the closed library door.

Only Melinda was not asleep, but she lay with her eyes wisely closed, so full of hate and plans that she could feel her body, as stiff as a board, and wished she could spring on them all and beat them to death. Mrs. Catlett hadn't sent darling sneaky Lewis away, only her; her teeth clenched against the unfairness of it. Then that little pale Miss Priss had slipped ahead of the approaching grown-ups and caught her just taking off the beautiful lady's bonnet. She had only tried it, just for a second, all she wanted to do was to look at herself in it for one second, she wouldn't have hurt it for the world. But Sara had told her she'd better take it off at once, it wasn't good manners to steal ladies' things and her mother would be mad. After all it was her mother's bonnet. She didn't have to say that about it being her mother when Melinda didn't have anybody, and about her hair being dirty and her being a thief and not having any manners. One day she would repay her; she moved her head just enough to watch Sara asleep beside her, her fingers in her hair, and her mouth slightly open and wet.

"I vow eternal revenge on you," she promised but didn't know she whispered it until she heard Minna mutter, half asleep, "Go sleep, Miss Lindy." The rocker creaked.

Melinda scrunched up her eyes to show how asleep she was and daydreamed that she was dropping, light as a feather, into Cousin Sally's milk-white arms. Cousin Sally said she looked like a very beautiful angel, and thank God she had found her little lost darling again after she had been stolen away from her for so painfully long.

The voices behind the library door faltered and hummed on.

What Sally Lacey couldn't understand was how she could have slept at all, obsessed with worry as she was. She came down earlier than the others, before four o'clock, trying to keep her skirts from rustling on the stairs and as she tiptoed past the library door, too frightened of being caught to pause and try to catch the separate words. All she could make out as she went into the parlor to wait were the two levels, Peregrine's quieter, lower voice, and Brandon's, raised once, and then subsiding.

There was nothing to do but wait. She sat on the edge of the sofa she had lounged on. The clock ticked loudly and began to whirr for the stroke of four. Sally jumped up, seeing her bonnet on the floor, threw it in a tiny teacup rage on top of the pianoforte, and sat down again without even bothering to look in the mirror. Every other sound except that of the men talking caught at her nerves. The clock pounded. She could hear the children, away in the distance, waking up, growing louder, Sara crying for a minute as she always did on waking. Sally folded her lips and resolved to speak to Maria about allowing the child to do it in other people's houses, even kin, even these kin. Sally felt a smile spreading and stopped the thought and the smile.

The library door was still closed. The clock struck.

The children's presence began to permeate the house. She could hear one of the boys say with authority, "P'like we're gathering the Clan. I start the Fiery Cross."

Sara asked, "What's that?" and the other little girl told her scornfully, *"Lady of the Lake*. Ain't you never heard of that?"

"Sara's only four"—a boy's voice.

"Can I be fair Ellen?" Sally could recognize now the girl with the tousled black hair, the little gypsy.

"You have to be Blanche of Devon," the authoritative voice went on, now at the top of the stairs. "Sara can be fair Ellen. She's company."

"I'm a cousin"—anger in the little gypsy's voice.

"She's a closer cousin than you are. If you won't be Blanche of Devon you cain't play. She's too little to jump over the cliff. She'd be afraid."

The gypsy was conquered. "I'm not afraid of anything," she said proudly.

"Who am I?" That was Johnny, the handsome child who had sat beside her.

"You be Rhoderick Dhu."

"I had to be him last time."

She could see their feet on the stairs. It was Lewis, the older boy, who said, as he came into view, leading them, "It's my turn to be James Fitz-James."

"It ain't," Johnny muttered, then saw her and looked away.

"All right! So help me heaven and my good blade, the Fiery Cross begins right here." Lewis stopped on the stairs and held his arm high. "Ho, ieroe! Fire and blood! The muster place is the mare-barn. Woe to the traitor. No law but the Clan's command!" He hadn't seen Sally yet, but Johnny had and was too shy to answer the Call of Blood.

She, forgetting them, withdrawing from their noise, whispered to herself, "I just don't know what to do," and watched the glitter of her rings as she rocked her hands. She nearly jumped up as the library door was wrenched open and Peregrine came out, looking stern, even angry, with worry. She could see that. She could see the unwilling no on his face.

"You children go and play somewhere else," he commanded, and slammed the door.

They ran together through the back hall. Now, completely alone, Sally leaned back hopelessly, deadened, too disheartened even to cry.

Chapter Six

THE TROUBLE began when Johnny stopped on the way to the mare-barn to show Sara the new puppies. She asked for one, and happened to pick the pretty spotted bitch with the two black eyes that Melinda had claimed, and Sara just squatted there, holding tight to the puppy as it wiggled and licked the tears from her face, crying for the puppy.

So Johnny told Sara she could have it so she would stop crying, and Sara pranced right back to the Clan, even letting the puppy tumble out of her lap, not caring in her excitement that it landed on its back.

Of course, because she was a girl, the first thing she did was to tell Melinda, so he had to explain that Sara was a cousin twice, through both sides, and that Melinda was only a cousin once, through one side, and besides, Sara was company. Melinda acted so mean he was glad he took the puppy back.

They had brought Sara home, a sad procession after gathering the Clan. She said Melinda had pushed her, but Melinda only bumped against the little old thing when Lewis chased her with the snake. It wasn't much of a snake anyhow. Lewis had said it was the Serpent after Eve and had teased Melinda with it until she screamed and screamed that she hadn't told a lie. Nobody said she told a lie. Sara only cut her arm a little bit when she fell down the hay chute, but it ruined the game.

As they filed slowly up to the porch, Johnny saw his father

through the twilight, looking angry, his face red as it was sometimes by evening. All the grownups but his grandmother were there. They looked like they hadn't said anything for some time. Sara told on them anyway, after she promised she wouldn't. She told as soon as she saw her mother. Her mother acted all fluttery over her, and took her in to find Minna and some vinegar and brown paper. He could hear Sara hollering all the way upstairs. His father took him and Lewis by the arms, tight. Cousin Annie sprang toward Melinda. "Where is my comb?" she hollered, when of course it didn't have anything to do with that.

None of this bothered Lewis. It never did. He could close something behind his eyes and wait, not saying a word.

Over their shoulders, his father said to Cousin Brandon, " 'Withhold not correction from the child: for if thou beatest him with the rod, he shall not die.' "

Cousin Brandon didn't answer. He didn't even pay any attention to Sara's cut. He just kept on staring through the darkening trees where the first lightning bugs were showing their bright flashes.

In the library his father waited until both of the boys knelt in front of him. Through his voice Johnny could hear Melinda calling, "I never took it. Please, I never took it."

"Liar and thief," Cousin Annie kept repeating. "Liar and thief," and whipping her.

At the same time his father told them that they had to take care of little girls who were frail and weak, and he said it was sinful to lie and make excuses. He told them they lived in a world where you had to discipline yourself before you could take on the burden of disciplining others. He always told them that. Then he whipped them hard with his leather strap. Lewis just stood there and didn't even cry or repent, but Johnny cried and ran off down the road to be by himself. He heard his father say as he ran, "Let him go. He has to think things over and nurse his wounds."

His mother answered, "He'll miss evening prayers. He'll miss his supper."

"He's not to have any supper." He heard his father through the trees, having the last word.

Johnny ran up the creek, back to the mare-barn where he had

his favorite hiding place. Hardly anybody else came there, except to feed the few mares, which were stalled when they came in heat and his father didn't want them bred.

He climbed up the ladder to the loft and found his hiding place, carved out of the hay by the door, where he could see the deepening twilight from outside and could hear the big creek behind him and watch the little run across the road. The loft ran around three sides of the barn, where the pitch darkness contained the ghosts of all their stories, the headless people, the pale specters, the walking skeletons, the cold, damp hands of life after death, always ready to caress. He could not have hidden there for the world.

"John—nee, Marse John—nee!" He could hear Minna away across the run in the side yard, and he burrowed farther into the hay. His father called out, far away from the porch, "Let the boy alone, Minna, he'll come back."

That was one thing his father always understood about him. He would whip, but then he would leave him alone and make everybody else leave him alone.

The tree frogs began their grating cry. Johnny could still see, in the shadow below, the one mare in the front stall change weight, click her shod feet, and blow out a trembling sigh, like a person. He thought he slept, and then he thought he dreamed, but he couldn't, at first, be sure.

Cousin Annie was standing below him, her white hand rubbing the mare's flank. She was humming; he never had heard her do that in his life. The moonlight caught shining in the coil of hair on top of her head and made it seem to move like a snake. As she turned he could just see that she had drawn some of her hair forward in sausage curls on her cheeks like Cousin Sally's. She stopped humming and glanced around at the open barn door so he could see the dark pits where her eyes belonged. She leaned her head down and rested it against the flank and let herself stroke the mare under her tail where Lewis had shown him the place, opening and shutting sometimes, like a mouth. The mare didn't mind. Its back rippled and caught the moonlight too.

Johnny didn't hear him coming either, but he was there. He seemed to slide in beside Cousin Annie. Big Dan O'Neill was right below him and he was laughing very softly at Cousin Annie. Johnny knew how much they hated each other. He held his breath.

" 'Tis the place fer you, my dear. Rut. Rutty." Big Dan went on laughing until Cousin Annie whispered, "Be quiet."

Johnny saw Big Dan's hand go up and thought he was going to slap her. She must have thought so too, because she stepped back and leaned against the stall boards. But he only reached up and took the pins out of her hair. It poured down from her head almost to her feet, a shadowy dark tent.

She said, "Don't—"

"Thin why did ye send me the orders?"

"I had to talk to you."

They were whispering. Johnny could hear his heart beat. He prayed that they would miss the sound.

"You want to hurt me. Humiliate me, you . . ." Her little white teeth gleamed as she spoke. Her tongue darted out from them like Melinda's when she made a face.

"Catlett. Catlett lady." Big Dan moved against her and Johnny had to shut his eyes to keep from seeing if he hurt her. She wasn't a Catlett anyway. She was a Brandon.

He heard them move. They were climbing up the ladder, coming nearer to him in the dark. Cousin Annie climbed first, panting; her breath filled the barn. She turned away and he could hear her stumbling through the hay making a sound like rats scurrying, toward the terrible black interior. Big Dan's body loomed in the light, and he followed Cousin Annie. Johnny could hear the heavy crackle of the hay as she sat or lay down.

"You've got to do something." Cousin Annie seemed to be crying.

"I've got nothing fer you, my fine lady, but this." Big Dan laughed softly.

Cousin Annie moaned. He could hear Big Dan shift his weight on the hay. The moaning grew louder; Johnny knew that covered by the dark, Big Dan was shaking her, hurting her. He could hear his breathing and the hay rustle to the rhythm of his beating like the fall of Father's strap, which was always in time with the clock.

He wanted to scream. It was cold.

Cousin Annie did call out at last, "Ahhh!"—a calling sigh—and stop her moaning. At the same time Big Dan said, "Oh Gawd, oh Gawd, oh . . ." and Johnny knew he was sorry for hurting her.

The barn was dead still for a few minutes. When Big Dan spoke again, he was quieter, as if the Mike had been taken out of him.

He said, "Name of God, Annie, what do you expect me to do?"

"We cain't wait." Cousin Annie seemed to be crying again. "I cain't hide it much longer. Leave her, Dan. She's only trash. I'll make a gentleman out of you. That's what you want, ain't it?" Her persuasive words tumbled out of the darkness faster and faster. "I can do that. After all, you've not always been as you are. You told me. You told me the kings of Ireland were your people."

"Annie, Annie, the pigs of Ireland air me people. Why do ye listen to me blather? I'm a Catholic paddy and me auld mither suckled me on beer and slops."

"Say 'Mother.' " Cousin Annie's voice was stern, as it was when she corrected Melinda.

"Mother," Big Dan imitated obediently.

"You will be Mr. Neill, and you can embrace Jesus as your Savior. Even a Catholic can do that. We can go away."

"Ye willful lady, can we now? I'll break ye yet. Damn you."

Then there was their breathing, pain from the sound, and the rustling of the hay.

Silence, and then she said, "Dan, you're hurting me."

"I want to hurt ye."

Johnny could feel the pressure, almost unbearable, of waiting for them to reappear at last. They climbed down into the moonlight, Cousin Annie winding up her hair. Big Dan must have been sorry he had hurt her, because he kissed her, holding her, and said, "Soon, me darling, call fer me soon." He burrowed his head in her shoulder as if she were his nurse.

She lifted his head and Johnny thought she said, "I hate you." At least he was sure she ran her hand over his face as she had the mare's flank, and suddenly, she laughed, one short, bitter laugh; and ran away down the creek path, her skirts flap-flapping behind her. Big Dan leaned in the doorway and watched the moon, his back to Johnny, until he thought he would never move.

After he had finally disappeared, Johnny lay for a long time. Then slowly, sure again it was a dream, he climbed down from the loft and ran toward home on the pale ribbon of a road, through a corridor of lightning bugs he didn't have time to catch.

He couldn't know how long he had been trapped in the barn, but it felt late. He could hear some of the field-hands singing to a banjo over against the hill at the quarters, so he knew at least it wasn't nine o'clock. Nine o'clock was the only time after dark he really knew. That was when his father made the hands leave off their singing and go to bed. Usually from his own bed, through the opened window, he would hear the singing cease, and the sound of Mr. McKarkle's horse clopping along by the quarters, his last job as overseer done for the day.

Johnny picked his way surely across the ford stones of the run, and climbed up the bank to the lawn where in the dark the white-washed trunks of the trees stood out like ghosts. The Mansion, through the branches, was a hulking shape, but the windows lit up from time to time on the second floor from candles being carried past them. They flashed and faded, guiding him. He knew that the other children had gone to bed, and that someone was in his mother's chamber. The only steady light was in the library window. As he sneaked closer he saw the lamp making a soft pool of light around the library table. His father was sitting there with his back to him; the cool blue smoke from his pipe curled upward out of the light.

He couldn't see Cousin Brandon; he could only hear his voice, almost dead now, not excited as it had been for a minute at the dinner table.

"It's wrong, and it's ruinous, but by God, what can we do? Let everything go to hell? If there was some place to take my people and start again . . ."

"Have you considered the West?" Johnny could hardly hear his father.

"I can see Miss Sally Crawford in Missouri."

Johnny slipped along under the sill in the protecting dark toward the back of the house. At least they didn't seem mad any more.

The nursery was so quiet when he sidled through the door that he tried to keep it from groaning as it always did, to give him away. He could feel sleep around him, all the other children. Minna sat beside the candle near the window. The light flicked over her face as she watched the bounding shadows that, from its blowing, made the room seem wave-tossed with the night. Johnny tiptoed up to her, and, as he knew she would, she hugged him without a word and kissed his face, then began to undress him, even as she heaved him onto her lap, being very careful not to wake the others. He nestled up to her, already nearly asleep.

The door behind them opened a crack. His mother whispered stridently, edgy, "Is he back yet, Minna?"

"Yessum," Minna said.

"Bring him right here to me."

Minna gathered him up, almost undressed, and carried him into Miss Leah's chamber.

She was standing in the middle of the floor, holding her candle in her hand. Her hair was down like Cousin Annie's had been, and her voice, when she spoke, trembled like Cousin Annie's when Big Dan hurt her.

"Johnny, where have you been?"

He turned his head into Minna's bosom. He could feel his mother's hands, picking him away from Minna's safety, and he struggled, but not enough. She walked back and forth with him, not holding him as Minna did, but clutching, as Sara had clutched the puppy, into the light of the candle, into the dark, the light, the dark, talking, talking; the room was full of it. The darkness changed shape, made bears in the corners.

"Oh you hurt your poor mother so when you run away, Johnny." He never meant to hurt her, yet she did breathe just like Cousin Annie when she was hurt by Big Dan. He hadn't done anything to her.

"You must cast out, my child, the terrible iniquity in your heart, the sin of forgetting your mother's feelings. Do you know what can happen to you in the dark with these fearsome blacks ready to rise at any moment?" The darkness was a tall tree. "Oh be careful in this wicked world." Now, as she passed in front of the candle, the darkness squatted, a huge dwarf.

She seemed to have forgotten Minna, and Johnny hoped Minna couldn't hear, but he knew she could. Parents just seemed to look through the blacks sometimes and talk about them as if they weren't there, or were sweet and charitable and talked about love and religion in special voices. Once he got caught undressing in front of Melinda to wash in the creek, and it was a sin, so he was given a good hiding. But Cousin Annie and his mother went around in their dishabille in front of Jim just as if he didn't exist and wasn't a man. He had heard Minna warn Jim about that. Jim was her husband. She said, "You be careful. . . ." The dwarf reared up, a horse. Everybody said, "Be careful." All be careful of each other. His mother had started to pray.

"Oh my God, my God"—just like Big Dan when he was sorry—"look Thou down upon a little sinful child. Take Thou his heart in Jesus before he dies a tiny sinner. . . ."

The shadows drifted and changed. Johnny was nearly asleep.

"Oh Thou who diest for sinners, save a wicked child that he may be spared the pains of hell if he should be taken from his loved ones this night. Teach him that disobedient children, unless they repent, come to a bad end, and that there is no blessing on such as do not honor their parents and respect them. . . ."

He was just conscious of being transferred into Minna's arms, and of her whisper, far away. "You go to bed, Miss Leah. The boy's asleep."

He wasn't quite asleep.

By midnight Beulah crouched lifeless under a full white moon in the center of the sky. Only Cuffee, the miller, was still awake. He took a last look at the pond side of the mill, where another moon floated in the water. He listened. A dog howled, and slept again.

Cuffee tiptoed across the creaking wooden floor, picked up a bundle which lay by the loading door, and let himself down carefully into the road. It was so light that the moon cast his shadow on the pale dirt. He stopped and felt again under his ragged flour-dusty shirt where he had tied the gold comb, found a stick to hoist his bundle to his shoulder, and slipped off the road across the creek where he could find the mare, the only horse unguarded, in the mare-barn. The pack was heavy from the food he had been saving, and the stick bruised his old shoulder. He crouched behind a tree and tried to keep from whimpering as the dog set up its howl again. He picked up a rock to kill it if it came near, but dropped it again as he found the direction of the sound. It was only Marse Johnny's Prance, tired of her pups, trying to get out of her pen. Cuffee slipped on, under the tree shadows, to the mare-barn.

Peregrine Catlett took longer than the others to go to sleep. He lay as far from Leah as he could, to keep from waking her, for the poor child's sleep seemed troubled too. From time to time she groaned and threw her arm above her head in that sweet gesture which made him feel such tenderness toward her.

He could hear, for a long time, the voices of Brandon and Cousin Sally across the hall, and knew, ashamed and impotent, as clearly as if he were there, what they were saying. As sleep flirted with him he felt guiltier and guiltier about them, and damned them for it. Who, in trouble with his mount, knew the tight reins in the hands of the man who seemed to ride so easily? As he dipped finally toward sleep, he thought he heard a horse canter by, and smiled at the irony of his image of himself as rider coming alive as he sank toward dreaming.

Chapter Seven

LEWIS WAS the first to see the nigger-catcher's wagon. He liked better than anything else to be first and inform the others. When they crowded around the wagon, not scared of the miller at all in the broad daylight, with so many of them there, Lewis couldn't help laughing. It was the only time he had ever seen Cuffee when he was washed clean black, except for the dust on him from rolling around in the back of the cart. He hadn't been gone but a week, but he was changed. He didn't look ghostly at all, just a plain old scared nigger in the same ragged nigger-cloth jeans he always wore, with his arms and legs all roped up like a hog. He wouldn't look at them when they hollered at him. He wouldn't look at anything but his big bare thick feet. He kept moving them as if the rope were too tight. The mare he'd stolen was tethered to the back of the cart.

When Lewis's father came over from the inn yard, he didn't even act as though he saw Cuffee. Lewis noticed that. He almost seemed to be trying to avoid looking at him. He looked at the mare, though, and bent down to inspect her legs. When he had done that, and run his hand over her coat and patted her, he turned around and spoke to that bundle of nigger laying there just like he was apologizing.

He said, "Cuffee, I been good to you, ain't I? Why did you do this to me?"

Cuffee mumbled something and then he started to cry that trickly kind of old-man cry like he was wetting himself and couldn't help it, and couldn't get his hands up to wipe the muddy water from his face.

Lewis turned away, disgusted, and inspected the nigger-catchers, just a couple of field-tackies anybody could hire. In their dirty straw hats and homespun, they looked off into the distance with their dumb blank faces, waiting to unload and get paid so they could go on back downriver before it was dark.

Mr. McKarkle, the overseer, rode up then and his father told them all to scat. The last thing Lewis saw was Mr. McKarkle with his gray beard blowing in the summer river wind like pictures of Moses, guiding the wagon up toward the abandoned smokehouse near the quarters.

They kept Cuffee there for a week. Lewis watched Aunt Tilly taking plates of food and waiting as patient as a skinny broke mule for Mr. McKarkle to open the door for her. She was Cuffee's mammy, and he was already as old as a rock. Lewis couldn't figure out why Cuffee was so clean of the flour until he heard his father tell his grandmother he had been caught trying to swim the Ohio river. "The poor fool," she said. "He might have been drowned."

Melinda told him they'd found Cousin Annie's prissy damned gold comb she was always hollering about still tied to Cuffee under his jeans; he hadn't even had sense enough to sell it. Cousin Annie didn't mention it to Melinda; she didn't apologize for whipping her about it. She just washed the comb over and over again with a worried look on her mean square face and stuck it in her horsetail of hair. Melinda swore eternal revenge on Cousin Annie in blood she pricked from her finger. That was one good thing about Melinda. She wasn't scared of the devil and hell, and she was always swearing eternal revenge. Lewis wanted to rassle her and hold her down. She was the only one he couldn't make do what he told them.

One night during that week, when the house was quiet and he lay awake, thinking everybody had gone to bed, he heard his parents' voices and slipped out of bed to listen. He wasn't scared; he'd done it so often and knew how to tiptoe through the dark hall and crouch down near the edge of the door, all ready to run if he heard one of them walk toward him. The moon touched him with light from the observatory door and he scrunched away from it into the shadow of the linen cupboard. Through the closed door of their chamber he could hear his father, sounding angry and bored.

". . . and for all, Leah, you cain't see what I have to do. We ain't had a runaway in our family before Cuffee, and I cain't have him contaminating the others."

"If I could just understand why he did it . . ." His mother had been crying.

"Hell and damnation, I don't know why; said the youngins hurt his feelings; said he asked me for a boy to keep him company." He heard his father sigh. "I cain't remember everything, so damn many people asking. A runaway and a thief after all this time. I feel a failure."

He knew his mother didn't answer because his father had sworn. He heard a chair groan as if she had got up.

"You just cain't tell when a runaway will show up." His father was talking to himself, he was sure. "They got it in their blood, some of them, like horses. Once for all, I cain't have a runaway contaminating the others. Root him out. If he don't like it here, let him go elsewhere. I've given my life to this passle of blacks. . . ." He sounded hurt.

Lewis knew why. His mother had told him. She even said once that his father seemed to pay more mind to the blacks than he did to his own blood. She said he ought to because of the sin. It was terrible to see your own father's sin all around you, black, ungrateful, taking everything. Lewis hated it when his mother talked like that and then wouldn't say what was right in front of the others. He willed her not to pay any attention to that close begging in the chamber which shut him out, not to give in, but willing in a dark hall was not as close as the touch of a hand. He knew; he knew she was touching the man, maybe even pushing his old rooster's comb of hair back as she did Lewis's bangs, for her voice, when she spoke, had softened. Lewis's hands curled into fists. He wanted to beat the door until it splintered.

All sweet soft, her voice said, "Mr. Catlett, I never dreamed you were upset about it. I didn't understand . . ."

"Maybe you will now, Leah. What use am I if I cain't keep my people contented under my care? I've got to keep my authority."

"I just cain't reconcile myself to the passing of money for a man," his mother answered as if she were asking a question.

There was not a sound in the room. Lewis held his breath for fear he'd missed something. Someone's weight shifted and made a chair squeak. He knew which chair by the sound. His father would be sitting by the fireplace, staring at the summer paper fan, and she would be standing there, close to him, her hand all soft and gentle, tickly.

"Have you ever considered how much money Cuffee's worth when we haven't had a red cent for three months?" The man broke the silence with a slight laugh, cruel to her when he had lured her so close. "Twelve hundred dollars, Miss Leah."

"Twelve hundred dollars!" Her voice had changed to another person's, someone Lewis didn't know. She repeated it. "Twelve hundred dollars!" She seemed to lick each word.

"You never bothered to find out, did you, my dear? You married, in human terms, a fairly rich man."

"Twelve hundred dollars. Dear Lord."

She said nothing more. Lewis, cramped and impatient, thought it was over, and was waiting for them to begin moving so he could slip back to bed without being heard. Then she said, "We must go to bed, Mr. Catlett, I'm just tired to death." He could hear her voice slide downward, defeated, as if it were her body, and he raged, willing it not to happen to her because she was right, she'd told him in deepest secrecy. Now there was only that betraying voice, sliding as his tears threatened to slide and melt when his father whipped him, even when he was right and his father was wrong, as his mother had told him in secret among those easy-going hateful fools.

There was only the door to will. He put his mouth against it and willed with all his strength, hard, hard, body-hard and mind-hard with anger, strong enough to make her do anything he wanted her to.

He heard her say, "I'm sorry," all timid like a nigger, and knew, right as she'd taught him to be, that if she was weak and lost, he wasn't. He *wasn't* lost. They were all lost, even her now. He never would be. He would never let himself give in to a weak living soul as she had.

Then something occurred to him so unbelievable, and at last such a simple answer, that he knew, with his face still pressed against the door and his nightshirt stuck to his hot body, that he was not their son at all. How could he be of that one, of those two stranger fools? He felt free of them for a minute, and then so desolate that he turned his cheek to the door for comfort and was afraid to breathe in that hall he didn't belong in, for fear he'd blubber and sob, and they'd all come running to whip him when they had no right, or tell him more lies. No. In that house full of strangers, he, Lewis Catlett, was a king; but there wasn't a soul to tell about it.

The next morning he didn't look at his mother at breakfast, and only mumbled and backed away when she said, "Good morning," and tried to kiss the top of his head, not enough to be called rude and punished, just enough to let her know—only her. His neck hurt with the choked feeling of a bridled yell, an uncalled whoop which made his throat swell. After breakfast he hid in the parlor, twirling the new piano stool and trying to think.

He heard the sound of fiddles, rising away above the wet swish of someone scrubbing the porch—the skirl of soapy water, the sweep of the broom on the brick—and there, coming downriver from the upper bend, the promise of entertainment, of presents, of maybe even a monkey to watch, of the fiddles and their high-stepping music. He ran to the window. Already the children, black and white, were running down the carriage path toward the main road and the sound.

"Little fools," he said to them through the window. "You'll get there first, but you ain't ever seen a monkey." He had, but the little fools wouldn't believe him and teased him all the time when he told them, and he even twisted Johnny's arm to make him believe. When his mother went down to the Court House at Canona, she took him and talked to him all the way, and that's where he saw the monkey. Little fools.

He paused just long enough to look at himself in the mirror and brush back his hateful thatch of hair with his fist, then, setting a stern face which was right for the eldest, he sauntered down the walk, not appearing to be in a hurry or to care that he was going to be last to see what the fiddles were bringing—not in front of that dirty nigger who had stopped scrubbing and was craning her neck toward the sound.

He didn't bother to climb up on the fence-rail with the others. He stood, dignified and alone, behind them, then forgot and let himself rise to his tiptoes as the fiddlers came into sight around the sun-drenched bend of the road, so bright it shimmered like the marching music.

It wasn't any entertainment at all, only a slave coffle, marching down the road two by two, dressed up in their trade clothes, while the speculator, a thin, worried-looking man in a low-pressure hat which hid his face from the sun, trotted his worn horse up and down beside the column, trying to make the children keep time to the music. He didn't look rich at all, not a bit rich, all road-dusty and skinny as a peddler. Lewis turned as if to tell his mother so; she said the speculators were the only people in Virginia with a red cent. As he looked toward the house, he saw her, away through the trees on the observatory, switch around and walk, straight-backed so that he knew she was mad and wouldn't watch with his grandmother and Cousin Annie. Even though she was as beaten as the rest, she could still make that silly show of disapproval.

"Dealers in black flaish." He could hear her saying it, and see her fold her lips. "You listen to me, Lewis!" But that was before she changed, before his father forced her to change.

The fools on the fence set up a yell, waving and calling back and forth to the grinning children in the procession. Several of the children were capering now to the music so that their audience on the fence would laugh.

He heard the speculator order a halt, and as the music stopped he saw his father walk slowly out of the inn and tip his hat to the trashy man as if he were a gentleman. Then he looked up and saw the children. Lewis had never seen him look so mad. He strode across the road toward them, doom in his walk, but they all scattered like crows before he could reach them. From behind a tree, Lewis watched him turn and trudge back slowly, looking weighed down because he hadn't caught anybody to whip. Lewis grinned and slapped his heinie at the retreating back; Uncle Telemachus had told them that was the worst insult an Indian brave could give.

Lewis didn't see the speculator again. He was gone, and so was Cuffee by the afternoon when he sneaked down to the road to watch again. Later his mother had cloth for a new dress and he got a jacket like a man; but she didn't speak to him about it as she would have before. She didn't say a word.

He told the children for a joke that he'd seen Cuffee again, lurking up near the mill like a ghost. After that they thought they saw him too, looking over their shoulders when they dared each other to gaze into the millpond. They were more scared of the mill than ever, little fools.

BOOK TWO

April 10–June 30, 1849

Chapter One

THE CLOUDS had hovered like smoke over the wet Albemarle hills for weeks, Monticello blotted out, Afton Mountain shrouded, distant Charlottesville a vague disturbance in the gloom. The wet lawn of the University of Virginia seemed an island in the mist, its bricks stained with streaks of water, its arcades grimed with damp and the smoke of winter. The dripping trees waited. The students huddled around hissing fires. The smell of wet wood, tobacco, books, and winter clothes, heavy and airless, permeated the little dark rooms.

Everybody at the university had the blues.

On the morning of April 10, 1849, if Johnny Catlett had been asked what in the wide wet world was his last interest, he would have yawned, blown his nose, and answered either life or Latin, but being alive, he did manage to drag his unhappy nineteen-year-old frame to an all too early Classics lecture.

Dull light filtered into the dirty windows of the lecture hall. The sound of coughing, and once in a while a suppressed yawn, mingled with the drone of Latin from the lecture platform, the dead language smothered once again, with boredom and the ever-present smell of musty boys too young to make decisions about linen for themselves.

"Deploratur in perpetuum libertas, nec vindex quisquam existit aut futurus videtur." The professor's vague and gentle voice floated far away.

Johnny, almost asleep as near the safety of one of the sunless walls as he could find, roused himself and began to search for the place in a sadly unused copy of Livy. The small youthful man behind the too big desk on the rostrum, yawned behind his hand, called a name, then watched with deep ironic, almost mothering eyes, belying a face whose Indian caste made it seem stern, a young man who was sadly unfolding from where he had been resting on his neck.

Since it was not Johnny's name he subsided again into staring at a scrap of paper on his desk, on which he had written and scratched out: "My dear Cousin"; then: "Fair April, my Melinda creeps, sleeps, peeps, oh goddam what's fair about April, pay Sanders *today.*"

All he had received from Dr. Harrison, Virginia's first classical scholar, Gessner the Great, was his yawn. That morning it was all Johnny was capable of catching. Youth was in the way, and floating dreams. He returned the yawn behind his hand.

Young Dan Neill, state student from Beulah, whose nose was scarlet and raw from a head cold, and who was twisting the last button from his green-black ancient jacket, finally blundered to his feet.

"Deploratur in perpetuum libertas," he muttered, "uh, liberty is allus gittin deplored—"

There was a patter of light laughter from those few who even on such a day were so out of touch with the demands of mood, age, and its entailed privacy, that they sat brightly demanding, hoping for notice from Harrison, or taking it for granted. He leaned forward, concentrating now. "Mr. Neill, you are a transmontane, traditionally a lover of liberty."

The young man sagged, mute and gross with embarrassment.

"Can you contemplate," the voice went on over his bowed head, its tempered irony lost on its unwilling victim, "a Roman such as Titus Livius writing such a line as 'liberty is allus gittin deplored'?" Love of his subject had won over kindness. Harrison turned with a sigh toward the front row of the lecture-room.

"Mr. Kregg, will you translate, sir?" Johnny closed his mind to further troubles as another student rose. He dimly heard, as the new voice began, even its eastern Virginian ease clipped a little with confidence, *"Deploratur in perpetuum libertas,* liberty was given up forever; *nec vindex quisquam existit aut futurus videtur,* nor did any defender step forth, or seem likely to in the future."

In this, at least, the orphaned Crawford Kregg, last heir at Kregg's Crossing, was absolutely and relievedly sure of himself.

Johnny did open his eyes when Crawford began to speak. He watched his cousin (fourth, once removed on the Lacey side), and couldn't help smiling a little, even in such deadening gloom, at a remark one of his friends had made about him. "It ain't Fish's fault he's so damned faultless."

Even on a day when everyone else's clothes looked slept in, and the cold shaving water had been, in most cases, ignored, Fish Kregg stood at ease, his Latin book balanced in his hand so that he held his head high to see the print, retaining the necessary and ill-suited arrogant poise his fine jacket, his Byronic collar, his flowing red cravat, and his knightly haircut demanded. These badges of fashionable approval would, in their studied abandon, have done credit to Mr. Maximilian Rudolph Schele de Vere, the University's Prussian arbiter of form and manners. In looks Fish was at that moment the best of sons the mother of states had trained and buffed to offer.

Johnny had to scratch his neck. His hand began to write, ". . . underneath that fashionable exterior, Crawfish's life gets drearier and drearier." He crossed that out, too, ashamed, as always, of that imp which made him see the tattered petticoat of fact under the gilded robes of fashion. He whistled silently to himself when he thought of that phrase, and decided to write it to Melinda. Melinda could laugh in the right places, or in the same wrong places that he did. She always had. Johnny grinned and retreated from the Albemarle lecture hall into a summer world, an uncomplicated world of homesick memory, habits, and what in his mind he termed his loved ones. Even the sentiment of homesickness, *Weltschmerz,* the accepted illusion, comforted him so near to sleep that his head jerked, shaking his now chestnut hair which in the dampness had an unfortunate tendency to curl and had earned him from some sharp unattainable little witch the nickname Byron. It was hard to bear, but he was secretly proud, and glanced more often in his shaving mirror in the rainy season. Indeed, who at nineteen would not have had a twinge of pride when every last girl one was afraid to dance with had the poet hidden from prying parents under her chaste pillow?

The now livelier questions and answers of the Latin lecture filtered through even to his dreaming. Fish still stood, doing as he had done all his life, what was expected of him, so carefully, and with such unquestioning gratefulness for the attentions showered on him by a never-ending series of paid teachers, riding masters, traveling companions, slaves, and female cousins whose one aim in life seemed to be to advise him on religion, money, and matrimony.

Crawford Kregg had learned, too young ever to fight it, the constant attrition of having to please his subordinates so that the world around him would not become silent but full of unspoken resentful words. Even his neatness, the way he organized his room, touched everything lightly, took up little space, Johnny knew was an effort to please by not demanding too much notice. He did not even push at his clothes with his slight body. To be like the others, and for the sake, he said, of self-discipline, he had sent his servant back to Kregg's Crossing, and used the university stoop nigger for his few wants as the others did. Even that had, in the long run, been following the fashion. Personal servants were considered ostentatious and unmanly in a school where most of the students couldn't even afford a horse. Johnny had hired his own servant, Tig, out to supplement his meager allowance. When Fish found out Tig was unhappy he kept him at Kregg's Crossing so that Johnny could use him in the holidays. Johnny had been too embarrassed to admit that he really did need the money, and he didn't want to hurt Fish by refusing. Johnny was probably the only person who secretly felt a little sorry for one of the richest young men in Virginia.

Fish's perfection and his guileless vulnerability always succeeded in making Johnny feel guilty. By that evening he too was trying to do his duty in the flickering light of a smelly lamp the servant had forgotten to trim. Through the door between the two rooms he shared with Fish, he could hear the scratch of a quill, and from time to time a slight movement, a sigh, the light creak of the wooden chair. Beyond the back window the rain murmured on, all the way to the mountains.

Rooming with Fish could be lonely. Johnny, in an unconcentrated fit of the blues, picked at the candle wax, letting all thought of Livy fly from his mind, birdlike. He rolled the wax into a ball, squashed it on the table, picked it off and threw it in the fire, watched it melt, wanted suddenly to smoke, forgot, sighed, yawned, went on staring at the smoldering green-wood fire. It was an effort to reach for his pipe. After several false starts he lit the meerschaum Fish had brought him from his last trip to Germany, and began to fill the room with belligerent smoke.

Fish coughed gently, almost unconsciously, while his quill scratched on. Johnny ran his hand up under his hair, pulled it slightly, whispered, "Damn," and decided to take both his blues and his pipe outside.

"Goddammit, I wish it was spring," he said to himself aloud, as he stepped down into the dimness of the Colonnade, where a few lamps in sconces reflected the rain. Almost at his door he collided with another student. He backed away and took his pipe from his mouth slowly.

"Howdee, Dan," Johnny said, feeling tired and drained of energy.

Above Dan Neill, the rain dropped steadily on the roof of the Colonnade as if it would go on forever. Dan was wet to the skin. He smelled of raw whisky.

"Come in and take a seat," Johnny had to say.

Without a word, Dan stamped into the room and pulled a chair close to the fire, shutting away its small heat with his body. Even with his awkwardness and the self-centered mood that permeated the little room, isolating him sorrowfully in the middle of it, he looked the way Big Dan used to look to Johnny when he was a child, but a Big Dan trussed up, confined, damp, poor, and respectable.

He didn't speak for some time, and when he did Johnny pulled another wax bit from the candle and prepared himself not to listen, not to be drawn in, in the unconscious protective habit caught from his mother.

"What's the matter with me, anyhow?" Dan asked the fire. "Johnny, I knowed that lesson. I—"

"Oh, hell and damnation, Dan, that ain't bothering you. I don't know. You just ain't . . ."

In spite of himself, Johnny had touched off the fuse of Dan's complaint.

"It don't make no difference to you. You got the world by the tail, you and Fish. You don't know what it's like. I'm the one's got to pull myself up by my bootstraps. By God, I will too. I'll pull myself up by my bootstraps. I'll show ye. I'll show ever' last one of ye. I don't know what it is happens, but by God . . ." He stopped at last and pulled his cold-red nose, then tried to push it into his face. "I'm agone to kiss a fool. Anyhow," he said bravely, "I only want a mite Latin to make me some speeches. I don't claim no more than to git into politics."

Johnny did laugh then, with his whole chest and mouth, his load of the blues gone.

"How in the hell did you get a scholarship, Dan?"

Dan grinned through his sorrow. "I reckon Ise more skeered of Miss Annie than I was of book larnin. It jest don't take on me though."

"I wonder," Johnny thought aloud.

But Dan refused to be comforted. "Him. Harrison . . ." he began again. He sounded so bitter about the kindly man that Johnny shut up and watched him, surprised.

"His own paw was agin us. Did you know that? Did you? Voted agin the western counties and went agin his own people."

"On what?"

"On suffrage. On *manhood* suffrage. That's what. Left usn in the west with a passel of nigger-owners runnin our business. You jest wait, Johnny Catlett, by God we're goin to cut right away from the Tidewater yit."

The quill stopped in the other room.

Dan looked up, annoyed. "I niver knowed *he* was here."

Fish came gently to the door, trying by habit to make amends before Dan had even turned round.

"Howdee, Dan," he told him, "I'm mighty glad to see you."

Dan ignored him. "You wouldn't happen to have a drink, would you, Johnny?" he said with a trace of that insolent grin which had always put Johnny in his place.

"No," Johnny lied, glancing at Fish. "You know damn well I ain't, Dan."

"Oh, I forget." Dan was suddenly struck with an idea as if it were new. "We got a Son of Temperance here." His grin turned to include Fish.

Fish's usually mild handsome face went a little pink. "You are aware of my strong sentiments on that score." He sat down on Johnny's bed, controlled himself with an effort, and smiled at Dan. To Johnny his face looked almost fatuous with sincerity. "We would like to have you with us, Dan." His sense of duty was beginning to make his face shine. He leaned farther toward Dan, who had retreated to staring, embarrassed, into the fire again.

Fish took a deep breath and began. "Why not turn from the poison cup before it is too late? That one, those two sips you think are no harm, but the poison acts through conviviality to make you its slave. Its foulness fills the prisons, leaves the widow—"

Dan stopped Fish at the rising of his voice. "How the hell do you know, Fish? You ain't niver been drunk in your damn life. Tell you what I'll do. You git drunk with me sometime, and I'll give a try at bein sober with you. Won't neither one of us enjoy it." He threw back his head and laughed at the ceiling, showing strong teeth, and dropping confining respectability with the gesture, as if it were an uncomfortable mask he was glad at last to shed.

"Anyhow, Fish, I ain't married and don't intend on it. That there and prison air much the same, eh Johnny?"

"Can you not think of your loved ones?" Fish tried again.

"Oh hell and damnation." Dan got up so quickly his chair fell to the floor.

"Sir!" Another button of Fish's attitudes had been punched. He rose at the same time, ready and stern.

Johnny yawned and said, "Excuse me," but no one paid any attention.

"Goddammit, I'm goin to pick me a fight. I'm all riled up." Dan ignored Fish, and blundered out of the door, slamming it behind him.

"Poor unhappy fellow." Fish watched the closed door, then neatly picked up the chair and sat down. "I wish I could help him."

He was so serious that the comment behind Johnny's lips went unsaid. He threw himself on his bed and concentrated on sending thick gusts of smoke to the ceiling, where it curled and clung. Fish succeeded deftly in getting the neglected fire to flick out tongues of flame. Johnny knew what was coming.

"He admires you, Johnny. Why don't you be an example, take the pledge? You can help him curb his strong spirit."

Johnny wanted to tell Fish about Dan's spirit, how he had seen it through the years curbed and dammed; how it was when Dan laughed and showed he had not quite been defeated. He saw him, once bigger than himself, until Johnny had outgrown him by an inch and a half and a set of rules which Dan rejected with contempt. He remembered how Dan was emulated by his own small self, how he copied his spitting in the road, and felt disloyally glad when once in a while the older McKarkle boys took him hunting instead, or when Dan had licked his big brother Lewis. These things and other things—thinking of them only made him answer, "You save him, Fish, he's your cousin. As for me, the Sons of Temperance are agin my pa's principles."

Fish, teased, subsided into safer channels. "You know," he said, "I don't remember Cousin Annie, but there were stories. She was supposed to be a great beauty and a fine horsewoman. I cain't understand her marrying—well, that sort of fellow."

Cousin Annie Neill, as Johnny had last seen her, walking slowly down the road at Beulah, shrunken and hard-bitten by life with Big Dan, her voice an incessant complaint for the cross she bore, was so far from the legend. Sometimes Fish wanted to gossip like the bird-twittering women, whose voices could be heard pecking until a man walked into the room and they turned silky.

"Annie made her bed," he had heard his grandmother say once.

Melinda had stopped in the hall, put her finger against her mouth, held his hand tight, and made him listen. There were tiny pretty beads of sweat around her mouth. That was when Cousin Annie had come back from Cincinnati, where she had gone for her Brandon nerves. She had stayed a year and when she came back Big Dan was a widower and he courted her, after they had been in living hate of each other for so long. "I would never have thought it of a Brandon. . . ."

His mother had answered shrilly, in a surprising voice for her. "We ought to forbid her the house. I won't have my children exposed. As sensitive to things as dear Lewis is . . ."

One rap of his grandmother's hand on the chair arm settled it, that rap of finality, then the statement, *"She was a Brandon,"* then silence, so long ago. Melinda giggled and ran.

Now, eleven years later, Fish imitated, "She *was* a Brandon"—and then leaned back to keep on talking.

Johnny shut his eyes and listened to the rain.

Rain. Its hard patter that night at Beulah drummed the back porch, roared down the drainpipe into the overflowing rain-barrel. As Johnny opened the door to slip in from a night so black he had had to feel his way blindly from tree to tree, soaked, exhausted, the candle guttered out. When he closed the door after that battering noise, the house was so quiet it made him hold his breath. Then, in the pitch-darkness of the hall, someone had laid a hand on his wet arm, and, as he jumped, his father whispered, close to him, "Come into the library, son."

The library was full of lingering smoke and the smell of old tobacco. That was how he knew his father had been waiting so long. That long wait made him freeze with fear of bad news, that and the unaccustomed gentleness of his father's voice, completely without banter or authority.

"Get yourself dry, son, and take a drink with me," his father said as he guided him to the fire, his arm around Johnny's shoulder. Johnny looked up, so startled that his father smiled.

"If I'm going to talk to you as a man, son, I reckon I'd better treat you as a man." Johnny had been sixteen for a week. He turned and warmed himself, feeling a new freedom at his father's words, still sensing the pressure of that arm across his shoulder, and watched his father pour whisky from a half-empty decanter which he had set under the shade of the lamp so that the movement of pouring made amber flecks of light on the dark, heavy cloth. But something lay so sternly on his father's face, belying his voice, that Johnny felt another pang of fear at what was to come and reviewed the things he could have been caught at.

His father motioned him to a chair by the fire, sat down slowly opposite him, and lit his pipe again, sending the smoke upward, white against the dark ceiling. Johnny could hardly keep from breaking the silence, but he managed to match his father's quiet until the man was ready to speak. It was the first time in his memory that Johnny had noticed the change of age in his father's face, which, once so controlled, now that he was fifty-two was taut instead of calm, gray with a fatigue he hadn't noticed before, runneled and creased with years of keeping his mouth tight, with bat's wings of wrinkles where his amused eyes had long belied his face. He still wore his hair high, in an old-fashioned lion's mane like General Jackson whom he had always hated, and the tall collar, left over from the apex of his manhood, kept his head stiffly erect. The whisky he was sipping made Johnny's blood tingle. He gradually relaxed and stopped being afraid.

His father decided to begin. He sighed and made a joke.

"Thank God, Johnny, you're old enough to talk to. You know, it gets damned lonesome being . . . the rooster with a flock of hens. Oh, we've always had company . . ." He didn't even seem to be talking to Johnny. He didn't look at him, and he spoke so softly that Johnny had to lean forward to study his mouth. "Oh, there's other men here, men in Beulah, to pass the time of day with . . . but friends . . . I meet men I love at the county court without the women. They're all the same. Farming is . . . everybody leaning on you. Blacks you feel are a burden you can't do without." He got up and wandered to the fireplace.

"Johnny, you and Lewis . . ." The sternness came back. "Before you govern others you have to learn to govern yourselves. I've consulted with Mr. McKarkle. You're to take over being overseers.

He wants to go out on his own. After all these years, for Beulah to lose the McKarkles . . . If I have a prayer to a merciful God it is that this cup pass from us, but what can we do? What in the hell can we do? If we are left ruined, what good will that do my people? I've thought—every decent gentleman in Virginia has thought about it. Protect our womanhood, face the responsibility we have, and rule ourselves with a hand of iron, not fear justice, or sternness. It is hard."

He had an almost bewildered look. When Cuffee the miller was brought back and said he ran away because the children hurt his feelings, he had had the same bewildered look before his anger. Johnny saw the old reins of his authority slip from his father's hands, saw him wilt without the control. He wanted to cut and run out through the rain, anywhere. . . . He shut the image away and listened.

All this had been said before. Both Johnny and his father knew it was not what had made the man wait up, alone, for his son on such a blustering night.

He began again. "We all—we men—have needs." He leaned his head on his hands, telling the shame to the floor. "Terrible fierce needs of the flesh. Vile whisperings unbecoming to a man of God. This lust, this other burden, must never touch a white woman. . . ."

Their tutor had taught them to declaim. Was it now as deep as the blood, to declaim and shatter?

His father had jumped up and was pacing to and fro before the fire so that Johnny had to move his feet.

"If the demon within us is too great, we cannot let it touch the innocence of those whom God has given us as responsibilities to the tender and the frail. Never, never let them know."

He threw himself down in his chair again, forgetting Johnny. "Never a white woman." Even then his father hadn't said it, said it directly.

"I would to God that you could go to the woman of your choice unsullied by passion, pure and undefiled." Now his voice was quiet. He turned his head away and his profile was that of an old man. . . .

"Johnny, Johnny, let me touch you there. Kiss me, Johnny," Teeny Neill had whispered while the hot soft breeze fanned her vixen face and lifted and parted and played with her hair. "Look at me, Johnny. Air you afeard? I ain't." The whisper, "Touch me, Johnny, touch me, hyar." Then the pain and the shame, hating her, even the sounds she made, but he had gone back. Even tonight, even this very night. Knowing his father would be so beyond such things, Johnny's eyes filled with tears of shame. He brushed his face with the back of his hand, hoping that they would not be noticed.

"If you must fall," his father was saying, "become like an animal in the dark." He sounded bitter with himself. "If prayer does not avail and discipline is not enough, don't let it be a white woman. Don't defile a white woman with your lust. I would in all mercy I did not have to say this. Nobody knows what we go through. *They* criticize . . ."

He got up again, sighed deeply, and laughed. "Well, Johnny, I reckon you are a man. I know you are a gentleman. I've watched you." The burden was gone from his voice. "Let's have a nightcap before we go to bed."

Johnny had thought with relief that he was finished, but he was not. More easily, now man to man, he went on. "Sometimes there can grow up real affection in relations with our people." He thought for a pause, and then said, "Real affection—of a kind. I know a man who has eleven children by a wench whom he dearly loves. He plans to free them all at his death. White men who commit the same crimes in the dark pass him in the street without lifting their hats. I only tell you this to warn you. Sacred love and lust are different things. They are opposed in God's ordinance." He said it so fiercely that he seemed to be persuading himself. "We Southron men are tempted and we know."

"Do you love me, Johnny?" she had whispered, a white girl and a connection, after what he had done to her, the vile thing he had done.

Peregrine Catlett's face relaxed, became more as it had always been, the mask in place, now that he had done his duty, painful as it was. He poured his nightcap, but this time forgot that he had offered one to Johnny.

They had never spoken of such things again.

It was not until Johnny had left the room, lit his candle, and watched his own huge shadow flick and dance on the wall beside him, climbing the stairs, that he realized that he had not said one word, not even goodnight.

"Are you asleep?" Fish called from the fire. Johnny opened his eyes and, feeling the old tears again in them, rubbed his face as if an ash had fallen on it from his pipe.

"Hell, no, I ain't asleep. I wish you wasn't so damn starn, Fish. I'd take a drink."

"Well, take it if your conscience will allow. I'll go into my room."

"Not with you in there apraying for me I won't." Johnny rolled himself off the bed, staggered, and stretched. If there was one thing he knew it was that Fish Crawford had never felt a craving lust that hurried him into the dark. Johnny envied him that peace with his whole nineteen-year-old healthy yearning soul.

Two weeks later Albemarle woke up, as if the ground, the trees, and Johnny, lying stretched on the grass of the lawn, had all been kissed by summer. The guilt and darkness, the saddening rain, the blues, had receded like the little running white clouds which seemed to swim in a faint breeze across the sky, chase on and on as Johnny watched. The faint swish of a scythe up on the first level of the lawn, where a Negro was rhythmically cutting the new meadow grass, green and strong from the spring rains, made him dream of girls walking in summer silk. The sweet scent of the new-cut grass permeated him.

Fish, leaning against a tree whose leaves, pale yellow-green, were not yet big enough to form a tent and shut out the sky, had conceded to the spring one tasseled cap and a yellow nankeen jacket. He was talking.

"It is time to read the nature poets." He leaned his head back against the bark, mindful of his cap, and closed his eyes. " 'Nature I loved, and next to nature, art.' That's new. It has been on my mind. It is important to catch the intuition of the poet as one reads. Now, at the castle of Chillon, what wild images, and at Weimar . . ."

Only the tall Virginia grass of the lawn answered him with a long sigh as the breeze played it. Johnny turned his head into it and stared at the tiny blue innocents which blanketed the ground. On such a day a man of nineteen need never feel ashamed. He was heavy with being alive, like another thing in the grass.

But Fish would keep on talking. "Do you ever consider the philosophical import of suicide? Goethe said it did not matter whether a man was weak or strong, but whether he could outlast . . ." Fish was trying to remember and translate for Johnny's sake, who was gently blowing the nearest innocent, watching it tremble, and not listening to a word, ". . . the full measure of his pain," Fish finished. "Who is that?"

Johnny sat up, looked, and lay down again. "It's Lancelot Stuart."

"The sun's in my eyes."

"Going fishing. Now I know it's spring." Johnny went back to his trancelike watching of the clouds as they skidded behind the filigree of new-leafed branches. As he watched, the clouds seemed to stop, the tree itself to ride across the air, and then the ground and himself with it began to roll under the unmoving sky; he was more and more aware of the world turning with him.

A kick from Lance interrupted Johnny's ride on earth. He grinned and sat up, dizzy.

"Quit that mooning, Johnny, and come on and fish."

Johnny grabbed Lance's ankle and knocked him down. Tackle, a worn book, his cap sprayed the grass. Fish watched, aloof, as they locked bodies and wrestled, rolled over and over together down the terraced lawn onto the next level. Fish waited patiently until they had stopped and struggled to their feet, to see if Lance would go so that he and Johnny could get back to their interesting talk.

Lance's face was red; his thick black hair hung in sweating ropes. He didn't bother to straighten his dirty weekday cravat.

"Dear God." He panted and flopped down on the ground. "It's hot as hell. I don't even want me a woman. I just want to lie down by a river and go to sleep. Maybe the Rapidan."

Fish, feeling left out, strolled sadly away, carefully looking as if his mind were on great matters.

"Fish, where are you agoing?" Lance called after him.

"Oh," Fish called back vaguely, "I have to study."

"Damnation," Lance muttered to his retreating back. "He's an odd fellow, ain't he now?" Beyond Fish he saw one of the lawn Negroes squatting patiently in the shade of the Colonnade near Johnny's room, waiting at his daily post for orders.

"It's three o'clock." He told time by the figure. "Hey, nigger!"

The Negro didn't hear him.

"He's deaf," Johnny murmured by habit, to keep the old man out of trouble.

"Boy! Get your damn black hide over here!" Lance's yell shook the calm sweet afternoon. The Negro ran toward him.

"Go get us some cold beer." Lance flicked a coin, which fell into the grass. The man, who had the ageless look of the Negro old, stooped down slowly and picked it up.

"Yassuh, boss," he said to the ground. It hurt his back to move more quickly.

"Hustle," Lance told him, and grinned at Johnny, who had hunkered down beside him, his back against the tree.

The old Negro grinned his expected grin and loped off as fast as he could.

Johnny called after him, "Nero!" The Negro stopped and Johnny went to meet him. "Buy me a lemon," he almost whispered, and gave him another coin. "Yassuh," the old man conspired seriously. Johnny strolled back to Lance, smiling at something of his own he didn't mean to share.

"Ain't this the life?" Lance's face was smooth in the satisfaction of the sun. "One more month and we'll be at the Springs. Are you going?"

"I aim on meeting my family there."

"Any pretty gals?"

"My sister—and my cousin."

"Oh hell." Lance flicked a fly from his forehead. "It almost makes a fellow feel like a goddamn knight of old." They were both quiet. "I wish I didn't have to work. Pa's hired me out on the canal where I won't see nothing but female black snakes."

This thought saddened him, but another chased it with resignation. "The damned cadets'll get all the gals anyhow. I wish Pa'd of sent me to the VMI. He said he wasn't aiming to have a son of his considered a bad subject."

He sat up. "Now seriously, Johnny, wouldn't you say I was bad subject enough to be a cadet?" He tried to look as lascivious as he could, but his square face only looked healthy and his sunken eyes as if he hadn't had enough sleep.

Johnny laughed with him.

"Oh hell, come on, let's flaish the maiden hook." Lance began to gather his scattered belongings from the grass. He hid the book.

Johnny knew what it was. Once when Lance was drunk he had knelt on the floor of a tavern and promised his sainted mother, as he had on her deathbed, that he would carry the Good Book with him always.

"Oh don't look down on me now, Ma," he had cried, "I ain't fitten to be et by hogs"—and had passed out right there until the others were ready to take him home.

"Ain't you going to wait for the beer?" Johnny reminded him.

Chapter Two

IN THAT suspension between sleep and waking, both dreams and yesterday mixed in memory, Melinda floated in joy. Time was tangled; she could still hear the twitter of busy women, the rush of skirts, the sweep and feel of shaken and smoothed cloth, the whisper of tissue paper folded carefully around acres of silk and poplin. She felt again under her fingers the thousand fine trails of stitches which made up their winter labor, stitches marching toward the summer while the snow lay over Beulah, while the spring rain beat outside, in the gray mornings and dismal evenings with Johnny gone. All those stitches were sewn with loving caresses no man would ever feel and it would be unseemly for them to know about (for there could be no antagonism against such hemmed, embroidered, ruched, tatted) . . . oh, she turned and sighed, women's love in the sounds of packing, hers, all hers, those bright clouds of delicate belongings.

The dream retreated, blew out. Melinda opened her eyes. The room she lay in was still asleep, the dawn not broken but softly there, the big wicker trunk all ready, strapped down. She could almost see the little gloves, the handkerchiefs, the sachets—all that movement gone now, Minna no longer stolidly working while Miss Leah gave incessant nervous orders, Lydia no longer whining with the vexation of her excitement every time she was crossed. It was as if all the energy had been imprisoned as well under the wicker lid.

With the reality of being awake, the bitterness returned. Melinda's small black trunk sat sensibly in the corner, no clouds suppressed in it to burst out like Pandora's feminine devils at the spring of the lock. She had no need to look inside it with her mind's angry eye. She knew every patch, genteel and seemly; she could have put her fingers around her two treasures, her locket and her one pair of kid gloves, as cared for as her own hands.

Melinda dimmed as reality caught her, but she was still tangled in some tendrils of the night power and of an excitement that even she, with her rigid training in facts, could not deny. She yawned and stretched her arms which she knew were whiter and rounder than Lydia's, smiled her most secret smile, her challenge, at a faint stain in the ceiling, created by her eye into a swooping bird.

Outside in the damp blue dawn, the Mansion at Beulah seemed exactly the same after twelve years, except that the trees were taller, and the rose bushes thick and tangled, drooping with their June burden, their dark red roses nearly black with dew. The house had settled down into its ownership of the ground, its rawness gone. With their new growth the cedars showed patches of richer green against their dark fringe. Not a soul moved.

Melinda turned over toward the window, smoothed back a veil of hair which had escaped her thick plait, and was sure she hadn't slept a wink. She eased herself out of her bed carefully, to have some time of her own before the house woke up and she was besieged by voices, and the sick panic which lurked caught her up, involved even her in the fear. What special day it was made her catch her breath with excitement.

Lydia was still sleeping, almost hidden in her feather bed. Melinda looked at her to make sure before she claimed the chamber as her own, for a little while.

It was the same room the girls had slept in always, but now it was no longer a nursery. The beds and toys had been cleared out, and by the addition of two high-posted bedsteads, a pink chaise longue with delicately patchworked pillows, by long pink curtains which Lydia had sniveled for, and by a large lozenge-shaped pier-glass, it had been turned into a chamber for young ladies. The studied abandon with which Lydia draped the room with her girlishness disgusted Melinda. Her soon neglected dulcimer, the music stand on which she had piled the few ladies' magazines they had to copy from—even the way she had set the pier-glass so that she could glance at herself on first rising up from her pillow—shouted Lydia, Lydia. She was underfoot, overhead, everywhere Melinda stumbled. She said she put the pier-glass there to practice waking up gracefully in case she ever married and had to sleep in the same bed as a man. Minna had slapped her when she said that and then laughed and repeated it to all the servants.

The most Melinda could see of Lydia were a few tendrils of brown hair which had escaped from the curl papers Minna made her wear, part of her high forehead, one closed slightly wet eye, and her nose. The buttermilk to fade the tiny bridge of freckles which so worried Minna had long since been brushed off by her pillow. That, and the gloves soaked in buttermilk which both the girls wore, made the curtained room smell sour, and the sweet tang of thieves' vinegar soaking in a sponge on the mantel was pungent in the closeness.

Melinda longed to fling the window wide, but for the moment she wanted more to be free of Lydia. There was no denying, though, that the girl looked pretty, lying in the secure repose of a child who has spent admired and warm time in her father's lap, where he had curled her hair in his fingers and called her his little princess. When Miss Leah made the picture for the parlor, the Prince of Wales feathers of all the children's delicate, fly-away baby curls, Johnny's blond, and Lewis's and Liddy's brown, and russet pink from the dead baby, she used Melinda's too, because it was black, she said, for contrast—for contrast.

"Little old pugnose." Melinda rejected Lydia and swung herself out of bed. She stopped, then remembered to sneak to the door of the porch to see if Toey and Lydia's servant were still asleep on their floor pallets. Her bare feet made dancing steps as she avoided the familiar creaking of the boards. The pallets were gone, and so were the servants. They had already tiptoed down the back stairs to heat the morning water without making any sound to wake the ladies.

Securely alone, Melinda tiptoed back and stood, critically, in front of the bureau mirror. The image she saw disappointed her almost to tears, but she cast that aside as unbecoming to a woman of twenty. First she drew in her lips to make them small and more demure, then had to giggle, once, that such rounded lips could ever be so prissy. She made a face, inspected her teeth, and was satisfied. Her gloves felt clammy against her palms; she stripped them off and slid her hands down her sides, wiping the dampness onto her nightgown, then let her hands rest at her waist, squeezed in, let out her breath so they would touch, took a relieved gulp of air when she found she could still do it.

She pushed aside with her elbows a pile of ribbons and an orris-root sachet Lydia's servant had left out of her handkerchiefs, almost tipping over the precious Florida water which had been her Christmas present, and which she had saved for summer. Lydia had opened it in February and then refused to own up to it, so part of it had already evaporated, even though Melinda sealed it again with jelly-wax. It took five minutes of holding her hands up to make them cool, useless-looking, and white enough to satisfy her. While she did this, she dreamed of dresses, whirls of whispering silk covered with tiny moving flowers, red to make her hair blacker, and her dark eyes were huge, impudent, fast, not caring as she flirted with herself in the mirror and tested several smiles.

"Darling Melinda," she murmured; then the sudden thought of Johnny's laughter made her finish with a sharp, "You're nothing but a damned fool," and straighten up at once.

A sob from Lydia's bed made her wheel, angry, caught.

"How long have you been awake, Liddy Boo?" she snapped.

Lydia was leaning on one elbow, her tears falling onto her book. She didn't hear.

"Liddy, what's the matter now?" Melinda sighed.

Lydia faced and stated the most banal discoveries of life with such an air of wonder and crisis that Melinda was not troubled by her sobs, which had begun to bounce the clover-patterned quilt as she gulped for air. "Oh, Linda," she finally was able to say, "she's so poor and so proud and they're so mean to her. They're going to break her noble heart." "Heart" she sang on four notes of sorrow.

Melinda had to laugh, having lately outgrown hiding novels under her pillow and reading them in secret in the morning. How could a child like Lydia know the real torture of a woman? "Real torture"—that was Byron. She ran to her bed, thinking of it, and buried Byron in her drawer so Miss Leah wouldn't find it.

Lydia's squall stopped as quickly as it had begun. She sat up in bed and began to pull off her gloves, watching herself with some care in the pier-glass.

"I wish you wouldn't call me Liddy Boo any more. Pa said I was to be called Lydia." She lay down again and rose up from her pillow more slowly, gracefully, toward the mirror. This gesture was better done. Lydia looked pleased at her reflection.

"That ain't all you'll be called if your ma catches you with a pernicious novel poisoning the fountain of your God-given wisdom." Melinda's imitation of Leah was so apt that Lydia giggled.

"You've read it your own self." She clasped her knees. "I won't be able to bear it if she don't marry him."

"Who?" Melinda was aloof.

"The young lord."

"You've read them before. They always do." Melinda snorted. "Real life!"

"Oh, wouldn't it be terrible though to lose all and have to be a governess?"

"Lose *what,* may I ask?"

The door opened. Only the plump little hand with its weighty ruby ring opening it warned Lydia in time. She hid the book quickly under her pillow.

Miss Leah's demands began as she jerked back Melinda's gown to inspect her throat.

"Put your camphor bag on at once. Won't you ever learn?" The intrusion of her grasping hand froze Melinda.

Standing there, insolence in her eyes, Melinda showed by her demurely folded hands, her slightly bent head, her figure, insolent too in its studied acquiescence, that she was very aware of having learned becoming meekness. She could have told Miss Leah, as she told herself over and over again, how she had learned to sit in a corner of the parlor instead of near the lamp, learned the piano to inspire Lydia to practice, learned to be a second cousin and eat the bread of charity, all the time whispering in her head, "Oh God, dear God, all I can do is stamp my feet in the smokehouse sometimes where nobody can hear me. Me. Me. Melinda Lacey, some kin but what is that? I don't want to be their kin. I want to be Melinda and have them kin to me."

Waiting coolly for the end of Miss Leah's frightened chatter, she answered with her eyes but not with her mouth: *I stand in a house that is rightfully mine.* When I told Johnny this I had tears in my lashes and I looked so pretty. Oh Lord, he just laughed, as if it wasn't important. He always laughed, but he sat in a corner with me instead of near the righteous lamp, and I ran to the piano once before I thought what I was up to, and played "My winsome handsome Johnny" right in front of everybody. Mr. Catlett said, "You play well, Melinda"; he said, "You play well"—and then he ruined it. He said, "Liddy, you play, you know what I like," in that soft voice of his like the whirr before the clock strikes or a snake's rattle. I went back to the corner with Johnny and the music just fishtailed through the room. Johnny touched my hand and I knew he was watching me, but I couldn't tell even him what the matter was, not even him—much less you.

Miss Leah was still fussing, without noticing that Melinda hadn't answered. "You won't mind me. None of you will mind me. Melinda, you ought to be an example after all . . ."

Melinda's secret voice shouted: After all we've done! You don't care if I catch the cholera. You don't care if I die. One day, she promised herself, I will put it all into words.

"Yes ma'am," she finally answered, and went in search of the hated camphor bag that made her skin smell sick.

"Why ain't you girls smoking?" Leah found the tiny unsmoked cigars on the mantel and shook them. "How long have you been awake? Oh dear Lord. Lydia, get up at once. I think you do it all to pester me."

Lydia had already jumped to attention behind her. "Oh Ma," she said, her voice full of easy expected tears, "the smell gets in my hair and smoking makes me sick."

Leah had not stopped to listen. She nagged on as she threw back covers and started sprinkling Melinda's bed with more thieves' vinegar from a vial, even though she wouldn't sleep in it again for two months at least.

"It's a God's mercy, a God's mercy without any of you taking the simplest precaution. Why, your father has a watch set downriver on the turnpike and upriver, too, though there's none been reported upriver yet, and he's put one at the boat-landing. We're leaving in an hour. Everything is packed. Are you sure everything's packed?" She inspected the closed trunks and then reached forward and absent-mindedly, very lightly, caressed the wicker one. "You gals . . ." Her voice trailed to nothing; she seemed to freeze for a second.

"It's all packed good. I know it's packed good," she went on sadly, all the tension gone from her battle-weary voice. "I saw to it myself. People can tell who you are. Their niggers watch and tell. They can tell by the way things are packed, especially your little personals, especially when you're kin to the best people in Virginia."

She had completely forgotten her panic of a few minutes before, and as she turned with her vial toward Lydia's bed, she looked satisfied. She was getting closer to the pillow. Lydia ran around her. "Ma, I'll do that," she squealed.

"If you want a thing done right . . ."

Melinda called out for diversion, playing on Leah, "It's the will of God whether the cholera comes or not anyhow"—and couldn't help grinning.

"Don't you be sassy, young lady," Leah snapped back. She pushed Lydia aside and flipped the pillow up to spray under it. The offending book lay exposed on the rumpled sheet. Leah laid the vial down gently and turned to Lydia, who had begun to cry.

"I'll . . . give . . . you . . . something . . . to . . . cry . . . about." Leah raised her flat hand and slapped the girl, who fell onto the bed, drew up her knees, and began to roll back and forth. She did not quite manage to roll over onto the book. Her mother picked it up with the tips of her fingers.

"How you get them I don't know. I watch and watch and watch the peddlers." She marched out of the room.

"If it had had a tail she would have carried it by that." Melinda, who had obediently begun to smoke, judged Lydia's outburst and knew it was nearly over.

"What a way to wake up! Oh, how dreadfully we live." Lydia sobbed her words, quoted almost perfectly from the novel. "I'm going away. Far away."

"Where?" Melinda asked practically. "Quit rolling around. Your hair's like a hoorah's nest."

"Oh, I don't know. To cousins, I reckon. It must be heavenly living with cousins. Parties all the time."

Melinda only stared at her.

"Nothing ever happens here, nothing ever happens. Oh I cain't wait for marriage and keeping a carriage!" Lydia moaned.

"Crambo!" both the girls called out together.

Cousin Annie was already there, at breakfast time. They could hear the light cough that punctuated her barbed party voice long before they got to the dining room. She sounded bright. Melinda glanced at Lydia and they both shook their heads patiently.

"Of course," she was saying as they opened the door, "I ain't saying it ain't the right thing to do. Oh dear to goodness, girls." She coughed dryly into her genteelly doubled fist. "Mr. Neill has concluded to send me with Teeny next year, he says. He says next year." Her voice went dead. Her hand, which had been rapping on the table woodpecker-like with a spoon, stayed clenched. "Melinda, it's a real privilege for you to go to the Spa too. I know you'll be of use to Miss Leah." The spoon began again, and the brightness. "Of course it's for your sakes. My, what beaux you'll see. I hope, Leah, you have a care they don't behave in too backwoods a manner. Manners there are not like Ohio." She coughed. "Of course I won't say you don't have education in Ohio. Book larning." She couldn't stop coughing. "Excuse me. I never saw such *earnestness*. Quite touching. We silly flighty Virginians must just seem—" She coughed again. "There ain't a book to tell you about —certain things."

"Lewis, say the blessing," Leah interrupted coldly.

Lewis obediently bowed his head and muttered. Now, at twenty-three, he had grown huge, his hands square, his thin dark face with its sunken eyes already set in solid lines of worry. As he prayed, his shock of hair fell over his forehead. The first thing he did when he finished muttering was brush it back carefully and glance at Melinda. Melinda wasn't even looking at him.

Cousin Annie went on as if she had been holding her breath until the amen. "Duty, Leah, does tear us so. I realize that it's my bounden duty to stay with my loved ones. The cholera might reach Beulah at any moment. They'll need someone in authority. It's so courageous of dear Peregrine to go. All these valuable niggers. I hear tell one of the Carter plantations was decimated. It just dropped on them like the angel of death." The spoon tapped faster. "Hovered, then dropped. It is my fondest hope," she finished at last, her square face rigid under the shadow of her sunbonnet, "that it doesn't strike at Egeria Springs. The Mask of the Red Death. Ah, while the wild dancers tried to flee. That's Poe, Leah, but of course you don't hold with reading."

No one at the table said a word. There was only the scrape of spoons. Cicero, waving the peacock feathers, watched her, his old face drawn with fear. No one else looked at her.

"Just to throw everything off. Throw it all off." Cousin Annie and the spoon began again. "I *don't* know of course whether I could have sold a nigger to go." She laughed. "When I was a gal, I went with my papa. He pinted some folks out to me. 'They're here eating nigger,' that's what he said to me. Of course, then, we didn't have to do that kind of thing. Sell a nigger to catch a rich beau, and you'll marry a beau that's had to sell a nigger to catch an heiress. Later, of course, things were different. But he never sold for pleasure. It was all done over his head."

Lewis lifted his large head slowly from staring at his untouched plate. "I never met a Virginian admitted to selling one," he muttered. "How come we're the biggest slave-exporting state in the Union?"

"Oh, Lewis, you're just a nigger-loving abolitionist." Lydia giggled.

"Quit that, Liddy, dammit," Lewis fought back.

Cousin Annie smiled.

"Lewis," his mother interrupted, *"pas devant les domestiques.* Eat your grits. You've got a long hard ride."

"Are you going to ride the new bay mare?" Cousin Annie was arch. "I hope you can handle her. Johnny will show her off well when you get there. Oh dear me, I must go." She jumped up, busy. "Mr. Neill is so strict." She staggered slightly as she reached the door.

"May God bless you and keep you from harm," she said, and it sounded more bitter than the rest.

"Oh Annie." Leah ran around the table to her. "Take care of yourself, my dear." She touched Cousin Annie's arm tenderly. "Oh my dear."

"You needn't to mind me, Leah, I know my duty." Annie watched her sternly. "Have your pleasures." She was gone, Leah drawn after her, into the hall.

Lewis got up slowly from his chair. By the time he reached the hall, he heard the front door slam, and Cousin Annie's straight back was sailing away down the walk. His mother was wiping her eyes with her apron. He didn't notice that. Lewis had something to say at last.

"Mother." His sharp voice made her turn toward him, her head still down. "Are we using the money from selling Loady's boy for pleasure? You told me 'twas needed. You told me Pa had to have the cash in hand for business. Pa said so too."

"Business, son?" Leah rapped at him through her tears. " 'Tis certainly business. The business of staying alive. I've got to get my family away from the valley. What does one nigger matter in the face of that? Talk about duty. I don't know where you pick up this foolishness." She stamped her foot like a child. "The Lord"—Leah retreated from the bleak, stern face which took so after her side of the family and stated a practical truth—"helps those who help themselves."

Melinda and Lydia stopped talking when she came back into the dining room, but not in time to keep her from hearing Melinda say, "She's *full* of laudanum."

"Melinda"—Leah's impotent fury finally mastered her—"never let me hear you speak of your cousin Annie in that manner again. She was fiercely devoted to you."

Melinda had never seen her look so angry. "Yes ma'am," she said meekly.

Far away down the path toward the carriage, the three bell-shaped women swayed, the heads of the girls up and expectant, as if in the first excitement of going they were practicing their gliding strut, working out like two fillies down the course of the walk. Peregrine, hot, worried with setting the downriver watch, reined in his horse to look at them, and catch his necessary moment of quiet before the long woman-laden trip across the mountains.

The girls moved slowly, so lightly that his heart could feel the pride like a strap around it—Lydia so fragile and gay, that dear child Melinda so demure to set her off perfectly, a contrasting frame, like a pace-setter for a fine trotter. Beyond them, around them, the summer was gross and heavy. They seemed to need protection from the ground itself—green-bearing, straddled, and pressed-against already by the ravishing sun he could feel on his back, as if he were in the way of it.

"Merciful Father," he whispered, "help me to protect their virgin innocence even from the sun. God in heaven keep my girls from all knowledge of good and evil. Vouchsafe them always the innocence they have today. Amen."

Instead of peace after his prayer, he found his eyes were closed and his teeth clenched in anger. He looked down at his fist, doubled on the reins, and couldn't help smiling at his fool self.

Lewis was already mounted on the mare. He could see that dark head bent toward Leah's hand as she touched the saddle to make a point of what she was saying. The mare's flank rippled nervously in the sun. Peregrine patted the chestnut neck of his own mount to calm the animal he couldn't reach.

"Goddammit," he muttered, "I wish Johnny was with us. Lord, how I miss him. Hell, Lewis, set that mare when she's standing still anyhow! That damn fool's got hands like traps. I've seen his knuckles white on the reins many a time. Nothing but a born fool."

The mare backed. Leah's voice rose to a nervous shriek—"Gently!"

The girls' pink and black parasols, matching their dresses, closed like flowers, and they climbed into the carriage. Now, nearer, Peregrine could hear the sound of Leah's voice, but not her words.

He sighed, touched his horse's flank delicately, and began to go toward the carriage at a walk, watching his wife. She was standing, solid with authority, her head turned partly away, and he could see the stretched tendon of her neck.

Those two women, the tug-of-war that never stopped until the day before his mother's death: from the great bed where they slept now, because it was expected of them, she had beckoned Leah close to her. Leah had been kneeling, a handkerchief over her mouth and nose as if death stank, or as if she were going to scream. Leah got up, awkwardly, stumbled on her skirt. He could not see her face, only his mother's. Leah's head was turned a little away and he noticed only the tendon of her neck, standing out. Mrs. Catlett's face went soft when she looked at Leah, as if she pitied her. He rejected that for sentiment—sentimental old woman . . .

And, merciful God, he thought. Poor old lady, she is doing what is expected of her even when she is dying. Then, irrelevantly: I wish I had no pity.

Hands which had never been clasped in true love met, and Mrs. Catlett found strength to slip the ruby ring from her now bow-thin finger and push it, thrust it, into Leah's waiting hand. The little ceremony was over.

"Well, now, that's over," the old lady whispered, and grinned, whether from pain like a baby or a thought of her own, he had never been able to fathom, and closed her sunken eyes.

One day later she had rallied strength, as people said, or fought for the last wild hour. Something was happening he could not be allowed, for delicacy's sake, to see. He could hear it through the closed door of the library.

Leah, her face gray and still, as if she had been some place and found out something she couldn't tell, came into the library. He could still hear her saying, "By God's grace it is over. She had been so unhappy for the last hour—so unhappy." Leah had cried, but she seemed to move with more grace than he had seen before in her, after his mother died. More authority, too. Now, in the sun, she was showing that authority with her whole small body.

Three weeks after his mother's death he looked up to see Leah coming over the lawn to the courting swing where he had retreated to read the *Tocsin* and think about his mother. He could still hear her voice tumbling ahead of her (the timbre of that voice, never far from his nerves) as she came toward him that day, walking fast in a great circle around one of the bad-tempered peacocks, nearly colliding with two orphan lambs that were nuzzling in the grass.

"Mr. Catlett, I have meant to speak to you for some time."

He put down the paper as she climbed into the swing and settled herself opposite him, her movement making it sway back and forth. He could feel the slatted floor shift slightly under his feet.

"We should have a church—a brick church like the house. God has put a hundred immortal souls in our care." How could a small woman, grown plump as a nesting hen, look so like her father? "Mr. Catlett, I know your duty."

"Do you, my dear?" he couldn't help saying, but she didn't hear him.

"I wanted to surprise you with this." Her hands were folded securely in her lap. "I have made a sketch, and figured about the bricks and the labor. A woman can do that, you know. Dear heavens!" She sighed and squinted at the sun. "What an elegant memorial it will be to your dear mother. A Gothic arch to the windows. A little bell-tower. We can put it up where the old fort was." She was no longer talking to him. She had started the swing with her foot, and leaned back to plan as he had seen his mother planning the house which rose behind them. "It's the *least* we can do," he heard her say.

"We will see," he told her, and picked up the protecting paper against her wishes, as weak as iron. The *Tocsin* spoke of the salt tariff, and how Benton and Polk were going to ruin the salt business in the valley if Polk were elected—revolution, ruin, rabble, and easy money, worse than Jackson. He tried to concentrate, finding the Whig sentiments more satisfying than the now waiting, demanding woman.

Light, sweet Lydia, the pretty child of ten, came running through the Catawba grape arbor from the house, her thin summer cotton flat against her tall, little girl's body, too young then for the dissemblance of a hoop. Strange, on that summer morning, he could still remember exactly how she looked, the leaf shadows racing across her head.

"Come here, pretty child," he had called, forgetting, until Leah's usual words broke into his smile.

"Don't say that. It's bad for her. Never tell a girl child she's pretty. It makes them vain." Then, louder, "Lydia, put your slippers on. Your feet are spreading worse than a nigger's." There was a jerk of the swing and Leah got up. "Little colts should be well broke," she finished. The light went out in Lydia's eyes and she turned and ran away, back through the arbor. Leah began to push the swing again, with a smile of complicity at Peregrine. . . .

Now she turned from what seemed to be an argument with Lewis behind the carriage and saw him. Lewis's horse backed again as she let go the saddle. "Let us hear no more of this, son," he heard her snap. "You have the *right* to speak your sentiments but you needn't embarrass us with them."

"Mr. Catlett, we are ready to travel," she called lightly, covering for Lewis. "I told you we would be ready, and we are ready. Where in heaven's name is Minna?"

The girls' servants had climbed onto the outside back seat of the carriage, and sat, heads down, demure as they had seen the ladies sit. Delilah, Lydia's girl, dug Toey in the ribs, but Toey was praying as she had prayed for three weeks, "Please Jesus, please Jesus, make Marse Peregrine jest shet his mouth."

But he went on and said it. "Leah, why do we have to take three servants to take care of you women in a one-roomed shack for the summer?"

"Mr. Catlett, let us not go on. You have yours—"

"He'll take care of the horses."

"Napoleon takes care of the horses."

Toey's mouth moved on.

Leah said the final word. *"Pas devant les domestiques."*

Toey sighed and stopped praying. She didn't know what it meant, and she didn't trust Miss Melinda at all, who had told her it meant the French for shut up and eat your grits, but she did know that Miss Leah had won again.

Just then they were drawn together as one pair of eyes by Minna, marching down the path, her blood already up to defend herself. Behind her, two of the Negro men carried the trunk which had been Colonel Peregrine Lacey's last possession; she had found it in the carriage house years before and had commandeered it for her "things." Every treasure she had acquired was kept in it. Without a word, she motioned to the grinning men to hoist it onto the carriage roof, already piled high with baggage strapped and ready.

"Minna," Leah almost shouted. "I *told* you."

Minna, watching the men climb up and unstrap the load, didn't say a word. Leah could have been stamping on one of the nameless stones on the hill clearing where the old graveyard had been.

"Mr. Catlett, do something," she finally appealed to Peregrine. He started to smile, then, with an effort, kept still, to keep from laughing, taking sides. Minna's massiveness silenced even Leah at last.

Ten minutes later Minna climbed, towing herself like a heavy-laden boat, into the carriage, after she had waited, politely, submissively, for Leah to get in before her. The girls were still giggling, but they stopped when they saw Leah's face, and turned away from each other to keep from catching eyes and beginning again.

Just as the door closed, a tiny white dog raced down the path and jumped into Lydia's arms. She hugged it and started at once, before her mother said anything, to cry.

"Oh for the love of heaven, take it!" Leah told her, tired of them all when they jostled and bumped her well-laid plans out of place with their capriciousness. Lydia stopped crying and kissed the dog, which had knocked her bonnet crooked and was scrabbling over her dress.

Minna finally spoke, softly. "I got to take my things. These hyar thievin niggers steals ever'thing left loose. And besides," she added, watching nothing out of the carriage window, forgetting them all, "I ain't decided if Ise comin back this way no more."

Lydia began to giggle again into the dog's fur.

With a yell from Napoleon, the carriage jerked, and began to roll. Both girls went quite still with excitement as they watched the Mansion recede from them.

Peregrine, leaning down toward the window, seeing them, thought, What girl wouldn't have visions while the old dream dreams? He forgot for the moment what they were leaving.

Leah was nervously going over the rules, the thousand rules she was so tired of. She knew Minna was watching her. Sometimes she felt that Minna could read her mind, with its load of fears of things the Virginians took so for granted. She knew Annie could. Annie, she told herself again, was a good woman, and had been chastened by life if anyone ever had been, but sometimes she had an idea that the devil got behind Annie's little faded eyes and tempted Leah to hate; talk about temptation, the black fiend never used the temptations on Leah she'd learned about. No, hers were dry temptations, to hurt back, to fling down her riches like a glove before the wreck who could still make her remember, whenever she wished, that she had been a stranger in the land of Egypt.

Ever since she'd been at Beulah, Annie had known how to dig, expose, and flick her wounds; the knell of her brittle tapping finger, or a spoon when she was at the table, tapping on and on like the telegraph, knocking at disaster, telling her secrets to her, probing at her weakness; just this morning, the way she, and even Lewis . . . Leah frowned. Dear Lewis; why was it so embarrassing to be told right and wrong, to be reminded of one's duty, for if ever a woman was certain of her duty, it was herself? She sighed, making Melinda look up, and they smiled communication.

Leah found comfort for herself: Why shouldn't I go and protect my own? I'm tired. I'm just dog-tired and that's a fact, obleeged to look after the blacks morning, noon, and night, doctor them, tend to them. They won't do a blessed thing for their own selves, dirty black things. All this talk of Lewis. I don't know where he picks it up. I'm just dog-tired. . . .

Now that the perils of leaving were over, and they were really on their way, the rhythmic trot of the horses lulled them all, isolating them from one another in their own dreams.

Ahead of them, at the crest of the old fort hill where the turnpike turned toward the east up the Great Kanawha, Leah's new church rose among the heavy, dark trees, clean red and white, its proud white clapboard bell-tower with the single field bell in it which rang sometimes when the wind cut through the slats, and made the field-hands look up, startled, from their work, frightened at the power of God, all moaning on His own. Peregrine saw the tower first, its bell now dead still in the breathless heat. As the little procession rolled and the horses clattered nearer, he could see among the parting trees his mother's tomb, the first one in the new churchyard. It stood, its funeral urn cold, its fluted pedestal already patinaed by the weather. The rambler roses on the iron fence around it tumbled like fulsome tears of blood. When he first heard a sound, he thought a new breeze had shaken the bell, but it was not that, it was the groan of Negro voices inside the church praying, from time to time punctuated by a sharp cry.

Leah and Minna heard the sound from the church at the same time and looked out toward it, frightened. Lydia was in a whirl of daydreams, dresses and flowers, the Queen of Love and Beauty. Melinda was smiling secretly, and humming to herself in time with the carriage wheels, "I know where I'm going, and I know who's going with me. . . ." They both stopped when they heard Minna say, awed, "Oh Miss Leah, they's all in the church. They's skeered, Miss Leah, they's jest plumb skeered."

Peregrine spurred his horse past them and galloped into the door of the church.

Lewis, seeing him go, tried to hold the mare to keep her from following, and didn't succeed. The groaning grew louder as he cantered up through the trees. He heard old Telemachus's voice above the others.

"Love of the Lamb, take Egypt's plag away. Oh take Egypt's plag away, take him away. Let the Angel of Death fly over like a big bird upriver. Don' let he light down on Beulah with his bloody beak, hootin and hollerin—"

Then dead silence and his father's stern voice, as Lewis saw his horse reined up in the vestibule of the church. The Negroes, through the windows, had turned, mute, as if one of the four horsemen had galloped straight out of the Bible.

"I told you niggers not to gather together," his father said quietly. "This is the worst thing you can do." Several of the Negroes were getting to their feet.

"I've posted a watch upriver and downriver. Cain't nobody get in to Beulah. There's no cases nearer than the Salines, and that's farther than most of you have ever been. Way far away, downriver. Now go on back to your work. Remember the Bible says to be contented and obey your masters. Merciful God bless you and keep you."

Peregrine backed his horse from the door, almost into Lewis, who had stopped behind him. He turned from the look of fear on the Negroes' faces, to lock eyes with his eldest son, and see such familiar hatred that he turned on and spurred to rejoin the carriage, away from it.

"Ain't you even going to let them pray while we . . ." Lewis yelled after him.

"What?" His father threw the word back at him.

". . . run away?"

"Don't be a damned fool. Have you no regard for your mother or sister? Clear those niggers out of there if you're so damned consarned." Peregrine cantered back to the carriage, which had stopped, the frightened women's faces bunched together at its narrow window. He waved the carriage on, falling in beside it, as if nothing had happened.

Lewis waited, sawing at the mare's mouth to keep her back, until the chant rose up again, quietly at first, then louder as the carriage and his father got out of hearing.

He smiled.

The mare succeeded in walking.

All the way up the blinding column of dust, which he welcomed to hide him, and could feel in his teeth and eyes, Lewis could hear the rumbling chant following him, now behind him, now strangely filtering down from the trees as they prayed, "Love of the Lamb, huh . . . love of the Lamb, huh . . ."

Toey, who had had a moment of fear again as the carriage stopped, was feeling peaceful and lucky, going to see her Tig, her own Tig, married like white folks, not like those common scared field-niggers in there. She had had a white dress, and a banquet with a cake, and words read over her by Marse Peregrine instead of old Telemachus, and she rested comforted in her faithfulness to Tig when he went away to be educated with Marse Johnny. She leaned back against the jolting carriage, holding her honey-colored arms to steady herself, and watched Marse Peregrine for a minute, wondering still why he didn't like her. She knew he didn't. Once, when she was twelve, he had come on her, just not doing anything, leaning against a tree, dog-tired. He had spoken to her so gently, and had even lifted her up in his arms to see how much she weighed. Then he looked over her head down the lawn and said, "Poor Toey. Don't look white folks in the eye. It's uppity."

It wasn't that he hadn't been good to her, and never complained when she only had one baby in four years, though Minna said she wasn't doing her duty by the family. It was just that ever since she was grown-up and married to Tig, Marse Peregrine hadn't liked her. She could tell, feel it in her skin, just like she could feel her fingers stroking now. It made her try to do things for him and they made him nervous and made Jim tell her to hoe her own row, and he'd hoe his. Now that Marse Lewis, she didn't like him at all. He was mean, had always been mean. Just him coming into a room made a person quit singing or humming or just moon-gazing. She felt then like the doves when he clipped their wings to keep them in the eaves where they belonged.

As for those in the church, Toey didn't hold with that kind of going on. She went to prayers with the white folks, and read from the Bible and the Prayer Book, because it had been Miss Annie's Christian duty to teach her.

"Ain't you skeered 'bout your boy?" Delilah, round-eyed with fear at the praying, asked her, interrupting.

Toey tossed her head, proud in Melinda's old bonnet. "He's gone be fine. He's just gone be fine. What kin I do? Best not to worry." She was annoyed at Delilah. She knew she ought to feel something, but the boy hardly even knew her when she went down on Sundays in her time off to the quarters. The rest of the time she was at Miss Melinda's beck and call. Now, going to see Tig, she had greater things to think about. That was ruined by Delilah. She didn't want to feel anything else. She just wanted to be happy. Now here Delilah went and spoiled everything, making her sad and ashamed. She could have pinched her. The tears started down her face.

Lewis, riding out of the dust, seeing Delilah misunderstand and put her arm around Toey to comfort her, looked from her to his father's invincible back, hating him for dragging the woman away and leaving her own child in danger. From the way his father sat his horse, to his cold, quiet voice, and his turning, always turning aside, as if his whole existence depended on the comfort of serving his own selfishness, Lewis felt the familiar wave of hatred for his father—now taking them to the Spa for sinful pleasures by eating nigger, the only one since Cuffee, and this time no excuse, not even the excuse of a runaway.

"Yet forty days and Nineveh shall be destroyed." He said that aloud, and didn't notice his father rein in beside him.

"You'll ride her better when you relax, Lewis." The man tried to smile, as if he were weakly making amends. "Don't let her get too close to the carriage."

They rode on side by side, not speaking, Lewis's wide feet already beginning to be cramped in the stirrups Uncle Telemachus had carved for Johnny.

At the inn gate, Annie clutched the gatepost with one hand while she shaded her eyes with the other, watching them drive out of sight. The sun was a weight on her head which made it hurt and buzz, but she couldn't go in, not until they had really left her.

She heard someone coming down the beaten dirt yard, and looked around long enough to see that it was only Mr. Neill, walking bent over as usual as if he were cold. She noticed that he had remembered his hat when he came out of the door, and was pleased. She turned back to see just a glimpse of the now tiny carriage and riders almost at the last bend beyond the church—just a glimpse through the trees. She thought she saw one horseman rein in beside the other.

"Dear Annie, now come into the house. Come, now," Mr. Neill touched her arm to persuade her.

She shook away. "Don't talk to me as if I was a child," she muttered, still trying to see the carriage. "Peregrine won't rest until he has Lewis off that pretty mare."

" 'Twill be all right." Mr. Neill tried again, not hearing her.

"It will. *It* will." He didn't know whether she was agreeing, or telling him about his brogue again. He never knew any more. Mr. Neill trudged up the yard, his stooped back feeling the sun too hot for a man who stayed so much indoors. He didn't feel good, not good at all. The inn stable hid the snaggle-toothed row of houses where he and his woman had lived until she died. That was too bad, now, but a man had to go on, had to rise in the world for the sake of the others. He could see Teeny at the window. She disappeared when she saw him frown, and with the faintest echo of Big Dan O'Neill he murmured, "Damn lazy slut, 'tis the back of me hand to her troublesome parts," then looked around to see if Annie could have heard him.

Seeing his own wench standing at the door watching, too, scared-looking sullen damn wench, he turned his mutter to a cough, spat roundly so that his tobacco juice bounced satisfactorily in the dry dust and called, not loudly, so that he wouldn't bother Annie, "Git me a toddy, damn ye."

After all, she was his own nigger, and he was a gentleman and could do as he pleased. He eased himself down on the bench by the door to wait and try to get Annie to bed, poor thing. He wished he felt better, but was afraid to tell Annie and make her take on.

She went on looking up the road after the carriage had disappeared and even the column of dust in the distance had settled back into the road. Annie felt cold. She closed her eyes and let both fists pound on the gatepost.

"My God, my God, why hast Thou forsaken me?" she whispered once, dry-eyed, her teeth clenched.

Chapter Three

FAR AWAY, the welcoming cow-horn from the gate at Egeria Springs reached through the air over the jostling of the carriage. Melinda's heart seemed to turn over, as the heart at the first shot of one committed to battle. It sounded again. She prayed, a biting little prayer in her mind that the others would please God, or her, by sleeping on. She wiped again at her dusty face, girded up her loins by patting her hair, bit-bit at her lips, controlled her body, ready to spring. One minute, she knew, was all she had, her one minute, her desperate chance, planned, planned. . . . She was hardly breathing, and her eyes shone. If she still had had her animal's tail, its tip would have flicked almost imperceptibly, lifting her skirt at the hem.

Having plodded for three days, the carriage whipped through the gate and under the trees, down the groomed, dappled white road, swept around a curve of the hill, bearing Melinda toward a bright green valley where she could see a round Roman temple, and a crowd of people gathered, moving, yet still, static, waiting. . . . The others were now awake, excited, looking toward the crowd. The wheels stopped.

Melinda tucked her whole body to spring, put one gloved hand on Lydia's excited stomach to hold her back, gave the other to Napoleon to help her down, and stepped daintily, prettily, ahead of Leah and Lydia, out of the carriage, her head high and her bonnet straight. She heard Leah gasp behind her. It was done, her secrecy committed to action.

Mr. Catlett drew reins beside them and leaned down to speak to a courtly man. She paid no attention to what they said, moved now through the waving mass of strangers with her family following.

Then she saw Johnny, sitting on a white fence beyond the crowd. He hadn't moved yet, just sat there holding her eyes with his, watching, grinning, damned Johnny Catlett. He unwound from the fence and was already behind her kissing his mother, before she could reach him.

She hadn't seen the other boy until she heard Johnny say, "Ma, this is Cousin Crawford." Melinda did turn then and look at Fish, straight, blond, and just like Sir Galahad, and behind him a woman she had seen some place before, and a tall, plain girl.

The woman took her arm possessively and burst into nervous words. "Why if it ain't dear little Lydia! My stars!"

"No, that's Cousin Melinda." Leah breathed hard some place below her, swooped, and brought Lydia to the center of the circle. "*This* is Lydia." Melinda finally found herself on the edge of the huddle of women, while Sally Lacey and Leah hugged each other, their bonnets lightly touching.

Johnny came around and kissed Melinda's cheek. Somewhere behind him she could hear Lydia's high-pitched squeal. "Ma! Everybody's a cousin!"

Close to her, so close, but with his face turned away toward the others, Johnny stood quietly in the whirl of skirts, Negroes, baskets, seeking arms. Melinda weakened for a second in her armor for public arrival. "I only wanted you to be proud of me," she whispered, but wouldn't have said it aloud, not to Johnny's easy laughter, not for the world.

Like fishes poured into the main stream, the Catlett family were guided, found direction, and were by evening floating, as if they had been there forever, in the way of going through the day at Egeria Springs.

The white cottages, built in long verandaed rows, lay around the hillsides in a horseshoe. In its center, the bigger wooden dining room with its fine white colonnades could be glimpsed through the huge virgin trees from the porch of the cottage where Leah sat and rocked. She had succeeded at the unpacking, at the placing of her charges, and at successfully impressing Sally Lacey, who sat beside her, rocking too. Quiet evening was coming to Egeria; only the sound of a banjo some place, and, once, someone laughing, disturbed the inevitability of Sally's voice, and the clack of ninepins falling in the distance beyond the springhouse.

"Crawford," Sally was saying in rhythm with her rocking; she had been talking on ever since she had come out from her nap and sat down to wait for the correct time to go down to the springhouse for the evening stroll. "Crawford." She had said the name over and over as if her mind anchored there and only floated a little away from it from time to time. Leah, watching the couples and single figures begin to gather again in the valley below them, finally listened.

". . . said the family ought to get together. He wanted his cousins together." The rocker banged. "I declare he is the thoughtfulest child, like my own son, more like a son to me. After all, he would consider us so; we're all he's got at Albion. If there's anything under heaven God intended me to do, it's make a home for that child. Oh there, down there, lookee!" She stopped rocking and pointed toward a fat man slowly sauntering toward the spring. "My stars! What's *he* doing all by himself? Mr. Wellington Smythe is the lion. He's elegant—all the gals are in love with him, but to my mind"—she sank back and smiled—"he prefers the older, more sophisticated ladies"—she looked at Leah—"who've traveled and know the world for what it is. He's *English.* My conjecture is that he's had a great sorrow. . . ."

Leah hadn't said a word. As always her mind was racing, squirrel-like and as pert, and she had nothing in common with Sally Lacey but age, relations, and memories of her which had filled her with surprise when she had seen Sally again.

Trouble had tightened Sally's strings. She seemed to have frozen, curls all in place, still in front of her ears now in 1849 when ladies were wearing their hair in smooth medieval coifs. Leah wondered if those taut curls had not stopped moving as watches are supposed to stop, the day Brandon took the only way out a gentleman could take under the circumstances, gone through with everything, even his people and Sally's jewels knocked down to his creditors. When Mr. Catlett heard, he locked himself in the library for a day, and when he came out he was the same as always, but exhausted. He only said, "I didn't know what to do about it," and never mentioned Brandon Lacey again, but would leave the room when the women discussed it.

Leah's whirling mind settled sadly on the way Sally had once looked, pretty, delicate, spoiled Tidewater doll-baby before time (Leah thought of it as retribution) had dried her in the perpetual winter of a shrunk apple in sawdust. Dust, dust on the Beulah road; Leah was away again, worried about Beulah. The strings of conscience hadn't loosened enough to let her feel pleasure at the damp, quiet evening, only relief at having got her brood in the safe mountains under the safe trees. At last she let her legs spread peacefully, hollowing her skirted lap.

Fortunately for Melinda she had already put out of her mind the minute's happening at the carriage. She was too concerned with a new set of problems. Mr. Catlett had disappeared with a gentleman in a wheel-chair whom she couldn't yet connect. Who was a close cousin, and who a distant cousin in this first trip to the divide where the rivers ran west and east too? There were still so many she couldn't connect, after all the years of trying, still spaces in the past, still that walled garden of people. It was not easy and never had been, being connected with the best people in Virginia. Leah sighed. She saw Lewis in the distance, sensitive, worrying Lewis, who wouldn't even leave his home to go away to school, coming along the path from Wolf Row, where the treasure of bachelors stayed. She frowned without knowing it. Sure enough, he turned up through the woods behind the cottages instead of down toward the spring like everybody else. How like her father he walked, the awkward boy.

"Everybody is here. Everybody," Sally was saying, excited. "Sara had a heap of beaux at last night's ball. I counted; twenty-seven Virginians spoke to her, five danced with her, and one young gentleman from South Carolina looked her over for a spell. It's very important to notice these things, very important. Of course South Carolinians stay together mostly. I find some of them a little *nouveau,* and as for those new cotton and tobacco people from Tennessee and Alabama! My stars in heaven! You know, not really established. Everyone knows cotton's down and they're stretching their credit just like everybody else. They put on so." She leaned forward. "They dress up too much in the morning. They wear their *rings* at *breakfast."* She emphasized this sin, but said it half-whispering as if she really didn't like to speak of such things but felt she must. "As for the Northern girls—silk dresses at breakfast. French! Did you ever hear tell? I don't know why they admire to come here. They have their own places."

Melinda listened from inside the cottage, sitting on her cot beyond the open window. She inspected her two cousins, went on buffing her fingernails, and smiled a slight smile. Sally's carefully modulated genteel voice, which carried in it the capability of nervous screaming, had slipped into that perpetual discussion of rules and personalities which passed for conversation when two or three Virginian ladies were gathered together, and Melinda was no longer interested. Why should she, a captured princess, jailed until she found her own key, pay attention to those edicts which placed her in bombazine, too young and dangerous, below the salt? Lydia, because of the push in the carriage, had put her in Coventry, but she did not mind, only listened to the two girls, mostly Lydia because Sara was very shy and tall for her age, and answered awkwardly. However, she was useful, in her quiet way. Melinda went on buffing her nails, letting her mind rest with Johnny. As she and Johnny were coming out of the new brick church, she like a dark angel all in white and Johnny securely holding her frail arm, there impinged as if she had been reading her mind the quick voice of Aunt Leah through the window, and her comfortable laugh.

"Oh no, only childhood friends. He's always been helpful and kind to her. My Johnny won't marry for a long time, and then not his cousin. He's far too attractive and independent, and I would never be willing to the match. No, I would never consent. I know what's best for my boys. Of course I want them to marry—sometime." Melinda could hear the boards of the porch groan.

Miss Sally was saying, "My hopes are set on Crawford. It's an inevitability. Everybody knows its an inevitability. I've never been so sure of anything in all my born days."

They went on easily, waiting for the cool of the evening, waving in unison their turkey-feather fans, never questioning their inalienable right to plan and manipulate the lives of others, expecting it of themselves as woman's duty. Leah had the last word. "It isn't of course that I don't pity the dear penniless child, and care for her as if she was my own daughter . . ."

As the key turned again in the prison door, Melinda glanced at Sara, who had heard too. Sara could not blush prettily. She blotched, and looked as if she were going to cry. Then Melinda remembered the pretty little girl in the kid slippers on a weekday, and her voice—"She's awfully dirty."

Lydia giggled but she stopped when she saw Melinda's face, and ran to put her arm around her as she would have done to anything alive that looked like that. "Don't pay Ma any mind," she whispered softly. "Aw, Lindy," she begged. "Have a good time. Please!" She sounded afraid.

Cousin Sally got up from her rocker and leaned into the window, stretching her neck like a swan. "Come, gals, it's time to take a little promenade before tea," she called in her sweetest thrilling, trilling, evening voice. Then, seeing Sara's red face, she hissed past Melinda's ear, no longer swan, but predatory goose, "Put a mite rice powder on and quit that blushing, Sara!" She disappeared from the window and went to stand beside Leah to wait, complaining, "*She* don't care."

Minna, dozing in a corner, woke up and waddled toward Lydia to pull her away from Melinda and inspect her. "Thim hands is too sweaty. Hold thim up. Let that trashy blood drain out. Now do what I tell you. You done got two freckles. You want to look like a horse done pooped bran on ye?" She was fierce as she twirled the girl around. Lydia spun and giggled, paying no attention. "I don' know what Ise gone do with you. Come hyar." The pungent mossy-green smell of the white bare wooden room was mingled with the scent of Florida water.

Melinda reached for hers too, calm as stone, and cold as stone, having made up her mind among her enemies. Pride forbade tears, but set her face in a mask which could have passed, she hoped, for the haughtiness of great ladies everywhere, especially in durance vile.

"Now we'll go down and listen to a heap of fire-eating from the men," Sally told them wisely as she guided them down the porch steps. "My stars, you know the way men carry on, sporting Pally Alty hats and talking big, just like leetle boys. They carry on so. Sara, come here."

As they walked together, the mother looked up commandingly at her tall child. "Don't talk politics, and don't talk books, and dear heavens, don't talk religion. You're inclined to. Men don't take to it. It scares them. There are some things a gal just don't talk about. Don't . . ." She was, for once, speaking so quietly and urgently that the others could hardly hear her. She was like a nervous rider who had to depend on a bad mount.

"Glide," she chattered, almost to herself. "Don't take long steps. Whoever wants to see a young lady's *skirt bounce?* It ain't genteel. Oh it's all very fine for the likes of some of those Richmond girls, putting on to be so dashing, but you, my girl, will please glide like I tell you to."

Sara's dull misery was making her move like a somnambulant, faded, careful.

Across the little valley, Cornelius Stuart, once Congressman from Virginia, sat in a wheel-chair with his black alter-ego beside him. His lined gray mask was lifted toward the western mountain with the eagerness of a child who begs for a last minute of the sun before being taken away. The veil of knowledge of death, embarrassing, unbreakable, between himself and the bright gathering crowd made him gasp, as he swung his chair from the touch of warmth and look hungrily down into the valley. After the past and the sights of a greater world in his long life, he sat contemplating Egeria as a man stares at his own fireside. Of all the personal worlds he knew, each with its center, believed in, taken for granted as if there were no other centers, only Egeria for him was home enough to die in—this taproot thrusting in the willing ground, this campfire, this porch, this main street, this Numa Lake, this Mall, this one round Roman temple set in a bowl-like valley within the bigger valley among the ancient oaks, the maples, here an aspen fluttering, there to stand near if the hair were black, a huge red rose-bush, making the perpetually damp, wood-rotting green bowl heavier with its scent.

He watched the temple through the milky lens of his old eyes, the shape swimming, the movement around it whirling, and grinned, satyr-like, to himself at the familiar small copy from some traveler's sketchbook of a Roman temple to Vesta he had once seen in the Forum Boarium—Vesta, sometimes called Nemesis because her women votaries destroyed with burial alive those who broke taboos. Its white columns held up a dome, faintly pink in the evening sun, which made the marble statue on its roof blush along her ample back, her face coyly turned away from the light, and her shadow long on the roof in front of her. Egeria watched down perpetually on the valley, the lowest leaves of the nearest oak brushing her head from time to time, making the shadows swim across her face and giving her movement as if she were alive. The over-zealous artist who had carved her in Italy had put into one hand, held outward, an umbilicus, which the proprietor of the Springs thought was a snake, which was just as well. Her breasts were uncovered, but she was foreign art and that, in itself, was a great draw for the ladies. At least her limbs were covered with flowing draperies. One of her feet had been broken in the long transit, which gave her a very satisfactory ancient quality. Cornelius Stuart remembered when she had been hoisted up there, in the days when the spring was still famous for its aid to fertility, but now, only twenty years later, when gentility had spread like a fog, this was discreetly forgotten, or not mentioned, which was the same thing. Under her guard, below the dome, the spring lay like a clear dark mirror in a well surrounded by a marble wall, where an old slave in red livery presided, remembering the various dosages, doling out the evil-smelling sulphur water for the crowd drawing from all directions across the long grass, which whispered at the touch of the ladies' skirts. They strolled and bowed, imitating one another—less alive to the old man than in the good old days when presidents and gentlemen from the Congress came, and everybody had money;

not riffraff and poor folks putting on with the bottom dropped out of everything, even cotton, and all the ladies in dimity, and a bunch of highfalutin strangers in silk.

At his feet on the grass, Peregrine Catlett lounged, watching too; for a catch of a minute, Cornelius Stuart saw things as they used to be. Used to be . . . used to be . . . The valley already murmured of used to be. He saw the old Negro ease back from the noisy clamor around the well, avoiding a gentleman who was spitting tobacco on his marble floor, and carry a cup of water lovingly up the southern slope.

"Hyar, Marse Cornelius. I come quick as I could. Don' make no face." Then the Negro saw the young man who sat on the grass. "Ifn it ain't Marse Peregrine Catlett! You ain't been hyar in more'n twenty yars!" Then, the old refrain, "Things sure ain't like they was."

Peregrine smiled. "I went and got married. Been rearing me a family." He spoke with an easy pride. "There's one of my boys." He pointed to the other side of the valley, where it widened into a large savanna, with a little creek wandering through it. On the near side of the creek a half-mile track had been fenced in. A young man was taking a mare through her paces around the dirt course.

"Lord, Marse Peregrine, he jest like you. Got your way of goin," the old Negro said politely. He couldn't see him, so far away. "How many more?"

"Two more living," Peregrine told him, "a daughter—"

"Wal now ain't that jest fine? We mighty glad you could finally afford to come back," the Negro finished simply, saying what he thought as the privilege of an old man, who, having so many masters, knew none but his well. He hobbled down the slope, back to the mob who were now milling around the springhouse, making the trodden mud seep through the grass.

Sally sailed ahead of her new relations down the path to where the ladies were gathering in their separate cliques, like little protected states, away from the crowd. Wooden seats had been built against the trunks of the largest surrounding trees.

The Louisiana and a few favored Alabama ladies held court under the south oak; a little to their right the South Carolina ladies spread themselves under its twin. The skirts of perpetual mourning for a child, a cousin, were pools of black, here and there relieved by the bird's-egg-colored dresses of the girls.

The huge maple northwest of the temple was still deserted. It was nearest the spring, and was tacitly reserved for the Virginians. Higher on the slope, full in the evening sun, just below Alabama Row, the ladies from the North spread their silk skirts and tried to shade their eyes until the sunset. Some of them had even brought books. A witty lady had barbed that it was as though they had no relatives to talk about.

This was what Sally whispered, as if the remark were her own, as their party, a close-assembled, entrenched group, walked slowly down the path for all the world to see.

Melinda dropped back a little to glance at the Northern ladies' dresses and keep their images in her mind. Away beyond them, in the valley below the cottages, the children played together as if they had no states. Beyond the babble of voices she could hear them singing, "London bridge is falling down," and see them flop upon the grass. Melinda looked away, envying them. She knew what it was to suffer greatly in her heart as she walked, head high, preferring to enter her next battlefield alone. No one could have known her knees were quaking and her mouth felt dry. Ahead of her Lydia bounced, as full of pleasure as a child at seeing more white people than she had ever seen before in all her life.

"Now here we sit," Sally called back to her, and settled herself on the bench under the maple. "That's why it's fine to be in Alabama Row. We can always get here before anybody from the Tidewater. Piedmont ladies first! Oh lookee, Leah." She motioned, but of course didn't point, toward the springhouse. "There's Mr. Wellington Smythe talking to Crawford. The *Englishman.* He's the lion, the *bon ton.* He is Egeria's beau, just like at Bath, a dictator. Even I am a leetle scared of him. He knows everybody, and, my stars, he's well connected." She patted Leah's skirt. "I know the English. Mr. Smythe looks very like the former king. I shouldn't be at all surprised—well, you know you *can* tell a gentleman . . ."

She let a hint of the delicious relationship hang in the air and not be spoken, just as Mr. Wellington Smythe had let it hover over her enchanted head a few days before.

"Naturally he wouldn't talk about it," she added wisely.

Melinda let her eyes sweep past the short fat man with the red face, standing beside Crawford, to see if she could find Johnny. She still refused to fade into being one of them. She saw the red rose-bush and wandered away to stand in front of it, glad for the first time for her smooth raven hair instead of Lydia's silly soft brown mop, bobbing in ringlets around her shoulders.

Among all the men who leaned on the columns, sat on the stone steps, wandered out of the temple considerately, now that so many ladies had come, to spit tobacco on the grass, she couldn't find Johnny. Betrayed, she waited, a lamb for a slaughter she feared might never happen, watching and trying not to watch for him.

Across the little valley, Peregrine was too busy with Cornelius Stuart to see them arrive. What he had noticed in the older man's face made him stand still before him when they met, shy and shut out from his dying.

Now that they had been quiet for a while, Cornelius Stuart had begun to talk, assuming, as he had assumed other privileges before in his rich, responsible life, the privileges of the dying. Peregrine caught a sense of urgency as he talked, as if he had to state it all quickly, let it be known.

His thin voice, which matched in its slight quaver the movement of the thin hands in his lap, went on over Peregrine's head as from time to time, guiltily, his glance and attention wandered to faraway Johnny exercising the precious mare.

"We are committing suicide, young man, in a cultural Sahara Desert." Cornelius Stuart's hand clenched in his lap. Peregrine was reminded that he had been in Congress.

"What's happened to us? Why, I remember twenty-five years ago when we in Virginia needed no poor white Garrison or upstart interfering Beecher to tell us what to do. We knew. Peregrine, goddammit, we knew as well as anybody. We talked of it then and tried to find a way. By God, we tried. They holler about rights and wrongs as if that's goin to help a man make up his mind. These young people don't even talk. They take it for granted that it's their privilege to own and trade in human flaish as if it was hawg meat. You ain't supposed to know it. I ain't supposed to know it, but the only damn thing we got to trade with in Virginny is niggers." He chortled. "Nice folks don't do it. No, we don't know about nice folks doing it."

Peregrine was so surprised, after so long, to hear the taboo stated so baldly by the old man, that he didn't know how to answer. "Well," he said slowly, "it's come more then a man's worth to air the subject these days. If you criticize it, you're an abolitionist."

"Oh, hell and damnation." The words made the old man pulse so that he pushed aside his knee-rug, and, as his servant adjusted it, spat. "Abolition, rights for women, free love—damned passel of socialists. Cain't even go to the theater—passel of reforming mollies, mealy-mouthed preachers won't let a man dance." He, so far from dancing, watched the couples slowly promenading on the grassy slopes. "Look at them solemn youngins strut; temperance and Germany and Pally Alty hats. Dear God!" Here he reached the neural point of his evening's exercise. "If I had that youth . . .

"When in the hell did free speech quit being good manners?" he went on, covering Peregrine's too understanding silence. "Eh? Remember when it wasn't a sin to speak your mind, and we didn't rear no passel of—oh hell. All we know how to do is boss and be bossed. That don't make a man."

Peregrine laughed. "Oh, we quit speaking up when St. George Tucker and Mr. Jefferson died, and Praise-God Minor and Hell-Far Bare-Bone Presbyterian McGuffey took over at the university. My Johnny told me three-quarters of the damned school took the temperance pledge. Concentrate on licker and let the country go to hell."

"When money went south to a passel of new-rich cotton-pickers, and we quit fighting and argying by God." The old man grinned, delighted. "Before God, Peregrine, we're losing our humor. Them fire-eating fellahs to the south will drag us into war yit."

"No." Peregrine was serious. "No. They had theirselves a good workout over Texas. I don't believe it."

"Worst thing could have happened to us. Honor and command! Hell's fire, what else have we got to do but fight? Damn sight easier to fight than think."

The old iconoclast, enjoying the evening, slashed away with his voice, too old to be called out, or make decisions any more that mattered.

"Marse Cornelius, it's time to go." The old servant beside him leaned down to his ear. "You gone die right hyar ifn you don' quit gittin so mad."

"Wait a minute. Just a minute. Peregrine, I ain't met your ladies yit." At the mention of the ladies the satyr face smoothed, prepared for pleasure and a few minutes of courtship, like a game, before he was trundled off to bed with the blasted children, who were having their game invaded by their black nurses.

"Just the same," Peregrine told him as he got up from the grass, "we got duties. These youngins have to larn them. My boys never took life easy," he added proudly. "Sometimes I reckon we had too much freedom—never taught to control our passions. My boys have been overseers since they was sixteen. I had to do it. They're better prepared than I was."

Across the grass a child set up a wail and was slapped by his nurse in mid-scream.

"Yes, I know." The satyr peeped around the old man's eyes again. "Pray and whip. Whip and pray. McGuffey! We got more pious attitudes than a dog has fleas. Goddammit, Julius, wheel me over to the ladies." He reached up a hand and clutched Peregrine's arm. "When you rear youngins only to obey, or be obeyed, you don't breed brains. Soldiers and rebels, that's all you git. You know what they got to the North we ain't got? Brains!"

Peregrine wisely said no more; the man who had been so bright and elegant a legal mind, he felt, was old and wandering. As he listened to the more passionate language and accent of his father's time, the past he had had to cope with in his own blood surged up at the irresponsible, crack-voiced barbs, and the thought of his own father, who would have been Cornelius Stuart's age if he had not succumbed to his passions and left Peregrine alone with only his mother to shield him from that vicious, unhappy, uncouth old miser, Grandfather Ezekiel Catlett, who had cracked over Beulah the whip of his anger and his broken, frozen heart.

He wanted to say, "Goddammit, old man, you don't have to deal with it any more," but, of course, he only walked casually beside the chair, saying nothing as Cornelius Stuart was wheeled through the warm and moving crowd toward the ladies. He pointed up behind the Virginia tree where a girl stood by the roses. He judged her coolly, as he would have judged an untried colt.

"Peregrine." He waved to Julius to stop. "Who is the gal with the white face and the handsome bitter eyes?"

But they were within hailing distance of the ladies, who had arranged themselves, feet crossed, to receive them. Peregrine didn't see whom Cornelius Stuart meant, but said instead, "That's my Lydia. She's fourteen. That one, talking to her cousin, Sara Lacey."

"Dear Lord, Miss Sally was a pretty gal." The old man motioned for the chair to be pushed on. "God and my nephew treated her like a dog. Poor little old thing." He said it as he had a good look at Peregrine's Miss Leah. Lord God, wasn't it like Peregrine Catlett, after he'd raced all over Virginia, to marry a plump, brown small Methodist partridge, who looked like a satisfied squaw, sitting there all motherly and calm. But there was something around her mouth they'd better watch out for. It sat too straight in her bland face. The old man wondered where it came from. It annoyed him that he didn't know her breeding.

Sally, having blessedly not heard his epitaph on her, sat expectant for attention. Leah, beside her, was pleased that it was a dear old gentleman and not one of those inquisitive ladies. Behind her, Sara whispered, "That's Great-Uncle Cornelius. He's got five hundred blacks, and the Jeems and Kanawha Company in the palm of his hand. You know the Dunlop Creek property?" Lydia shook her head, wide-eyed. "He inherited that through the Crawfords. It wasn't worth a cent until the canal—"

Sally heard Sara and leaned back. "Don't talk about money, Sara. It ain't genteel. My stars, nobody talks about money but Yankees."

Sara, having had this information drummed into her, and having heard her mother talk about nothing else since her father's death, subsided without question.

Melinda looked once at the old man, rejecting the formal, ancient flirtation she knew would come, and stayed where she was before the roses. Sadly, she turned away and watched the opposite hill, her triumphant dreams so clashing with what she saw before her—nothing, nothing new at all. Glimpses of a vaster life swept by, as elusive as the Northern ladies in their fine gowns. Whatever it was, it was not here, and not with the people sitting under the tree. She had seen such a lady once, but that was only Miss Sally, and look at her. . . .

Two fine horses cantered lightly on the road which topped the opposite hill, carrying two high-handed girls across the air. She wished herself with them, above the others, riding against the sky. She started, realizing that Crawford Kregg, elegant Crawford Kregg himself, was standing right beside her and was actually speaking to her. She stared, then made herself glance away; the two girls were already reining in by the race-track in the distance, where at last she saw Johnny and his damned mare.

"You looked," Crawford said shyly, "like the muse of poesy. Johnny says you read. I do too, of course." Then he rejected Egeria Springs with a slow wave of his hand. "You are bored with all this?"

"The blues possess me in the evening," Melinda told him, watching beyond his head to where Johnny had started cavorting like a damned fool, maniacking his mare, showing off before the girls. "I prefer to commune with nature, and the peaceful dead." She drooped and sighed, as carefully as if she were practicing before her mirror in the morning.

"May I escort you to the graveyard?" Crawford matched her sadness. "There we can watch the valley; the—the dumb-show."

Melinda had spied a rustic seat, spread over with a vine on a log trellis, a little farther up the hill, where they could see and be seen, and Johnny Catlett, when he pleased to leave his horse and his flirting, after her two years of waiting, could find them, and, she hoped, be jealous.

"I am too fatigued by my journey for a long walk. Perhaps tomorrow. I would admire to go tomorrow." She began to stroll toward the rustic seat, noting as she turned that Miss Sally had stopped jabbering and was staring at them. Melinda put a frail hand on Crawford's arm and let him lead her to the seat.

"I'm glad you chose this." Crawford let her sit, and stood in front of her, trying not to look too closely. It clearly was fate which made this mysterious girl choose his favorite spot at Egeria, the place where he, the only child, had played so often, always alone. He had dreamed of courting there, but had never had the nerve before, so hid behind his own grandness and avoided the girls when he could. Aunt Sally had warned him about their scheming so many times; he knew they couldn't really like him anyhow.

To him all of the pale, poetic creatures he had searched for among the silly girls and never could find, had formed into one image suddenly before him—an orphan, too, a proud, aloof orphaned heroine. So once again Fish Kregg faced the expected and bowed to his fate, acquiescent to his image of himself. Crawford was at Egeria Springs. You fell in love at Egeria Springs. Crawford, polite to the last, decided to fall in love with Melinda. His nerves sang, and he froze so that his jacket fell gracefully, afraid to move.

He watched her lean her night-dark hair on her white hand, her arm across the bench back. An escaping curl touched her white, swanlike neck. Crawford moved aside to keep from touching it; he could almost feel it spring against his fingers.

Melinda had to shift her position. She couldn't see that blasted Johnny past Crawford's shoulder, talking to the girls. "Sit here beside me." She smiled wanly. Carefully adjusting his trousers, Crawford obeyed, and at the same time set his Pally Alty hat beside him on the bench. Behind his blond hair Melinda saw Johnny dismount and lead the mare over to a Negro at the fence. The girls had ridden on at last.

" 'Where every prospect pleases, and only man is vile.' " Crawford's hand swept over the valley below them, obscuring her vision again. She turned, bestowing on him the full light of her magnificent eyes, then let her lashes drop. Crawford, having failed to make her look at the valley, found something else to tell her.

"This stone we rest on"—he followed her glance down to a great flat stone, to where her small shoes rested lightly on its darkened center—"was once an ancient hearth. When I was a child a chimney still stood over it. I thought of it as a mute sentinel of the past. See the fossils imbedded here." He went on one knee to point at a minute cornucopia, and traced with his finger a hollow whirl, like the spring of a watch or a frozen curl.

Melinda had never been flattered by confidence from a near stranger before. She leaned down, and traced one of the spirals with her finger. "Frozen perpetually in death. How peaceful," she said. It was not what she was thinking. Crawford, looking up at her, saw her relax against the seatback and let the lucky dying sun touch her cheek.

She closed her eyes and sighed. "If we but trust, there is a way," he heard her whisper, so beautifully. Sitting above the hearth of what had once been the first cabin in the land of Goshen, and now was Dunkard's Valley, she felt a ghostly sense of peace and safety, as if she were going to survive and have her dreams come true. She opened her eyes again to a new valley, seeing it for the first time in a lull in her private battle, which might mean that it could end at last.

Away below them, Sally saw him go on one knee and gasped. "Sara, my dear, carry me up some water. I feel faint. Oh my stars, something's come over me." She swayed back against the treetrunk, fanning herself, the turkey feathers shaking in her hand.

Cornelius Stuart, afraid of missing one move in the game he might not see again, chuckled to himself, too old to interfere, but never too old to enjoy it.

Between the rose-bush and the maple two ladies strolled, their bell-skirts undulating, hiding the loveseat. A twinge of breeze touched the maple and wing-seeds floated down around them all in a breath of silence. One of the ladies, unaware of the moment, shattered it, picking a wing-seed from her sleeve.

"My son cain't get shet of the shingles," she said. "The water don't do no good."

"Be patient till he gets cleaned out. I always abide by a good old-fashioned physic," the other lady commiserated. They were out of hearing.

Cornelius Stuart leaned toward Sally to pleasure her a bit. "You went to Versailles?"

"Ah, Versailles. My stars, yes." Sally's light shone again. "The fountains of Versailles!"

"There is one," he turned to tell Leah, "where people are being changed into frogs. Leto, beloved of Jupiter, was escaping from his jealous wife Juno with her twin children, Apollo and Diana. She stopped at a beautiful spring. When the peasants muddied up the pool with their feet to keep her from drinking because she was a stranger, she turned them into frogs. . . ."

Leah, deciding he was trying to bait her to find out if she were cultured, said nothing, but nodded wisely, as if she already knew.

She told herself, turning the story into a sensible plan, If Melinda will draw me the picture, I will embroidery it on black velvet, with the sweet little babies in her arms. Mr. Catlett likes the classical subjects, and it's something to occupy myself in the winter. At least it wasn't wasted, she decided.

Cornelius Stuart went on, "I reckon I thought of that because—listen."

"What a pretty sound," Sally said, smoothing the wing-seeds from her dress. The frogs sang all across Egeria, bringing the evening down.

It was so quiet.

Somewhere in the distance a dog barked, once.

Melinda leaned her head back charmingly and sighed an evening sigh. The sun had gone down behind the mountain across the savanna, and the valley was blue under the traces of clouds in the east, floating, brushed with the last pink. Down beyond the race-track, the creek wandered through the wide meadow and away between the distant hills—no sound, only a faint mist rising from it. Now she could, from high above it, see all Egeria spread out under the sheltering trees, the semicircle of white cottages, now in shadow, the fine springhouse, around it beautiful people, peacefully moving, changing places, some fallen here and there on the grass, as quiet from where she sat as if they were all enchanted by the evening, and all of it protected by the charmed circle of mountains.

She turned her head, and caught Crawford with her smile. He followed obediently where she watched and saw Johnny Catlett wandering up the slope. For the first time since he had known him, Crawford wished with his whole body that Johnny would go away.

Johnny was mad. He had tried to ride his madness out on the mare, but he hadn't succeeded. Now he had a double reason for feeling the way he did. Melinda had acted almost as if she didn't even see him, after all that time and all that waiting, and thinking about her every day as somebody who was almost with him when he had to be so far from home. Damn Melinda. He never knew when she was going to act like that, or when her self was going to break through all the hoity-toity she put on sometimes and laugh as only she could laugh with him. Seeing her from the fence as she had come down from the carriage, putting on a lot of queenly airs, and then hardly speaking to him so that he couldn't concentrate on the best horse his father had ever given him—that was a fine beginning for a holiday, prissing and capering and behaving as if she hardly knew him.

"Goddammit to hell," he said aloud to himself, and didn't realize until he looked up that he had climbed to the top of the slope and was face to face with a gaggle of ladies.

"That's the seventeenth g-damn I've counted since we got here," the lady whose son had the shingles muttered to her friend.

"I'm sure it's all these Westerners. Transmontane riffraff. Not like the Valley of Virginny when we were gals," her friend reassured her.

Johnny heard and backed away, awkward and embarrassed. He hadn't meant to cuss in front of the ladies. Goddammit, he knew better than that. He felt trapped by ladies, not able to speak his mind. As he tried to skirt around them, he looked up the hill and saw her at last, Miss Priss Lindy, waving languidly, acting as if she had the blind staggers. He climbed up toward her slowly, to show he didn't care when he got there.

"The *mare* goes good," Melinda finally roused herself to say when he had dropped onto the stone in front of them.

All three waited for someone to speak. Crawford was flushed first.

"There is a grand ball tonight," he told Melinda.

"I'm agoing fox-hunting," Johnny said over his shoulder, sulking.

Melinda smiled so brightly at Crawford that it surprised him. Her eyes looked mad. He smiled back, tentatively.

Johnny whirled around then and saw them, looking as secretly at each other as if he weren't there. He jumped to his feet.

"I got to see a fellah," he mumbled, and walked fast, trying to keep from running down the slope.

Melinda's smile was gone as quickly as it had come. Crawford's misery was, as quickly, sharp.

"Do you—uh—read the *Southern Literary Messenger?"* he asked her humbly.

"No. Oh, sometimes." Melinda said, but Crawford was far too mesmerized to catch the sting of her voice.

He straightened himself to launch into a lecture on the latest issue. But he never began.

From the far hill the evening was pierced by the thin whistle of a fife. The people began to stir and move toward the road. A rumble of drums could be heard under the fife as it came toward the valley. The girls streaked across the grass, billowing their light summer dresses, all color converging at the road in a long line. Melinda saw Lydia and Sara h'ist skirts and run like children across the meadow.

Into her sight around the hill, soldiers in gray marched in double file, precise and tiny as tin soldiers, so small it seemed that she could have bowled a ball down across the valley, and knocked a hole in the line of toys. The air was filled with reedy martial music.

In the distance she heard, like a sigh, "Ha—alt." Egeria itself seemed to take the command. Nothing moved.

"Shun!" Faintly a flutter of faraway feet banged softly. "Ri—ight tun!"

A shift of movement rippled along the gray line. The little toys faced the ladies.

"Pree—sent ahms!" A hollow slap of palms on wood; straight, tiny sticks of rifles thrust up toward the trees.

"They wear the uniform of the young guard of France," Crawford explained.

Melinda, for the world, would not have shown excitement. "The young guard?" she questioned, still watching; she didn't know she was whispering.

"Napoleon's splendid guard. *L'esprit de France!*" He made it sound, to Melinda, like foreign Florida water.

Down near the tall, elegant, handsome boys, Lydia jumped and jumped to see over the heads of the crowd. She thought it would be fitting to cry, but she didn't. They were too magnificent to let herself cry.

"There's Cousin Willie, and Cousin Virginius, and Cousin Eustacius and Cousin Tertius . . ." Sara grabbed Lydia's arm and was so excited that she forgot her manners and pointed. To Lydia they all looked exactly alike, very beautiful. "Oh, Sara, it seems like the whole world is made up of cousins!" Lydia hugged her new best friend.

Behind them two nankeen-trousered figures lay on the ground, pointedly ignoring the whole performance. One of them finally lifted his hat from his face.

"It's them goddamned VMI cadets, Dan. We ain't got a chance in hell with the ladies. We might as well go on back to Bewchanon." Lancelot Stuart put the hat back to shut out the sight.

The other figure went on lying with his wide hat over his eyes.

"I sure wish Pa had of let me be a sodjer," Lancelot complained, defeated.

"What air you acarin?" a muffled voice answered. "Damn bunch of nigger-ownin Easterners. *The* military institute. *The* university. *The* damned all-farred Springs. Who the hell . . . ?"

"Now Dan Neill, if you're agoing to start in I'll have to whup you. I ain't going to pass my time digging no canal with nary but a passel of niggers and you doing nothing but grinding your goddamned Irish ax."

Dan Neill sat up slowly, letting his hat drop and roll away. "You and how many other Tidewater bastards air goin to whup who?" he demanded quietly.

"Oh quit that." Lancelot flopped on his stomach and talked to the grass. "I ain't aiming to fight nobody. I just want to be peaceful and get drunk when I want to and be a sodjer."

"Di—ismiss!" The last command rolled over them. Lancelot sat up and watched sadly while the cadets broke ranks and ran down the slope to find their sweethearts.

"Oh hell, what's the use? Let's you and me go on back to Bewchanon. The gals there ain't seen nothing." Lancelot groaned.

Up among the dark trees on the hill behind Alabama Row, Toey and Tig lay asleep. At the distant sound of music, Tig woke up, and floated for a precious minute, hardly knowing where he was. Then he made himself wake all the way, and turned over to look at Toey, the one human being in the world who was his own. A pang of fear caught him, and he leaned down toward her parted sleeping lips as if he were going to suck up water from a pool. Instead he stopped himself, just over her, and whispered, "Toey. Toey, you wake up. They comin back pretty soon."

Toey opened her eyes and stretched, with her hands made into fists. Her sleepy mouth widened into a smile. Then she remembered.

"Lord God." She jumped up. "Miss Lindy gone tan my hide. I got to wash her hair." She didn't even look at Tig.

"You don' belong to Miss Melinda nohow," Tig complained, following her.

Chapter Four

THE WARM and secret night protected Crawford as he felt his way along the path up the center of the valley, in a black bowl surrounded by lights appearing, disappearing as a door slammed, casting long fingers between heavy columns from the windows of the dining room which, once tea was over, had become the mysterious, inviting ballroom.

Crawford turned and paced and turned again into the moonless darkness, aware of the easy security of his faultless evening dress. His pumps were new and pinched his insteps. Even that sensation he welcomed as part of the task that he was performing, pacing unknown, conjuring up loneliness as if he could touch it around him with the tips of his fingers, up and down in the protecting blackness, looking, looking again at the dim lights of the cottage windows of Alabama Row. He hadn't been able to tell which one behind the familiar long porch, made magic by the night, was the right cottage, so he let his longing rest on each of the windows in turn, imagining the mysteries in the women's voices which he could hear faintly behind them. Once a door opened, and he heard a burst of loud giggles. He listened longingly, waiting in an infinity of time, for the ball to begin, for life to begin.

He wanted to fling himself on the ground, and stare up at the cold ignoring stars and lose himself in trying to remember exactly what she really looked like, what she really said. It bothered him that he could not recall her face, only the constricting sensation of his breath, seeing it. But Crawford could not fling himself down and abandon himself to the stars. He couldn't go to the ball with grass-stains on his pantaloons. He even had to keep carefully to the path; he could smell the heavy dew on the night grass and was afraid of going to the ball in damp pumps. He sadly flicked imaginary dust from his sleeve, and walked on and on, now to the springhouse, a ghostly dome in the night which made the only focus at the other end of the black hollow, with its pale lantern swinging a little, making a moving pool of its dim light; now almost to the ballroom, stopped by the discovering fingers of light from the windows; and turned to pace again, away from the heavy scent of night-blooming flowers. His shoes were hurting a little less. The ball was still an hour away.

From Wolf Row, the last of the cottage rows, he heard a yell, and the answering easy call of a boy's voice. He wanted now to go back into the noisy brightness of his room, but he knew that they were drinking, even Johnny, whom he had last seen stretched out on his cot, his boots in the air, a toddy on the floor beside him, as if he didn't give a damn for anything fine, listening to nigger stories from those two fools, Lancelot Stuart and Dan Neill, whom Johnny persuaded to stay over for the fox-hunt. Crawford felt shut out from his own cottage. Even in his own meticulous corner he had stumbled over a pair of boots before his servant could get into the room through the rowdy mess to move them, knowing how particular he was. After he had dressed, he had managed to slip out of the cottage door without their seeing him. He didn't dare go back for fear of careless Johnny reading what was in his face.

So he kept on walking.

"Melinda." He whispered the name in the dark. She hadn't come to tea. She was sick! She wasn't coming to the ball! Crawford, now near enough the light from the ballroom to look at his watch, studied its face with some longing as if the dial were responsible for the time, and put it back, gracefully, draping its gold chain correctly on his trousers.

Inside their cottage, under two exposing analytical lamps, the girls were being groomed. Leah was dressing quickly, in her best black, to clear the way, making Lydia and Melinda lie still on their cots, straight too, so as not to wrinkle their petticoats. Lydia was tense with fright. She lay, following her mother's movements with her eyes, finding it painful to turn her head with the cluster of twisted curl papers which bit into her scalp. Melinda had had her hair washed in a dozen eggs by Toey. It lay loose in a great dark curtain down to the floor for its last drying. From time to time Toey picked it up in both arms and let it fall, showering it loosely, shaking it gently so that it undulated, catching the light. Her face turned to the white wall, Melinda lay as still as if she were asleep.

Miss Leah finished and stood back from the mirror. "Now," she stated and swooped toward Lydia with her hands out. Lydia's young servant Delilah, with nothing to do, stood as far out of the way in the small room as she could. Minna and Miss Leah pulled the girl up from her cot, and led her, docile with fright, to the chair before the mirror. Minna unwound the papers from her hair, and brushed it long, and let it spring into curls, brushed it long again and let it spring.

"Don't take all the curl out," Leah warned.

Minna didn't even look up, intent on the hair. All of them, even Melinda and Toey, were hypnotized for a minute as Minna touched the brush to a bowl of beaten egg-white and began to set the curls in place.

Melinda sat up on the end of her cot and whispered to Toey, who began to brush too; Toey had to bend down to reach the end of Melinda's for the long polishing stroke. Melinda sat, obedient for once, listening to the sound of the brushes sliding over her clean hair.

"Now." Minna stood back to admire Miss Lydia's crowning glory. Leah stepped back critically, and leaned against the wall, moving the remains of a sandwich on the bureau with her hand so she could lean and concentrate.

Lydia's hair tumbled now to her shoulders, a pile of shining corkscrew curls, with here and there a few spitcurls on her temples and around her ears. She was pleased. She tossed her head once, watching the curls bob and settle.

"Quit!" Minna ordered. "Now stand up."

The girl rose, forlorn in her camisole, its ruffles heaving over her small breasts as she tried to breathe, but was too frightened to breathe, too excited, and felt cold and skinny with them all watching her. Then she remembered that she was going to a ball, really going to a ball.

"Oh Ma," she screamed. "Ma!" She hid her face in her hands, and began to sob, her new curls falling over her face.

"I knew she'd bawl," Melinda whispered to Toey.

"Get some ice. Quick," Minna called over her shoulder to Delilah. "She'll be red as a beet." Leah had already unscrewed her sal volatile with an impatient sigh and, forcing Lydia's hand down, she held it under her nose.

Melinda pulled away from Toey, and walked over to where her white cambric dress hung against the wall, damned hated thing with its acre of fine-sewn ruffles to hide its cheapness.

"Get me the scissors and a needle and thread," she told Toey.

"Miss Melinda, what are you adoin?" Toey tried to take the dress out of her hands.

"I know what I'm adoin. Get," Melinda ordered, and sank down on her cot, the months of patient work across her lap.

Toey inched her way through the noise and cluster of women and inched the scissors off the bureau before Miss Leah could notice her and stop her. Melinda grabbed them from Toey and snipped delicately at the pile of white cotton, her mass of black hair falling around it. From time to time she whispered, "Hurry, oh hurry"—as if there were anything Toey could do.

Toey watched, horrified, as ruffle after ruffle that had stood all the way out around the shoulders and hid Melinda's bosom, and made her head look just like she was sticking it out of a huge white dahlia, was ripped and flung in a growing pile on the floor.

"Oh, Miss Melinda." Toey stooped down to the poor rags that had been so pretty.

"I know what I'm doing." Melinda didn't look up from the dress. "Fetch a needle and start tacking the ruffles to my petticoat."

"It already got ruffles," Toey said, then hopefully, "Kin I have 'em?"

"My second petticoat. Quick," Melinda ordered. She closed her eyes and tried to recall the exact shape of the Northern ladies' Paris dresses, how they looked like they had risen out of clear water and not like a big gob of soapsuds.

"I know what I'm doing," she muttered again to herself, as she began to rehem the now bare neck. Fifteen minutes later the dress was hung up again. It looked forlorn, the bare neck, the bare sleeves, like an old nightgown.

Toey wound Melinda's hair in a long snake, now smoothed its errant waves against her head, now coiled the snake around and around. Melinda's interfering hands raised, touched it. She ordered, "Lower, put it lower." It lay pinned huge above her neck. Gently Toey released her neck curls and fluttered them, making them escape from the rest, as if they had been touched by a breeze.

As soon as Toey had finished, Melinda pushed her away, grabbed her morning robe, and slid out of the chamber. Toey heard the outside cottage door close quietly and moaned to herself. "You cain't go out thar in your dishabille. Oh Gawd, Miss Lindy, you jest gone to ruin ever'thing." She picked up the ruffles sadly and began tacking them to Melinda's second old petticoat, working faster and faster.

Lydia stood shaking, holding her mother's hands hard while Minna laced her, crooning, "Breathe out, honey. Again. Again!" Lydia had only been corseted once before, to try it. It was horrible.

"Now bend your limbs a leetle and breathe out. Thar!" Minna was finished. She put both hands around the girl's waist, and when they touched was satisfied. Lydia's face had gone white. The smell of sperm oil from the lamps made the room so close that she was afraid she was going to faint. Minna dropped the hoop over her head, caged her pantalooned young thighs and legs in a bell of iron. Its size forced them to stand farther away from her. Minna brought her petticoats fluffed across her arms. At last it was time for her dress, dear sprigs of flowers and ruffles, dear, dear first ball-dress she had already planned to put away for her grandchildren. She put out her hand to touch it.

"Don't wrinkle it," Minna ordered, and billowed it high in the air to settle over corset, petticoats, hoop, thinness and all, and cover them.

Leah blinked back some tears herself. The child stood so pretty now, delicate, beautiful, just the most beautiful—not like her own black and solemn girlhood, not like that at all.

"Shouldn't it come up a leetle in the front?" It seemed somehow wrong that such a child should show quite so much of her bosom.

Minna powdered Lydia and sprinkled Florida water, and, hoping Miss Leah wouldn't notice, pinched her cheeks, once.

Leah inspected, frowning, then put both hands into her jewel-box. "Oh Ma!" Lydia sighed as her mother's pearls went cold around her neck. "Can I, Ma?"

"Just this once. This one time." Leah pulled earrings out. "Your ears ain't pierced. We'll have to do that." She dropped them back into the box. "Never mind rings. It's evening."

Now garlanded, Lydia was ready, a cloud of ruched, tatted ruffles around her shoulders, in a tent of sprigged, tucked, starched, faintly pink mousseline from Cincinnati, for all the world, Leah couldn't help but realize, like a little grown-up poor lamb for the slaughter.

"Melinda, you get ready now. There ain't room for three hoops in here." Her eyes still on Lydia, she led her out to her father to be admired, not realizing Melinda was gone.

Crawford had hesitated in the pool made by the springhouse lantern when he saw the pale figure run out of the cottage and down the steps. At first he thought he was seeing a flitting ghost, then realized, feeling foolish when he saw Melinda, that he had been yearning up at the wrong cottage.

She disappeared in darkness and he could only hear her, lightly breathing. She appeared again beside the rose-bush, just on the edge of the pale pool as he stepped behind a tree and watched her stop and hover near it. She stood there, delicate, alone, smelling the dark flowers while lesser girls giggled and prepared in their secret chambers. She was above caring, the frail lonely figure.

The sight of her in the moonlight mothering the dark roses was more than Crawford felt his soul could bear. He sneaked away behind the trees, praying she wouldn't notice the movement and catch him spying.

"Hell and damnation," Melinda whispered, too far away for him to hear, and stuck her pricked finger in her mouth.

Melinda was intent on what she was doing, clipping the buds and dropping them into the held-up apron of her morning gown, frowning, counting, until a black mass from the stripped bush lay in the hollow of her gown.

The family were standing with their solid backs to her when she slipped into the cottage. Mr. Catlett was saying to the pink soapsuds, "You'll be the prettiest gal at the ball"—as if men didn't always say such things. Melinda bit her lip. Even Lewis was there, looking like a big embarrassed bull in his evening dress.

"There comes a time," Melinda said to herself in the mirror, letting Toey hear, "when a gal of spirit has to be her own fairy godmother." Even scared Toey had to admit she was right.

All the winter buttermilk had done its work. Melinda's skin, if she did admit it, was like alabaster. Melinda had never seen alabaster, but she had read about it. She grabbed the bedpost firmly and ordered Toey to pull like blazes.

Just as she was pinning the last of the red rosebuds around the neck of her dress, Leah opened the door. She didn't say a word, but Melinda, watching her in the mirror, saw her pause and look shocked, sad envy on her little old round face that made Melinda feel triumph like a stab. She lifted the little circle of rosebuds she had made, and crowned herself.

"You look half naked!" Leah muttered.

Melinda passed her, head rising high from a wide low rim of rosebuds. The rosebuds in her hair made it as black as night. Melinda sailed.

Mr. Catlett saw her and comforted her with a smile.

"Where's Johnny?" She had to ask, but she knew already. He wasn't there.

"It's nine o'clock," Mr. Catlett told her instead of answering.

Leah, behind her, said, "He ain't coming. The pesky, selfish boy. Fox-hunting with those trashy McKarkles."

Mr. Catlett interrupted softly, "Mr. McKarkle is a friend of mine, Leah."

Leah didn't hear. "He don't consider nobody but his own self," she complained. "Lewis, you can escort me. Your pa can squar the gals."

Lewis couldn't have touched Melinda. She looked so splendid and unashamed it was just plain brazen. He stumbled past her and took his mother's arm.

Some of the families from the cottages had torches bobbing along in the darkness before them. Leah wondered, when they saw them, if it was correct to do the same, but Mr. Catlett didn't seem to be worried, and Mr. Catlett knew. They went down the steps with Toey and Delilah and old Minna watching at the porch-rail. Toey's hands clutched tight to the railing as she gazed at the other world of ghostly people passing by in an almost silent parade.

All up the valley lights winked and flickered, vague shapes moved toward the ballroom. Ahead, on the hill, the steady glow from the windows swooped and rose upward. The Spa servants were lighting the chandelier. The thin, complaining sound of a fiddle being tuned made the hands of the two silent girls tighten on Mr. Catlett's arms when they heard it. He squeezed back, knowing they were excited.

Melinda had to be brave. This was the way it was, when the bugle warned of battle. Her traitor legs carried her on toward the baptism of fire. They seemed not to be part of her at all. Yet she went on, not running, not hiding, not feeling at all like a savage princess, but cold as stone.

She hadn't even danced before with a man, not really, just once with Mr. Catlett, and round and round with Lydia to the sawing of Telemachus's fiddle. "Relax and let the man do it. Just relax, honey," she had heard Minna call to Lydia once, laughing fit to die.

It was too late to turn back. The ballroom doors yawned open, the enemies, relaxed, waited inside in a great space to swallow her, under the magnificent glitter of chandelier, a huge aloof star of prisms and spermaceti candles. Melinda took as deep a breath as she could in her corset, and stepped, as she had practiced so many times, across the Rubicon alone.

At eight-thirty by his watch, Mr. Wellington Smythe stood in front of his own mirror, fighting that fatigue which had whispered, "What does it matter?" far too often of late. Letting down was a luxury he couldn't afford. He concentrated hard and made himself begin to enjoy tying his white cravat, laying it around his high collar which stood out just enough, neatly folding and turning it. He was pleased. Sometimes cravats were as stubborn as people. Sometimes, as on this most important night, at least clothes obeyed. Mr. Smythe stood still for a moment, poised at the top of the *ton,* inspecting the cravat, the ruffles, the coat which encased him. His pudgy body relaxed with pleasure. He liked himself. He liked, for just a minute, his large nose which gave him, he decided, a faint (not too much) arrogance which suited. He even liked his thin lips, which worried him sometimes, but they did balance his ruddy face, and give it just that touch of control he needed to show discipline.

Mr. Smythe picked up his gloves and considered their cleanliness, turning them over in his thank God thin enough small hands. His servant Nash looked relieved when he saw Mr. Wellington smile and begin to draw the left glove precisely on each finger. At least he wasn't going to demand water to wash his hands again. Mr. Smythe even nodded a little to the boy, now really pleased. It had been a caprice which he enjoyed every time he thought of it, changing his boy's name to Nash, after the great Beau. If he could never train him to tie a cravat, at least he could launder gloves, and on such small details great reputations could be built. Mr. Smythe was sure of this. It was one of his maxims. Of course, being against it, he couldn't actually own Nash (even if he could have afforded him). It gave him a feeling of a problem well faced that he was hiring him from Mr. Mason of Alexandria, who had assured him that he was using the money to put a lovely child through school. So he felt he was really being useful. Mr. Smythe loved little girls and old ladies and he always did what he could for them in his quiet way.

He fitted on his right glove, and glanced around his room to see if everything was in place, peaceful for him to come back to after he had done his bounden duty. The white china phrenological head stood naked and veined with blue lines on the dresser, so benign. Sometimes, in this wilderness, Mr. Smythe felt sadly that it was the only friend he had, carried all the way from England, wrapped in his second coat. It, at least, had arrived without a scratch. His eye caught the area of benevolence on its china pate and he lightly touched his own bump of benevolence, almost as if he wanted to see if it were still there—very lightly of course, for his coxcomb had been perfectly pomaded and he didn't want to soil the glove. He was sorry that there was no bump of decorum that was recognized by the science, nor one of gentility. It was another of his maxims that without them a man had no rudder as he pulled for life's shore. He was sure that had there been such bumps they would have stood on his head like two commanding splendid horns. His books were all in place: *The Language of the Flowers, Burke's Landed Gentry* (more useful to Mr. Smythe than Debrett; it held almost every English name he had come across in his travels), *The Phrenological Guide,* dear Mr. Lockhart's *Life of Walter Scott,* the very necessary *Edinburgh Review,* several tracts from the Tractarian Society which he had sent from England—he always believed in carrying his books wherever he went, and he went, oh dear, how often! It wasn't that Mr. Smythe made a living from these things, but he did have certain interests, and the ladies were not averse to the right guidance and, when cotton and tobacco and—he had to admit it—Negroes were selling high, delightful, peaceful, long visits. Mr. Smythe loved the country. His narrow white cot waited without a wrinkle to mar its perfection. The inspection was complete.

The mood of pleasure passed as Mr. Smythe turned from the safety of his mirror. He remembered again that his plans had been ruined, absolutely ruined by recalcitrant savages, after all he tried to do for them. He had picked the two sisters as twin deities, practically laid hands on them as the belles of Egeria. He knew their backgrounds, their expectations, and their looks, everything which made them eligible, and they, ungratefully, had got very out of hand, had actually ridden at the wrong time of day and reined up, right before his eyes, at the track fence to talk to a young Western cousin of Crawford Kregg's, to whom they had not been properly introduced. He knew that. Mr. Smythe made it his work to know everything that went on at Egeria. Next they'd be smoking cigars and crossing their limbs.

If there was one thing Mr. Smythe would not brook it was insubordination. Let it happen once, and all authority was gone, Mr. Smythe cut adrift. The only thing a sensible man could do was revise, but he found this hard after his mistake. He let his mind go blank to help him make a brilliant makeshift plan, and lit at last on Crawford Kregg. The earnest young man was rich, the finest type of young Virginian, without that knowledgeable cool arrogance some of them had which had more than once forced Mr. Smythe to lay his small and valuable hands to a four-in-hand and dash along, his heart against his throat, just to wipe the look out of their eyes. Crawford was traveled, and seemed to have missed that traveler's itch so many of these people had when they returned. Crawford had no brag.

Mr. Smythe ran quickly in his mind's eye over this afternoon. He silently thanked his stars for the *Quarterly Review,* for Lockhart, who never made a mistake in the literary fashions. He saw again Crawford leave his side and go up the hill with the new arrival. Even more important, he had seen him come down again. Mr. Smythe thanked heaven and earth he hadn't actually said who he'd pick to lead the german. It was better that way, kept the gals on their hopeful toes.

Mr. Smythe was elated—a dark horse, he would be brave and back a dark horse and she, out of that sweet gratitude these provincial girls seemed to have—well, at least their dear mamas had it —would, almost sheeplike, ask him to stay at Albion after they were married, and . . .

He caught himself in his dreaming and marched back to the mirror for a last cold look and the facing of hard facts which kept him from that kind of foolishness which had made him err too many times and exposed him to the betrayals of ladies who used him and really thought only of themselves, leaving him high and dry with no real home. First, he reminded himself that he was fifty-four years old. Plans, not dreams, were Mr. Smythe's forte. He recited the facts to himself, cruelly, flicking himself with them.

Second, the materials he had to work with—a pinched small ballroom, one chandelier, a group of girls like frightened or obstreperous colts, and their mamas as full of outmoded rules and fears as governesses, a class of pious women he particularly despised. This glorified camp meeting, this perpetual picnic—tobacco-spitting, cursing, violent, genteel, timid at the same time—was not Bath, was not Baden, was really nothing—was only tentative raw material for him, Mr. Wellington Smythe, to mold in a pale image of the world he should by rights have been in, and never could attain; no marble columns, no vague brushes with the *ton,* none, never again. He shivered; these wild people said it meant someone was walking over your grave. He could see himself, sinking in the ground, a perpetual visitor in someone else's graveyard. Stop.

There was no denying the pleasure he took in his work. He could make the provincials swoon at the sound of a duke, just as he used to his old mother when, after her housekeeping years, she lived on vicariously in her chimney, lapping up his stories of the people he had seen (sometimes very close to) like an old cat lapping cream. The Virginians could learn, too; it gave him real joy to hear the ladies' voices begin to change with time and travel. What if they did still say "esteet" like the Irish, and "ketch" and "heap," and said everything was handsome or elegant, from a table to a calf, and called their lifeline river the Jeems? It had its charm. They were at least beginning to use the more fashionable broad "a." Mr. Smythe felt that he had left one footstep on the red Virginia clay. The wonderful thing was that they cared so, that was it; caring itself made them provincial, waddling like little ducks across polished floors, the dear ladies, and they loved the words "lady" and "gentleman" as much as their Irish predecessors. They even said "gintleman." Mr. Smythe smiled. America, except for some smart travelers he could avoid, was so trusting. If a man said he was a gintleman, he was. At last, undeniably, he was.

He even let himself miss his mother for a minute. The dear old biddy. How these same ladies would rend her and him, if he, like a wounded chicken, showed blood! Holy Jasus! Mr. Smythe always said he had no family to speak of. Speak of! Mr. Smythe giggled aloud so that Nash looked up at him. He stopped giggling. Caution. Always caution.

There was not a man of them out there, whatever dancing pumps and knightly poses they assumed, who had not seen a man killed or at least beaten by the time he was fifteen. He sensed a catlike violence, ready to spring in the darkness outside the delicate illusion of safety they constructed for the ladies. Mr. Smythe preferred the ladies.

He had known frailty in a Liverpool street, terrible frailty in the face of brute, animal gang toughness. Mr. Smythe's small teeth went together. He had arrived at the moment of strengthening therapeutic truth.

"Ay, gormless bleeding barstards," he whispered to himself, and let hatred pulse through him. Then he relaxed all over. His body, his soul, and his accent felt very clean. At last he was ready for the ball. Mr. Smythe trotted to the door, and out into the night among the many torches.

Mr. Smythe was standing beside Crawford, carrying on his conversation about a conversation with a man who had actually had a conversation with Mr. Lockhart. (Mr. Smythe prided himself on being able to take up a topic where he had left off. It gave a faint illusion of flattery.) Crawford's eye and mind kept wandering, and, frankly, so did his.

Mr. Smythe sighed with relief when Melinda stepped into the ballroom. She was frightened, white with fright, but she had a good carriage, a wide deep chest which meant she had stamina; that black hair and white skin became her and she walked as if she knew it. Those cat-eyes, Indian blood most likely, but then they seemed proud of it. Irish, Scotch, and Indian, they still had killer eyes—demure, yet savage. The dear girl had a spirit which had made her strip her cheap white dress and deck herself with rosebuds so that she looked quite elegant. Lesser girls, like the plain pale child on the other arm of one of those wary fathers he disliked, would have covered themselves with those painful, nervous ruffles he detested. She took a step forward, looking straight ahead, a backwoods unbroken filly, the whites of her eyes showing. Well, it was the best he could do, and it was delightful, for once, to take a little chance and show his power—just to remind the ladies.

He touched Crawford's arm. "What a primitive wild beauty—what dash—what bumps of sublimity!" He poured it on, sweet warm water of praise on the young man's pleased and tentative head. "Will you do me the honor of presenting me?"

Mr. Catlett guided the two girls to straight chairs against the far wall, making them walk all the way across the exposed floor because he knew it would deaden their fear.

Lydia promptly forgot a pinching corset, a rulebook of admonitions, and, like a child exposed to real fairies in a garden when they had only been in books before, she stared, neither believing nor unbelieving, just plainly and simply there. More silk than she could have believed swished on the polished floor as the great, aloof rich ladies from the Deep South and the North promenaded by, like big boats on the Kanawha. Everyone moved, stirred, as the fiddles were tuned. They all seemed to know one another. Ladies looked up and smiled at gentlemen in black evening dress, who seemed to lean protectingly forward to them. She didn't know anybody, anybody at all. She straightened her back against the wall and moved a little closer to her father. Two young ladies in white dresses sailed by, as much at ease as if it were all real. They had a whole group of gentleman cousins following, surrounding them, who bowed and took miniature books from their hands and wrote in them.

Her father was gone. She was exposed, alone. There was only Lewis, almost stamping his feet, standing beside her mother, and Melinda on her other side, looking a way she'd never seen her look before, except in the early morning when she thought no one was watching. Poor Melinda. Lydia touched her dress to reassure herself. Miss Sally looked like thunder, just beyond, and she couldn't see her new best friend, who had shrunk behind her mother as if the whole beautiful party were an ordeal and not the prettiest thing Lydia had ever seen in all her life. Two young cadets in their fine gray stood very straight and were looking for someone, because they both looked carefully over the faces of all the girls who sat, as she did, with their mas against the wall. One of them caught her eye, and she almost smiled at him, but she remembered in time and looked down at her folded hands. Her whole pink lap was trembling, and she was really surprised. She had forgotten, for a second, how scared she was. Her father stood over her with three little white books in his hand, one for her—it had a gold tassel—one for Melinda, who took it as if she'd seen such a thing before and dropped it in her lap, and one for Sara. She could see Sara's gloved hand reach out and grab it.

Sally was more angry than she could remember that Crawford hadn't escorted them to the ball. Of course she hadn't said anything to him about it; witless, she had taken it for granted. She watched the floor. The crowd parted and she could see him at last. Her anger vanished. The dear boy was actually bringing Beau Smythe over to them. "Sit up, Sara," she hissed and fixed her smile for them.

Mr. Smythe saw it, saw the mouth opened, heard again the blather he had had to take from the silly woman. He knew her kind; perpetual, useless aunts he had to flatter from time to time. "You'll find us very English here." That's the first thing she had said to him, as he knew she would, as they all did, and told him about how in Papa's time they'd served toddies in silver cups on a big tray that came from England, on an English sideboard. With such ladies the great days had always been in their papas' time, and would be again, if they had their way, in their sons-in-law's time. He hated pretentious poverty. Mr. Smythe smiled back at her. After all, she was Crawford's aunt. He had to remember that. Those inevitable shrines to England which he was always taken to admire—well, he, too, was a sort of shrine. He hadn't said a lie, he had only become what they wished him to be. He wondered, from time to time, why they had bothered to revolt at all. He hoped at least the new girl wouldn't be between generations of money and silver goblets—most Virginians seemed to be. But like all worshiped things the word money itself was taboo.

Mr. Smythe had successfully given the cut direct, the cut admonishing, to the two sisters with their retinue of beaux, and left them astonished, at least he hoped so. He did think he heard a man's laugh behind him, but that could have been at something else. "Mr. Smythe!" Sally's happy voice intruded.

Sally beamed at Crawford. So this was the surprise. She hoped Sara wouldn't tremble too much and make a fool of herself when Mr. Smythe picked her to lead the german, and to think, as carefully as she watched, she didn't . . .

It *could* have been at someone else—that damned laughter.

Mr. Smythe bowed and said, "Good evening." He moved over to Melinda before Sally could answer.

Looking into Melinda's untrainable eyes, Mr. Smythe nearly had a sinking spell. He had made his worst mistake. He knew he was committed. The whole room was watching him. He hardly heard Crawford's introduction.

Melinda had watched them all the way across the floor, Crawford, rescuing again, steady branch to grasp in the deep swirling water of riches in which she had no part. The roses were feeling smaller, deader, cheaper by the minute as she saw the ladies' jewelry glitter and heard their commanding silk. The two young ladies she had seen riding toward Johnny were as high-handed, high-stepping as they had been in the afternoon, balanced in their element. The only reason she hadn't run was because she was too far away from the door. Her forlorn dress drooped around her. Then Crawford came, handsome; he was handsomer, handsomer than Johnny—at least handsomer *there* than Johnny was foxhunting. The funny podgy man beside him was looking through her, stripping her not of clothes but of the fool idea that she could carry off any plan she might ever have. He was the same one Miss Sally had pointed out at the springhouse.

She looked up at him, and saw a fear in his eyes as tentative as her own. *You* tell on me, sir, and I'll tell on you, her eyes told him; she felt triumphant.

"Miss Lacey, may I compliment you on the message of the roses!" Mr. Smythe turned to Crawford. "The damask rose for bashful love, the rosebud for confession. What a dear conceit." Crawford could only stare at her, and she at him. She had forgotten the Language of the Flowers.

"May I have the honor of leading your lovely niece in the german?" Mr. Smythe bowed to Mrs. Catlett.

Leah nodded and smiled. After all, it wasn't Lydia, not Lydia the silly little man asked for. She didn't care what Sally said, the man looked an utter fool.

Mr. Smythe nodded, once, toward the quartet of Negroes squeezed in the tiny gallery. He took Melinda's hand and helped her to rise. Crawford picked up the program she let fall.

"You are the center of all eyes," Mr. Smythe whispered to Melinda as he led her to the end of the now empty floor. "Eyes up, girl, head straight. Just do what I do, and don't balk." He almost jerked her arm shoulder high. The string music cut the waiting quiet, filled the room. She knew only that she was walking slowly, to a march, across the bare floor. It was not until they turned at the other end and he grasped her other hand to form a high arch that she realized that she was actually leading the german. Couple after couple, who had followed behind them, dipped and passed under her arms to form a long line down the ballroom. Mr. Smythe led her between them, still watching, relieved as her eyes began to shine at last as she passed the envious line of ladies. At least the girl could march.

"Behind them now. You're on your own. Up to the other end," he whispered, and left her to sink. Full sail, Melinda walked back up the ballroom past the wall of mas. When she met Mr. Smythe again, she smiled at last.

"Splendid, my dear," he whispered professionally, relieved. "Can you waltz?"

"No," she whispered back.

"Polka?"

"Yes."

"Same step. Don't bounce." Mr. Smythe grasped her waist and pushed her around the floor as the figure broke into partners.

Leah gasped. Whatever else, she had specifically told both girls they were not to waltz, evil disgusting thing for young girls, with men holding them like that. At least Lydia didn't have to do it.

Lydia sat between her father and Lewis, watching Melinda, too sick with disappointment for tears.

At last it was over. Mr. Smythe led Melinda back to her seat. The room burst into a roar of talking. Ladies' smooth heads nearly touched as they questioned one another.

One of the sisters told the other that he was a dreadful toady after all.

Crawford led Sara to her ma, and came over to Melinda. She looked up at him as grateful as a child. Mr. Smythe hoped that puppy-dog look didn't show to anyone else. Crawford handed her program back. "I took the liberty of stealing several dances," he begged.

So that's what it was for. Melinda fingered the tassel. She couldn't speak.

Leah leaned across her. "Crawford, dear, no waltzing. My girls ain't allowed to waltz," she said sweetly, then glared at the strange man.

"My girls." Melinda watched the tassel as it flicked in her hand.

"If the queen cannot waltz, then perhaps the madame would not be averse to her dancing a reel." Mr. Smythe swallowed ire. He hated the sweaty things, but would not be put down by a solid small farmer's wife in a cap.

Leah was defeated at last. "Perhaps a reel," she conceded.

Crawford had already reached for Melinda's hand.

"Who are they, anyhow?" Melinda heard a lady say.

"Miss Obscurity of Obscurity Hall," the wittier of the sisters said to her beaux. Melinda and Crawford passed by too quickly for her to hear any more comment.

"That's Fish Kregg. He's as rich as the inside of a dog, Viny," her brother teased back.

"Well, present him. What are you for?" she demanded.

" 'Pears like she's hooked the fish," her brother whispered.

"He's not yet in the dish," Viny finished, playing Crambo, which she reveled in. Her beaux laughed dutifully. Viny had been known to send more than one aspiring upstart away with a barb of rhyme in his eye, and then melt his heart to water ten minutes later with a sad, sweet song.

But when Mr. Smythe circled the floor again and was close to her, her brother saw her smile at him as tentatively as a backwoods filly and wanted to kick the damned fool.

"Toadying to that goddam governess," he whispered.

She muttered, "You wouldn't have to, Wilson. You're a man!"

Through that sweet darkness which smelt of perfect trailing, animal-scented damp, Johnny was riding into peace. They wound slowly up the valley, the thin wiry pitch of the violins fading behind them until they were gone and he was free at last. He could hear the lead horse rather than see it, but as his eyes accepted the blackness he made out, faintly, its rump and the shape of Gideon McKarkle riding the wide path. Behind him Lance's borrowed nag stumbled and recovered, now in rhythm with his own mare, lovely girl under him who was not afraid of the dark even though he had ridden her only one day. Hoofs struck rock, clattered quietly. Away to the back the rumble of the cart carrying the McKarkle dogs and driven by Gideon's brother, Jeb, grew quieter too as they struck clay and the rocky road was left behind. He sensed climbing, in his forward body, in the pulling tread of the mare.

Johnny looked up at the moving stars above him, and let the reins fall, not even wanting to constrict the mare, or any creature on such a night. He was impatient to stop and release the dogs. They waited, only a fine complaint from time to time as they jostled in the cart, not free yet, not free to give tongue.

They began a steeper climb into the trees where even the stars were hidden and an underwater blackness pressed around him. The mare felt her way slowly, sensing the horses ahead, trained for the night. The tunnel of woods constricted, covered. Johnny would not have told a moment of panic then to a soul on earth. His mother's disappointed face intruded in the dark. He didn't want to think of his mother, or his father, or of Melinda, all of them in the light, wheeling automatons to fiddles.

Once out of the woods, he could have lifted his arms to the high free stars. They were on top of the world in the night wind, unhampered as sea breeze. Around them one of the wide crests of the Alleghenies curved, dropping at its edges downward somewhere in the distance. It was too dark to see the slopes, under the dipping sky, but he knew them, as he knew his hand, now loosely holding the reins. The dark hulk of a deserted cabin loomed up as they passed. The stars seemed lower, brighter, and the sky flattened out, not confining, but infinite carbon space above them.

There had not been a word said all the way up the long hollow. Every man rode alone.

They reined their horses to a line of thin trees on the plateau edge. When Johnny turned to feel his way across the high brush grass, he could already see Gideon McKarkle's figure outlined against the fire, which he kept there ready in the field, caring for it as his own hearth.

The dogs babbled as his brother Jeb walked around the cart, tuning up for their wide miles of song.

"Would ye take to a mite whisky, Johnny?" Gideon hunkered down beside the fire and handed the jug to Johnny as he flung himself on the damp, green smell of earth and grass beside him.

Johnny took the jug and drank, letting the liquor warm his fingers and his chest. He felt bodiless on the ground after the two-hour ride. The moving yellow light of the little fire lit Lancelot's and Dan Neill's faces as they sat waiting.

Johnny hoped no one would say a word, but Dan Neill did, as he took the jug, never quite at peace.

"I wisht we had our dogs hyar, Johnny. Ain't neither one of us took our dogs out fer two years. Edication!" He spat sorrowfully.

"I remember that dog of yourn, Dan. Turkey-mouth dog, redbone." Gideon spoke low in his throat as if he were unused to speech, or didn't expect to be heard.

"Naw, I ain't got him. He gotten kilt by a painter, bobcat, I don't know. My best one is by him out of Johnny's black and tan bitch. She's turkey-mouth too, fell heir to her paw's voice."

The dogs, released, moved out through the field and away, discordant, searching, not yet a pack. Johnny could hear them swish through the grass, slip down over the far slope, their tonguing changing key as they flowed down a far hollow. Higher than the others, farther away, a sustained note came back, soft bellow out of a soft mouth.

"That thar's Bathsheba. She found down Walker's holler three nights ago, ole male down thar. He'll allus give a run," Gideon explained, then was quiet. No one spoke. They listened until the dogs were out of hearing, lost in the soft slur of the constantly moving woods.

It was not sleep, but its opposite, awareness of the ear, concentrated, so that there was nobody demanding but only the ear, and the rest drifting under the black night.

Gideon's soft voice rumbled in his throat; he the talkative one of the brothers, who had left Beulah when Johnny was fifteen. Once when he was ten they had taken him with them in the night, away up the hollow behind the mill. He could still hear Gideon telling him over his shoulder, "You got to keep up if you're agoin with us." No possibility of quarter, no help. "Keep up, Johnny Catlett." After that Gideon had given him a pup out of Bathsheba's grandmother. But he had never raised a dog out of her yet like the one who had just sung her way into the dark.

"They belong to be sum'ers near Dead Man's Cave. Oncet a fox led the dogs in thar, them goin so fast, I reckon, jest feelin the sand at the mouth under their pads. We lost three dogs that night. Fell forty feet. We couldn't even git down to them. Jeb went next mornin and shot straight down. He said it sounded like thunder. They's a camp meeting a mile from thar. You ought to take your maw. She used to like them things. Hope that fox don' break it up." Gideon allowed himself one low bark of laughter.

Jeb, beyond Gideon, nodded while Gideon told.

Later—no time, just a space later like the space of night itself revolving toward morning—Jeb spoke. "Listen!"

Far beyond the hum of the woods, Johnny heard the thin song.

"They done found." Gideon moved a little. "Circled round to the back. Listen."

Now stronger, the wind carried the single tonguing of the pack.

"He's agittin sweet." Sweet, the sweet fox smell remembered, as the runner trailed his hot musk over the ground, fast, free.

Either the wind or the fox veered. The baying died out.

"Downriver . . ." Gideon charted the course by ear. "Johnny, you got to come and see Paw. Your paw never done no man a better turn helpin him to locate up hyar. Good land and not no niggers. 'Twas a queer thing 'bout Paw, dealin with niggers all his life like he done at Beulah. Now he'll say, I'm a free man. You keep free, Gideon, he'll say. Keep free of ownin niggers, as if 'twas the whites that got freed after all."

"You git that canal up into these hyar mountains and we'll lose ye like we lost Rockbridge County when it come. You'll git your niggers," Dan called from across the fire.

"Wal, Dan, you're ahelpin to dig the thing. We-uns air fer it. I tell you thim drivers delivers some mighty lean hawgs oncet they've drove them all the way down to Bewchanon on the hoof. It ain't good dependin on foot produce for your whul livelihood."

Dan was still dwelling on Gideon's words about being free. It made him angry, angry to remember his father shrinking down there, given McKarkle's inn because he had been blessed by becoming a connection of the Catletts.

"Listen!" Jeb said again.

A swirl of sound, nearer, rising up a far, long hollow; he could hear Bathsheba bugle, the turkey-gobble of the rest of the pack following, sweeping toward them. A thrill touched the back of Johnny's neck with cold.

"They're two mile away," Gideon judged. "Oh Gawd, listen to the music of thim hounds!"

"I ain't raised nothing like her." Johnny spoke sadly.

"Tuken me twenty-five years." Gideon spat his tobacco into the fire. "You're too young, Johnny. One dog, one woman, that's all a man's entitled to. Got to wait long enough to know what you've got."

"What about the woman?" Johnny jogged him into keeping on talking.

"She'll come," Gideon said, sure and patient. "Paw been arter me iver since Maw died. He don' want to breed Jeb. I might go to the tent-meeting," he added, thinking he was changing the subject.

Later, when the pack had veered out of hearing again, Dan spoke low, still worrying his bone. "Rockbridge. Lookee at Rockbridge—led the western vote till the canal got to Bewchanon—"

"Hell, Dan, shut up," Lance told him. "You're digging the goddam canal, ain't ye? You ain't never going to be satisfied. One of these days you're going to rile me up so I'm going to eat you blood raw."

"Ifn it wasn't fer the damn Tidewater we'd be layin a railroad." Dan had to win.

Lance wouldn't let him. "It's mostly their money, ain't it?"

"Whose fault is it we're so goddam poor?" Dan's anger was like a night-jar.

"Oh shut up." Johnny spoke low. It quieted both of them and they sat for a minute, ashamed, letting the night come back.

"Thim hawgs is mighty lean oncet they git to the Jeems, that's all I know." Gideon had managed peacefully to have the last word on the subject.

The endless night rolled across the mountain crest. The fire no longer danced, but lay, hot red embers. Johnny didn't know how long he had been watching Gideon's still face, concentrated on far-away wisps of dog-sound, through the faint roar of darkness as if, quiet enough, a man could hear the sea, all the way across Virginia. Gideon's dark sunken eyes looked nowhere, the hollow of his face and his wide high cheekbones were etched in light; he knew with his whole body the meaning of patience, not counting any time.

Down in Egeria Valley, confined to his cot beside the window, Cornelius Stuart waited too, by the light of one low candle so he could see the dark and later the torches in the night. He was listening to the violins, judging the time by their gathering speed. Beyond the race-track and the creek, the dogs swept through the inner valley, their wide-throated bass moan mingling for a few minutes with the sharp high strings.

The dying man shifted in his bed.

His servant was there as he heard him move. "You go to sleep, Marse Cornelius," he whispered as to a child. "You hungry?"

"No, goddammit, I ain't hungry. Don't just sit there dumb giving me slops and waiting to blow out the light." The Negro touched Cornelius Stuart's fleshless head with his own old hand. "Quit that!" The Negro sat down again to wait.

"Oh Julius," he whispered later, "you do ever'thing else for me. I told you my will freed you, didn't I?"

"Yes, Marse Cornelius. You tole me." There was not a sound in the room. Julius was nearly asleep.

"Git out on that porch and notice for me," the old man complained. "Cain't you notice for me? Damn youngins, profligates, take it all for granted . . ."

"Sure, Marse Cornelius. I gone notice fer you."

"The way the girls—"

"You go to sleep."

"I cain't sleep. Maybe tomorrow I'll git back to work. It ain't good for a man like me to be useless, Julius. Ain't no sense in it. I sure would admire to go . . ." The dogs had veered again up toward the mountain. The old man was quiet, yearning up through the valley with them. He closed his eyes.

It took only a sigh to blow the candle, which was beginning to gutter out. Dutifully, as he heard the music stop, Julius hobbled out onto the cottage porch to notice the first guests to leave the ball—the young, the old who would not stay for supper.

A few burning torches began to weave down toward the cottage.

Just then Julius knew with a wave of blank loss that the man inside was dead.

Chapter Five

AT HALF-PAST THREE on a Sunday afternoon, five days later, Colonel Peregrine Lacey's granddaughter lay in the hammock on the cottage porch and managed to smile just once over her Bible at Crawford Kregg, who was dutifully paying court to the ladies. At the far end of the porch, Lydia sat in a rocking chair. Two cadets leaned against the porch railing, waiting for somebody to say something. Lydia was looking at them as if she'd counted them over and over.

Melinda wore black with the rest of the ladies. Early in the morning before church she had practiced managing her hoop on the hammock, and now could be safely abandoned about it. Cornelius Stuart's death, after the first wondering if it would ruin their visit, had been, in its way, a blessing. Black showed you were really kin. She only had three dresses and couldn't have worn the black without looking like a poor relation and ruining everything she had built up. Besides, it gave her, after her triumph at the ball, a mysterious respite which Mr. Smythe enjoyed, spreading the word about her being a granddaughter of a famous American hero and telling her once quite firmly to keep quiet, just like she heard Mr. Catlett tell what Mr. Biddle of the United States Bank had said about poor President Harrison—"Don't let him speak." It was one of Mr. Catlett's sayings. Melinda enjoyed the unaccustomed attention of being groomed by Mr. Smythe. It was like being touched. She feasted on it, swinging slightly in the sleepy afternoon.

The ladies, having decided at once to go into deep mourning, discussed their kinship for the hundredth time, Melinda was sure, since Cornelius Stuart's funeral, reciting the rules, even of death.

"Let's see. I know I'm right." Sally broke the silence and used her fingers to help her figure it out. "Montague Lacey's daughter—that was a niece of Peregrine's grandma—married Cousin Cornelius. That's where he got his fortune; of course, it's nothing now to what it was. Nothing is." She sighed. "I always think Presbyterian money is somehow safer." She had forgotten Crawford for a minute as she mused and rocked. He, so used to hearing her voice drift on, heard it no more than he would have heard a breeze without listening, and watched the way Melinda's dress lay like a black pool, obscuring her in mystery.

"If he was seventy-four when he died"—Sally hadn't stopped—"that would make him Lydia's—let me see? He was a distant cousin of mine on the Crawford side, but of course a much closer connection through Brandon." Then she added delicately, as if she had not said it every time Mr. Stuart's death came up to intrude on illness, and gossip, the pleasure of vicarious crises, "I wonder how he left things."

Melinda swayed the hammock with her body, and let the breeze it made relax her. She tried to catch Johnny's eye, but he wouldn't look, just kept on shuffling up and down the path below the steps. She decided, pleasure blotted out, that if there was one of them she hated most, it was Johnny, making the only real attention she had ever had seem somehow silly when he did deign to notice her at all.

"Of course he was only a second cousin twice removed to Melinda." Sally rocked.

"No, my first cousin once removed," Melinda told her, looking up from her book, which she was not reading.

Sally's voice was shrill. "No, dear child, you're not the right generation. It goes in generations."

"Age doesn't have anything to do with it," Melinda sassed, forgetting her guard, as sharp in return. "He married my father's first cousin." She couldn't help teasing, even with Crawford watching her.

"I forgot. There's no use arguing with Melinda. She's always right," Sally told Leah sweetly. Leah was placidly paying little attention to anyone.

"She always was like that," Leah murmured, forgetting that it was a new and dangerous change she had noted in the child, which worried her.

Melinda appealed to Crawford helplessly. She didn't need to say anything. Then she looked back at Sally and forgave her with a gentle smile which said, There's not a bit of use to pick on me, ma'am. I'm going to marry Crawford Kregg and never go back to Beulah. Never, as long as I live. She glanced at Crawford, her anger dying a little.

Sally stopping rocking. "Crawford, you *are* taking us to the picnic tomorrow, ain't you? We thought it would be pleasant to go on to the camp meeting. Of course, it's not our persuasion, but many of the ladies go. You and Sara have so much in common with your faith."

Johnny slouched up onto the porch and sat on the step, turning his back to Melinda. He stared out over the afternoon-dead valley and decided that the time since dinner had already lasted three days. She had paid him back enough for the fox-hunt, making a damned fool out of herself over Crawford, going for walks, mooning around about poetry, acting the trained pony for Mr. Smythe, attention gone to her head.

He sighed, full of trouble. "Linda," he almost yelled, having said nothing for so long, "you can ride the mare."

Leah glanced up and answered for her, "Melinda is not a tomboy any more. She is a young lady and ought to learn to behave as one. No lady rides in the evening here, especially on Sunday."

"Richmond girls ride when they take a notion," Johnny muttered.

"I consider Richmond girls a little fast. They waltz and polka and put on airs and graces." Leah glanced sternly at Melinda for her disobedience on the night of the ball, waltzing the minute her protecting back was turned.

Her disapproval brought Melinda up from the hammock so quickly that it twirled over and back behind her. The Bible clattered to the floor. She stood quite still, the women watching her, and made herself be quiet. It was not time yet—no, not time.

"Melinda, you dropped the Bible to the floor." Leah gasped. "It's dreadful bad luck."

"Crawford," Melinda said quietly, "didn't you promise to show me the Indian grave?"

"With your permission, ma'am." Crawford had already picked up the Bible. He bowed to Leah. She nodded, glad to get the bad-tempered girl out of the way. Melinda heard her murmur, "Airs and graces, hoity-toity," as she went sedately down the steps, tying on her leghorn and trying to ignore Johnny.

After Sally had excused herself and Sara, and Melinda and Crawford had strolled up the path, Leah felt she had to speak to Johnny.

"Come and sit by me, son." She was pleased to have him for a while to herself. But try as she might, she couldn't get the boy to talk to her. He only threw himself into the hammock, still swinging from Melinda's body, and watched sightlessly out through the trees.

"If you would only confide in your mother, son." Leah tried again.

"Oh, Ma, there's nothing wrong," was all the boy would say. "I wish you and Pa would let me go back to Beulah. There's nothing to do here."

Leah had concentrated on her Bible and only heard the word "wish." "If wishes were horses beggars would ride," she said almost unconsciously, as she always did to the children when wishes were mentioned. A few minutes later she looked up, and Johnny had gone. He was walking fast down toward the stable. Leah smiled to herself that he had found something to do.

Later, inside the cottage, Sara's voice rose once. "Oh, Ma," she wailed, "you never was a plain girl. Let me be!"

Up on the path behind the cottages Melinda was crying, with Crawford's arm across her shoulder, hiding her face from him.

"I can never go back. Never!" She whispered, "You don't know."

He comforted her, but he did not say the words. Melinda was tired of battle.

She looked up again and dried her eyes carefully. They had reached the woods, and the wide path through the virgin trees made her walk on it as if it were the peaceful aisle of some huge empty church.

"Oh, you know so well, Crawford. This peaceful place. When I am too weary, sometimes I go and lie across the grave of one of the peaceful dead at Beulah. In the still hour of evening . . ." She looked so sad that Crawford almost caught her hand, but her private sorrow made him shy of intruding.

"Is your grandfather buried there?" He couldn't forget the hero.

"No, he was buried with great honor at the county seat." She had her face still hidden by her handkerchief and he could hardly hear her. He could sense her waiting, that strange attendance on what he would say and then withdrawal when he spoke that made him afraid that he bored her, even though they had so much in common.

"Melinda," Crawford said, and cleared his throat. The sound of it humiliated him. Both the girl and the woods, even the birds, seemed suspended in stillness, waiting for him to speak. At last he went on, "Here is the Indian grave."

A great pile of stones rose up beside the path. Crawford relaxed. He had something to lean on to counter the silence.

"The legend is that an Indian princess loved a young brave." He patted the rock ledge for support. A lizard, interrupted in the one place where the sun made a thin line through the thick ceiling of trees, slithered away. Melinda saw it and moved close to Crawford. She touched his arm and held it, not knowing why she was suddenly so afraid. He turned then, drawn at last, and kissed her so shyly that she thought she was going to cry again, this time for the boy.

"I cannot bear this kindness," she whispered, her face against his slim erect body. He smoothed her hair, as if he were her nurse, and when he spoke his voice trembled, but he spoke about the Indian princess.

"Her father, the princess's father, was a great chief. He wouldn't let them . . ." Crawford paused, as if he had forgotten a word. "He wouldn't let the princess out of his sight. So one night she slipped away and she and her lover went across the mountain—

you know, to the west—where there is a huge rock which juts out above the canyon. They are supposed to have thrown themselves from it. Their bodies were found together in the river below, where it cuts through the mountains. They call the rock Lovers' Leap."

Whatever moment there had been was gone. He was at ease now, telling his story. Melinda dropped his arm and stood, swinging her hat against her skirt, dutifully looking at the stone pile.

"It's only a legend," Crawford apologized to the girl. She was withdrawn again in that surprising way she had, when he least expected her to. "Several years ago my tutor and I were here; we came up with some boys and brought a picnic, and we took away the rocks. He wanted to show us how Indians were buried, and find some artifacts. It took the whole morning to move the stones. Down about three feet, we found remains, but they were only of one body, so at least the lovers weren't buried together. The warrior lay nobly, with his arms crossed, and there were two coins that had been on his eyes and had fallen into his skull.

"Lookee." He brought out of his pocket a dull coin. "My tutor gave me one to keep in memory of the noble dead of a warrior race. It is my charm. Lookee, it's an English shilling. See the picture of the King, Georgius Secundus, and the date, 1750." Melinda turned the coin in her hand, under the beam of sun.

"Then we put all the stones back," Crawford went on behind her.

"He said, my tutor said, that they buried valuable things to help them on their way to their heaven, and they must have thought of the coins as magic. Poor heathens." He was telling her quickly now, in full retreat from the kiss. Crawford had never kissed a girl before. The possibility of Melinda's allowing him to kiss her was so remote to him that he hardly believed he had done it, though he could still feel the cool skin of her forehead against his dry mouth.

"He said . . ." But she had already turned as if she wanted to walk back. He fell in beside her, in full spate. "My tutor told me that whenever an Indian passed he would add another stone to the heap. They buried their dead like Absalom in the Bible. 'They took Absalom and cast him into a great pit in the wood, and laid a very great heap of stones upon him.' That's what he told me. He said it was one of the proofs that the American Indians were really the lost tribes of Israel."

Even though she kept on walking, not looking, Crawford was easier with her, and took her hand. She did not draw it away, but let it lie lightly in his. Crawford felt his heart unlock. "I wish you had known him, my tutor, he would have loved you. He thought women should have minds of their own. He had some very socialistic ideas," he went on happily, holding her hand. "He took me abroad. We went down the Rhine and saw the castles and we climbed the Matterhorn—well, I mean we climbed up a ways. He was going to be a minister. He taught me—"

"Where is he now?" Melinda's voice was as sharp as it had been for that minute on the porch, a sharpness he couldn't believe could come from her mouth.

"He caught the consumption and he didn't tell me. One day when we were reading, I remember he was standing at the window, he looked at me as if he was surprised, and he fell down dead off his feet. I recollect he sighed," Crawford said humbly, longing to tell her everything, about all the losses, about his home he didn't like to go to even though Aunt Sally had done her best to make it a home for him, about the times he did love it when he and Johnny went from the university, about how it looked down on the meeting of the rivers where the Gloriana ran into the James. All these things were locked inside him and for some reason he didn't want to mention either his Aunt Sally's or Johnny's names. Besides, there was that sharpness in Melinda's voice. He didn't want to call it forth again.

"Poor Crawford!" Melinda had stopped. She took her hand away and stood studying his face with such deep concern that she seemed to be trying to memorize it. "Oh, Crawford"—she was beginning to cry—"I truly am sorry. Remember that!" She ran away down the path, her hat flapping behind her, leaving him in the woods above the white cottages.

Crawford realized that she must have been touched about the tutor, and had sense enough not to follow her.

After family prayers, Melinda had the chamber to herself, that Sunday pleasure while Lydia sat and read to her father and mother, a ceremony for only the immediate family, when Mr. Catlett liked to have his daughter alone. She could hear the dull special singsong voice of the girl in the next room, reading a tract, which was allowed on Sunday. She laid her head back on the chair and let her whole body relax while Toey brushed her hair. Out of her hoops and corset, in her nightgown, she felt bodiless, so peaceful that she cried and cried as though her heart were going to break, not paying any attention to the tears, just letting them flow down on her shoulders.

Toey was pleased. She said to Melinda as she brushed, "I tole Mammy you was heavin and cryin 'bout half the time and she say that was right, that was real good. She say you in love. Lord Gawd, you ought to hyar what Tig done tol me about Albion. He say it lord it over the Jeems way up on this bluff and got big old-fashioned furniture—real quality. He say it got one piano come all the way from England with the Lacey name put on the inside in gold letters. Tig kin read jest like I kin. That piano is so polished you kin see your face in it, sound like bees buzzin when you play it, and floors a fly could slip and break its neck, and land and more niggers than you ever saw. He say it jest *lords* it over the Jeems. The name in the piano proves you're kin. He say Mista Kregg is the fines' young man. He don' drink or nothin. The steamboat stop thar. It ain't *nothin* like Beulah. He say he thought Beulah was handsome but it ain't nothin. He got these fountains runs all the time and oh Gawd, I dunno what all. . . ."

Melinda never moved. She just for once let Toey's soft murmuring go on above her head.

"Mammy say you gone git married first too. She tole it in her tea leaves, and las' night I dreamt somebody died—big funeral, that means a weddin. Wouldn't that be somethin now? You jest show 'em, the way they done treated you." Since she had been six years old Toey had been the recipient of Melinda's griefs and her anger. She saw white humanity with her eyes. It never would have occurred to her that Miss Melinda had ever been anything but downtrodden, even though Minna told her she was a fool.

There was a long pause. The dark arms smoothed her hair as the dark hands tangled deep into it.

"Has he *ask* you yit?" Toey finally wanted to know.

"That's none of your business, Toey. Remember your place!" Melinda jumped up straight with anger. Toey still held her hair; she just pulled her back gently, unperturbed.

"That mean he ain't. Now you listen to me." She went on with the comforting brush. Melinda had stopped crying and the tears were dry on her face as she listened. "They things you white ladies don' know 'bout. It ain't fittin and I ain't gone tell you. It ain't fer white ladies."

"What?" Melinda asked.

"Neb mind. I jest tell you, git him in the dark. He got to suspect you got somethin besides heaves and sighs and pretty eyes. That all I'm gone tell you"—and then she added with some pride, "from a married woman."

"Oh, Toey, I do feel sorry for him." Melinda tried to tell; she couldn't tell anybody else. "I don't know what to do. He's dreadful handsome. He's so kind to me." She was really, at last, trying to say it, but Toey interrupted.

"Lord, you don' want to marry a man that's *mean* to you, do you?" Toey was troubled. She never had seen Miss Melinda so gentle, like she really was sorrowful instead of going about her business to catch a beau. She decided on a little sensible frankness.

"Don' you want to be rich? Don' you want to live in a fine house?" She could see her new home on the James receding dangerously. Toey was tired of Beulah, with Minna fussing at her all the time, and Tig never there. "I reckon you jest want lay around Beulah the rest of your life. Ain't nothin else fer you. Lay around waitin ten years like Miss Annie, moonin for Mista Johnny till you're mean as a snake, or marry the first white trash gits that fur upriver. One man ain't much different from another. Git a good one." Toey was annoyed. She brushed so hard that Melinda said, "Ouch, quit that," and pulled away. Her sorrow was gone. Toey had said the right thing.

Melinda smiled, and then began to laugh. She laughed as hard as she had cried. She laughed until more tears came and she scared Toey worse than ever.

The door was flung open. Leah called, "Behave yourself. It's Sunday!" And closed the door again.

After Toey had put her to bed, Melinda looked up and told her, "I'll be good to him, Toey. You believe that, don't you?"

"Course you will. Now git your beauty sleep. Gala picnic tomorrow." Toey went to the door.

"Toey," she called after her, "you're getting uppity. I forbid you to talk about this any more."

"Yes ma'am." Toey paused, then added, "Miss Melinda, it ain't good to let things slide along." She shut the door and left before Melinda could call her down again.

Long after Lydia had come to bed and told her in confidence that she couldn't make up her mind between the two cadets, and had used the chamber-pot and been fussed over and buttermilked by Minna and kissed by Leah, and Leah had kissed Melinda too and smiled down at her as she did sometimes, and the flurry was at last over, and the candle out, Melinda lay awake, staring at a pale tree in front of the open window. The sickle moon rose, so young that it was fine as a bone. Melinda turned so that she could see it over her own thin left shoulder, and whispered to it, "New moon, new moon, tell me who my love shall be. Color of his eyes, color of his hair, color of the clothes he's going to wear," and made herself wish something sensible, then turned her head to the wall and went on thinking.

Chapter Six

MR. SMYTHE knew it was important to keep the ladies busy and, what he liked to think and often said, "the swains adoring." As the morning went on ideally, not too hot, lush and soft, toward time for the picnic, he took his constitutional in the valley and surveyed his domain. The gala picnic was a good idea. It made a ceremony of going to Dead Man's Cave, and occasions made the ladies dress more carefully. There had to be occasions, especially this year, with the outside world stabbing at their peace from time to time. Mr. Smythe knew the signs, the gathering of the men around the Richmond *Enquirer* when it came, the news of sweeping cholera in the lowlands casting a pall over Egeria. Joy and ceremony—Mr. Smythe believed in them to counteract the gloom. In the last week, he knew of three families who had retired to their cottages, outcasting themselves because of cholera and ruin on their places, and afraid to return home.

He had to watch the temper of the Western gentlemen against the Eastern gentlemen; the mention of the tariff could ruin an afternoon, the ladies forgotten. There were times when the men talked angrily together, rumbling like shut-in animals, harried on all sides about the territories. There were silences so dead when the gentlemen from the North came too close and heard their talking that it made him nervous enough to dance a jig in their midst to break the unspoken tension.

The morning was perfect for the gala picnic of the Turtle-Dove

Society which the girls had formed with Mr. Smythe's always willing help. The nosegays had gone around after the girls' committee had gathered the flowers and bound them. He had tried to get Melinda on the committee, but all he had succeeded in doing was having her and her family included. His plans weren't working well there. A week of waiting—nearly a week anyway—and young Kregg hadn't made her the first engaged girl at Egeria, which by rights, with his blessing, she should have been. Never mind, the morning was perfect. Mr. Smythe wanted to skip like an old fat faun.

The young ladies carefully carried their bouquets of bridal roses for happy love, china roses for grace, bachelor's buttons for hope in love, daisies for beauty and innocence, and sweetbriar for green and simplicity, in fine paper ruffles sent from Richmond. They lolled against the backs of barouches, sulkies, and chairs which wound slowly, dappled by shade, down Egeria Road on the five-mile drive to the cave. The heavy wagon from the dining room trundled behind the long procession. Mr. Smythe had to ride instead of drive. There was so much to do in the cavalcade.

Johnny rode on one side of the Catletts' hired surrey, Crawford on the other. Mr. Smythe approved of the young men as outriders. It gave an almost medieval air of the chase in the forest, especially when they flirted and maniacked their horses to make the girls scream. Mr. Smythe smiled with pleasure when he heard the light affected cries of fear. There was hardly a farm-girl in any carriage who couldn't ride anything that could be saddled. They had to, usually, isolated as they were, or stay at home, and he knew they loved company, like savages.

He rode up beside the Catlett carriage. "You ought to have a hawk on your arm, Miss Melinda! Afternoon, madame"—to Leah, who looked surprised. "Ah! What a beauteous day. We could be wending out from Windsor, lords and ladies, following the train of the glorious Elizabeth on a hunting day!" It was time for a little singing.

" 'Ahunting we will go, ahunting we will go'—lords and ladies, sing together!" Dutifully they joined all down the way, making a dream of lords and ladies, ladies all dressed in pink and yellow and white, singing softly until they ran into a wild man of a drover with a herd of hogs, and the carriages had to drive off the road and wait until the silent man and the squealing mass of pigs passed slowly among them.

One of the girls, carried away by the afternoon, called out, "Whither, gentle swineherd?" and the taciturn man, who had walked all day, glowered through a pretty shower of giggles.

They halted at the top of a rise, and Mr. Smythe passed the word that they must walk down the winding mountain path to the cave mouth. Girls shook out their dresses and checked their bouquets.

"Mrs. Catlett, have I your permission to escort Miss Melinda up to the top of the hill? I want to show her the magnificent view." Crawford begged so for permission, as if he had had the speech long made up and was only waiting for the carriage to stop, that Leah couldn't deny the boy.

Johnny and Lewis looked on dumbly while he took her away.

"Johnny!" His mother called him back to duty. "You take Lydia and Sara down the path. Lewis will take me and Miss Sally. Now be careful. It's narry and it looks a mite steep."

Johnny made himself stop staring up the hill path and took the girls' arms dutifully. They picked their way down toward Dead Man's Cave.

"What a beauteous day!" Sara said politely.

Lydia whispered in his other ear, "Sara thinks you're the handsomest man in Egeria. She told me."

"Oh Liddy." Sara had heard. "I never."

"My little sister is not to be trusted," Johnny teased.

Sara decided she would give him her bouquet. "I never told you. My dog only died three years ago. Every time you came to Albion I was too shy to tell you," she said to the flowers.

"The puppy. I had forgotten about the puppy!"

"I know you had."

There were rustic seats in the tiny valley, dominated by the huge black mouth of Dead Man's Cave. Above it the mountain cliff rose as far as they could see, when they tipped their heads back as prettily as they could. A little bubbling creek ran along the valley and was perpetually swallowed by the cave. Sara would have sat on the green mat of grass, but her mother wouldn't let her. Some of the girls did, though, and more than one looked up at the two tiny figures on the cliff where the breeze whipped at a line of distant evergreens.

But Johnny went off to join the group around the sisters from Richmond when one of the boys called to him. He wasn't even listening to them, but kept looking up to where Melinda and Crawford stood. Lewis stayed, though, and he looked so gloomy that Sara decided to give him her bouquet instead.

Mr. Smythe bustled about the tiny Eden, saying it was a tiny Eden, and forming parties to tour the cave.

Where the trees cast their roots over the cliff edge, so near for the wild thrill of it that Crawford wanted to pull her back, Melinda stood, letting her skirt sway and pitch in the mountain breeze, watching the long slope of the green-covered mountain opposite. It almost seemed possible to spread wings and fly across the deep wild chasm, or to take one more step and float down through the air to the people below, strewn flower-like around the tiny cup of the creek valley. Melinda could feel herself landing, as softly as a leaf, among them. She made herself look down the cliff to where the ground called, and the green creepers hung for life on little ledges. Far below the top of a valley tree looked like a welcoming nest.

"Miss Melinda, come back." Crawford touched her arm fearfully, as he would have a somnambulant. She did seem to him, head high in the wind, her curls escaped to lash gently at her face, frozen in flight at the edge, as if she were really entranced by the wild chasm, the great dwarfing trees, a bird woman in her natural element of the somber mountains.

" 'Nature I loved, and next to nature, art.' " Crawford remembered the last time he had quoted that, and threw up his hand as if he were trying to shut out the memory, or offer her with a gesture the far furrows of the endless Alleghenies.

When she turned back her eyes were wet with tears, or the wind.

"Do you know 'The sounding cataract haunted me like a passion'?"

Crawford did know. Relieved, he took her hand and finished for her. " 'The tall rock, the mountain, and the deep and gloomy wood, their colors and their forms were then to me an appetite; a feeling and a love. . . .' "

In their pause above the cliff, only the warning whisper, "Miss Melinda, come back," had been words of his own.

Sally saw them finally coming down the path, Crawford helping the girl as if she couldn't run down it barefooted like an Indian. She fought a sense of doom. After all, she had seen Crawford wave his arm as if he were offering her the whole range of Allegheny Mountains.

After the picnic, which only Leah and the two girls ate much of, and the round of toasts to the ladies, to love and beauty, to the Turtle-Doves in wine cooled in the creek, which Crawford refused, watching Melinda for approval, it was time to go to the cave.

Mr. Smythe, who carefully read the signs of Melinda's aloof patience, picked them to go with the first party. Johnny, seeing her disappear into the wide black mouth, which lifted at one side as if it were mocking him with a half-smile, was suddenly so animated that Miss Viny, even though she had been told he was only a younger brother, bestowed a smile. He lay on his stomach for her, his head over the ledge of a rock, and put his hand, fishlike itself, into the clear water to tickle a trout for her.

The cave party surrendered to the hollow silence after the first shock of excitement of having nerve to enter the great mouth, and the easy walk across the sandy floor onto a narrow rock path high above the black chasm below. Ahead of them the guiding torch of the old Negro Egeria kept as guide fluttered its light like something alive, trying to climb up to the ceiling of rock, into the darkness out of sight. Behind them another torch flickered. They moved as fearfully as deer on ice with little steps in the pale place between the lights.

"Dis King Solomon's banket hall," the guide's small voice drifted back, making an echo across the huge cave-room. He stepped to the edge and shoved the pitch-pine torch down into the hollow. Far below, sunk in space, the tops of rock stalagmites were frosted by the light.

"Three hundred wives." The guide spoke to the chasm, bored.

Polite, frightened laughter flirted small in the huge vault. Melinda clutched at Crawford's arm.

"Now," he heard her say, as if she were praying. "Now!" He caught her other arm to hold her.

The corridor narrowed. They bent low under the rock. What had been silence turned into new sounds, the far drip of water, as if it had never stopped since time began, the sigh of the creek below them, a thin scurry of claws somewhere, scuttering in the dark.

In the next rise of the vault they huddled together, close now against the cold space which never in all time would see the sun or the stars. The light reflected in a mirror pool, made stars of its own. It seemed near enough to touch, until the guide dutifully threw a rock down and told them to count. They counted to twelve seconds before it hit the water far away, and shivered the pool surface.

A snake dislodged and flowed down out of the light. Melinda felt her knees give.

"Take me out, please take me out," she whispered, shaking. "I cain't stand them. Please, Crawford."

He held her hard to him until she stopped quivering, not noticing the others.

"I cain't. We have no light. I'm with you, I'm right here." He pressed her hard against his chest.

She heard the guide speak again, comforting too, knowing the hollowness like a home. He held the torch flaming up to a mass of stalagmites, flickered with crystal as cold as ice.

"Dis hyar the ha'nted palace of the snow queen, all covered with di'monds." The crystals winked back, filling the room with more cold flashes of light. They could feel the air blow from somewhere beyond where wind had never been.

"Feel that," the guide said at the right time, as he had been taught. "Come from the hell of the Norsemen, cold not hot, and hyar." He waved the torch to the right wall and picked out a small upthrust of rock, pink, brown, veined with black, in a wall niche. It looked as if a great hand had twisted it. The floor of the niche was covered with the small beginnings of other upthrusts where a fine rain of water dropped.

"That Jesus and His flock."

The Negro with the other torch came around them and stood by the guide, both of their faces solemn, black, against the lofty, glittering, haunted palace of the snow queen.

"Ladies and gintlemen, we a mile inside the bowels of the earth now. Hyar no light ever come. Ifn nobody against it we gone blow out these lights fer half a minute. Ifn anybody against it say so. Don' move while the lights is out."

No one spoke. Melinda's hand bit into Crawford's arm. She moved her body against him and whispered, it seemed to herself, "Now," again, tearful. He could feel her panic pulse at him.

The lights blotted out. The black which had retreated to the far walls engulfed them. Black pushing over them, black without breath or sound, the black of all absence of life, all negative, dead, stultifying black. Melinda moved once against Crawford, pressing hard for dear life. He felt her whole body, where her legs parted, where her living small breasts thrust against the blackness. Her mouth was wild and warm, open against his lips. Black with his eyes open but as if they were more closed than they could ever be and live, he opened his own mouth against hers.

Somewhere a fine nervous giggle fluttered. The small flame of a long locofoco heralded the lighting of the torches.

In their new warmth they sighed and began to talk loudly, unafraid of the now familiar room.

So no one but Melinda heard when Crawford asked, as if he were surprised, picking his words as carefully as they had picked their way through the cave miles, if she would do him the honor to accept his hand in marriage.

"You must speak first to Mr. Catlett. He is my guardian," she told him formally as if the dark had never happened. But at least—he was dazed about it—she didn't say no.

"It was so exciting! Dreadful frightening!" one of the girls called to her ma as they came out, released from the cave. Only Johnny, who had laid two trout at the feet of Miss Viny, and Lewis, who had not moved or spoken since they left, knew at once from Crawford's face what had happened. Lewis stumbled to his feet and walked away, so quickly he surprised his mother, who had thought he was asleep. Miss Viny, watching Johnny, looking so alive and careless, but with that hidden cold sorrow that curly-headed boys had sometimes, which made them so attractive and a little cruel, decided she didn't care at all if he was the younger son. The older one was dreadful anyway.

"Marry west," her mother had told her. "Of course in Virginia, but nobody east of the fall line has a red cent, my girl, that ain't tied up in land and pesky niggers." Then added, smiling, "Remember your blood and your breeding. We don't marry for money, but—"

"Marry where money is," her sister had called out. "Oh, Ma, quit saying that."

Viny knew who she was, and didn't care.

Sally had her back to the cave when the party came up the path. It was only when the two of them were almost on her that she turned and saw and read, sick once again, and getting older, and more afraid, with disappointment.

"Europe has nothing to the wonders of American nature," Crawford told the ladies. Melinda wished he would, one time, be quiet. She bit her lip, annoyed at her first disloyal thought about Crawford.

Even Leah recognized with some relief that the girl had changed, lightened somehow, her gloom gone. She seemed to Crawford as unattainable as the air, somehow imp-like in her new gaiety. Once she laughed aloud and caught her breath, just over nothing, not even looking at him.

Johnny, lying on the bank tensely calm, waiting for another fish to flash across his submerged hand, heard that gay ironic familiar sound for the first time at Egeria, for the first time in two years, and knew with a relief that made his whole body feel weightless against the ground that all was well again and that she had answered "No." He felt the fish and caught it, threw it at Miss Viny's side still wriggling, and sauntered away, his wet hand in his pocket. Without a word he dropped beside Melinda, at home.

There was singing as the night came on, soft singing in that time of day when everything, even the trees, the air, are quiet, demanding peace. Mr. Smythe picked the young ladies to sing; and one by one their thin young voices trembled obediently to a banjo as they had learned at their own pianos, nasal and with feeling. "Annie Laurie" and "Lord Randall," "Flow Gently, Sweet Afton," "Sweet Alice, Ben Bolt" . . .

Miss Viny sent her lovely, cold, sweet voice softly to the trees, not to human ears " '. . . . Oh yes! I am poisoned; Mother, make my bed soon, for I'm sick at the heart, and fain would lee doon. . . .' " She sang, and smiled to herself as she heard a strangled sob. After she finished there was a hush of sorrow.

It was Melinda's turn. In the softening night she gently touched her curls to bring them forward and soulfully looked at Crawford before she lifted her head as if she were going to cry plaintively to the trees, after all the sad singing, and matched, mimicking, Miss Viny's cool voice which still seemed to linger.

" 'Gooo tell A'nt Nancy, go tell A'nt Nancy.' " Her wicked parody of all the moving songs stilled the valley. Then someone tittered, and another. She had broken the evening peace as frail as a bird's eggshell.

" 'She died in the millpond,' " Johnny joined in, Lydia, even Crawford. The singing moved across the valley.

" '. . . standing on her head. The goslings are cry–ing. . . .' "

Mr. Smythe didn't know whether to be furious or delighted. He could tell that something important had happened, something successful, and that the sweet voice had a savage edge of triumph, but he couldn't imagine what it was. This was not the correct genteel behavior for newly engaged girls.

Only a small shy cat belonging to the Negro guide's cabin, and his mother, had noticed Lewis leave. Perversely, having escaped the attempted petting of the girls at the picnic, the cat now chose to follow him, from time to time trying to rub against his leg, though he kicked at it, as he almost ran, distracted, back up the deep twilight of the road. It followed for a while behind the trees, flirting, so that he thought it was gone at last. His walk now steadied, had more purpose in its stride. His hands were clenched at his sides but he was not aware of that, not aware of his body at all, only a burning in his head, beyond anger, beyond anything but the need to walk on and on, faster. Far in the now deep twilight distance he heard at last a low moan that could have been the wind or many people somewhere off to his right in the great woods. A bowl of light hovered in the sky above the distant trees. He walked faster, the calls of evening animals that made the woods alive ignored.

Unknown to him the cat, playing its game, gamboled after him, now ready to pounce. It slid out onto the white road and curled with a winning howl against his leg.

Lewis stopped, tall above the cat. She came again to his foot, flirting. It met her and lifted her on the air as if she were a stone. She landed off the road, stone hard, her back already broken by the kick. He had to walk even faster to get away from her thin screams.

In a huge clearing, surrounded only by miles of trees, lit by hundreds of fires from family camps in a semicircle under them, the saplings had been left a few feet apart, shoulder high. Across the clearing on a platform under a tabernacle tent, the figures of men danced to the flickering pitch-pine torches as they sat, waiting for the camp meeting to gather for the evening. The roar was the unconcentrated noise of thousands, eating and waiting too, deeper and deeper among the trees. Nearest Lewis, so that he hid himself in the dark, the hulk of a covered farm wagon sat, looming between him and a family cookfire, where he could see, through its wheels, legs walking. A woman knelt down and threw something on the fire. A few early comers, their dinner over, had gathered already near the platform. One of the men squatted down on the platform edge and gestured to the nearest of them. Lewis, leaning against a huge tree-trunk on the periphery of the meeting, heard them begin to sing, calling the others, charming, inviting in their distant voices which seemed to call even to him, beckoning and reedy.

" 'There is a fountain feeled with blood' "—far away and soft, the women's voices—" 'drawn from Emmanuel's veins.' " The voices were already swelling toward him as by the signal more and more people walked singing out of the circle of woods. Now stronger, lifting, filling the space in front of the tent: " 'And sin-ners plunged beneath that flood, lose all their guilty stains.' "

It had taken only the first verse to fill the open tent; outside the people were a dark mass, the song a roar of thousands who had waited. " 'The dying thief rejoiced to see, that fountain in his day; and there may I, though vile as he . . .' " The "he" was carried like a cry through the trees into the sky-bowl of light.

Leah heard it in the carriage over the horse's trot, sitting with the silent women. Johnny and Crawford followed behind, not talking. From time to time Melinda turned in her seat, bothering Leah, to glance back at them. The carriage lamp cast a crazy jiggling reflection at the quick-passing trees. Over them they could already see the bowl of light, and now all of them heard the rhythmic moan of singing.

"They've already begun," Leah muttered. "I'd admire for once—"

It was Sara who interrupted her. "Listen!" A tiny breathing scream ahead, along the road, came nearer as she spoke. "Somebody's been hurt!"

Melinda listened. "It's only an animal."

The carriage was already beside whatever it was. "Stop!" Sara called. "Stop." The urgency of her voice made the driver jerk at the reins. The horses dead still, the little screaming seemed to fill the night.

Sara was already out of the carriage before her mother could stop her. Johnny dismounted and threw his bridle to Crawford. By the time he got to Sara she was kneeling beside the road, touching something, crying.

"Oh, Johnny, it's a cat. It's hurt. Oh, it's hurt."

By the light of the carriage lamp he could see its small pink mouth opened as it drew in breath to scream, its eyes glossy, blind to them with pain.

"Don't pick it up." Johnny grabbed her hand. "Its back is broken."

Sara cried, "I've got to do something to stop it suffering. I cain't stand it."

"You get back in the carriage," Johnny lifted her. "Now git."

"Do something." The girl's face was in her hands, but she turned away obediently.

"I'll do something."

Leah could not see Johnny after he had motioned the carriage on and taken his reins from Crawford. She looked back with the rest, but he disappeared out of the light into the dark road with its tiny screaming.

They had not gone far when the screaming stopped, and they could hear the clatter of horse's hoofs as Johnny caught up with them.

The crowd was so thick that Crawford insisted on the driver's stopping in the woods where they could watch from the carriage, protected.

The invitation roared up, asking, "Are you washed in the blood of the Lamb? Are ye white as snow?"

"There must be thousands of people, black and white. Lord, I didn't know so many people out this far owned blacks. Imagine!" Sally said complacently, amused, not noticing that Sara was as white as if she had really been washed in the Lamb's blood.

It was instinct more than sight that made Leah pick Lewis out in the huge crowd.

The singing stopped. The crowd strained forward for the first low sounds of the preacher.

Small, frail, dulcet-voiced in the distance, he began his sweet persuasion. "Friends, brothers and sisters in Christ . . ." The preacher was too far away for them to see him clearly. He yelled, "Have you embraced Jesus as your Savior? Are you steeped in his blood? Or do you come here under the mighty canopy of God steeped and wallowing in abominable sin? Are you dead in affliction and suffering?"

"Yes. Yes"—murmurs in the dark around them. The murmurs rose as the high night wind rose. Leah shivered and huddled in her shawl, never taking her worried eyes from Lewis. "Are you with the Almighty and terrible God who seeth into your foulness and marketh your passage as the slime of the foul serpent of sin?"

In the bowl of silence the preacher's voice dropped again, fluttered over their heads. "Oh God, God, forgive the abominations of these hosts in sin. They are happy. They wallow in worldly wisdom."

"This is all the entertainment these folks get," Sally whispered to Sara, thinking she ought to explain.

Gideon McKarkle was enjoying himself, but he hadn't yet found anybody he wanted to stand by. He only wandered through the crowd, warming in its presence after the lonesome year with hardly a damn soul to talk to except his paw and Jeb, and Jeb wasn't much.

"In the hills and in the valleys, I hear the sound of timbrels and dulcimers and the cry of women dancing, baring their shoulders like harlots, casting wanton eyes, steeped in sin and riches. I see the eating of fancy foods and hear the laughter of those who care only for their own selfish plaisures, brothers, amusements of the flaish, women that never stooped to pick up a handkerchief! At this very moment, not fur from here, the clink of devil's coin at the gambling table, men when they spit got niggers to wipe their chins." The far voice rose again, like a wind-rise. "Befouled as hogs with the lurking fiend of spiritous liquor, toiling in the coils of the tobacco habit, trafficking in the seduction of human flaish. Did we come into the great mountains, brothers, to make a new Israel or a new Babylon? A new Zion or a new Sodom?"

There was a murmuring between Lewis and the platform where he could pick out here and there black faces.

The preacher caught the murmur and crushed it.

"HELL! Hell on this blessed earth. What if at this moment the last almighty judgment of Jehovah should open up the wide heavens and call you to your hour of death? If at this moment the sound of profane music and laughter would not drown out the awful warning? Brothers and sisters, the plague of God stalks even now in the sinful towns—judgment on the dying sinner. What if at this very moment these great trees lit up with the fars of God's anger, mile after mile of hell-far to trap you with His revenge and burn your souls and bodies forever where you stand?"

Near Lewis a woman began to moan and caught onto a sapling with each hand.

"Amen, hyar, amen." He was besieged by the calls in the dim mass of people.

"Is your flaish ready to rot with the rot of evil lusting men? Is your sinful body ready to cross to Glory? Or is it eensensible to the ghastly flicker that draws ever nearer of the pit of hell itself, ready to receive you, ready to burn your soul in the everlasting affliction of the dying sinner?

"Are you afraid to die? Do you know the word everlasting, what it means, the word forever? Alone, in these mountains without a friend, brothers and sisters, alone, disinherited and weary in the poverty of your seenful lusts!"

The woman's moaning was now rhythmic. She swayed back and forth between the saplings, laboring, her legs wide, her weather-exposed, thin, hard-worn face creased with pain, her eyes closed.

"Uh . . . uh . . . uh Christ take me, oh Christ . . ." she called to the aloof trees.

"Come! Throw yourselves under the wings of the cherubim before the mercy seat. Mourn and weep together, hold each other and give a torrent of your tears to God Almighty in His Glory, feast your seen-sick vile bodies on the eternal mercy of the ever-receiving Arms of Jesus."

"Amen." A groan shot through Lewis. He did not know he had done it.

The woman tore her hands loose from the saplings and screamed, "Hailp me, oh hailp me." The crowd parted to let her through. Lewis followed her, groaning in a sea of groaning. Behind him a small child began to wail, lost in the crowd. "Whur's Maw agoin? Whur's she agoin?" "Haish that," someone commanded.

Sara was afraid to move. She could no longer hear the preacher through the roar of people, but she could see Lewis as the dark crowd parted and swayed, drop onto his knees at a long bench. She longed to go and touch his troubled head, the way his body drooped, as if it were hurt, like the cat. Then she saw a black-coated man lift up his head and speak to him as if he were a father.

One of the other preachers caught the woman in front of Lewis by both arms. She relaxed, babbling, and began to shake.

"It don't take larnin, it don't take worldly wisdom to speak in the tongues of the Holy Spirit! The Holy Spirit is in her, Oh God. Come all ye to this saved one, blessed with the unknown tongues. Be saved, oh brothers."

Someone above Lewis shook him from his blind trance. "O Jesus, look down on this Thy sheep who gives up his wickedness to battle against transgression and the foul stains of the flaish and the blind amusements of the world. Who is trying to turn from the primrose path of seen and freevolity to the stern rocky straight and narrow path that leads to redemption." It was miraculous how the man knew what was in his mind.

"He seems to know his Bible," Leah whispered to Sally, who nodded approvingly but said, "Of course, it *ain't* the kind of thing I'm used to." Leah had lost Lewis for a minute and turned again to find him.

"Hear the great beating of the wings of death even now in the night. They are ever there, ever ready to swoop upon the just and the unjust . . ." In a short lull they heard the preacher's voice again. "Let them hear your sacrifeecial groans and tears. 'How' "—he began to sing, holding up his hands—" 'lost was my condeetion!' "

Gideon McKarkle finally found a family he thought he'd sit by. He was tired of wandering around the edges of the huge crowd. Families sat with children, just enjoying the crowd and the singing, and Gideon was lonesome. There was a nice sensible-looking girl sitting with her paw and maw and a whole passel of brothers and sisters.

" 'There is a baam in Gilead.' " He got near enough to listen. She sang pretty well, carried the tune and didn't holler or, what he hated worse, sing with that awful suffering waver. He wouldn't have any woman around the kitchen moaning and trembling when she sang, but something sweet and clear. He hunkered down beside the father, and went on listening. She had pretty good hands, too, laying in her lap there.

"Pretty fine singin," her father told him.

"Haish," his wife said.

"How fur ye come?" the old man whispered.

"Six mile."

"That's nary a fur piece. We-uns come eighty mile, from Fayette County."

"Then thar's a fur piece."

"I do admire a good meetin. All these folks. Meet some fine folks."

"Haish, Carver. I cain't hyar the preacher," his wife said placidly again.

He reckoned he might as well listen, too, now that he had found some place to sit with people. The end of the song had quieted the crowd. They strained forward for a new preacher, while he could see others, moving toward the mercy seat for the melting time. There must have been a hundred of them, he never had seen so many preachers, walking among the crowd, scanning people's faces and stopping by the saplings to pray where someone had caught onto them with the shakes. Just down between Gideon and the platform, he could see a whole group who had the shakes together. Their heads bobbed as if they were dancing. He was sure this girl wouldn't get religion and act that way in front of people. Down in front of the platform, a whole row of people knelt or were fallen across the mourners' bench with their hands outstretched. He thought from there it looked like a hog trough with the preachers passing back and forth, feeding them, but he decided that, although it was all right with him, he liked pigs, it might not be polite to say something like that. Some of the saved had already been led over to the amen corner. They stood, close together, looking shy and proud.

"Bless God, bless God, hope and glory!" one old woman called happily, every time the new preacher took a breath.

". . . this great country of ours, this hyar blessed land, this heritage of our forefathers given to them in fee by Jehovah. This American land for Americans, oh hear me. . . . Terror stalks it, evil squats in its valleys, already in the west the great Whore of Babylon, oh! 'And upon her forehead was a name written, MYSTERY, BABYLON THE GREAT, THE MOTHER OF HARLOTS AND ABOMINATIONS OF THE EARTH.' The seven heads are the seven hills of Rome. . . . The Catholic Church the abomination of the seven mountains. Acre by acre they wrest land from the native-born and plan in secret conclave and secret meeting and even in secret armies the overthrow of our great and glorious . . ."

Johnny, leaning on the carriage side, had heard this sermon so often that he ignored it and looked up again at his mother. He hated what such a place did to her; he could see her face softening as she listened into that loose piety which could end with the loosening of her hair and the terrible seduction of her tears. It had been so long since he had known the tentacles of her God that he had almost forgotten. Now his beloved woods themselves seemed, in the night, to pulse and throb with this hateful melting power of his pity and if he prayed, it was to be free of it. Free of the noise, of that slackness. He reached up and touched Leah's skirt.

"Mother." He wanted to beg her to take the girls away, but she paid no attention. She was too intent, and shook his hand away with a small benign pat.

The very young Reverend Charles McAndrews wandered where God led him through the crowds, seeking souls in the half-dark and the noise. He stopped for a minute with a group of Negroes who stood intently at the side of the—"arena" was the word Charles McAndrews called the clearing. They were listening so hard to the terrible menace of the Pope of Rome to their America that he smiled sadly to himself and passed by them without attracting notice.

Then behind the dense mass of crowd, flicked at as a still picture by the light from the campfires, he saw a carriage and stopped, recognizing, in the spectators, the familiarity of his own. Two young men, expressionless, lounged casually against the carriage in a studied aloofness from the crowd, their identical wide hats pushed back, their hair escaping. They could have been brothers, both slim, both graceful, both littered in Virginia and schooled in Charlottesville. Charles McAndrews knew every nuance of them. He had left the university five years before. Up behind them in the carriage, a little plump woman in black leaned forward, listening. Only her position set her apart from the woman beside her; both of them were bonneted, both were in black, but the second woman lounged against the back, advertising ennui for no one to notice. She changed her position once, and seemed to be trying to attract the attention of one of the three girls who sat opposite with their backs to him, except that one there, too, was different from the others. He could see the vulnerability of the line of her shoulder and her neck under her mourning, and the tragic droop of her head as she seemed to stare over the crowd toward the platform, seeing none of them, aware of no one in the carriage. She was watching a kneeling man at the anxious bench.

Charles McAndrews decided that whatever bereavement there was to put them all in black had touched her most closely, and he stepped forward just as one of the young men turned and touched the intent woman's skirt. Behind him, he took the young girl's hand carefully so he wouldn't startle her.

Sara looked down at a small, slight figure with the gentlest pale face she had ever seen on a man, so gentle that she was not startled, but only waited for him to speak to her.

"Child," he said simply, "you look troubled in spirit."

Sara could feel her mother tug suddenly at her skirt.

"I am," she said, wanting to tell him about the cat, and about Lewis like a hurt animal up there with all the strangers.

"Would you like to come with me down to the throne of mercy and give your soul into God's hands?"

"Yes," she told him.

Johnny interrupted. "Take your hand off that lady's arm and git, sir"—furious when he turned, having failed with his mother, to find one of them sidling so near the carriage. "If you wasn't a preacher I'd call you out, sir."

Crawford came and stood beside Johnny. The small man looked at them both familiarly, and grinned, or at least smiled happily. Johnny could have sworn for years, for he was never to forget the man's face, that he grinned—just as Johnny grinned sometimes to himself, privately with joy.

"Brother, what quarrel do you have with me?"

Sara was climbing down out of the carriage.

"Sara, come back here. Oh Crawford, stop her," Sally moaned up behind them.

Johnny could not stop looking at the man.

Gideon McKarkle was at his elbow. "Johnny," he told him, "ifn this hyar fellow is annoyin ye, give me the plaisure of tearin him apart. He ain't nothin but a damned abolitionist wants to let all the niggers run free and take up land. We-uns aim to put him out of this county with a lynchin party one of these days if he don't git."

It was the longest, most impassioned speech the helpful Gideon had ever made, but he was more excited than he let on by the meeting and he wanted to see justice done.

Johnny said, low, "No, Gideon, we ain't having no trouble."

"Oh, I thought you was havin trouble." Gideon, heavily embarrassed, stumbled back to his courting, having done his duty.

Crawford didn't know what to say. He felt left out, in that closing of ranks between Johnny and the stranger he never could understand when he saw it, as if they had known each other instead of being strangers. He couldn't believe that the small man facing them was an abolitionist. He looked like a gentleman to him; Crawford prided himself that he could always tell.

"What does it matter how a man goes to God?" Charles McAndrews answered the unspoken questions about the night in Johnny's troubled face with a question of his own.

Johnny stood back to let him pass with Sara. "Come, child, and pray," he heard him say. "It will do you good, and do others good to see your sweet face."

They went through the crowd away while Sally was still moaning. "He cain't talk that familiar. Oh my stars! Sara, come back, it's *tacky!* We're not this kind of people. We don't know people like this." She went on muttering in her corner, watching the girl's thin back go toward the mourners' bench. Melinda couldn't help wanting to tease her, but she felt too excited to tease anyone, poised as isolated as if she were perched atop the tallest tree in the night wind, ignoring them all.

But Sara had been led by the little stranger to kneel beside Lewis. When she saw that, Sally's trained mind flipped to hope again, and she sat up in the carriage and moved closer to Leah to pat her hand, sharing the solemnity of it all with a heavy sigh. It was strange how things worked out. She hadn't calculated on Lewis at all, and he was the eldest.

He, still crouched below the preacher, in an agony of sinfulness which did make his face like the cat's in its pain, waiting, tense with impatience, for mercy to descend on him like a cloak, did not notice the slight slim girl kneeling beside him, praying. Some others did. Women, seeing Sara look beautiful for the first time since she was a small child, touched her shoulder with their big solid hands, and whispered, "God in glory, sister. Bless the Lord. Praise the Lamb." She went on kneeling, under the comfort of their solid motherly welcoming hands, until Charles McAndrews lifted her to lead her up to the amen corner. She hesitated, and touched Lewis's hand, took it in hers to lead him with her, shuffling bearlike with shyness, among the women.

A rising sound of movement filtered through the woods as some of the families slipped away to be out of the crowd before the singing of the final triumphant hymn, but Leah saw that they would have to wait, trapped by Lewis and Sara, even though Johnny seemed so impatient. Surrounded by the meeting, their own voices floated in the rush of voices calling back the final hymn of victory over the indifferent roar of the miles of mountain space.

" 'I've reached the land of corn and wine, and all its riches freely mine,' " they called to the trees.

" 'Here shines undimmed one blissful day, for all my night has passed away.' "

The singing drew them in; the girls sang and Crawford, and even Johnny at last, sang. Sally let Leah's hand go to adjust her bonnet.

" 'O Beulah Land, sweet Beulah Land . . .' " Gideon drew his hand across his eyes at the weight of that many voices in the air.

" 'As on thy highest mount I stand, I look away across the sea, where mansions are prepared for me . . .' "

It couldn't grow fuller, the sound; the wave swelled.

" 'And view the shining Glory Shore, my Heaven, my Home, forevermore.' "

The singing ended, broke, receded and was replaced by a babble of good-nights and shuffling. It had been a good meeting. The preachers talked among themselves, feeling successful, but Charles McAndrews, following with his eyes the slight, wise-looking, lovely girl from the carriage, saw her lead the dark man back with her to their own people. He was overcome by the temptation of despair, loss of home, and aching loneliness, even after the song, which still lingered as if it crouched in the trees. He yearned to follow them. Instead he stepped back into the woods alone to pray that the temptation of illusive beauty, home, and worldly joys be conquered, until the carriage was gone.

Melinda made room for Sara. Something about the way the girl looked, not ugly and blotched any more, nor frightened, made her envy her for the first time since she had stood in kid slippers at the top of the stairs. The way she was now had the same complacency of security about it. Instead of running from it like a wild thing, though, Melinda wanted more than anything else to hug Sara, put the girl's head against her throat, where her life pulsed. She did draw her, so peaceful she seemed nearly asleep, against her and stroked her hair as they rode toward Egeria, now with only the woods making their perpetual night-sigh. They slipped gracefully through the night under the stars. Melinda, catching peace, wished for nothing more than that the carriage would slide on and on and that it would never be day again.

Sally stared with her mouth narrow. Miss Leah and Lydia were already dozing. Behind them Lewis rode pillion with Johnny. Johnny heard his brother sigh once, but he said nothing. Melinda went on stroking Sara's hair.

Johnny could feel Lewis behind him, hard and stanch as a stone. He murmured once and Johnny knew he was still praying. He reached back and touched his leg to show his brother he was there. There was nothing he could say.

Chapter Seven

AT LEAST the pesky girl had the good taste to be sickly the next day. Sally thanked God for small blessings. Sara hadn't even let their servant curl her hair and came out to breakfast wearing it as common as a farm wife and wouldn't do a thing to it even though Sally told her she looked plain enough always, God knew, without helping it along. The only thing fashionable about the girl was her pallor, which was quite becoming. She looked as though she were going to faint, and dim blue shadows under her eyes made even Sally see that they were much improved, more genteel. If there was one thing Sally knew, it was that men didn't like healthy, common women who looked as if they did their own work. Ladies were frail; many a quart of Virginia vinegar had been drunk in secret to the gentlemen. She did have the humor to smile to herself as she managed to drape an unprotesting Sara into the hammock before Melinda got to it.

After all, strict religion was not entirely unacceptable, she told Sara, trying to see the good side. She knew several ladies of the Episcopal Church who forswore dancing and the amusements of the world. Nobody danced with the disappointing girl anyway. That might as well be turned into a weapon.

"You ain't paying attention to a word I say," she fussed at the dreaming girl. "I think you might watch the tournament from here," she planned as she tapped at her front tooth with a well-buffed fingernail, in deep thought.

It had to work. Sara wasn't even wearing any colors for the tournament. She had already seen the two ribbons of Crawford's blue and white flutter from his hand to Melinda's, and Sally was too realistic from sad experience to do any less than gird herself quickly for a surer battle to go on living the only way she knew how. "Dear God, who ought to know more than *me?*" she muttered. As if in answer to a prayer she saw dear serious Lewis coming down the walk and bounced down the steps to stop him.

"Her experience has unsettled her. She's hardly of this world," she whispered, making it a secret between them. At least anyone passing would see that Sara had a beau. "Do come and comfort her when the tournament starts."

"Yes, ma'am," the awkward man mumbled, standing like a farm-hand on the pretty walk, and then trudged off. Sally watched his heavy back, trying not to feel disheartened, disgusted with the whole green world around her. Then she rushed back to cope with Sara.

"You, my girl, are going to stay right there on that hammock. That's an order."

Melinda sat in the girls' chamber, threading Crawford's colors through her fingers. Crawford, she knew, had gone to find Mr. Catlett to speak to him before the tournament. She had to make herself blank, let happen—not cry again. She had known as instinctively as a trained dog, or a slave, what to do; now she was sick with shame. She prayed a little, concentrated on faith in God, while she watched the pattern of a bat the smoking lamp had made on the whitewashed wall. She tried to concentrate on the evil thing she had done in the cave and the perpetual warning voice of Cousin Annie, and the preacher the night before, telling of the evil of the body in a terrible God's sight. She couldn't do it. She jumped up, ran, the ribbons still in her hand, across the porch, down the steps, pride gone, not caring, praying in a whisper to find Johnny.

At the race-course she could see Negroes putting up the striped pavilion tents in a cluster at the end of the track. Nearer, at the small grandstand, a boy shinnied up the last of the flagpoles, with Crawford's blue and white flag like a cloak over him. A hot summer wind drove the flags, made them whip and flick in the air. For a second as he hung the pennant it stretched so that she could read Crawford's motto, *Sans peur et sans reproche;* then it whirled again. Down below, where the ring-poles were being put up, a few horsemen wheeled and turned, practicing for the afternoon. A lock of her hair whipped her face like one of the flags. It hurt. She held it back, braced herself against a post of the fence to keep her skirt from swinging, and shaded her eyes to search the course.

Johnny was taking the mare through figure eights in the middle of the field, quite alone, leaning forward in his saddle, concentrated on her small feet as she touched them precisely to the ground.

Melinda called, but the words whipped away and she knew he couldn't hear her. She grabbed the ribbons she carried in her fist to keep them quiet.

It was five minutes at least before he looked up and saw her. By then she had lost the courage that had made her run all the way down the valley, not caring what anybody thought of her there, with no hat, in the morning.

Johnny cantered the mare over to the fence as soon as he saw her. She thought he said, "Watch, lookee!" He wheeled again, then thundered toward the fence. She saw the mare crouch, lengthen her neck, and sail in a high arch, her forelegs tucked, then stretch them from flight to touch the earth near her. Johnny cantered back to Melinda.

"She'll do anything," he called from the mare's back, and drew up beside her.

"Johnny?" She tried to tell him.

"You ain't been down before to see her." He gazed down at Melinda. That heartsickness which had disappeared with her laughter at the picnic and left him joyful in the lovely morning came back when he saw her strange face.

"I—Johnny—"

She hadn't even petted the horse, hadn't come near it. She looked ugly with fear, as if her face were going to soften and melt.

"What's the matter with you?" he asked her, gruff with worry.

"Come down here." At least then she walked up and touched the mare's wither. The bay silk coat rippled under her fingers.

For the first time in her life Melinda couldn't look at Johnny.

She could only hear him dismount, and she did see his hands tying the reins to the fence.

"Can we walk some place?" Melinda asked the ground.

"Come on." He took her arm and led her up to the empty grandstand out of the wind. They sat on the lowest seat, watching the field.

"I wanted you to write to me in lemon so it would be secret." That wasn't what she meant to say. The silly thing just came out.

Johnny concentrated miserably on a lone rider who was charging, pulling up, charging again, wanting to shake the fool, shake her until her teeth clattered and she was at least herself, angry and red, not this fool.

"I bought a lemon," he mumbled.

"I didn't get a letter."

"I used it for a toddy," he confessed, and wanted to drive away the misery by laughter but didn't dare.

She said something.

"What?" he asked.

"Crawford asked me to marry him, I said."

"Ain't that what you been trying to make him do? Sashaying around here like a damn fool."

"Yes." She looked at him then, but he was watching the field, cold and withdrawn as he could look sometimes.

"I'd just like to slap you," she told his head.

"What have I done?"

"Oh nothing."

"Are you going to?" he asked the lone rider, far away.

"I don't know. Johnny—please—"

"I don't want to marry anybody yet," he told the ground. "Cain't you give me time, Melinda?"

"How much time?" She wanted to take his arm, but he stood up then.

"I cain't help you. I'm not going to be . . ." He turned his back on her and walked away so that she had to call out.

"You just want me to wait around like Cousin Annie, getting meaner and skinnier, just wait and wait and end up marrying the first white trash that comes up the river."

Johnny stood for a long time, it seemed to her, and now looked at her.

Melinda crouched, her hands clenched in her lap, her face a wish that seemed to engulf him with its power, as if she were trying to will him into his paces, as he had willed the horse.

"You have to have it all in your own time, your own way," he told the wishing. "It's for you to decide."

"What can I do?"

"It's for you—"

"I never had anything." She stood up then. "I'm scared. I don't want to end up like Cousin Annie. You don't know what it's like for a woman to have nothing, and all the other women to treat her like a poor relation."

"Melinda, honey, that ain't why you get married."

"Ain't it?" She shouted, "Women don't have a chance in this world. It's all a woman can do."

"Goddammit, if that's all . . ." He walked away from her, trudging, unable to give another word.

"Johnny," he heard her call. He walked faster, out of the sound of her panicked voice.

"I ain't going to persuade her," he said, and didn't realize he had spoken until the mare backed and pricked her ears.

"Wooah, darling, don't *you* start," he said softly to pacify the horse, and mounted.

He didn't see Melinda leave, didn't dare look toward the stand, for fear of seeing the lone girl still crouching there in her dim black dress.

Miss Viny's brother cantered up beside him. "If this wind don't die, we ain't going to have much of a show," he called, looking worried at the telltale whipping of the flags.

By early afternoon it had almost died. Only a breath from time to time lifted the drooping pennants and in the empty field made the six-inch ring, which would concentrate the day, quiver, then fall. It was suspended six feet in the air, from a cord between two high posts which were decorated with colored paper like two wrapped Maypoles. The open space opposite the grandstand was already filled with people, a dark moving mass of Negroes at one end, and over the rest of the western slope a crowd of farmers with their wives sat on the grass, while children ran around them like pups, unable to keep still from excitement at so pretty a sight.

Peregrine saw Gideon McKarkle and his brother standing on the edge of the crowd. On Gideon's arm was a calm, solid-looking woman. Peregrine called over the heads of the crowd as he helped Leah and Sally pick their way through it, decorously managing their skirts.

"Gideon, you're a sight for sore eyes! I want to see you as soon as I've escorted the ladies to their places!"

Gideon grinned shyly and nodded to the madame. Leah smiled and tipped her bonnet just the right amount for the ex-overseer's son.

Up on the road, in a jumble of farm carts, chairs, and open surreys, one large worn-looking covered wagon stood, a row of children with their mother standing beside it, quiet with amazement at the noisy crowd and the colors. Their father had wandered down behind Gideon, and when he caught his eye and found someone to talk to, he kept saying, over and over, "We-uns is on our way to Californy. Ain't nowheres else to go. Ain't nothin in Virginny for usn. We-uns stopped fer water, but that thar well stinks turrble. I ain't goin to let my youngins drink it."

Having stated this to an attentive Gideon every time their small silence got too intense in all the noise, he did add, "Gawd, ain't this hyar a purty sight?"

That was what Peregrine had murmured, in not quite the same way, as he followed the ladies while they strolled around the track fence across the meadow grass toward the grandstand.

"I'm sartain there's nothing like it any place in the whole world!" Sally stopped and looked with him. "This is my first tournament! Nothing like Virginny in the whole world," she said solemnly, a thin-voiced liturgy as she stood still in the grass. "God's chosen people . . ."

Leah sent her a dark look from under her bonnet. "The devil can quote scripture for his purposes," she said. Leah had had a hard time with Melinda, who had had a sobbing fit from excitement, upsetting the girls. She had finally given the pesky girl vinegar to drink so she would look respectable for the afternoon, not red as a love-apple. Resentment and duty went so together that snappishness remained after the act. She wouldn't admit to herself that her annoyance was concern. The girl had fallen off to a shadow when she should be on top of the world, and Leah took it as a personal insult, after all her trouble.

Over the front of the grandstand a long banner was tacked, swathed and draped at either end, slightly sagging in the middle. It had painted on it bright red hearts and pink flowers with drooping green leaves. The words *La Royne de Las Beaulté et des Amours* were printed across it in large letters, shaky to show they were medieval.

"It's old French, not like French now. See *beaulté* don't have an *l* any more." Sally grabbed Leah's arm to inform her.

"I knew that," Leah snapped. It was dead hot now that there was no caressing breeze, and Leah was loaded with sweat under her hoop. She was tired of being informed about things, as if, as she had finally let Sally know, she hadn't come from the center of education in the West.

"The girls in the Turtle-Dove Society painted it," Sally told Peregrine sadly, wanting to discuss it all with somebody.

Peregrine walked, proud with a feeling that the boys and girls who were going to entertain him had something remarkable about them that he had given up long ago and now was going to have once again. He found himself being guiltily glad, not that Cousin Cornelius had died, but that the insistent wheel-chair which had met him with its burden of death as he came into Egeria, and the tongue of longing and cynical truth, were no longer there to deaden the sight for him.

He could see, in the center of the grandstand as they began to climb it, the cluster of girls in pink and yellow and white, except for ones in black, their gossip and laughter twittering like birds. Even over the tournament death intruded itself among the young in spots of formal family memory. Peregrine shook off presentiment, which almost seemed to have Cousin Cornelius's voice, and tried to pick out Lydia.

He found her, sitting straight and frightened, her red, white, and yellow colors from one of the cadets, he couldn't remember which one, pinned to her white dress. The women had decided that Lydia was too young to wear black for more than a week, and that she could go into white, but Melinda, who had at last proved her closer kinship in what had seemed to Peregrine an interminable argument among the ladies, still wore her black. He smiled to himself. It did become the girl. She looked as frail as a winter birch, with Crawford's blue and white pinned to her shoulder, straight as Lydia, not saying a word or looking around, gossiping, and laughing like the others.

He could not deny, watching Melinda, that he had been relieved when young Crawford had spoken to him in the morning. At least that problem was settled. He remembered the interview, short as it was, with amused embarrassment. In order to be kind to the boy, he had cut into what was obviously a rehearsed and frightened speech, to give his blessing and offer him a toddy, recalling too late something the ladies said about the young man's strong feelings about drinking. He didn't look like he had strong feelings about anything, but he was a fine young man. Peregrine settled himself comfortably beside the ladies and looked down at the waiting field.

Crawford was rich, he had a perfect seat on a horse, he was serious and intelligent. There was nothing wrong with him. That, in a way, was the trouble. Peregrine's old imp whispered to him and he shrugged it aside as none of his business, but it made him feel a tenderness toward the quiet girl, whose slim back he could see now, never moving.

The sunny field leapt alive with a drummed and trumpeted march. The bright parade wound down the green valley toward the racecourse, and brought the crowd to its feet to see it. Higher than all the sound—the roar, the surprise, the drums—the mounted cadet bugler chanted the ancient post-call which could have sounded over some such green hills in Scotland to alert the tragic queen.

The cadets came first, their marching caught up by a troop of small Negroes who had run into the field with no one to notice and stop them. They formed a ragged line beside the cadets and, in their own way, double-marched and capered in rhythm with the bugle instead of the solemn soldier timing. The crowd watched them cut their monkeyshines, and a sweep of laughter ran through it. From behind the cadets the king-at-arms, a fat gentleman dressed in the red and purple silk shirt of the judges, looking as red with annoyance as his shirt, and showing by his solemn straight-backed assurance that tournaments for gentlemen were to him no laughing matter, called to a pursuivant, "Git them neegurs off the field!"

The pursuivant wheeled out of the parade, came fast at them with his overseer's horse in its rocking walk, and chased them away.

Now the parade could go on with suitable solemnity. The prospective queens of love and beauty settled back into their seats. The pursuivant took his place again in the line.

After the cadets, and the tournament officials, the young knights rode, pacing carefully. Lydia had already picked out her beau among the cadets, so she sat back to enjoy it while the other girls pointed and whispered, here and there smiling to themselves, or sitting upright and worried, hoping the stitches which had made the young men's colored heraldic shirts would hold in the strain of their riding. Some way, the great pile of crash helmets sent from Richmond had been divided among them so that each knight wore one piece at least of shining armor with a full waving feather. Most of them still looked embarrassed at being in fancy dress.

Crawford rode in splendor. His blue and white tunic looked most like the pictures. It had been bought from a real military store, and his helmet, heavier than the others, he had actually brought back from Europe. It gave Melinda a pang of pleasure to see him, but she could not help scanning the long line of horses, now moving in front of the grandstand, prancing color on the brown ring, even though she had sworn to herself she never would look for Johnny.

The cadets had marched to their places at the end of the field, and the knights rode on around the track to line up in front of them.

Peregrine could hardly hear the first contestant announced, only the cut of the bugle again in the air.

"Wilfred of Ivanhoe." Sally nudged Peregrine and craned as far as she could to see. "That's Toddy Jemison from Broadlands.

Broadlands! Hunh. I hear tell it's down to two hundred acres. They've had to sell most of their people. His ma was a—"

Even Sally stopped talking as Wilfred of Ivanhoe, leaning low in the saddle, his lance held at eye level, galloped the length of the field alone toward the ring. In his nervousness at being first, he missed it by a foot and wheeled to trot back to the line, followed by a polite patter of applause.

Leah tugged at Peregrine's arm. "I cain't see Johnny," she whispered. "I cain't see Johnny or Lewis."

"Lewis gave up the afternoon to sit with Sara, the dear boy," Sally told her. "He is the thoughtfulest boy." Peregrine glanced at her, astonished, but her face was set in her new belief. She didn't even see him.

The faraway voice had gained strength. "Sir Brian de Boy Gilbert," the fat king-at-arms shouted, reading from his scroll.

A chant of *"Beau séant, beau séant,"* began among the girls, started by Miss Viny and her sister. The bugle called, and their brother rode out of the lists to take his place. He scanned the banners to judge the wind, and paused for a minute. Sally's inevitable information could no more be halted than the slight wind which sprang up. "His ma is an invalid, and his sisters bring him up here to marry him off to an heiress, but his heart is set on a Richmond gal they don't approve of. It's very sad. They'll never let him marry any . . ."

The wind dropped and the horseman was away across the field. He drove his lance through the ring and carried it as he turned in a canter, his horse seeming to dance to the applause. Now that the girls had started chanting from other parts of the grandstand, there were isolated shouts, "Love of the ladies," or "Glory to the brave," subsiding again as the crowd's attention was brought back to the field.

As a string was being stretched again between the poles, and the sun caught the second dangling ring, the pursuivant called the crowd's eyes back to the other end of the field.

"The Chevaleer de Bayard!"

Crawford cantered quickly to his place and studied his banner for the wind. He won his first ring easily.

Several of the girls turned their heads to stare at Melinda during the applause, but she hardly seemed to be noticing.

"Miss Obscurity is right high and mighty," Miss Viny began in a whisper to her own group, but she couldn't think of a Crambo before the next contestant was called.

Sir Launcelot of Tuckahoe Springs leaned too far, lost his balance, and fell halfway down the field. He rolled over, picked up his helmet, and caught the bridle of his waiting mount to get it off the field, limping in time to silence after the frightened gasp from the stands. His Guinevere turned red for him, but the other girls had the grace not to look at her.

In the quietness, as the bugler lifted his bugle to blow a tantivy for the next contestant, a cow-horn blare from up among the trees made a rude bawl over the valley. At first the bugler thought it was a cow and put his bugle to his lips again. The cow, if it was that, must have been watching him, for it blared again. This time there was a slight titter which swept lightly as they waited for the next attempt to blow the bugle.

The king-at-arms turned his horse to dash, if fat man and horse could dash, up to the hill to see what it was. He had already begun to roll when the people crowded around the lower end of the grandstand saw two horsemen coming out of the woods. One of them punched the other and he made a cup of his hands to shout. The king-at-arms was almost to them, when a scream started with the crowd who could see, and swept along the grandstand as they came into full view.

The king-at-arms came first, an angry but already defeated man, the shriek of delight from the crowd drawing him back.

"Oh my God." Peregrine grabbed Leah's arm to pull her up so she could see over the risen roaring people in front. "It's Johnny!"

Johnny rode with simple dignity through the field gate. He had on a crooked paper helmet that rose three feet high, like an enormous stovepipe, with a bill. Beside him, prodding a mule, and hollering at Johnny to wait for him, Lance sat on enormous saddlebags, with a pillow protecting him from the mule's ridge back. He finally prodded the mule up to the king-at-arms and handed him a tightly rolled scroll.

The king-at-arms by now saw fit to succumb to the crowd. He raised the scroll and let it unwind with a suitable flourish. A fish fell out; the crowd shrieked. He began to read, and raised his hand to bawl over the noise even of the knights, who were slapping one another, bending over their saddles, helmets askew.

The hand quieted them for a minute. "The Erring Knight, he calls hisself, Don Quixote de la Mancha, desireth to shiver a lance with yon splendid array." Johnny was quietly taking a string of sausages and a skin of some liquid from his Sancho Panza, while the crowd chanted him into line.

By the late afternoon there were only three contestants left in the race. Crawford had missed once, the wind had tipped the ring for Miss Viny's brother so that he missed, and Johnny's hat had fallen over his eyes as he galloped toward the ring, making him miss, and promoting another roar from the grandstand. Miss Viny's brother lost again to a sudden gust of wind which came up and shook the ring when he was within ten feet of it. He rode to the side, followed by *"Beau séant, beau séant,"* and the growing tension of the contest centered on the two riders, waiting side by side at the end of the field.

Neither of them spoke, or looked at each other. The young Don Quixote, hatless curly-headed boy, was calm; the now dirt-splattered Chevalier de Bayard's horse was dark with sweat. Even the murmur of so many people seemed to cease. The shadows from the trees of the western slope covered the mass of farmers, most of whom stood to watch the end.

Leah, having sat firm-mouthed during most of the contest, seemed to sense at last that Johnny was not drunk, as she had hissed at Peregrine, furious, under her bonnet so that Sally wouldn't hear. This had taken, for a minute, some of the pleasure of the joke from Peregrine, but not for long. He was proud of the boy, proud of himself, involved in each gesture, each success.

Seven rings later neither had missed. As Peregrine saw them try again, he realized that something was happening, something he couldn't fathom. This, begun lightheartedly, was no longer only afternoon folly, warm and gay.

Crawford galloped down the field where the shadows were lapping at its side. It was Johnny's turn. Neither of them missed.

The shadows were long over the course. The girls sat tired, ribbons drooping; the banner had ripped away on one side from a gust of wind, and now hung with its "La Royne" drooping in the late-wearing sun. The sense that something was wrong, the sense that Peregrine had caught, had spread among the others. Even Leah sat erect with worry, trying not to look at Sally for fear she would jabber, but Sally said nothing. She only sat with her handkerchief curled tight around her lace-gloved hand.

Peregrine saw Johnny glance at Crawford as they waited for the eighth ring to be strung, saw him look surprised, and then, as Crawford rode forward, saw Johnny bow his head as if his mind were far from the end of the tournament, far from the field. Johnny seemed not to realize his turn had come, and the king-at-arms rode over to him.

"What's the matter?" Leah grabbed at Peregrine's arm. He didn't answer.

Down below them, for the first time, he saw Melinda rise. Lydia tugged at her dress, and someone behind her reached forward to motion her down, but she seemed like a sleepwalker, only watching the horse, her head turning as Johnny, after the delay, cantered down the field. He seemed to be watching the mare's feet instead of the ring as he leaned to the side and balanced his lance. He missed by a foot.

The fence was solid with pushing people as he rode back around the field to line up with the defeated knights, threw his reins to Lance, and dismounted to stroke his horse and let her nuzzle at his face. He didn't seem to hear the disappointed sigh, and then the new wave of applause for Crawford when he rode up to the grandstand and dipped his lance to the ladies. The applause grew into movement, into a new event, into relief that the contest was over.

The king-at-arms, full of new duties, rode up beside Crawford and called out, "The Chevaleer de Bayard, Mr. Crawford Kregg of Kregg's Crossing, claims right as winner of this tournament to crown the Queen of Love and Beauty."

Mr. Wellington Smythe could find no fault with his protégée as she came down the stands to the garlanded empty "throne" to receive her crown, handed from the end of Crawford's lance. Melinda stood modest, pale, and straight. Something about her made even Viny keep quiet as Melinda received the coronet of woven flowers and bent her head a little, hardly looking at Crawford, showing no unseemly enthusiasm as she placed it on her hair and sat down to watch the other six best-scoring knights choose the ladies-in-waiting. Johnny chose Lydia, not looking at Melinda as he dipped his lance to his sister.

Mr. Wellington Smythe was tired in his legs from sitting so long, but he was enchanted, too, at the innocent provincial simplicity of it all. He said as much to a new lady from New York, a widow traveling with a companion, whom he had escorted to the tournament. Mr. Smythe had a yearning to see New York again under more pleasant and genteel circumstances than he had seen it on landing. Besides, Virginia would soon be farmed out for him, to use one of their phrases. He could see the image of a sea of genteel heads whose bumps he felt, and flattered, singing for a perpetual supper. Mr. Smythe had to think ahead.

"Don't it make you a youth again to see that primitive beauty?" he said to the lady from New York, who had actually lived in Florence for a little while. "Every dream she has ever had on some secluded plantation retreat is coming live at this moment."

The lady nodded, feeling it deeply under his guidance. He had told her earlier in the afternoon that her bump of sublimity was just like the Queen's. He hadn't said "of England." They had taken that for granted. She had found Egeria a failure, its manner alien and herself on some small valley of the moon. She had a lofty point to view it all with. She felt, as her escort wished her to, royal and sublime.

Mr. Smythe did have something, maybe it was the painful tiredness in his legs or the strain of living too long in his own dreamed image, that made him add to himself: Poor ignorant stupid little biddy.

"So this is the flower of Southern womanhood," the lady from New York was saying, surprised.

Sally managed to guide the others near Mr. Smythe in the crowd, but he was busy with a new lady and didn't seem to notice her.

"Have you noticed how they say 'heap' for everything from a heap of people to a heap of money?" he was saying. His imitation made the lady laugh.

"My stars! What do you say when you want to say 'heap'?" Sally asked herself, worried, then faded back to walk with Leah and Peregrine.

The farmer who was going to California walked slowly up the slope with Gideon. "Wal ifn that warn't a purty sight," he said. "Reckon they ain't nothin like that thar in Californy."

From the cottage porch Lewis watched them all the way up the slope through the breaking, wandering mass of people, Melinda in the center with a garland of flowers on her head and Crawford Kregg beside her. They did not seem to be coming nearer, only looming larger, his father's bantering smile turned on Johnny. His mother looked small and stern, as if she were trying to shut them all away. Even in the late cooler afternoon, her face looked pink with heat. Lewis tried to pray. He had, for much of the afternoon, lost consciousness even of Sara's presence on the porch, seeing only the riders in the distance, and hearing faraway wind in the valley, the changing yells and the spaces of waiting silence. He was even surprised when after so long Sara did begin speaking. Perhaps she had before. He neither knew nor cared. Now the hot, tired, sinful family who he knew were his cross loitered in the shadows as if they had not spent the afternoon in lascivious pleasure with their minds on nothing while the awful wrath of God lingered somewhere, a fearful presence behind the mountains ready to rush, roar, not in the cheering of fools on horseback, but in awful wrath.

"I know four horsemen," he said, letting Sara hear him. "They are pride, and war and famine and death. God have mercy upon this drunken and foolish generation."

"Amen," Sara said to help him. She had sat there waiting all afternoon for him to pay attention to her, watching his stern shy face when he couldn't see that she was looking. The sadness for him came back. She could feel pity for his awkwardness stir in her.

It felt warm, pity. Sara knew what it was like to be a constant disappointment, but envy had never entered her head. She wanted to tell Lewis that it was all right if he was awkward and stumbling, but his thoughts were on such a high plane that she could only admire him silently, astonished that he could be so holy and yet look so sad.

"Oh!" She caught sight of Melinda. "Melinda is the queen. Crawford must have won the tournament."

"She looks like a fool," Lewis muttered, and then added, "poor thing." But Sara had already gone down the porch stairs to meet them.

The porch was filled with fluttering, chattering fools. Lewis backed into a corner to watch them and listen. He saw Melinda go up to Johnny and touch his arm, and lead him, almost pull him, as if she were angry, out of the way of the others. They were so close, without noticing him, that he could hear them.

She murmured, "Why did you do it?"

"I never . . ." Johnny looked surprised, even through his gloom. Lewis supposed that was because he didn't win, and couldn't help a slight twist of a smile. He seemed to have trouble hiding it, too, for his voice stumbled. "I never," he began again, "saw him want a damn thing before, Melinda. Don't you know?"

"I do not." They were quarreling.

"He never cared that much before. I couldn't care that much for something so foolish."

"Thank you." Melinda's face was frozen with the anger that Lewis knew well.

"Don't you see? Just a game . . ." Johnny said.

"Yes."

"No you don't. Oh, I thought you would see."

"I *do* see." Melinda turned away then and Lewis watched her skirts swing as she pushed through the others to Crawford. She whispered to him and Lewis saw his face go red with pleasure.

Melinda ran to Lewis's father and stood on tiptoe to whisper to him. He smiled and tapped on the doorpost for silence. The serenaders, who had just come to the steps to dutifully serenade the queen, stopped and waited. The waiting spread until it even quieted Sally, who was talking urgently to Sara.

"Ladies and gentlemen"—that light sardonic whipping voice—"I have the honor to announce the betrothal of my cousin, Melinda Lacey, to as dear a cousin to us all, Crawford Kregg. May God . . ." Whatever else he was saying was shut off in the noise. Leah grabbed at Melinda to hug her; Lydia began to giggle and call something. Miss Sally stood up, white-faced, as if she were going to faint or be ill, but no one except Lewis saw her go into the cottage and heard the vomiting inside her room.

No time passed for him. There was just the engulfing noise and the numbness inside him. His eyes felt slapped, his face unable to move. There was music; the music became a polka. Somebody pushed a chair against his leg without seeing him as they cleared the porch. Girls in garlands whirled by in the sinful awful polka, Melinda gay as if she were going to break apart. He looked for Johnny, but Johnny had disappeared. Johnny didn't care. He never cared. He had never cared in his life, like his damned father.

Lewis didn't know he groaned, but Sara heard him and came over to take his dangling huge hand.

"Lewis," she whispered, "come and dance. I would dearly love—"

The touch of her cold hand was like a shock running through him. He wanted to hold it, crush it to him, put it against his mouth and press until the numbness was gone. He knew temptation, knew it in his whole body, temptation to take the quiet girl and whirl her around, around, around against and through the others, faster and faster.

He conquered. He thrust her hand away and dropped to his knees. "O God, O terrible and everlasting God, protect Thy servant from this evil and adulterous generation. Open not Thy blazing hell for sinners while they dance and play the dulcimer. Save us, O merciful Father, from Thy wrath."

Sara didn't know how to help him. She knelt down beside him and bowed her head, ashamed that she had fallen into the temptation of such pleasures.

The dancers slowed and stopped. Miss Viny began to laugh, then stopped when she realized no one else was laughing. Peregrine got up, furious, from his rocker at the other side of the porch and started toward Lewis, but Leah caught his arm.

"Don't," she whispered, "lay hands on him for fear of God's wrath."

Peregrine remembered Leah's father on the quay, sick again with disgust as he had been sick then, his barrier of silence closing against it.

Lewis was still praying, but he was quieter now. Several of the girls began to kneel too, thinking they ought to.

Sally opened her eyes at the stopping of the music. Her servant held a cold rag to her head, her servant who wasn't even hers, but Crawford's, as everything she had, even her clothes, was Crawford's. She could see that woods girl's cold, locked face in the dark. Lewis's prayer came through to her and she had one of those visions made from sickness, of being trapped forever by that deep, accusing voice, unable to laugh, unable to breathe for fear, ever again.

Chapter Eight

JOHNNY WANDERED away from the music and the sound of their voices, shut away from them all. Down the path, almost to the deserted track, he stopped and stood as if, in the center of his being, the world was a circle with all directions and none for him to run to. If he could have run just then, he would have, to which mountain, to which valley he didn't know or even sense—just away.

Someone was speaking to him, and he answered a muttered "Good evening" before he realized that it was Gideon.

"Johnny," he said, almost sharply, as if he were trying to wake him up, "I want you to meet my woman."

Johnny's smile, his pleasure, was so automatic that when they walked away he felt guilty that he couldn't remember what she looked like. He had to turn and watch them, only her straight solid back now as the woman walked beside the tall, thin man, matching his stride, her linsey dress blown around her, showing the strong contour of her legs.

He walked fast to catch up with them, shamed out of his blankness. By the time he got to them they had marched up the opposite hill and had stopped to talk to an ugly grinning man beside a covered wagon. From the inside of the wagon children peeped like shy dogs.

"Johnny." Gideon caught him by the arm. "I reckon you wouldn't know this hyar is a Crawford. Maybe he's kin to you."

"They's a passel of Crawfords," the man said proudly, "all good people, all real fine people. Myself," he explained, "I'm agoin off to Californy. They ain't nothin in Virginny fer the likes of usn."

The river, the life's blood of the Old Dominion—Johnny didn't know whether he'd said it or not, his father's old angry phrase was so strong in his head. He only wanted to get away.

"You rid that mare mighty well today, Johnny," Gideon was saying. "What in the hell—oh, excuse me, Miss Abby." He turned to Johnny again, seriously. "I done promised Miss Abby I wouldn't cuss, but Lord God, Johnny, it's a angry habit to break right off with."

"I'm mighty glad to have met you, Miss Abby." Johnny grinned at her. "I have to see to her, the mare. I have to see to the mare." He almost ran.

"You ain't agoin to forgit your pup, air ye?" Gideon called after him.

Johnny didn't hear.

It was the gentle quiet time of pale evening when he went into the woods. It was dark, and the cottages were warm lighted rows under the trees when he came back, not wandering but walking straight up the path toward Wolf Row. He slammed into the cottage as Crawford was getting dressed.

"Johnny." He looked over his servant's back as he pushed into his shoe. "I'm mighty glad to see you." Crawford's relief made him seem more relaxed than Johnny had ever seen him. His reserve, his solemnity, were not in the young man lolling back on the bed.

"Fish, I ain't had a chance to congratulate you." They shook hands over the Negro's back.

Crawford, watching him fling himself down on the bed, couldn't help saying, "Johnny, I thought you'd—I was afraid you'd—"

"Tig!" Johnny yelled. "Oh hell, Fish, what do you think I am?"

Crawford, looking at his face for the first time, had no more to say.

The numbness in Johnny had given way to an almost drunken vision of the people around him. He had seen Fish, really seen him for the first time, when he had glanced at him before the last ring of the tournament. Now he saw how young, how unfinished he looked, his blond hair thin like a child's hair, his hand, as he got up and began to smooth his evening coat, as slim and tentative in movement as a woman's, a safe boy, growing into a safe man, for his bright imp to cower behind, for his coon girl, wild girl . . .

"Tig!" Johnny yelled again.

If Tig had been his twin he couldn't have sauntered in more like Johnny, offhand, casual, black-mirror image. Johnny saw the parody of all his young affectations come toward him, and was repulsed, not by the devilish ease of the Negro, but by what he saw of himself. He got up from the bed and motioned Tig onto the porch, to get on with part of what he had decided in the woods.

In the dark of the porch, Tig waited for whatever foolishness Marse Johnny wanted him to do. He liked the Spa, the pleasure of all the young men in Wolf Row raising a ruckus without any women to bother them.

"If you don't keep your mouth shut, Tig, I'll horsewhip you," Johnny began.

"I ain't said nothin, Marse Johnny," Tig muttered, surprised. He could not see Marse Johnny, but he could hear him across the steps, jingling his watch fob as he did when he had waited long enough.

"Listen here, Tig, I'm going out of here tonight. I'm going West. Now I could tell you to come with me, but . . ."

Tig waited, not saying a word.

"I ain't going to tell you. I'm going to ask you. Tig, come with me."

Tig waited for so long that he flushed Marse Johnny into saying sharply, "Ain't you got anything to say?"

It still took time for Tig to answer. "You makin me think too quick." His whisper in the night was almost a plea. "You ain't niver let me decide nothin before in my life." Tig could hear Marse Johnny sigh, impatient.

"Make me run whin I ain't hardly walked—"

"Goddammit, Tig, are you coming or not?" Tig could see Marse Johnny leaning against the porch post in that withdrawn gesture of arrogant patience he knew so well.

"Marse Johnny," he tried to tell him, "you remember whin we used to sit out and watch the wagons? Remember thin we was goin

West?" In the darkness his voice faltered. He thought Marse Johnny turned away.

"I don' want to," Tig muttered.

Johnny closed his eyes, sick in the darkness. He could not plead, he could only open to the other boy, that new shadow across the steps. For the first time in his life he sensed Tig as a separate man. When he answered, he spoke to himself. "I thought I could depend on you, Tig—your—"

A group of young men tumbled out of the next cottage and lit a flambeau. It flashed the porches into light. Tig had turned away, hiding his face. They both watched the flambeau wind crazily down toward the faro house at the end of Wolf Row, as if that bright wavering light could make them concentrate, each to make the other understand.

In the dark again, he heard Tig say, "I got things to tell you, Marse Johnny. You don' know—"

"I don't want to hear them." Johnny wanted to run again, but leaned, tired to death, against the thin column of the porch corner.

"You kin have me whupped ifn you . . ." Johnny could hardly hear him.

"Goddammit, shut that up, Tig."

By now Tig seemed hardly to know he was there. He murmured on in the darkness. He seemed to be trying to explain. "You 'member, Christmas time you'd get apples come all the way from the West. Marse Lewis, he jest give his nigger the core. You allus give me half—split right down the middle. Marse Johnny, it was your apple. It was allus your apple."

"I don't want to hear this, Tig." Johnny started off the porch.

"I cain't lay a hand on you to stop you goin', Marse Johnny." Tig's voice held Johnny as forcefully as if he had. It was as if the isolation of the woods had followed him, shutting him off from anything but truth. He could not stop Tig.

"'Member whin you had to recite your Latin book and you larned me, too?" The Negro was reminiscing softly, destroying the sweet dependable memories, forcing his hurt into Johnny's mind. "I'd watch in the window whin you stood in front of your paw, hopin fer you, you wouldn't git whupped."

"I know you did, Tig. I know you did that." Johnny pacified to stop him.

"Well, nobody niver whupped me. Your paw would call me out on the porch in front of men and he'd say, 'Tig, give the gintlemen Cato's speech before the Senate.' He wouldn't whup me. He would jest laugh. They'd all laugh fit to kill whin I finished, and he'd say, 'Ain't he a smart little nigger?' And they'd say in front of me, 'Smart nigger—take off on anythin like monkeys.' I sure Lord got my larnin laughed out of me."

"Do you want to be freed, Tig? Is that what you want?" Johnny came back toward him so fast to get the damn new pain over that Tig shrank back without either of them noticing.

Tig didn't answer for so long that the night sounds intruded. Johnny could hear the fiddles tuning up in the distance. When he turned to try to make Tig answer, he saw his shadow figure, leaning against the other column of the steps, looking as if he'd been horsewhipped.

"No, Marse Johnny, I doesn't," Tig whispered at last. "I got me a wife. She's slave all the way to her soul—you cain't jest *decide*. Sometime I wanted to. I used to pray, git out in the woods and holler up whar I thought God was, in the top of the trees. I don't keer no more. I cain't be nothin but a nigger." Something made him laugh, one short sound. "You niver thought when you wanted me to pick up and go off on a wild-goose chase I couldn't go as a man. You niver done nothin all your life but take orders from your Pa and give orders to me. Jest took it for granted. You goin to find out it ain't all orders—Tig do this Tig do that. Love me like you love your dog—"

"I couldn't have believed you felt this way, Tig." They could both hear Crawford's footsteps in the cottage; it made them urgent.

"You didn't look. No, you let me be a slave, Marse Johnny. I ain't fitten fer nothin else. I'll jest play nigger, nigger boy till I'm ole, but underneath whar your people cain't git, I'll be a man, and you'll know it, anyhow."

"I don't want to go alone." This plea of Johnny's he hardly knew he said. It was to himself.

"I feel sorry fer you. It's you got the burden—women and slaves.

I seen what it did. Telemachus say he don' know who the most slave. We got ways. Live a whole life in secret, then play nigger. Be a clown, he say, nobody don' iver know what a clown's thinkin. You think all I larned was Cato's speech?"

The frogs set up their evening call, at first so loudly that Johnny could hardly hear Tig. "A big tree don' crush you till it gits weak and falls. That's what you got"—his words tumbling now as if he had been waiting to whisper them, as he was doing now, all his life. "You ain't got no more freedom than we got. Tears, and people leanin on you—free, white, and twenty-one!"

"I thought you'd want freedom—"

"I wants it, but not like this, not handed like apples, not doled out. You jest leave us be. You jest leave me be."

Johnny stood, longer than he knew, and Tig waited.

"It's you, Marse Johnny, it's all you white folks cain't do without us—that's how we win, cain't pick up a handkerchief without crickin your back. We been wipin the spit off your chins too long. Talk all you like. Who own who, I'd like to know? The water break the rock and the grass break the pavement—"

"I don't want to hear any more." Tig could hardly hear him.

Johnny turned so quickly that Tig backed away, his long accustomed physical shrinkage a reflex.

Johnny stopped and laughed. "What are you cringin for, nigger? I ain't going to hit you. I thought you was a man."

"Marse Johnny, I don' deserve that," Tig moaned.

"I know you don't, Tig. God forgive me." Johnny didn't speak again for a long time. Tig could hear his watch-fob turning and turning in his hand. Finally he blurted, "Oh Tig, I'm sorry . . ." He strode into the cottage and let the door slam behind him, leaving the Negro waiting to be dismissed.

In the light, blinding after the darkness, he could see Crawford turning before the mirror.

"I can't give you the nigger," Johnny blurted out. "Will you buy Tig off me, right now?"

At the mention of money Crawford's face became blank with protection. "I don't know, Johnny. I'll have to think it over." He began to slip on a white glove. "Are you coming to the ball?"

Johnny couldn't move any nearer to him. He could only say because he had to, "He's worth more. I'll sell him to you for a thousand dollars."

"Why, Johnny, he's—"

"I need the money."

"Oh." Crawford was relieved to understand so easily. He opened the drawer of the dresser. "As a gentleman I can't lecture you, Johnny, but you're riding a loose rein, the company you— So that's what you've been up to—gambling. I thought . . ."

Johnny stopped listening and turned his back. He could see the dark figure of Tig waiting.

Behind him Crawford was saying, "Of course, between gentlemen, a debt of honor. Don't think I don't understand. . . .

"There's no one," he said magnanimously, bringing the draft to Johnny, "I'd rather help out."

"Debt of honor," Johnny said to the floor and looked back at Crawford's face, peaceful with understanding. "Thank you," he made himself tell the face, and went back to the porch.

"You belong to Marse Crawford now, Tig. That's what you want, ain't it?"

Tig couldn't answer.

Johnny slipped away in the dark. Tig couldn't even hear his footsteps, only the loud croaking of the frogs filling the evening. Tig didn't want to cry. He hadn't cried since he was a little nigger. He just stood in the dark, still waiting.

Johnny walked blindly, drawing, without realizing it, nearer to his family's cottage. The sense of loss made him heavy, no words, no planning, just the sight of the lighted cottage ahead, throwing out its beckoning paths of paleness onto the dark slope. The blinds were drawn in the girls' room; once he saw a huge dark shape pass and a pang of longing made his breath stop. Even as he did it he was ashamed that it was Minna he wanted, to listen and to nod until the sense of loss was gone and himself soothed to strength again. He could see by the busy shadows that Minna was helping to dress the girls. He slipped up the slope between the paths of light, vaguely hoping that he could tap on the window and bring her out.

His father and mother were sitting on the porch. The whole cottage hummed with the triviality of evening, everyday noises, more rejecting than any wall to breach.

"I do reckon we can spare Toey for a wedding present," he could hear his mother saying, as if she had been discussing the thing for some time. "I don't know whether we can go as far as Tig, too. He's very valuable." He heard her sigh.

"Tig belongs to Johnny, my dear"—his father's quiet voice, too peaceful in the evening to be shattered.

Johnny clung to the wall of the cottage, watching as if for one second the wall of evening would crash down and he could tell his father . . .

"We can't spare two, Mr. Catlett." His mother's voice rose to her familiar tone of frightened possession. "You know how difficult times are."

In the light Johnny could just see the bland barrier of her face, a face demanding that things go on as they had always been, that everyone stay in his place.

"We'll see, my dear." His father ended the conversation by shutting her out.

Johnny could hear her rocker creak comfortably. "To tell the truth, I am relieved," she said.

What she was relieved about, his father didn't seem to care to know. He didn't answer. Johnny could see a tinder box flare as Jim lit his pipe for him. It was the last image of them both, black and white, leaning into the light, his father, in concentrating on the pipe, farther away from him than he had ever been, shut out, and tired with sadness of his own. The light flared and faded. He knew then, as if he had seen their faces of trouble, the reaction to the change in him that would happen if he tried to tell them; his mother's moist heartbroken blackmailing eyes, resisting his words, and then the dissolving tears he feared, the wild hair, the square mouth, the prayers. He could see that quiet face of his father frozen with anger, hear the wit turned to flaying words, the shouting down of change; he would be stripped as if he were still kneeling to receive the corrective strap of anger, and then, defeated, be comforted with his father's sorrow and compassion after he had won.

"Did you hear something out there, Jim?" Peregrine asked when he had settled back.

Jim came down the porch steps to look, but there was no one there.

Toey was excited about Miss Melinda being the queen. She thought Miss Melinda must be excited too, for she didn't even fuss about her white dress any more.

Toey tried to help. She told her it was the last time in her life she'd have to have just one old white dress.

"It will jest pleasure my soul ifn you'll give me this ole dress to remember ever'thing by," she hinted as she flung it once more over Melinda's head. She could already almost feel it on herself, already almost see herself at Kregg's Crossing, mistress-maid and no Minna to take her down a notch.

"Find Johnny," Melinda whispered. "You find him, Toey. Tell him there's nothing else I can see to do. Tell him to find me."

"I'll tell him," Toey whispered, sullen with worry that it was all going to begin again, go on and on, after everything had been settled.

"Git now." Melinda had turned her back as if she wouldn't tell any more, and Toey ran out, forgetting how afraid of the dark she'd always been.

She didn't dare go back without finding him. The men scared her, but they didn't scare her as much as not doing what Miss Melinda told her to. Neither he nor Tig was at the Wolf Row cottage. Nobody was. She peeped in the door, and found the kind of easy-going mess that men let their servants leave; she smelled wet leather, and clothes, and turned back down the steps, annoyed with women's annoyance at their ways, shaking her head.

He wasn't at the faro table. She could see, peeking through the open door, where the click of counters and the almost silent playing of the gamblers came through the night, that he wasn't there.

Down by the stables only a single lantern showed. One Negro was asleep, leaning back against the wall on an old chair. She could hear the horses puff and sigh, but there was no one else there.

An hour later she could hear the sound of the ball beginning and it was easier to search in the flicking valley lights. Then they were gone, and she was left in the dark valley. She didn't dare go up the wood path behind the cottages, but she had to dare. She just had to. There was no place else left to look.

She could feel her skin ripple with fear as she climbed the first steep part of the path, feeling her way up through the darkness, the twigs all snakes, every scutter a wildcat. She was out in the open path and could see ahead of her where the trees let the moon dapple the ground.

"Marse Johnny. Marse Johnny." She began to whisper to herself to keep her spirits up.

It was the sound of her whispering voice coming closer that made the tears unlock from Johnny's eyes at last. He had stood there, hidden by the Indian grave, waiting for Egeria to sleep so that he could leave, not daring to hope that anyone would find him, deadened to time, only waiting, hearing, when he let himself, the sound of the fiddles away in the distance. He ground his hand across his betraying eyes, disgusted at himself for his weakness.

"Toey, what are you doing out here? Get on back," he called back at her.

She had heard that single awful sob coming from a man, more real than the demanding ladies' easier tears, and she could feel her skin no longer quivering with fear but with that physical sympathy for the sorrow of men that made her stumble toward his voice, forgetting Melinda's message, forgetting everything, as startled into protective movement as an animal hearing its young cry.

"Marse Johnny." She felt for him in the darkness; her hands found him leaning against the stones.

"For God's sake go away, Toey." But he had buried his head on her shoulder, taking into himself the soft feel of her skin where her linsey had slipped down, her long neck, the gentle slope to her arm, and that unquestioning obedient physical compassion of women.

Toey did not say a word, only held on to him against the darkness, against the questions, knowing with her body that a man was comforted, not with words and not with ways to live, but with moments and surrender, as to a child sometimes. She fell under him on the dark summer earth, her skin drenched in Melinda's Florida water.

"Oh my Christ." Johnny turned from her on the ground and moaned, alone.

"Don' be 'shamed, Marse Johnny," she whispered, close to him; he drew away. "I knows. I always knows. We ain't got the same pappy fer nothin. I allus felt the closest to you."

Minna, dark Minna, dark as the night, welcoming the other tears of his father, not only his own: dark safe mountain where his father had lost himself, too, away from expectations, away from the thin, frail, breakable demands.

He knew he had gone so far that there was no one left; the final thing had been found out, the final deed done, the trap closed. There was nothing to do but go. Almost lightly he turned and stared up at the moon. Toey could see his face, peaceful, withdrawn. He seemed to be listening to something she couldn't hear. Suddenly he bolted up so quickly she had to roll aside. He began to retch, long breathless dry gagging.

"I won't tell," she began.

"Go on back, Toey, just go on back."

He glanced up once after the retching had stopped. Her figure, far away now in the moonlight, looked exhausted, as if she were carrying a load on her back.

The dawn came up behind Johnny as he put the mare on one of the down-winding curves of the turnpike. He had ridden most of the night, walking slowly, sometimes half asleep, surprised on waking that he could ever sleep again. The mare was not tired. Twice he had rested her and had lain, listening to her move and drink, by creeks on grass verges that he could feel more than see. Once on the last part of the huge savanna trail, where he could see, sometimes two within the same mile, the night-shut farmhouses, he heard a dog begin to bark and spurred her to a trot. In the last of night, he had looked up and watched the bright pre-dawn stars, and felt the loss unclamp from him, and at that minute, forgetting, felt as free as the stars themselves.

By the first clean dampness of morning he was on the highest mountain before the westward valley. After the silence the calls of birds rode him, wild and high in the trees. He tethered the mare to a tree where a path ran to his left through the woods, taking off the saddle and heavy saddlebags, so quickly stuffed with what he thought he needed. For the first time he could grin to himself—two saddlebags to take him to California.

He realized then that he had not thought of any of them; they had all lifted from his mind since the dawn; their faces came back, now stranger faces than they had ever been in an old world where he had taken them all and all their places for granted. They were back as heavy as before. Perhaps it was because it was his twentieth birthday. Johnny told himself aloud not to be a molly.

He knew the path, a stopping place for the coaches where the ladies were escorted to the jutting rock called Lovers' Leap, well protected while they viewed the great range and talked about it. He wandered down the path to stretch his legs and see his last of the mountains.

They lay, layer behind layer, bluer and bluer in the morning sun. Down below, the river ran in a great semicircle, the barrier of stone and rushing water so far below he could not hear it but seemed poised in flight over it as in a dream—the barrier river that kept the West from the East, and he alone over it as if it all belonged to him.

"I wonder, by God," he said aloud, "if you could put a railroad through that gorge." He leaned and planned and did not realize that he had spoken aloud until a great bird, he thought an eagle, soared disturbed from another high cliff and sailed free below him down the wind currents of the gorge.

BOOK THREE

August 10, 1856–June 3, 1861

Chapter One

LOOKING BACK on it, Johnny realized that there had been something in him all the time, not in his mind, but in that part of him which cared at all, which had lain fallow with neglect for seven years. What it was in the beginning of that day that began to wake him, he couldn't trace.

Perhaps it had started with the auction.

That hot morning he stood on the wooden porch of the county clerk's office with the man's belongings, still in a small paper trunk, and waited for the crowd to gather in the dust of the wide street. By twos and threes they sidled up and waited, slung-hipped, as if they didn't give a damn. It was easy to auction fine clothes, and any clothes but "Ruffian" shirts and homespun pants were fine in St. Jo, Missouri, in 1856. They brought war-inflated prices.

Down below him idle men stood muttering to one another. It was too early in the morning to get drunk, mount, and ride across to hunt in Kansas.

He began with his mind not on the auction, but on the clothes themselves. One watch and rigging, five shirts, dickies, collars, drawers, socks, pantaloons, frock coat, close-bodied coat, shaving gear, nutmeg-grater, silver toddy glass, stovepipe hat, saddlebags, Blackstone's Law, one Bible, a whip, and the trunk—there lay the whole fortune of one strange gentleman who had died without identity in a place where a man was who he said he was, residue of his existence in a paper trunk. Where he had come from Lord only knew.

What was your name in the States?
Was it Thompson or Johnson or Bates?
Did you murder your wife
And run for your life . . .

The men sang it as they rode over into Kansas Territory.

Johnny finished calling, ". . . make sale by public auction to the highest bidder."

Already the August sun pounded through his shirt sleeves. A little welcome breeze sprang up from the Missouri River and danced the dust behind in the dark crowd of men.

Seven years—like Jacob working for Rachel and he hadn't even earned Leah, among drifting men like the dust of the street. Johnny held up the frock coat and laughter rustled through the crowd. Cherokee Henry bought it for two hundred dollars and grabbed it from Johnny. He walked solemnly through the jeers of the men, inspecting it. "Hit'll come in right handy," he grumbled to himself, pleased.

"He's agoin to run fer office. Know Nothin," somebody yelled.

Johnny rapped on the porch rail for attention. He held up the first white shirt.

"Two dollars." A quiet voice close to him began the bidding—a Virginia voice. Johnny looked down at a small calm man and knew he had seen him before. Under his frown of half-recognition the man smiled. The shirt went for twenty dollars.

No identity. Johnny thought of the silver-handled crop that came from England which his father had given him when he was fifteen, of his own watch, his own copy of Blackstone—no difference between him and the other unattached free man, his epitaph an auction in a strange street to pay his last hotel bill. The auction dragged on in the growing heat.

Johnny looked up from counting the money. The other men had drifted away, but the Virginian waited.

"I have seen you before," Johnny blurted out, trying to remember. "I know you."

"Oh yes." The man smiled again. "You once offered to call me out."

Night, the carriage, flickering firelights—the camp meeting.

"Well I'll be damned." Johnny shook his hand. "The preacher!"

"Charles McAndrews, at your sarvice." The man bowed as if he were amused at the greeting.

"You don't look much like a preacher." Johnny glanced at the homesteader's shirt.

"I don't aim to," Charles McAndrews explained. "People have so much respect for the cloth they don't listen to the man."

"Come with me." Johnny stepped off the porch. "I want to pay a hotel bill."

Charles McAndrews fell into step beside him.

"Oh." Johnny stopped, partly because the cooling breeze was ruffling his hair, his shirt, flicking his tie, and it felt good. Charles McAndrews watched the leaner, darker man to whom something had happened which had stripped him of the old pose, had written secrets in the new sun-lines of his face, but underneath it all, like his skeleton, there was the same knowing, aware movement of his body, the same set of the head.

"I'm Jonathan Catlett, sir," Johnny remembered to tell him.

They walked on down the wide street flanked with wooden buildings the color of dust.

"I didn't want the shirt," Charles McAndrews explained. "I wanted to talk with you."

The guard went up in Johnny's face. "Sir?"

"I intend on going over into Kansas Territory."

Then Johnny knew what it was he had been trying to recall about the man. "Let me pay this hotel bill," he said wearily, as if he only wanted to be left alone.

They sat apart from the crowd in the hotel bar. Over them the morning roared toward its climax. Outside, the line of horses tethered to the long hitch-rack champed their bits against the flying dust. Behind them the Missouri rippled its yellow skin. The ferry waited.

Johnny knew what he had to say, but Charles McAndrews had taken the reins before he could. "What are you doing here, a man like you?" he asked.

After seven years Johnny Catlett had no answer. "Don't ask that question this far west." He tried to reject the man by teasing. "I wouldn't go over into Kansas if I was you." Something in Charles McAndrews' smile made him try to persuade.

"I rode over," Johnny told him. "In an evil hour I was persuaded to go. I think I go to see what I can do. Sometimes a calm man can stop these devils. Sometimes . . ."

He wanted to tell the innocent fool about the stranger who had stood at the door of his shake cabin, grinning into the night when they rode up. By the time Johnny dismounted, the first man to the door had slapped the stranger's face. He went on grinning as if he were too surprised to stop, with the blood running down his chin.

He stood in the glare of the torches, not able to get his tongue back in his mouth, still trying to be friendly with a piece of meat for a face, explaining that he didn't give a damn about any of it, he just didn't hold with niggers doing his farming for him and he just wanted to be left alone.

Someone yelled, "Git his Bible. I could use me a goddam Beecher's Bible."

Johnny pushed his way through the mob at the shack door. He heard another slap.

"You come here with an Immigrant Aid mob."

The man, still trying to grin, mumbled, "Yah, I come."

"You like niggers," somebody yelled.

"No." The man threw his hand up to shield his head. "I ain't got no niggers. Farmer . . ."

A big barefooted woman pushed through the door, her eyes and mouth still wet with sleep. *"Lieber Gott,* he's seek. We don't want no niggers. We don't quarrel." She tried to pull her husband back inside the door. Johnny got to them just as the man was hit again.

"You're a Free Soiler, ain't ye?" They were trying to make the man speak when he was too scared to understand a word.

"All right, get back to your horses," Johnny yelled. "These folks ain't done a thing."

"Mister, we ain't done nothin," the woman whispered. She was trying to wipe the man's face. "Christ Gott, his teeth. They knock out his teeth."

"Damn lucky we don't hang him. Whose side are you on anyhow?" someone yelled at Johnny. "Mugwump!"

When Johnny pulled his gun, there was movement in the tight huddle of men, but no one spoke.

"This ain't who we're looking for, men," Johnny called. "We're looking for Brown."

Somebody had already set fire to the shack. The big woman, beyond screaming, turned back into the one room, dazed. Johnny helped her carry out the rough bedstead.

"His teeth, *lieber Gott,* his teeth," was all she could say. Her husband stood in the yard dumbly, nursing his mouth.

Johnny ran back for the one lamp, the skillet, and the gun. It was too late to save any more. In the night the flames lit the silent tears on the woman's face.

Johnny saw them again the next day on the dirt road which stretched straight across the flat fields. They were headed for Missouri. He turned his troop off the road, his hand on his gun, to let them pass.

"Don't worry. They-uns'll be back. They allus comes back. Ye cain't root em out," a man behind him muttered.

They did come back, back from the South, and back from the North, not great believers like Henry Ward Beecher, hiring men in the name of God; or men like Stephen Douglas, who wanted to be President; or mad dogs like Osawatomie Brown, who murdered and then prayed to his blood-red God with his sacrifice running down his arms before he ate in the morning; or polite gentlemen to the south like Mr. Washington, who sent out paid loose wanderers, casual loud men from the New South under white banners saying *Southern Rights,* sent them out to do work a gentleman wouldn't have soiled his hands with. No, the immigrants just came back, dumbly, and replanted in the fine soil, between the clashes, the violence and disaster, winning in the long run through what was known as courage because they had no place else to go.

But all Johnny said to Charles McAndrews was, "Don't go over into the Territory, Mr. McAndrews. I remember your sentiments."

"I have to," Charles McAndrews interrupted.

"Look at these men." Johnny spoke quietly. "You speak to any one of them and they'll tell you they're Southron gintleman and how they're connected. They're nothing but border ruffians. Shut disagreement up with a slap. Hang a man for speaking his mind. Southron gentlemen! It's like seeing all our weaknesses. Caricatures of ourselves."

"No. Ourselves." Charles McAndrews seemed to have forgotten him for a minute. He had a kind of anger in his eyes that made his face wince as if he had been hit. "Terrible men. I love them because they are part of me, but we are terrible men."

He had said "we" but didn't seem to realize it. He went on. "I have to go. You know, a man gets torn when some integrity inside him—conscience, God—fights with his loyalty."

"They can kill you." Johnny's worry came out as anger. "Why cain't you go to the Free Soil part? You'll be safe there."

"It isn't—I cain't persuade—I have to live in a certain way among my own people."

Somebody yelled over the noise of the bar that the ferry was leaving. Most of the men jostled through the door, which kept on swinging after the last man had gone.

"Damned fools," a man in a stovepipe hat who was left said after them.

"Too many folks ain't got nothin better to do. Half horse and half alligator! Holy hell! Hit's all on account of that Stephen Douglas awantin to be the President."

The man in the stovepipe hat nodded, full of wisdom. "Wal, he niver got no nomination. I'll lay ten dollars down Mr. Bewchanon's the next President."

"Oh, Mr. Bewchanon's got a right smart chancet."

The door gradually stopped squeaking and swinging. The nearly empty room settled. A fly buzzed, caught in a hanging lamp.

"I wouldn't have spoken to you if I hadn't recognized you, Mr. Catlett," Charles McAndrews began again. "I have to explain to somebody before I go across the river. Why is it easier with a stranger?"

The two men at the bar laughed, shattering the silence. ". . . so he said, they warn't no goddamned Know Nothings west of the Ohio, said he was an old-fashioned Whig like what his paw was, withdrew from the ballot, got drunk, and preached a Universalist sermon on the courthouse steps. Best damned sermon I ever hyared . . ."

Charles McAndrews said softly, "Perhaps I'm just plain skeered, as a man, I mean."

"Don't go." Johnny was sullen with concern.

"There's a Scotch saying, 'Dree your ain weird.' " Charles McAndrews relaxed and grinned, that disconcerting gesture wiping the pain from his face. "Tote your own shadow. Though how a man knows it's his ain and not just all he's been taught . . . Here I am apologizing to you. When does the next ferry go?"

"Oh, he'll be back when he gets a load." Johnny knew no words could help the small man, who had turned away shyly. His slim hand twitched once on the dirty table. He had the profile of a man who dreamed and called it thought, who in another time might have gone into politics when revolutionary men were listened to, or in another place might have been a poet. At last the little preacher came to the point.

"If you go back and you are in Alexandria, will you go to see my mother? Tell her I had no choice. Tell her"—he was trying to find the words—"I had to love my enemies. It was my tragedy that they were my own people." He sighed, having confessed, and looked at Johnny. "She lives on Princess Street in Alexandria. Anyone can tell you." Johnny could hardly hear him.

"I'll tell her," he said. That was when he knew that sometime he would go back.

As if Charles McAndrews had read his mind and cut through the formality of strangeness to an accord beyond the barrier of both their manners, he said again, more sharply, "What are you doing here?"

"Oh, I came to seek my fortune." Johnny tried to push him away, push that which rose in minutes and caught him off guard, when his mind melted and let in the past—sometimes at night, sometimes after Lydia's childish proper letters, or his father's and mother's few notes over the years, still cold with hurt and anger. Beyond the fact of her marriage Melinda had been wiped from their scant news.

"I went to California like a fool," Johnny went on lightly. "It ain't easy to find out what a useless cuss you are. Well, let's say I decided to use my brains and read for the Missouri bar. Everybody ain't a muleskinner's a lawyer hereabouts. So I got elected the county clerk in Saint Jo, Missouri. I own about enough to tote in a carpet-bag."

Charles McAndrews broke in. "Perhaps you are the kind loyalty's more important to. Greater love hath no man . . . A man like you cain't try to lead a heartless life."

A heartless life. The part of Johnny which had been asleep stirred at last. He could feel it physically, a sinking warming pain. He didn't know, until he tried to answer, that he was holding his breath to stop it, or to keep from making some sound as private and exposing as a groan.

"Are you trying to preachify me?" he said lightly, when he could.

The man, so dedicated to his own straight way he seemed for a minute to Johnny to have a kind of arrogance in his humility, laughed at him. "Who am I?" he said. "I've seen duty corrupt men. So have you. Certain kinds of men."

Johnny nodded. Outer duty, as he had known it, had changed, silenced, and shrunk his father. Suddenly he missed him so he wanted to cry.

He got up from the table. "You can come and sit in my office until the ferry goes," he told Charles McAndrews, and then, because he had to look at him, he promised, "I will go and see your mother."

An hour later he watched the little stranger walk down the road toward the crowded noisy quay, the sun casting his ain weird behind him, purple in the pale dirt.

He did not see him again for three weeks. A mile outside of Franklin, Kansas Territory, three men lay beside the road as if they had been flung aside. They had been dead for a day. The flies were black pools on their eyes and mouths. A horse had stepped on Charles McAndrews' hand, as if he had been shot and ridden over only because he was in somebody's way. Johnny dismounted and buried him, and cursed the stupid useless failure of his unknown death, his immortality a face and voice in Johnny's mind.

He rode alone toward Franklin under the noon sun, following his troop.

Chapter Two

AT FIVE-THIRTY on the sixth of November, it was deep still dusk. A few snowflakes drifted, some upwards in the light of the stage lamp as it stopped before the inn at Beulah. Johnny stood in the snap-cold November air. He smelled the smoke of the sweet wood fire rising from the row of houses down the road beside the inn. A single dim glow from the porch lantern splashed out onto the old yard, but in the cold the inn seemed deserted. Johnny could barely read a part of a torn Know Nothing election poster flapping forgotten in the wind: *American ticket! Put none but* AMERICANS *on guard* . . . There was no sound. No one came out to meet the stage. It was so quiet that if Johnny had met anyone he would have whispered, as the cedar trees whispered on the distant lawn of the Mansion.

His carpet-bag was thrown from the stage-top, and the driver cracked the horses ahead before Johnny could do more than step back out of the way. Its pale lights were disappearing around the wide upriver bend of the road before he moved.

He bent down slowly, picked up the carpet-bag, walked across the road and up the carriage drive. The trees, now bare, were only great patterns of black branches in the way of the warm-lit Mansion. Johnny glanced at the horse-field by habit to see if there were any colts. It, too, was deserted. The pall of winter, or of the bare desertion itself, made him walk faster, hold his thin coat closer to him and lean into the slight wind from the mill hollow. The first sound he heard was the tock-tock of someone splitting kindling beyond the house. In the cold night the sound carried clear and sharp.

Almost beside him, making his heart jump and his skin quiver after so long, a single grouse whirred up from the dead leaves and flew ahead of him into the deep twilight. He stopped, all senses keen, free as the bird itself, and for the first time he sighed. That evasive mountain bird, after the years of flat land, with the birds rising together, heavy, massive to the sky from the prairies and the cornfields of Kansas, made time slip and memory close while he stood there where he belonged.

Johnny went quietly up the steps of the Mansion and pushed open the door. Inside the warm hall, even the smell of it, wood-smoke, lamp oil, and the shuttering down for winter after the out-side tang of wide cold; Johnny was a boy, a child, never away, a fool, he even smiled. Then he caught it—every object was the same, but dull, the hall hollow, empty. It was the emptiness of neglect while people waited. It was death, already in the house. He tiptoed without realizing it, as he had when his grandmother died, to the shut parlor door. Behind it he could hear a voice, lightly dropping words to the waiting room, and listening closer he knew, as he had known they would be, that the family were gathered around the fire, eating apples and cookies, and reading the paper aloud.

He recognized Lydia's dry reading-task voice. " 'My first step to ruin,' exclaimed a wretched youth, as he tossed from side to side on his straw bed in one corner of his prison house, 'was going fishing on the Sabbath. I knew it was wrong. My mother taught me better; my Bible taught me better, but I would heed none of them.' " Lydia's reading was monotonous, as if she had reached almost the end of her evening chore. " 'I did not think it would come to this,' " she went on reading flatly. " 'I am undone. I am lost.' "

He heard a crinkle of the paper being turned, the creak of a chair, a low murmur that he couldn't understand. Johnny opened the parlor door.

Their faces at the door's opening, looking around as avid with expectancy as wide-mouthed birds in a nest, made him sense them for a second, as still with surprise as a tableau-vivant, and before they moved he wanted to run again, after all that time. It was as if they had waited for him for seven years. His mother had grown round and pink. She sat beside the fire, now in the master chair. Across from her Cousin Sally Lacey nodded her head as if she had been saying a twittering yes to something for some time and could no longer stop. She had not changed, but she had shrunk a little. There by the table on one side of the lamp Cousin Annie stared belligerently at his invasion.

Lydia began it, the movement after that pause. She threw the paper aside and ran to him. Under his hands she felt thin and slight, and he wondered, backing her away from him and listening to the now rising voices of welcome engulfing him, if she had been ill.

He took Lydia across the room in his wake before his mother had quite risen from her chair.

"Son, I knew you'd come," she said simply, factually, and lifted her calm face to be kissed. She was completely controlled, but she kept holding on to his arm while the others moved around them. Where her hand was, the ruby caught the firelight and sent long messages of fire back.

Sally Lacey rose with dignity, still nodding her head, and came to be kissed. She was tiny, frail against him. "My stars," she told him, flirting, "you've grown into a fine figure of a man. Thank heavens you ain't grown a beard. I ain't seen a man's whole face here for a while." She went on talking, a panicked maze of words, but something in the seven years had taken the stridency from her voice and she spoke hardly above a running, nervous whisper.

Cousin Annie leaned toward him as if she would break. There seemed only will and bones left of her; she was as thin as the bare trees brittle in the wind. Her eyes, which he remembered as small, now were sunk in pools of wrinkles in her white square face; the last gray strands of her once massive hair escaped feebly from her cap. She was in deep mourning.

"Why did you come back, Johnny? You always was a fool," she sadly greeted him, her hand in his, a turkey's claw. Sally stopped talking for a pause to giggle at something she had said, took a breath, and began again, excited. Leah stood watch. They were all so close to Johnny he couldn't move his foot for fear of treading on delicate slippers. Lydia decided he was cold. She pushed him into the master chair and knelt to take off his boots, but he pushed her away gently.

"I meant to come—" The first words he said were swallowed up in questions.

"Your father's been calling for you," Leah stated.

Johnny got up so quickly that the ladies were scattered. Miss Sally flicked her skirt back from the fire, frightened.

"May I see Pa?"

His mother set her face. "We have to talk first," she told him, hoping the others wouldn't hear.

Then he heard the laugh stabbing the solemn moment and thought, for the instant before looking beyond the women, that it was a ghost he heard and now he saw.

When Melinda, drowsing on the sofa, trying to shut out Lydia's interminable reading, saw the door open slowly, then saw Johnny step so tentatively into the shadow beyond the lamp, she could not speak or move. He was simply there, crashed into the dull evening, after all the waiting, after the waiting that had seemed spatial, timeless, and now was over. He had changed—his face had begun to line, not in lines of age, but those to keep a man's mouth controlled, and his eyes watching into the distance for too long. He held his soft light Western hat easily at his side; his hair was darker, heavier, falling to just above his collar, his black wide cravat negligently tied as if he had forgotten that it mattered. He looked exhausted, not just the exhaustion of a day, but as if he had seen too much and heard too much and wanted only peace. She could not move, only watch, waiting for him to see her and tell her by seeing whether in his mind she was still alive. He looked stricken, even when he opened his mouth to speak, as if to him the dullness of the room were too sacred to be disturbed.

Then Lydia looked up and saw him and the room rocked, the movements of swooping anxious women tossing the fire- and lamplight. Even his smile, easy as ever, was sadder. It was not until he got up from the chair, scattering them, and made Melinda think of the chicken yard at feeding time, that she laughed. She had to; he was so weak against the onslaught of the small women who welcomed him.

When he looked over and saw her she knew she was still alive. They met behind the table, away from the closely watching women, and he took her hand.

"My stars," Miss Sally called, "she's still kissin kin even if she has been ever' place under the living sun!" She ended in a giggle.

Johnny leaned down and kissed her temple. He could feel it pulse against his mouth.

"You look fine, Johnny," she told him, lightly lying.

"I didn't know you would be here."

"Crawford came out to stump the western counties for the election."

He watched the civilized woman, cool, protected, as if the affectations of the girl had become tempered, real, in her now modulated almost accentless voice, her easy way of standing, the way her dress and hair went beyond fashion to a poise that made him feel shy and poor, rugged and awkward as the West he had come from. Then he began to smile at her, amused at her new self as he had been at the girl, sensing behind her assurance an eagerness as evocative as the scent of women's flowers, the same wild girl looking from the woman's controlled face.

Leah couldn't pull Johnny's eyes from Melinda. It hurt her, after she had waited so long for her child, to see it. She took his arm again. "Come to your father." She was formal about it.

Behind him, he heard Melinda sigh as if she had not breathed for too long.

On the stairs ahead of him Leah stopped. As she did the swish of her skirts made the flame of the lamp below flick. She turned now above him, looking down at his face.

"Of course, you know you broke your father's heart," she said as if she had been waiting to say it for a long time. Her shadow on the landing wall danced like a huge bear. "I think you know what you owe him. He is a dying man." She said it as bland with certainty as she had said the other. "We wrote little about Lewis. He has been a disappointment." Then, with a spurt of anger, "If his is religion, God deliver my soul from it."

She turned and went on up the stairs, leaving Johnny to follow, without letting him answer.

"I will not go in. Too many tires him," she whispered at the chamber door, the formidable chamber of his grandmother, then of his parents, now of death, set apart as always from the rest of the house.

Leah couldn't help it. She couldn't stay stern forever, though she knew it was the right thing to do. She looked up at this tall, new strong man who was her son, and threw herself for safety against his chest. It was the first time she had ever let herself go like that before the children. "Oh, Johnny," she moaned against his coat where she could feel his healthy heart beat. "I'm so glad you've come. I haven't known what on earth to do."

He put his arms slowly around the small, plump, weeping woman to comfort her.

They heard someone call from inside the chamber, but not what he said.

"Your father wants you. Oh my darling boy!" Leah ran as he had seen her run when he was a child, lightly, her handkerchief against her face, into the opposite chamber.

Inside the hot airless invalid room, Peregrine lay in the center of the high wide bed, watching the door. Johnny saw first that he was holding Jim's hand, and that Jim's hair had gone as white as tufted cotton. His father watched him so calmly that Johnny knew at first that he did not recognize him. As he did realize who it was he looked at him with that suppliant look of the dying that made Johnny feel a horror of embarrassment, and then so tender that tears stung in his eyes for the first time in seven years.

Peregrine tried to smile, and it was twisted. The left side of the old man's face was paralyzed. It made his smile so mocking that it was not until Johnny stood close beside the bed, and had taken his father's hand from Jim, that he saw there was no mockery in the faded dusty eyes, only relief.

He managed to speak, his voice windy as rustling paper. "God-dammit, son," he whispered. "It's about time you turned up." He tried to tighten his grasp of Johnny's hand.

"Pa . . ." Johnny began to tell him. That face had faded,

his toothless gap of mouth, his cheeks sunken until his bones showed like ridges, no longer red, but white, dull—his father, no lashing wit, now frail and waiting; he did not know how to tell him.

"Get on out of here, Jim," his father whispered. Jim, behind Johnny, touched his back, then put his palm flat against it, and slapped him gently. Johnny heard the door close.

"Oh, son, what in the hell did you come back for?"

Johnny stood, saying nothing, holding the cold hand in his.

The twisted grin again, attempt at smiling. "How did you know? It takes so damn long for a letter."

"Pa." Because he couldn't tell him about the preacher, Johnny found relief saying, "Remember Lance Stuart?"

"Lord God, I had an idea he was courting Lydia," the dry-grass voice answered. "He come through here, rattling West Point spurs, and smart talk . . . on his way to Kansas."

Johnny had sunk down in the chair left by Jim. "He found me."

The dusty man-filled street of Lawrence, Kansas Territory, jostling looting crowd in the flatter sun on the utility board houses. "Pa, Lance found me in Lawrence, Kansas. I was swept aside by a troop of United States Cavalry. One of them reined in and I looked up and saw it was Lance." Johnny laughed, remembering. "I heard somebody yell, 'What in the hell are you doing out here with this passel of poor whites, Johnny Catlett?' Pa, a Virginia voice . . .

"I asked him what the devil he was doing in the Army. He always wanted it. 'Why, Pa got elected,' he told me. Lance didn't say any more then, but told me where to find him and rode on after his troop. After that sickening disgusting day, I managed to get to his camp without getting shot."

Johnny could no longer look at his father's questioning eyes, but stared over his frail body where it hardly lifted the quilt, at the fire.

"Lance told me to go on home. He said I could do more good at home." He couldn't tell him that until he had walked into the hall and sensed the neglected space of death he had not known his father was even ill, how he had seen it in the waiting women, read it in his mother's sitting in the master chair, not yet in mourning, taut with that coiled sorrow that means someone has not yet died. There was so much he had to read in them, so much they, living in it, would take for granted and not tell him, so much that they didn't know, within their water, not seeing the shape of the river or where it was going.

"You never made much headway, did you?" he heard his father whisper.

"Pa! I wasn't fitted for nothing. Men like us are only fit to give orders," Johnny told the fire. "Those Bible-thumping farmers could outwork me, the unscrupulous could outtrade me, and the border scum who called themselves Southern gintlemen"—Johnny sounded bitter—"could outfight any decent man. In Missouri, after I reckoned I wasn't going to make a fortune—not by their rules—I was called to the bar. Things were better. There was use there for a civilized man. That license they called liberty . . . I was making my way. Then I went to Kansas," he went on, forgetting death, at last able to tell his father.

"Why?" Peregrine whispered, his head away, watching their images in the night window.

"To see, like any decent man, what I could do."

He looked back at his father, but he saw that the old man wasn't listening. He was busy dying and Kansas was far away from the close, hot, comfortable room. After the violence, the quick, obscene death of Charles McAndrews in the ditch beside the dusty road, this death seemed steeped in luxury—the luxury of dignity and care. The secure—he could not say this—even die differently, but he said instead, "Pa, do you want to sleep? I'll be right here."

"Johnny, things ain't going as they ought." Peregrine tried to tell him, from far away, as if he only wanted to get rid of it, not caring much. "I've had to sell a heap of niggers. Dammit, that's all we got to trade with now. The mother of states"—some of the sardonic humor Johnny remembered returned to the mobile part of his face—"a damned nigger farm. We ain't got much else to sell. Land ain't worth much. The salt business is poor."

Johnny suddenly realized why it had been so quiet outside at Beulah. The thump-thump of the salt drill, like a pulse of the little valley for as long as he could remember, was dead.

"Don't you go letting Liddy run off with that damn Dan O'Neill," his father whimpered, as querulous as a child. "All he wants is to get his damned Irish hands on our property."

"Dan . . ." Johnny echoed. He hadn't thought of him in so long.

"Politics. Goddam politics. Never thought I'd be glad to see a Dimocrat like Bewchanon win an election. It's the death of the Whigs, Johnny. They voted Know Nothing hereabouts. Next the damned traitors'll be agoing black Republican." His father turned his head away and after a few minutes of quiet, the room glowing from the fire, and the old man's chest hardly moving the quilt, his hand went limp in Johnny's and he realized his father was asleep.

Johnny thought when he eased his way out of the chamber door that the upper hall was empty, but even as he turned, he was engulfed in fat black arms and Minna crooned through her tears, always as easy as laughter, "Mista Johnny, you come home. Ever'-thing gone be all right." Old Minna, mother of his father's child, crooned at him.

Then she pushed him back, stern. "They ain't nothin in that old carpet-bag fitten to put on a gintleman's back. I found ye somethin of your paw's. And you looks thin as a rake. Who been lookin after ye?"

She didn't wait for an answer. "You been lookin after your own-self. Ain't a gintlemen fittin to do it." He went obediently to be fed. No one, in the excitement, had thought, except Minna, that he might be hungry.

Johnny sat at the head of the dinner table, trying to eat as they watched him. When the hall door shut, no one moved.

"That will be Crawford," Melinda told him, but she sat, her chin resting in her hand, amused.

Late in the evening Dan Neill called from the hallway and came in, cold before the fire. He kissed Cousin Annie's cheek dutifully. She didn't lift her head from spearing the petit-point that covered her lap. Dan motioned to Johnny over her head, then caught Crawford's eye. He didn't look at Lydia, now sitting tense with excitement on the sofa. The three men went into the library.

Johnny could listen to them as they drank together, ignoring his seven years away in the heat of discussing the election, men at ease with each other, Dan too much at ease, Johnny noticed, as he tipped his own drink from the decanter and rocked back with his feet on the library table.

"Why, Crawford," Johnny told the man now withdrawn and strange to him, Melinda's husband in the opposite chair, "I thought you were a cold-water man."

"I found it not to be expedient in politics," Crawford said, lightly. The man seemed brittle, and cold, rid of the tentativeness Johnny had always known in him.

"You ought to see Fish here electioneerin." Dan leaned into the light, grinning, to interrupt their concentration on studying each other, shutting him out. "I larned him, didn't I, Fish?" The edge of malice in Dan's voice seemed to be lost on Crawford. At least he took it as if he were used to it. Johnny saw in young Dan the ghost of Big Dan's sass, and Big Dan's body, bonier perhaps, in keeping with his black clothes, and his clean but rowdy linen.

"By God, Johnny, I told Fish, I told him if you git out hyar takin on to talk to folk thataway, you must not hanker after no office. Well, he done right good, but not good enough. You hang on, Fish." Dan reached for the decanter again. "Ifn you wasn't a damn fool, you'd throw in your lot with the western counties. Our turn's acomin. West Virginia." He raised his glass.

Something in Johnny's face made Crawford mutter, as if to himself, "I know you hate me, Mr. Neill, but—"

Dan rocked back and laughed. "No, I don't hate ye, Fish. I jest ain't got no use fer you damn East Virginians, lettin on to tell us what—"

"Hell, Dan, you still tooting that old horn?" Johnny interrupted.

"I say any man that casts a vote for the Dimocrats is a damned ass-licker from the Tidewater! Bewchanon!"

"Oh my God," Johnny muttered, exhausted.

"Oh the devil." Dan grinned at Crawford to seek complicity. "Johnny hyar's been in the big West. He don't want to hyar no politics. Catholics took over Kansas, didn't they?" he baited.

"With that passel of rock-ribbed Baptists there ain't a Catholic in the territory will admit to being one," Johnny told him.

"Our information is different," Crawford interrupted.

Dan just looked at him, tired of him. His conversation retreated from Crawford.

"Johnny, your pup Tear turned into a fine dog. Pheasant dog. I trained her. I reckoned you'd come back."

"My God, that little pup."

Someone knocked on the door. Lydia called, "Mr. Neill? You in there?"

"I'll be out presently, ma'am," Dan yelled.

Johnny could hear Lydia retreat slowly from the door.

"You wouldn't even have your own larning if it wasn't for East Virginia," Crawford told Dan, worrying the point to keep them from talking about the dog.

"Larnin didn't do all that much good at the polls, sir, now did it? Folks hereabouts are damn sick of talkin rum and niggers. They don't want no foreigners. They don't hanker after no black Catholics risin up to kill all the Protestants. Anyhow we carried the western counties; they stuck together. Voted for Fillmore and Donaldson." Dan threw his head back and laughed, his mouth wide. "That's what we run on, wasn't it, Fish? Know Nothin! Now that took a heap o' larnin, didn't it, though?"

Something of the old high seriousness came back to Crawford. Johnny also saw that he had drunk a lot. "The foreign menace surrounds true Americans," he began to intone. "If your ancestors and mine, Johnny, could see the hungry, evil-talking scum that inherit this fair land. Our forebears came here for freedom, not because they couldn't make a living, or were the spawn of foreign jails—"

"Oh quit that, Fish. The election's over." Dan tipped his feet to the floor. "Wouldn't Paw git the old shillelagh after me, Johnny, if he seen what politics had tied me up with?" His now good-natured insolence, breaking through, infected the room. Johnny couldn't help laughing with him, but his laughter broke off when Dan struggled to his feet.

"You wouldn't know my paw, Fish, but I'm kin to ye." He

banged the table and it shook. "Don't you forgit for one damn minute, Fish Kregg. *I'm kin to ye.*"

"I think you might lower your voice in my father's house, Dan. He is very ill." Johnny jumped up to face him.

When Dan Neill saw the coolness he had forgotten, his face went red. It took him a minute of thinking to say, "Now, Johnny, I apologize. I apologize, Johnny."

Another knock stopped them.

"Johnny," his mother called, "come here." At the door she drew him out and whispered, "Your father's awake. He's calling for you. Sit with him tonight, Johnny. I've got to get some sleep.

"Of course"—she turned at the stairs—"with my clothes on in case he calls. He won't call for me." She went on talking to herself sadly as she dragged up the stairs. "Not with you here."

The night was timeless, divided only by old Jim tiptoeing in and building up the fire coal by coal with his fingers to keep from disturbing the two men. For the rest, as his father slept, the house was so quiet he could hear the ticking of the parlor clock below. Once, when Jim came in, Johnny had let his head drop onto the quilt and was asleep, but the movement by the fire woke the old man, and his whispered "Son?" roused him so quickly that Johnny knew he had let himself doze.

"Johnny," Peregrine said as the door closed again softly, "what in the hell are we going to do?" His eyes glistened, huge in his sunken, chalky face.

"Pa, it'll be all right." Johnny thought he meant the place.

"I cain't understand no more, Johnny. If it wasn't the damnedest thing. The old Whig party turned into this trashy Know Nothing business. What a devil of a couple of fellows Dan and Crawford are, putting on to keep the Union together." He sighed and closed his eyes, murmuring himself toward sleep. "Dammit, counties splitting up. Families splitting up. Even the goddam state. You know what Lewis done?"

"Pa, go to sleep."

"He took to preaching abolition. Said God told him to. Nothing of the kind. I never saw him be decent to a nigger in his life. Didn't have it in him. I'm sick and tired of hell and damnation,

Johnny. That ain't it, is it?" He turned his head away and watched the fire leap up, alive again. It made the ceiling billow with waves of light.

Johnny watched the fire, too, not wanting to excite his father, knowing that if he didn't answer the old man would sleep again, but Peregrine went on murmuring to the fire. "If they're for the niggers . . ."

"There ain't nobody for them that way, Pa. Fools in Boston . . . First thing the Free Soilers voted in Kansas was to keep all niggers, free and slave, out of the Territory. There ain't a one safe there. It's all talk." His father was asleep again.

In the stretching of the night Johnny couldn't keep from dozing, and the nightmare always on the edge of his mind came back—Charles McAndrews, always lying there beside the road.

"Pa." He didn't realize that he had waked again and called to his father, until he saw his eyes opened, questioning, as if he had been watching him for a long time. "They called themselves Southron gintlemen, a back of border ruffians. Killed men when they got in the way. Southron gintlemen. They was like children dressed up to act like ladies and gintlemen in their parents' old clothes."

His father, father again, reassured, explained, patting his hand, "Johnny, it's Jackson's fault"—as if he hadn't really heard. "Know Nothings. By God, ain't nobody been better named. Cousin Crawford threw in with them. I didn't. I might be a Whig but I ain't having none of that. Used knee pads at the polls to keep the foreign vote down." Something of his old laugh sounded weakly. "We ain't even got no foreigners but them damned O'Neills. He's a Know Nothing. That upstart's a Know Nothing! Put naught but Americans on guard! Him!"

Johnny, now wide awake, smelled the sweetness of the fire, the gentle peace of the room.

"They did right well out here, didn't they, Pa?"

"Carried the western counties, Johnny. People who ought to have known better threw in with them. They put on to stand for the Union. God knows nobody else stood for the Union. I'm tired, Johnny." He was asleep again.

The first dawn was changing the shadows of the sick chamber. His father moved a little, and Johnny leapt, cold with fear. He only whispered, "Son, a little water."

Johnny held his head up in his arm and fed him the water as if he were a child. It was the first physical act he had ever done for his father. He put the old man's head down tenderly and let his hand rest on the cold forehead, pushing back the wisps of hair.

"You going to run the farm until I can get back on my feet, ain't ye?" he begged.

"I will, Pa. Go to sleep," Johnny whispered.

"I want Jim. Damn, it's embarrassing for a man to be ailing."

Johnny found Jim sitting wide awake in the hall. When Jim heard the door open, he jumped up, looking sick with fear.

"Pa wants you," Johnny told him, and went out onto the observatory in the dim freezing dawn.

It was seven o'clock in the quiet morning. Johnny counted the chimes of the parlor clock. It seemed strange—no sound of children in the house. Down the stairs he could hear the rustle of skirts and whispering. He heard Jim come out of the sickchamber and tiptoed back.

"Johnny." His father had had Jim prop him up a little on the pillows now that the cold white November day was filtering into the windows, turning the fire blue. "Be good to them. Poor innocent things. I've always taught you that, ain't I, Johnny? Women and niggers. They ain't fitten to look after theirselves."

Johnny adjusted the pillow, and his father was quiet. That half-mobile face winced in moving. "Lewis took her up there to live with them as his duty."

"Ain't he here, Pa?"

"No, thank God. I give him two hundred acres—the hill farm where the second orchard was. He wouldn't have no niggers. He's out preaching hell-far while that well-nurtured gal works like a dog. One hired gal. Johnny, if we hadn't abrought that poor little fool thing down here, she'd died of grief. She just set there, not saying a word. Ever'thing she stood for was a sin in Lewis's eyes, ever' time she laughed. He wouldn't even let her talk foolishness, and she cain't talk nothing else. Man of God!" The old man tried to laugh.

"I warn ye, she ain't quit talking since we moved her down here."

It wasn't until then that Johnny realized his father was talking about Sally Lacey.

"She was the prettiest gal . . ." Peregrine murmured just as Leah came in, rushing, as she always had, toward duty. "God is merciful," she whispered to Johnny. "He lasted the night."

She studied his father's face. "He looks better, quieter. You've done him good." She paused and whispered, "He didn't talk foolish, did he? His mind wanders. It's nothing but that." The man in the bed stirred. She didn't wait for Johnny to answer.

"We must pray, Mr. Catlett," she told her husband, leaning down to kiss his forehead. When she turned to motion him away, Johnny saw her eyes were wet with tears, like the woman's eyes, the woman in Kansas watching the night fire.

Johnny was too tired to sleep, too tired to talk to the women, light and bodiless with fatigue. He did not realize it until he walked out onto the porch and smelled the fresh cold mist from the creek, lifting slowly under the pale sun. Beulah lay in its whiteness.

None of them saw him get his gun, go and call Tear from the kennel, and walk out behind her by the creek path, up past the field-hands' quarters where smoke rose, disturbing the mist. He could see no one there. It was as if they, at least, were waiting for all of him to come home—if that could ever happen. He felt as cold inside as out, and stopped at last trying to care.

The millpond had a thin layer of clear ice; the millwheel was still. He passed it slowly, his eyes taking in the need for repairs—later, but now up into the mill-hollow the mist had lifted to the height of the trees, and ahead of him the empty waiting path skeletal with winter, fallen leaves cracking underfoot. Tear went on ahead, still stiff with cold, hunting close, and looking behind her from time to time.

Johnny stopped and breathed deeply, his let-out breath a mist, his body light but feeling peace at last. Far ahead he heard a single bird get up, wild in the cold morning.

Melinda had won. She had informed Crawford that since her foster father was so near death it was necessary for them to stay a little longer. She let Toey put her into her winter habit and told her to run and find the stable-boy, she couldn't remember his name, to saddle her horse. Toey, shy, now silent, asked her, "Whar Marse Johnny?" She had to ask, but Melinda didn't answer her. She only set her mouth and walked to the chamber door.

"Do as I say," she said coolly to the brown woman, and went out to wait in the cold.

Crawford followed her, not saying a word.

"I'm going to see Sara." Melinda leaned against the porch post and watched the mist. "She hasn't got a soul to talk to."

"It was only that I reckoned we ought to get back to the children. . . ." Crawford tried to begin the argument again.

"With a hundred people to look after them?" Melinda didn't look at him to speak.

When the stable-boy brought her horse, she mounted and cantered away, up the main hollow through the trees. Crawford watched her pass the mare-barn and disappear in the now sun-laden mist before he stepped off the porch and wandered, strolling down the walk toward the inn.

Sally Lacey paused at the upstairs window. "Ain't he the finest figure of a man?" she said, hoping somebody would answer.

But nobody did.

A ragged line of black children heard the thud of the horse's hoofs and scattered to the ditch beside the hill road. Melinda cantered past them, past the old graveyard overlooking Beulah, now so overgrown with brambles that the black tendrils covered the neglected old stones where she had sat so often. She let the horse trot on up the hill to the plateau where Lewis had built his solemn wooden farmhouse, unredeemed now in the sunny cold morning by any sinful beauty at all. It stood, foursquare, two stories high against the sky. The wind was cold. The cornstalks were gathered, neat rustling dry sentinels. She rode between them, the fields gleaned clean as far as she could see.

Ahead she saw Sara come out of the barn and walk slowly toward the house on the horizon, which made her look huge. Her back was bent as if the bucket she carried was heavy. One of the children was following her. Melinda could see the other two staring across the bare field at her. She brought her horse to a canter again.

Sara's face was suffused with joy to see her. It had not changed with all her trouble, her harsh life they complained about down the hill. Melinda once told her she looked dazed by God, hypnotized, but Sara had laughed and said, "Don't talk that way."

Sara put down the heavy wooden bucket and helped Melinda from her horse.

"How is he this morning?" she asked, squinting with the wind and worry.

"Some better." Melinda led the horse to the porch and tethered it. "You've got to go and see him, Sara."

Sara didn't answer.

"I don't care what's happened, Sara. Where's your religion if it can't forgive an old man? He did nothing to you."

"I . . ." Melinda thought Sara was going to cry, but instead she fought for that blind brightness and said, smiling again, "God forgives, not we poor sinners. Oh"—she turned, shutting out the subject—"there are my dear children." The Negro children from Beulah had reached the plateau and walked, far away, in solemn single file to school.

"They wouldn't be up here, letting you disobey the law, if Mr. Catlett hadn't honored your wishes." Melinda, annoyed, stamped up onto the porch.

"Crawford had a school for his people, Melinda. I used to teach them there. How can you talk so about the law?" Sara followed her.

"Things have changed. They get stirred up. *You* wouldn't be received in East Virginia. Oh, *I* don't care." Melinda threw herself into the only comfortable chair in the clean bare wood parlor. Because it was so bare, without color, the fire didn't seem to warm it. Melinda shivered under the habit, even after the exercise that had made her cheeks glow and her eyes bright.

"I think you do care. That's why I love you." Sara laughed and patted Melinda's fist. She was so pretty Sara couldn't help touching her hair.

Somewhere in the distance the cold clear air split with the sound of a shot.

"Is Lewis hunting?" Melinda sat up.

"Lewis has gone to a poor soul downriver who called for him," Sara told her calmly.

"But not his father!"

"I must ask you, Melinda . . ." Sara was as stern as she could be, armed with sweetness. "Don't you see, I must honor the wishes of my husband. Saint Paul says—" Sara couldn't say it straight to Melinda. She wandered to the window to watch her patient charges, each with a Bible sent from Cincinnati, saw her own shy children run to meet them. "Saint Paul says," she said more strongly, "that we must bend to the will of our husbands. The way Mr. Catlett lives is wrong and the way you live is wrong. You are a weak woman and cain't do anything about it."

Another shot cracked, far away. It brought Melinda to her feet.

"Johnny came home last night," Melinda told her, listening now for the direction of the shot.

"Oh, thank God." Sara ran to her. "Thank a merciful God. The prodigal has returned!"

Melinda smiled. "From what he says he's not been in the fleshpots, Sara. What a little judge you are!"

"I only meant—"

"You mean he can take the responsibility and ease your conscience."

Sara took Melinda's arm. "I don't care if you talk to me that way, my dear."

Nothing could penetrate that serenity, no fact of life, no brutality, no death. "It is the will of God," Melinda finished aloud.

"Amen, sister," Sara answered proudly, thinking she had made Melinda see, really see, at last.

"I must go."

"Not yet!"

Melinda almost ran to the door, stumbling once over her long heavy train.

"That's so pretty," Sara said sadly, touching the fine wool.

She watched, as Crawford had, from the porch, as Melinda rode away through the dry cornfield, looking as free as the air she seemed to float across.

At the old graveyard Melinda reined up, all senses tense, to listen again. She could feel her heart pound. Beulah lay now in the bright November day, bare of leaves so that the bend of the river was a clear cut shining, and only the smoke from the Mansion's chimneys disturbed the air.

The shot came from up the mill-hollow.

It was all she could do to keep from cantering headlong down the hill, but she held herself and the horse in until she reached the level road, and turned and thrashed her mount up the mill road, past the mill, never slowing until she was under the trees on the steep path up the mill branch.

She was afraid to ride too far and disturb the birds. A mile up the hollow she tethered her horse and climbed the steep path in the silent woods. Her feet hit a stone, dislodged it. She heard it clatter away behind her. It was hard to walk in the skirt, and the rocks made her ankles hurt. She could not turn back. The woods felt cold and barren to her, exposed by the winter.

This time the shot was just ahead, a loud crack, reverberating toward her, rolling through the trees, and then silence. She heard Johnny call, "Hunt dead, Tear." She heard him running. The thick laurel at the path's turn hid him, even so near.

Around it she saw him on the straight path bend down beside the dog, pick up something from under a clump of vines, and pet the dog with his free hand.

"Johnny!" In the silence she spoke so quietly that at first he couldn't believe he heard her.

He stood, the still live grouse in his hand, the heart thumping against his palm, its wing shattered. He could not look up.

Melinda said again, "Johnny." He looked at her then, but didn't speak, watched while she came and touched his arm.

The bird tried to flutter. Johnny turned away from her and lifted it to his mouth. When he turned back, it was dead, its neck broken. He still had a drop of blood on his lower lip.

"It's the quickest way," he said, and held out the bird, all the colors of the winter woods, subtle elusive color, the rocks, the bark, the winter leaves, the dappled sunlight, reflected in its feathers. "Oh God, Melinda, what a fool thing to do. You could have been shot."

Melinda threw her body against his. He had waited so long. Longing—a long time. That's what it meant. She found his mouth. When she let her head drop to his chest and he held her, the drop of blood was gone.

The rock Melinda and Toey had run away to was smaller under the tree by the tiny pool, now still in winter, under a film of ice so thin it pulsed, no rushing water, so that the gnarled roots of the tree were exposed, clutching the bank over the water.

"Johnny . . ." Melinda put her head on his lap.

He stroked her cheek. It was the same girl, her fine habit forgotten. She huddled against his lap on the cold ground.

"I won't have it this way any more," the rebel he remembered said, her mouth muffled. She rolled over and looked up at him. "What can we do?"

"Still want it your way. Oh, my girl . . ." The longing faded from his face and left it drained with sorrow. "My girl, leave me alone to mourn for my father."

She didn't hear him. She had waited too long.

"Johnny, it was not my fault"—that plea of the innocent. He thought she was going to cry.

She could feel him withdraw. "You let it happen," he whispered. He didn't even sound bitter.

To bring him back, she held his arm and pressed close to him, trying to tell him. "Do you know what they can do? Do you know how you can be pushed—"

"By your own pride."

"What else are we taught?"

She sat up and clasped her knees, planning. "We will do something, Johnny. Crawford—"

"I don't wish to talk about Crawford."

Melinda began to giggle. "No. It's dishonorable for gentlemen. I forgot. Facts and manners don't go together, do they?" She glanced at him, trying to goad him into truth, but his face was set in that control she had seen the night before, an old control of sadness, more rigid than the pulsing ice.

He didn't answer for a while, but leaned against the tree, staring across the creek. He pulled her back into his lap and stroked her face, her hair, her hands until they lay peacefully, one on his knee, the other cold hand against her breast. He let himself touch and hold her breast and then, deliberately, covered her hand with her long train to warm it. She was as quiet as if she were a child he was putting to sleep. Once she tried to speak, but he touched her mouth, let her kiss his hand and hold it. He whispered, "Shhh! Not yet."

She could feel his body tremble, but he didn't move. "Please, not yet," he whispered again, as if any movement would explode the silence of the whole mountain of woods.

He finally said, "What I have to tell you is that other people live, too." It didn't seem to be enough. She didn't look at him, but watched the pulsing ice, waiting. "You never are alone." He hesitated as if that were not it either.

"What is a crime, Melinda?" he finally asked her, and withdrew his hand.

She waited until he told her.

"I reckon a crime is when you take what you want when you know somebody else will have to pay. I saw men—arrogant irresponsible proud men taking what they wanted instead of earning it. Don't let me hurt you."

"You wouldn't," she told the ice.

"By telling you that when I saw you last night you had that look, that way of going—pride, but of the devil. It belongs to beautiful animals, but not to men. It is not courage. I saw a man once who looked like a man. At the tent meeting when Lewis got himself saved. I saw him again seven years later. The stallions had run him down because he was in their way. He went by the name of Charles McAndrews." Johnny was talking now to himself and then seemed to remember the shivering girl in his lap. "I'm so sorry," he whispered. "You cain't just take what you want."

"There are some that buy or push. Crawford bought me." Her bitterness was an open wound.

"No, he didn't." He stroked her face again, gently. "You pushed him, too, Melinda. You made Crawford do what you wanted him to. What do you think to yourself in the night?"

"Quit it, Johnny." He could hardly hear her.

His hand grasped hers until it hurt. "I said what do you think? What do you tell yourself?"

She began to laugh. It disturbed the woods; it brought the curious Tear to investigate and lick her face. She went on laughing, not caring, pushing the dog away.

Her laughter reverberated against the trees as the shot had, shattering the sweet silence. She struggled up in her long skirt, whipping it so that it broke the ice film and flicked the freed water.

"Well, I will tell you, Johnny Catlett, Mr. High and Mighty, what I thought in the middle of the night." She was panting, her voice lashed as the laughter had. "I thought about a woman who dressed me every day and how her nearly white child that should have been mine was born nine months after handsome Johnny went West and left us all to do the best we could. Now you'll say, 'I don't want to hear this.' That's what you always said—never break the charm. I thought how I have watched your child that should have been my child grow up—little nigger Johnny Catlett—and how Tig that you didn't even think about run away when he found out and got took by nigger-catchers and they killed him in the woods and brought him back dead for the reward, and how Crawford paid them, not saying a word. How he paid them . . ." She was crying against the tree almost too hard for him to understand her. "He hates you, Johnny. He thinks it's because of Toey, but it ain't. It's me. It's almost as if I was Toey and she was me. How could you touch her that you didn't care for, and not me that you did care for?" She looked at him then and was quiet, her hair loose, no genteel lady who had everything she wanted and had been to Europe and wore a French habit like a princess, but a crying girl escaped from her poise, slipped back the years to place and time where the chance was taken.

"Oh, I am a lady and I'm not supposed to know anything. Ladies and slaves, look after their wants and rule their minds and keep them innocent. You men!"

She laughed again. "It's a woman's joke. Ladies always know the father of the mulattos on the next plantation. Never their own. How do you think *we* feel?" She waved her hand, pushing at him blindly. "I don't care for your fine ideals. I reckon women are more consarned with the facts. Lord God"—she sighed—"we have to be. You . . ."

She stopped, was still, so that the words covered them again with silence. She turned and looked at his face and was beyond caring that he looked gray with shock.

"You never trod on anybody, did you? It's in your damned soul, Johnny Catlett. You take your ownership for granted."

"Oh my God, Melinda. Tig . . . You ought not to want to touch a man like me," was all he said.

She came toward him and he held her so tightly she could feel her body hurt and go weak, leaning against the tree. He would not kiss her mouth again, but held his face against her neck as if to reassure himself.

Tear sat waiting, and when a grouse whirred up in the distance, she began to bark.

They walked together without a word down to where Melinda's horse was tethered. He hoisted her into the saddle and held her hand for a minute against his eyes. He had made no sound, but she could feel her hand wet.

"I'll come back later," he said. "Pa and Tig . . . I've got to think things out." He didn't look back. She watched now as he disappeared around the bend behind the laurel thicket, and turned her horse to walk slowly down the path. She felt will-less, dependent on mercy, with no fight left in her and nothing to say.

It was late afternoon when Johnny passed the mill house. Far away at the gate he saw Minna shading her eyes. She opened the back gate and started up the mill road. At first he walked to meet her, then, nearer, seeing her face, he began to run.

He caught her, her whole great old body heaving against him.

". . . in his sleep, Marse Johnny. He's asleep in Jesus after the perils of this wicked world—as if he waited fer you to come home and run the place so he could go. He tole me ifn you ain't got no son the land ain't worth holdin on to. . . ."

Chapter Three

WITH THOSE expected acts so deep that they were a satisfying formal liturgy to the reality of death, the women moved through the laying-out of Peregrine, the feasting and the funeral, without the indignity of letting down. As the quick march is played returning from the grave, on the day after the funeral the November wind found its way through opened windows; the house was alive with cleaning, Leah directing it from her room where she sat in deep mourning in a chair beside the fire, receiving the others as they tiptoed in to ask her in low voices what to do. She kept Lydia with her on the other side of the fire, but when there was no one else but Lydia in the room, she sat without saying a word.

Sally and Cousin Annie mourned by action, expecting it of themselves, while they oversaw the sweeping, shaking, pounding of death out of the furniture, the rugs, the air itself. Minna saw to it that the rest of the servants obeyed their flurried commands though she moved through the days dumb with a kind of wonder in her face.

Once she went into Leah's room, forgetting to knock, and found her alone in an ecstasy of tears, but Leah pushed the air in front of Minna with her plump hand and sobbed like a child in the dark for her to find Johnny.

When he came and scooped her plump figure against his chest, he heard her say once, through her heaving sobs, "At least now I'll know where he is all the time," and then moan a little about the dark before he got her to go to sleep.

No one else but Minna and Johnny saw that outburst. She let Lewis in to her, but what passed between them no one knew. Once Minna heard Lewis laugh, as if it were long ago when he and his mother were so close, before differences parted them.

Crawford told Melinda to be ready to leave. He had sat through the women-filled hours, the mourning conversations, the food, with the other men, who for the few days after Peregrine's death seemed to lose their identity, and melt, even Johnny, silently into the background. They met and sat in the library, seeking one another out, but having little to say.

Lewis walked up onto the porch when he heard of his father's death and shook Johnny's hand without speaking, but afterward he and Johnny were noticed by the others walking together out on the empty road or in the dead winter garden, early enough in the morning for the white frost. Sara had come to do what she could, and she paused once during the cleaning day and watched them. They seemed closer to each other than they had been since they were children.

In the public movements of the funeral, Melinda found no time when she could talk to Johnny. She felt the attrition of minutes crawling by while he moved through his duties, close to his mother and his brother, not seeming to see her, not needing her at all. She could feel the current of other people's lives sweeping them apart again, and herself drowning in it.

Cousin Annie and Melinda, as the old unthought-of relationships were reasserted in the strangeness of the time, drew together, feeling more in common with each other than with the entrenched, blind mourners. Cousin Annie put it into words, those words that ever since Peregrine's death the women had been shocked into saying, as if through mourning for his death they were released from his life, and in an anarchy of truth were for once letting what had been on their minds show through rifts of their habits.

They sat, keeping out of the way, on the observatory in the gray November day, wrapped against the cold. A few snowflakes whirled down and lingered for a second before melting, on Melinda's black hair and the sable fur of her cape. Cousin Annie stared straight ahead, and Melinda, free to study her profile, the emaciated square jaw, the sunken pocket of her eye, and her still fine nose, realized that it could have been true that Cousin Annie had once been a beauty. The memory of it showed in her peaceful face that morning. When Cousin Annie did speak it was as if she had, being at peace at last, found a way into Melinda's mind, but she didn't speak to her, only murmured to herself, for once all tension gone from her defeated voice.

"Poor Cousin Annie," she told herself, and smiled so terribly that Melinda couldn't look at her. "I never wanted it to happen to you, child. If you thought sometimes I was starn . . ." She reached across the space between them and let her hand linger on the soft sable, stroking it, then hitting it with each word, to make herself clear. "Not that waiting . . ."

She took her hand away and went on staring at the bare trees. "Do you know what I brought here? I brought dash. Pa and I had lived in Richmond before he died. Aunt Mamie, that was Cousin Peregrine's ma, couldn't wait for me to come. I never loved a woman more. She was like my mother. I waited fifteen years."

Her voice sank almost to a whisper. "You don't know what it is to love a person and know you won't have a chance to live because they won't let you.

"Well, it was a long time before I realized that they were bored, and wanted to be entertained. That was all. They were amused by my dash. When time passed I didn't have it any more. That is what waiting does to a woman."

She was suddenly angry. "These people don't need us. They charm and use everybody who comes their way to entertain them. That's all they need, and they use their security and their charm to get it, make you love them, make you . . . love them, and they never know for a minute that they *have no right to do it.*"

Melinda knew that there was something more killing about this lancing of old despair than she had known herself. For the first time since she was a child, she was frozen in awe of Cousin Annie —not of her wrath, but of her stripped raw naked truth.

"They were kind. They gave you food and let you stay when

you didn't have any place to go and you could feel them withdrawing more and more into daily habit. You were just around. It was all so easy. I stayed fifteen years to entertain Cousin Peregrine's mother. They never dreamed that they were asking anything."

The hour with Johnny, the overpowering of death, and now these bitter words she could not stop made Melinda docile with sorrow. She watched a snowflake on her fur, tiny perfect crystal, melt to nothing. There was no energy left in her. She suspected for the first time in her life that she had stopped fighting, and that all her life's reason was slipping, melting from her body. Her strength, that Johnny had called arrogance, was no longer in her, only dead courage to resolve at least, as he had, to do her duty. She wondered if this was what was called defeat, the weight of her world, all the unthinking demands and blood relationships on her shoulders.

That hand was at her lap, patting the fur to get her attention. Cousin Annie had been speaking again. Now she had to listen. ". . . even her piety was an entertainment to pass the time. I let it happen because they bound me with just enough love . . . they were too satisfied. When Cousin Peregrine went downriver and got himself a wife he didn't even know, they didn't tell me, just let me find out. You thought I didn't know. You only saw me losing my teeth and you thought I didn't know what was happening to me. . . ."

She sighed. "When Mr. Neill died of the cholera, and thirty of their people died, who took the burden? Cousin Annie. It was a dreadful time. . . .

"I don't care any more. . . ." Her remarks came now only at the top of her thoughts. Melinda could no longer follow what she said—whether it was about her, or herself, or the old lady she seemed still to dwell on.

"Innocent . . ." she said once, and, "at least you've larned decorum and are genteel. *I* taught you that. . . ." Later she murmured, "She didn't know what she was doing. She never thought . . . horrible . . ."

At last she was quiet, and then she sighed once, deeply, and smiled. "Ah! The satisfied are unjust," she told the girl, or herself, or the bare trees.

But when Sara came to the observatory door and called Cousin Annie to see to the dinner and count how many there would be, she almost upset her chair, jumping up so fast to go and help.

Out the window from the bed she had slept in as a girl Melinda watched the full moon climb until it was remote and white in the night sky. The room was so full of its pale light that she could make out the crack on the ceiling above her where the bird swooped. Beside her Crawford slept, as he always did, quietly and deeply, his back to her.

She had prayed to sleep, but the closeness of Johnny in the next room was heartbreaking in the night. Her senses extended with fatigue. Long after she had seen the light stop staining the floor from the space under his closed door, she heard him walking. He sat down several times, as if he were trying to go to bed; once he walked toward his window and must have looked out for a long time. Later, in his bed, she could hear him turning and turning. She lay still. Far away the parlor clock whispered three.

At last he stopped and she knew he was asleep. She longed to go and look at him, just once, just once to remember, but she didn't dare. The house creaked and settled. There was not a sound.

The clock struck four.

The longing, the power of his nearness made her breathe faintly so she would sense him awake again. Time and the night finally blotted out.

Melinda, slung suspended just under waking, found herself standing, barefooted, beside her bed. She looked back once at Crawford. It was cold.

She opened Johnny's door so slowly to keep it from groaning that she thought it would never be opened enough to let her in. He lay, eyes closed, his bed rumpled from his restless tossing, now still. She wanted with her whole yearning to straighten the quilt, not wake him, just comfort that much, but she turned away after her watch, hopeless, and tiptoed toward the door again.

"Linda," she heard him whisper, as if he were dreaming, or couldn't believe she was there. She stopped still and shook her hands and let them drop.

"Linda."

She rushed back and was half kneeling beside him, whispering, "Yes," and "Yes" again. Her body was against his, and she was crying. "Don't make me go away anymore, Johnny. Please don't send me away. Please, Johnny."

"Little sweetheart," he soothed her, "I wouldn't. If it was mine to say."

"I wasn't going to ask again. I wasn't." She curled up, safe, against his chest and legs. "I wasn't. I only couldn't keep from coming to look at you."

She was quiet at last, and in his arms. His body grew closer to her. She pulled him over her. He whispered, "Please. Oh, God, please . . ."

After the longing they hardly needed to move.

Someone was walking in the hall. There was a knock. The peace and quiet, the whole relief of years turned ugly and frozen with fear. Johnny covered Melinda and kissed her eyes and opened the door, blocking it with his body. He went out into the hall.

"Johnny, I'm a little afraid in the night," Melinda heard Leah say. "I thought I heard somebody moving about."

"Mother, go back to bed. It's nothing . . ."

"I could swear. I had this feeling . . ."

That was the way Leah would always be, vigilant, commanding, pacing the house on the winter nights, watching, checking, owning. She seemed to see Leah again in the girls' room, rushing in with that light demanding run to catch them with their novels, their secrets, their hidden souls, which nobody had a right to keep to themselves. Melinda was lost in the defeat of it.

"Mother, go on back to bed. It's too cold for you."

Leah wandered away to her own room and looked behind her to reassure herself that Johnny was still standing there and she was safe.

"There was somebody," Melinda heard her say as she went back across the hall into her room. "I can always tell."

When Johnny came back to his bed Melinda was gone. She and Crawford left the next morning before the will-reading. Johnny stood watching the carriage from the porch, unable to believe it or to move. She paused only once, on the carriage steps, and looked back. Then she put her head down and got into the carriage and was gone.

Crawford was relieved to go, and surprised at Melinda's quietness, after she had waked him sobbing in the night, her feet as cold as ice so that he had to move away from her to keep from freezing. She didn't even look back at Beulah, but laid her head against the cushion they held for her and went at once into a sleep so deep he couldn't wake her at the first halt.

There was little to do in November when the authority to put the field-hands to work was changing. They were forgotten except by the young master, who came into every cabin on the day after the old master's funeral and remembered, after seven years, to call all of them by name. They had seen him in the family bench the day before and, having done their mourning duty, a low expected moan that swept among them like the groan of trees in wind when the old master was carried underground into the family vault, they trudged back to the quarters, herding the children. The old women said among themselves that Marse Johnny looked ha'nted by something and as if he hadn't eaten as well as they did. "Death written on his brow," Aunt Tilly, the oldest, said.

But that day there was death everywhere; it could be smelled in the air and read in the dry rustling cornstalks, in the dead leaves and in the shivers under their winter smocks like someone stepping on their graves. They talked about the vault. One of the boys had been near enough to the stone steps going into the ground when Marse Peregrine's coffin was carried down to peer in and see two stone shelves like a smokehouse, waiting. He said he could just make out the old lady's coffin and Marse Peregrine's father's. They remembered Telemachus telling them how his coffin was moved from the old hill graveyard in the middle of the night by lantern light, so the children wouldn't be scared, to lie beside his wife. He said there wasn't a thing left of him but hair and bones and a part of a red cravat. The rest was dust and rags. A root had grown around his thighbone and had to be sawed away.

They were quiet with awe, even when Johnny came to see them

all. He wandered up to the long double row of cabins, seeing in the distance how they came slowly to their doors and leaned with that elaborate casualness of the Negro body waiting, taught to wait, for decision, staring at him with their sad alien eyes, as if he were disturbing some secret world of their own. Johnny liked the field-hands and the workmen. They had about them a dignity that no indignity could touch, unlike the house servants who, in too close contact with the family, played "nigger" sometimes for attention and approval, like children. He wondered if they, too, even as close as bed and table, had a secret life where they kept their dignity, a world he could not penetrate and could only dimly sense. He understood why the women, haters of the natural, the secretive, the unknown, were afraid of the Negroes. Even as he strolled, coming nearer and seeing more and more quiet men come to stand in their doors, or squat in the dirt yards as if they had not seen him, he remembered the glimpse into that secrecy that helped them to survive which Tig had given him. He felt hot with sorrow and yearning to make up to them for what he had done, to care for them.

A huge black man named Withrow, a nigger-driver who had belonged to a man named Withrow downriver and had been transferred to Johnny's father in payment of a debt, walked forward from his cabin, smiling just enough to warm his face. As if they had waited for someone to move first, the other men came out and surrounded him, the women hanging back except for old Aunt Tilly, who with the privilege of the old pushed the men aside and thrust her gnarled face close to study him; all that was left of her seemed to be distilled defiance in her tiny spindled graying frame. She had been the hands' midwife for many years, and could cure with herbs. She was believed to be able to judge the value, if times were good, of a male baby at two days old, like the men could judge a litter of pigs by the strength of their suckling. She shook her finger up at him and said, "Marse Johnny, you been drinkin licker. It got worms in it, eat your stummick."

The men tittered with infinite politeness at her uppity ways.

Coming back down the hill, calculating how few able-bodied men there seemed to be left to run the huge place, Johnny realized again the warmth of the race, how quiet they had been out of deference to his father's memory, their sorrow of the day before, the pall of grief that hung about the cabins.

It was the grief that comes of fear. The master was dead; that white horseman who swooped down on them in the fields, who held decision like the horsewhip he carried, never using it, the final man, not human, like people they worked beside, slept with, quarreled with, danced with, ate with, buried, but a man beyond any contact but admiration and fear. When the unapproachable man died, a new unapproachable man, or men, took his place. His dying could shake them like corn in a can to spew them out, rearrange, sell as he had sold before, give away. They couldn't know him. He joked with them at Christmas and called them by their names when he laid down the law or told them it was time to marry. That didn't bother the men any. If the woman didn't produce children they didn't have to stay married. They considered that they had more freedom than the house servants, who ate better and drove good horses. At least they didn't have to be on hand all the time, and could draw their own shadows instead of being someone else's. But the women were drab with envy when they saw the favorites, prettier or brighter, taken to the Mansion to be trained and perhaps really married in a white dress with a cake, prancing by, high-stepping, looking down on them, even sometimes going away from Beulah, to some place they couldn't fathom; most of them had never been beyond Beulah's surrounding hills.

So the old women sat together, not like the ladies at the Mansion thinking of the past and the personality of the man, but thinking and talking a little of how much they were worth in dollars and whom they would belong to. The day for them was not the day of death but of disposition. They stood in the cabin doors, talked low in little groups, waiting like prisoners for a verdict, for the reading of the will, wondering over and over how they would be split four ways.

On the morning after Johnny's visit one of the children saw a black-coated stranger they knew was Lawyer Carver drive up to the Mansion in a one-horse shay, and ran to tell his mammy. He knew what a lawyer was. There was one in the Bible Miss Sara made him read. He could recite, "Woe unto ye also, ye lawyers! For ye lade men with burdens grievous to be borne. . . ." He had heard talk permeating the quarters of lawyer and will. He knew what will was too, but he could not remember. He was scared.

Gradually a few of the men moved closer to the Mansion, then the women, until, when the family gathered in the library, they were pressed against the windows to listen, and hearing nothing through the thick glass, faltered into the forbidden hall where the house servants were huddled in their own frightened knot. Only the old people had ever heard a will before, but they all knew what the piece of thick paper they could see in the lawyer's hand could do to them.

Miss Leah looked up once and saw them through the black mist of her heavy mourning veil, but was too intent or dazed to send anyone away. She even tried to smile sadly at Aunt Tilly, who had forced herself to the front and stood chomping her toothless gums nervously, wearing the old bonnet that Leah had worn to Beulah as a bride. It was as if Leah, too, were at the mercy of the dead man's will, as she had been in his life. Aunt Tilly understood the smile, and nodded, but Leah had already bent her head and was gazing at her hands in her black silk lap, rubbing, rubbing at the ruby. She put her hand on Johnny's sleeve to touch him and reassure herself and left her hand there as she had through the funeral, holding so tightly that her knuckles showed white without realizing she was doing it. The only relief to her black clothes was the ruby; now even that seemed dull in the gray morning light of the library.

"I, Peregrine Catlett, of the county of Fincastle in the state of Virginia, being very sick and weak in body, but of perfect mind and memory . . ."

Minna pushed her way through the huddle of house servants, trying to get away from the dry voice and the words that were like him speaking. Her eyes were blinded with tears and she couldn't find a way, so she stood there with her back to the door, trying to shut out the voice.

". . . first of all I give and recommend my soul into the hands of Almighty God who gave it, and my body I recommend to the earth, nothing doubting that I shall receive the same again at the General Resurrection."

"Firstly I give and bequeath to my beloved wife, Leah, my whole real estate comprising the farm of Beulah to be used by her during her natural life, and after her death I devize and bequeath that my estate be divided in the following manner."

Not understanding the words before, the Negroes in the hall stirred at the word "divided." Johnny looked up and so did Lewis, who made a move to shut the door, but Johnny motioned him back.

"Whereas the conduct of my son, Lewis Catlett, has been in constant opposition to that which he owed himself and the society into which he was born, and has persisted in direct violation of friendly warnings and paternal counsels, virtuous admonitions, and fatherly care, and whereas he continues in the name of religion to disseminate sentiments derogatory and dangerous to our institutions, and whereas he is already in possession of the two-hundred-acre tract known as the orchard farm, I give and bequeath, after the demise of my wife, one third of the real property remaining to his children in trust, one third of said share for the use of his wife, Sara, should she survive him, out of love to the children he may leave and in friendship to him as well as to be a lesson to all prodigal disobedient sons, and a dutiful precedent to all afflicted and offended fathers, with this last warning. That if he persist in the downward traitorous course he has taken in violation of his family wishes, he confine his activities to those places beyond the borders of Beulah, so as to be out of the offended sight of his mother."

Leah saw the tears spurt from Lewis's eyes. So did Sara, but he shook her hand away and blundered out of the library door into the dining room. The only sound in the room was the memory of the slammed door. Lawyer Carver cleared his throat and coughed. He began again in a low, embarrassed voice that some of the Negroes in the hall couldn't hear. They shuffled forward, whispering to one another to hush.

"And whereas the conduct of my second son, Jonathan, has been in direct violation of his parents' wishes and has offended against the command of God to honor his father and his mother, it is my wish that he return at once from Missouri in order to take up his responsibilities at Beulah which it has pleased Almighty God to lay upon his shoulders because of his brother's attitude toward our people. If he heeds my wishes and returns to Beulah, I hereby give and bequeath to him at his mother's death, one third of the real property of Beulah, the remaining third I give and bequeath at her mother's death to my daughter Lydia, in the pious hope that she will marry someone who is capable of understanding her sacred charge, and of cooperating with her brother Jonathan in keeping Beulah intact as a working property. These admonitions for my children I have set down here in love and fatherly duty trusting in an Almighty and Merciful God that they in turn shall recognize their duty.

"It is my will and desire that all personal property remain on the land as at present in charge of my son Jonathan, and at his mother's death that the Negroes and all other personal property and chattels be divided between himself and his sister Lydia, without share for Lewis or for his issue. It is my desire that my son Jonathan and my daughter Lydia pay in trust to his wife Sara, and after her death to his children the appraised value of one third of the Negroes as their fair share without subjecting them to parental pressure as to the actual ownership of said Negroes, in understanding of the pernicious influence to which they will have been subjected and in fairness to the Negroes, with the following exceptions.

"First, that Fielding, the son of Louisa, be hired out during the rest of the natural life of my cousin, Ann Brandon Neill, she being without funds and in a low state of health and without dependable support, the proceeds to be hers as income without let or hindrance.

"Second, that Solomon, the son of Winney, be hired out during the rest of the natural life of my cousin, Sally Lacey, she being without funds and in a low state of health and without dependable support, the proceeds to be hers without let or hindrance."

Sally put her face in her handkerchief and began to sob. When Sara tiptoed over to her and held her, she muttered, "The dear man, my stars. Everybody was sorry for me but nobody ever left me any money before," and went on muttering, not able to stop, so low that no one heard what she said.

By the time the family had heard the last formal paragraph of the will and were beginning to move slowly, saying nothing, inside the library, the slaves had faltered out of the hall and were wandering in a long ragged line back toward the cabins. Only Lucy Ann, a tall erect ugly Negress who had been married to Fielding after the writing of Peregrine's will, walked beside Fielding, neither of them saying a word, avoided by the others in their trouble.

Cousin Annie still sat straight in her chair, staring at Leah, who had thrown back her veil. Leah came toward her, firmer in step, bigger than she had ever seen her before.

"Annie," she said, "Mr. Catlett was a fine man to think of such a thing. I hope that with your bitter tongue you appreciate what he has done." She turned to Johnny, not noticing that the lash of his dead father had left his face still white.

"Though how I'm going to manage without two prime hands, I don't know. Johnny, your father was a sentimental man."

He could see that she was angry, even after she owned the whole of Beulah she was angry, and he wanted to turn away.

"Johnny, would you see that the matched grays are sold or traded for driving mules as soon as possible? I have always had a particular terror of those horses." She turned and marched out of the room, pulling down her veil again as she left, but she went toward the dining room.

When Sara got her mother to bed and came down to see to the dinner and a chamber for Lawyer Carver, Leah was still in the dining room with Lewis.

She heard him say in a low voice as she came to the door, "Ma, why did Pa hate me so? Why?

She saw Leah reach out and touch his clenched fist on the lace cloth. "I don't know, son. I don't know. You were more like my blessed father . . . God rest his soul."

Sara had never heard Leah mention her father before. She turned without disturbing them.

"I made over every penny to Mr. Catlett, Lewis. It was expected of me," she heard Leah say sharply in answer to an unheard question.

Down by the rose-garden gate, Dan Neill waited, hidden from the house by the thick matted honeysuckle fence. The house, for what seemed hours, was as still as the recent death. At last he saw the slaves come out, and read by their walk, relieved, that there had been no division. He felt a stab of annoyance.

When he saw Lydia run across the lawn and circle the honeysuckle fence with the light nervous little leaps she thought so sweet and childish because her father had kept her doing it, he almost hated her. Her face had gone so drawn in the last two days, he could see how drab she would be in time.

She put her hands up to his face, questioning whether he would kiss her or not, a flicker of fright in her eyes.

He waited.

"Oh, Mr. Neill, my beloved Pa didn't say no. Anyway he didn't say no, as we feared."

"My darling little girl," Dan Neill said and put his arms around her and let her kiss him.

Johnny had had to drag his mind again and again to what was happening in the library, back from the dead weight of his despair, his father's last lash, given in the only kind of love he knew—imperial love, demanding—and his other loss. He trudged through the bare honeysuckle tendrils, which caught at his coat, and only looked up from watching the hard ground in time to see Lydia in Dan Neill's arms as if she had flown, birdlike, from one protection to another.

Instinctively, he livened with anger, felt a surge of whipping words, then stopped. He hardly realized that he had gone not toward them, but away, back toward the house. Who am I? Who in God's name am I to interfere? he asked himself. There's been enough of that. Let be.

He was surprised at his own lightness, suddenly, as if the sun had come out of the gray sky, and even looked up to see if it had.

Lydia and Dan neither saw nor heard him.

Chapter Four

ON SUNDAY, October 16, 1859, it rained at Harpers Ferry, Virginia, so that after the Sunday night protracted meeting, people scudded into warmth and shut their doors. No one but the watchman at the arsenal saw John Brown and his small band of men ride into the dark drenched town.

On Monday, the first rumor of the raid got to Beulah that the Negroes had risen in northern Virginia and that an abolitionist army had invaded Harpers Ferry. Leah remembered that all Sunday she'd had a feeling; she looked back on it and was certain that she had smelled danger. Every fear she'd ever had was pushed to the surface of her mind. Leah felt set upon from all sides. Even Cousin Annie knocked on doors and flung them open, avoided unlit places in the hall, though she said nothing could frighten her. Shadows from the lamplight jumped, played with Leah's fear-blinded eyes.

It was strange how at such a time normal, unimportant things went on. She stood stock-still in the hall, on the sunny Thursday morning, with Cousin Crawford's letter in her hand. Through the glass of the door she could see her Johnny talking to a group of men. Thank God at least it was daylight, a beautiful October day, as if nothing had happened. October—when the hay was dry and racked, when the corn could burn. She could smell fire for a second, see it lick eating the banisters, and shook herself free of such thoughts because Johnny had told her, Johnny had sworn that there was nothing to be afraid of, and that it was the duty of the women not to spread alarm and despondency.

Not to spread fear, as if it could be helped, this infection, this opening of an abyss before your safe feet. She sensed it all around her, except from those two old gabbling fools in the drawing room; if she'd heard it once she'd heard it twenty times in the last three days. "*Nothing* to Nat Turner. *You* should have been in Virginia in those days." Leah really felt as if she, who owned it all, had no place to go in her own house.

It was Thursday and nothing had happened yet. Only four days after the horrible news had filtered upriver, and the whole farm was tense with men. Why did men face all their problems in quiet groups, some standing on the edge of the porch, some gathered around the door of the office Johnny had built for himself in the garden? They stood waiting, talking and waiting, just like men, not really knowing what to do. Leah set her teeth, and then relaxed, dreaming of Johnny. Trouble gathered men to him more than she could ever remember in Beulah, and he, patient—she could see him, patient and cool like his father—tried to pour oil on their troubled minds.

At least she didn't have to worry him with the letter. At least she could do that for her boy.

Leah wandered into the parlor and sat in the half-dark with her head in her hands, trying to think what she had to do. Outside she could hear the patrol ride up and stop, and strained to listen for news. Everything was being kept from her, she was sure of that. She jumped up, panicked, and raised the front window enough to hear them. One of the men who had just dismounted switched around when he heard the window open.

Leah had to smile grimly as she stepped back so they wouldn't see her and stop talking. They were just as scared as she was. She could see that.

She could hear one of the men almost yelling. She thought it was Kelly. "Downriver they're half crazy. They ain't a nigger safe nowheres at night, don't care who he belongs to. My God, Johnny, you cain't trust nobody at a time like this. I hyar they got a whole damn abolition army ready in Pinnsylvainy—"

"Don't nobody have to look as far as Pinnsylvainy," somebody she didn't know interrupted.

She heard Johnny beginning to calm them. "Now listen, Kelly, there ain't a man living but old Brown would have carried this off. Our job I reckon is to scotch rumors. Don't add fuel to the fire. The latest news I've heard is that not a nigger joined him."

"Governor Wise says—"

"Hell and damnation to Governor Wise. He's making political capital," somebody yelled.

"They do say they's five hundred abolitionists on the Ohio River makin ready to come right up the Kanawha and burn everthing in sight and let free the niggers—"

"They been ready for years. I hyared they found a whole basement full of pikes and rifles downriver." She couldn't tell who that was.

"Did anybody see these things?" Johnny questioned.

"No, Cap'n Johnny, but I got it from an unimpeachable source." That was that damn fool Maury Carver, always putting on to talk big.

She noticed Dan Neill still hadn't turned up.

Captain Johnny. Leah was proud. The militia had elected him captain because he'd been in Kansas and knew all about Brown. Johnny told her about Osawatomie Brown the crazy man, who everybody said had eaten human flesh in Kansas. Johnny said nobody would listen to a madman. He said madmen sprang up from time to time and had to be cut down like mad dogs. He said he'd seen John Brown in Kansas and that he was . . .

"Listen here, Cap'n Johnny. We ain't gittin the turnout for muster downriver we ought to. They's plenty down there ain't no more with us than that thar brother of yourn."

Leah walked slowly back and sank into the chair again, too troubled in her soul to listen any more. She felt that the whole weight of the fear was on her own back, and she couldn't say a word. She was a young girl again, and with her father, watching the flames and listening to the speeches, seeing the stripes on beaten black backs exhibited by torchlight. She wasn't born in Ohio, anyhow. Her mother said she was born across the river in Kentucky, and the Cutwrights came from Virginia. Nobody could have shown her loyalty more. Nobody.

One of the men yelled and intruded his voice into the quiet parlor. "My God, Cap'n Johnny, I hyar tell they killed a hundred people at Harpers Ferry, armed them niggers with pikes, and they're loose all over the damn country up there."

Johnny interrupted, "Dammit. Spread the word around, Kelly, since you're so good at talking. We muster at four o'clock—everybody sober and no fighting."

The nights were horrible. She had known every creak as her house settled, every jar of a door. Now, all strange, they made her sit up in bed, shaking, afraid to take her eyes off the door, or lie there counting the hours as the patrol clopped by and made Beulah sound like an armed camp. Last night, finally, in troubled sleep, she had dreamed, and the dream came back to choke her. She had dreamed big Withrow got into her room and he was coming at her saying in that gentle voice he had for such a big brute of a man, "Ise sorry, Miss Leah. I got to. I got to." His big hands were up and his body was naked, naked and gleaming like a black panther in the moonlight. She was sure she was awake.

She had whispered, "Don't, Withrow, we never did you harm."

"I got to, Miss Leah. I got to." It was like a song, the huge man swooping down covering her with darkness, but it wasn't Withrow, it was Mr. Catlett, young as he'd once been. She had tried to scream and Johnny ran in not even touching the floor and floated over the darkness and wrestled it off, whatever it was, a huge catlike thing with stripes on its back.

Dear Johnny. The letter in her hand shook. She felt sick and knew the foretaste in her mouth and in her swimming eyes of one of her headaches. Remembering the dream had brought it on. She wanted desperately to sleep, but she had to concentrate.

Everything they had in the world was tied up at Beulah. That reminded her of the murmur of voices in the drawing room across the hall, which had once been the library until she just had to have it for a drawing room, and Johnny moved his father's old desk and table and his own law books out to the new office, even the old ugly tomahawk his father had used as a paperweight, and the silver-handled crop, no use any more, that showed they were well connected in England. What he'd wanted that battered junk for she couldn't imagine. The new drawing room was so pretty now, just as she'd always wanted it—if she could set foot in it ever without getting sick and tired of niggers and who they were kin to and how much they used to own in eastern Virginia before Mr. Catlett passeled them off with money that rightfully belonged to her. It still rankled, Fielding and Solomon hired out, worth their weight in gold. She had known many a time since '57 when the worst panic hit, when she, worth nearly a million dollars on the tax-books in land that wouldn't sell and salt that hardly fetched its shipping cost, and niggers that wouldn't work and had to be clothed, and stock that had to be fed—*she,* owing five hundred dollars to a Cincinnati merchant for nigger cloth alone, had not a dime in her pocket to send downriver for ribbon and not wishing any more credit, while Annie and Sally sat knitting and playing their incessant brag, putting by money, year after year. . . .

She could almost hear the voice of Mr. Catlett, and it made her smile. "Oh, honey, don't fuss. Let them play brag. They've little enough else, God knows. Lord God, Sally brags a relation, poor old Annie has to go it or bolt—only instead of one-eyed Jacks and nines they use pride and pretension."

"It is not Christian, Mr. Catlett," she had said.

"Lord, honey, what is?" She could still hear his light laugh. "Anyhow, my dear, you're as bad as they are. You Methodists take out your envy in moral judgments. Episcopalians envy by social judgments. Just more brag."

She didn't know anything about cards, of course, but it helped to think of it that way. She smiled at Mr. Catlett's voice, missing him now, feeling closer than ever to her memory of him, now that he could no longer surprise her image of him.

Any company was better than none. She stuffed the letter into her reticule and wondered at herself, putting things off like that. She knocked at the door of the drawing room, and the voices stopped.

It was Annie's turn to wind. Sally sat caught in the wool skein, obediently holding out her skinny little arms. Even the sight of the gray wool made Leah wince. They'd had the money to send downriver and pay for the small hill of gray which covered one of her brocade chairs. She'd had to buy hers, and even Johnny's uniform, which she ordered to surprise him all the way from Philadelphia, on credit till the salt agent came back from Cincinnati. She felt her forehead twinge. When the uniform was ready and they sewed on all the braid Johnny would stand for, to make it like the picture of the English Hussar at Balaklava they cut out of *Harper's* magazine to copy, Cousin Annie came in with an ostrich plume she'd saved all those years without telling a soul about it, often as Leah could have used it for Lydia, and stuck it in Johnny's hat with a big gesture. That fool Sally kept saying, "It's just like getting ready for a tournament; just like the tournaments when I was a girl," when Leah knew absolutely she hadn't set eyes on her first and only tournament until she was thirty-six years old exactly.

Already Sally and Cousin Annie had finished four pairs of gray socks for the Fincastle Greys.

When Cousin Annie saw who it was, she went on talking. "Sally, you just don't recollect. He was a third cousin of Crawford's on his mother's side."

"That's *my* side so I ought to know. I expect I recollect better than you do, Annie. After all I used to stay there long after you did."

"They had sterling silver doorknobs, and juleps in silver cups. . . ." Cousin Annie dreamed.

It was Sally's turn to move at brag, but instead she ignored Cousin Annie and turned to Leah brightly. "We have set a goal of socks for the whole company by the end of the week."

"You'll put out your eyes."

Sally's eyes were far from being put out. They flashed. "Perhaps, being an Ohio girl, *you* wouldn't know how important it was . . ."

Leah couldn't find a chair to sit down in. She was shaking so she had to grab the table. "There's nobody more loyal than I am, Sally. How dare you talk like that. I've got everything in the world to lose." Tears started in her eyes.

Cousin Annie saw them and said, "Never mind, Leah, I always say as Papa did, the farther west you get, the more people *care.*

They're more Virginia than we are." She smiled. "They have to be. That's what Papa said. Though he never dreamed his own daughter would end her days in western Virginia. In Richmond we never knew the western counties existed." She tapped her foot, because her hands were busy whirling the wool faster and faster.

Sally giggled.

Leah burst into tears and embarrassed them, for a minute, into silence.

"You don't know what it's like. *You* don't know." She fought her way, blinded, out of the room to lie down, ashamed that she had showed blood.

Inside the drawing room, Sally said sadly, "She never will get used to niggers. . . . My stars. *You* ain't really worried, are you, Annie?"

"About a passel of Yankee trash!" Cousin Annie snorted.

But when the outside door slammed they both jumped and avoided each other's eyes, trying to recognize the footsteps in the hall.

"It's Johnny," Cousin Annie said.

"I wish they'd bolt the door." Sally muttered in the way that made Cousin Annie realize, annoyed, that she was going to go on for a while talking to herself. Cousin Annie went on winding the gray wool. Even that gadfly chatter was better than being alone.

Leah couldn't sleep. Pain began to stab at her head. She found her reticule and, delving in it for laudanum, couldn't find that, but found the letter instead. She wandered down to the drawing room, her cap crooked from lying on the bed.

"Cousin Annie." She put her head around the door. *"You* always have laudanum. I so seldom indulge in it I have none. Could you lend me some for a headache?"

Cousin Annie set the huge ball of wool down, careful with anger. She handed Leah a bottle from her pocket.

"I'll fetch it back quickly. I know you don't like to be without it," Leah said sweetly. She was gone before Cousin Annie could say, "Your cap's on crooked."

There was only the closed door to speak to. *"Fetch! Fetch* and *egg* money, instead of *tote* and *pin* money, and she's larning my grandchildren to talk that way." She snatched up the wool again.

Sally Lacey, her awkward ally in the house she was made to feel a stranger in so often since Cousin Peregrine's death, shook her head sadly, her thin pale curls bobbing. "Annie, we can keep up the standard at least. Remember who we are."

But agreeing was far from appeasing Cousin Annie. She wound silently, pulling so hard she hurt Sally's arms. "When are you going to be your age and wear a cap over that fool hair of yours?" she stabbed. Leah's cap had reminded her.

They wound on in silence. Sally glanced at the window and saw that the men had gone. "I just wonder," she said to herself secretly.

The tone made Cousin Annie question, as she knew it would. "You just wonder what?"

"Who Cousin Leah's letter was from."

"Probably from Pocahontas. She's descended from Pocahontas."

Sally giggled. "Oh my stars!" Then she stopped. "I *really* am, you know, Annie, through the Brandons."

"That's only a connection. After all, I'm a blood relation . . ."

They had begun to play brag again, family nines and one-eyed Jacks.

Leah paced up and down her chamber, tapping the letter against her skirt. She looked around at last at the closed door, then at the bed Mr. Catlett and his mother had both died in. Then painfully, because of her joints, she knelt down and looked under the bed to assure herself there was no one there.

Finally she sat down at her writing-table and opened the troublesome letter to read it again.

"Dear Cousin Leah." Crawford was always such a polite man. Leah was pleased again when she saw how he addressed her.

> I have kept from you the news of our misfortune at my dear Melinda's request. She is taken very sick. I have traveled with her to Baden to the waters. We have tried several of the spas nearer to you, but for some reason a manifestation of her illness was that she did not wish to return to Beulah. Now her mind wanders there and I fear it is almost too late.
>
> I am writing to you because you have been, of all, most nearly

her mother. It began, I realize now, soon after we left Beulah after the passing over of my beloved cousin, Mr. Catlett, God rest his soul. Melinda slept in the carriage going across the mountains. I thought it was fatigue of the mind after her foster father's death. We rested a while at Egeria. She seemed more docile and settled in her spirits than I have ever known her, and talked, as she seemed to convalesce, more of religion and duty than she had ever done before. I thought it a great miracle. She prayed much and seemed sustained by prayer.

A few months after we returned to Kregg's Crossing there was a relapse. She was with child. I took her abroad. Again this drowsiness, which seemed to be a sign of the illness, overcame her. She fell off in weight and by evening her temperature rose. She took no interest in her former activities. After the child was born, our second daughter, as you know, one of the manifestations of her illness was that she refused to be near it. I wish you to know that every physician who could help her has been consulted. Even with the serious financial crisis in Virginia I have spared no expense. Nobody but one physician could name a cause except for a malaise of spirit, affecting her heart.

Leah put the letter down, annoyed. She knew that was nonsense. Leah told herself it wasn't that she didn't worry about the child and feel affection for her as she always had, but she really had done enough for the girl, and now, with everything exploding all around her . . .

She thought again of Johnny. It was always Johnny she dwelt on, neither Lydia nor Lewis entered her mind much any more, and, realizing it, she felt ashamed, but after all she didn't have them. She had Johnny, more dependable than either of the others leading their own more selfish lives. If ever a man had made up to his family for youthful selfishness and prodigality, Johnny had. She did worry about him sometimes. He took his duty so seriously and seemed more silent than ever. Sometimes she could see the light in his office burning until late at night and when she went across the lawn to tell him it was late and time for bed, pleased to do it since she felt that he was her only charge left, she would find him with his head on his desk and the account books piled high around him or his law books scattered over the floor. He rested that way, but he was never asleep. She knew he wasn't drinking. She'd looked for a bottle and never had found one. She tapped the letter on the table and thought. If the times weren't so ominous she might consider asking one of the young girl cousins from Cincinnati to cheer him up. After all, Johnny had told her that there was no real danger. She knew her Cousin Amelia would appreciate a stay in the country. The poor girl had had to become a teacher after her father's death. It was the only respectable thing she could do. Besides it would be entertainment for her to have one of her own people for a while to talk to. She was sick of listening to East Virginia, East Virginia, East Virginia. Once she had been proud of being connected, as Cousin Annie said, to all the first families in East Virginia, but she was tired, bone-tired of being reminded that being connected wasn't quite being family. More and more often since Mr. Catlett had passed on, her girlhood had rushed back at her, the intellectual pleasures, the music, the talk of things instead of people. She was, after all, from a city, where you could buy a tract without having to wait for a peddler.

She made herself finish the letter.

> She has spoken lately for the first time in three years of visiting Beulah. It seems to be all that cheers her. I have tried so many things, but I cannot reach her, although she appreciates it and tries to please. She could not stand the six-day journey across the mountains, but I thought of coming by water down the James and around the Gulf, up the Mississippi. The sea voyage would cheer her, knowing she was coming home.

The rest of the letter was news of the politics, intended for Dan and Johnny. Leah thought of Johnny's work and his peace being destroyed. Melinda always had a secretive way with him she hated, and was sure was a bad influence on him. Besides, he was the one anchor she needed in a storm of worries. Leah knew, hard as it was, what her duty had to be. With all her trouble, she couldn't stand any more of them, couldn't stand it. She tore the letter across once and then precisely across again.

She made herself, even with a headache untouched by the laudanum, write two letters. One was an affectionate letter to Crawford and Melinda, wishing a return of health but pointing out, since the trouble at Harpers Ferry, the unwiseness of coming so near the border at the present time. Something stirred so deeply in her, telling her she was doing the right thing, that she excused herself for putting her worry on paper, when Johnny had told her not to.

The other letter went to Cincinnati. She pointed out that, in view of the present trouble, she would be more than pleased if one of her own people would come and see for herself that affairs were not so dreadful in Virginia as they were painted.

She called Minna to take the letters to the afternoon stage, and, duty done, lay down at last to surrender to her headache. But she still could not sleep. A rooster crowed at midafternoon, a terrible omen.

Johnny sat in his office watching down through the trees to the creek. Now that some of the leaves had fallen, he could see the barn clearly, and down-creek from it where the great stump of the old sycamore tree still jutted into the water and made the swimming-hole, with its water-cleaned dead roots.

Beyond it he could see the hills upriver from Beulah, now yellow and red in October. That firelike beauty in another time would not have permeated the air itself with terror, like a forest fire that could spurt from one mind to another as fire in the wind leaps from treetop to treetop. He remembered once that lightning had struck in the hills and how they fought, the boys, the men from downriver, and the Negroes, to trench and cut until they isolated it. His father had had a bullock killed and cleaved. They had dragged its half-carcass thick with blood across the fire-break. He wondered then how many bloody carcasses would have to be dragged to stop the new fire. The recurring thought of fire made him glance at the full barn again, remembering with some pride the fine harvest, now ready, not for the winter feeding, but for the furtive night-torch, hatred-driven, lit by Brown. Downriver on patrol he had seen a haystack flare up and pierce the black sky with its wild light. It was only boys, catching the fear and turning it into action as boys did. They had cantered up, expecting Ohio fanatics or wild Negroes, and found the two scared boys, hiding, horrified but excited at what they had done.

He picked up the old tomahawk his father had kept on the desk and, only half looking at it, traced its eagle design with his finger, now dreaming and, for the moment, at peace to consider what he should do. There was something he missed somewhere along the way, some time of decision; he searched back in his mind for it like a lost thing, a lost moment, but he could not find it. He saw again in his mind's eye Charles McAndrews' hand, crushed, but found no answer for himself. Instinct had driven him back to Beulah like an animal as soon as he sensed that he was needed. Instinct and sense, love and need—those had been taught and demanded; action he had learned in Kansas. These were all he had. Now, watching the yellow and red hills from the vantage point of his office window, his mind clicked as his eyes turned down the slopes of Beulah to where the harvested farm rolled out, and the inn, now deserted, with no one to run it, seemed to sink abandoned into the ground. Beyond it, he could see light smoke of what salt he could boil, with the slaves he could spare; now to the Irish cabins, where he had moved two of the Negro families, and on downriver, seeing only the empty road where the patrol had gone.

Usually at such a time, and at night when he could escape from the nervous cribbage the ladies played without running the gamut of their disappointment and affection, they having waited all day for him, he found peace and sanctuary in his office. He had moved the memory of his father there, his desk, his books, the round scarred table and his lamp, the few objects left of his life. In the Mansion nothing was left of the man. The sweeping-out, which had begun at his death, was complete. It was permeated to its corners with the voices, the movements, the activities of women. It had taken sixty-two years for Peregrine Catlett to die; it had taken a year for the women, with that power of survival he did not see in men, to kill his memory and his influence after his death. Having never quite caught him, they made images of what he could have been to them, and Johnny listened at the dinner table, to these images that were not the man, to the sweet sentiments over cards. He wondered if the gulf were too great to cross from responsibility to innocence, from honesty to the perpetual attrition of affectionate good manners.

Now the upriver wind that shook the gold oaks in the garden brought violence, even to them, and he was afraid suddenly, and realized with a start that he had dreamed, not thinking of the crisis for too long. How it had come, fed by small decisions and fears as deep as the taproots of the trees, to Beulah he could, for the moment, see, but only as through a glass darkly. He was afraid, not for himself, but for the inability to speak clearly enough in a strong enough voice, to stop it. He wondered if, outside of the easy-going farm days and the splitting of a man's mind into infinite small decisions, as a flint breaks, there were any place on earth where men were taught to think instead of being taught to love and feel and decide blindly under the pressure of dependence and events.

It was easy to call it the will of God. Two madmen had called it that. Twice in his lifetime men in Virginia had tried to think. The first time he could hear his father tell how they had conferred over the black pall that sucked Virginia's blood. That time Nat Turner, the crazy nigger, had set the fires of violence and killing that made the mind shrink in fear until men could not think but only react. They had lost their last chance to abolish slavery in Virginia. Now this man, this other man who said he was ordered by God, had waked the old nightmare just after men had gone to the polls and elected a governor who had struck the chord of balance they needed to set the western counties at least free. Perhaps they were right and it was the will of God, Lewis's God, blood-drinker, and he, impotent with anger and sorrow, caught up in this will and not knowing, alone there in his dusty office, what in the name of a more merciful God to do.

He could hear a skirt swishing close to the office door, and he held his breath and prayed against a timid demanding knock, but it was only Cousin Annie, busy on one of her interminable attempts to make herself useful, going down to the chicken-yard by the creek to gather eggs.

At the moment, pushed as he was, if he could have had two wishes, not even these would have been great ones—only that there be someone to talk to, and the freedom of a shut door he could trust, but there was only one person in all his life to whom he had done, not the violence of desire or the blackmail of care, but that thing people called opening the heart, only one with whom he had gone beyond the armor of politeness and aloofness he had been taught was the protection and duty of a man, and she was gone.

Some nights, sitting there not sleeping, trying to read, but drifting into that waiting he tried to guard against, time suspended, he would be jarred with hope at the opening of the door, that time had not taken so much, and that it was Melinda, bright brave tongue and laughter. But it would be his mother, bringing her worried awareness of him in her face, as if she half expected him each time to be gone again, flown like a grouse into the safety of freedom. When she did, flirting like a girl with him to make him "look after himself," the night settled heavily around him again and he would rouse awake, to the time of his life, and realize that he was tired enough for bed again.

So by the day he sat, watching the creek, his arms flung across a desk filled more and more with duty. If he had prayed, it would not even have been that Melinda come back; that had deadened from a piercing wish to a dull heavy hope that made him know sometimes that it would not be such a weight if she were dead and he released from hope altogether. No, the prayer would have been simply that no one, for one more hour, knock on his door and rouse him to decision.

His prayer was not answered. The knock was loud; he knew at once that it was big Withrow, whose great hand could not knock gently.

"Come in, Withrow," he called.

The Negro opened the door tentatively, trying as always to figure out how Marse Johnny knew it was him.

"Marse Johnny." That soft voice, worried, roused him to listen.

"What is it, Withrow?" He did not know the sound of his own irritation.

"Aunt Tilly gone die tonight."

"I'll be up there presently."

"Want me to sind somebody to dig her grave?"

"Good God no, Withrow." Johnny laughed. "Aunt Tilly's died four times in the last year. She'll be madder'n hell if she hears we dug her a grave."

"She wanted us to make her a coffin." Withrow grinned with him.

"Oh, she wanted to boss that and keep it to look at."

He waited for Withrow to go, but the man stood still, flatfooted and sullen with some worry he hadn't yet voiced. Johnny knew him too well to prod him. He waited, as usual, patient and aware.

"Marse Johnny," the Negro mumbled at last.

"All right, Withrow, what is it?" Johnny stared at the tomahawk, still waiting.

"Fielding done run away to Canady."

"Hell, Withrow, Fielding don't even know where Canady is. What are you trying to tell me?"

"He done run off last night from the warehouse, two o'clock in the mornin, downriver."

"Did he get away?"

"Yessir."

"Thank God for that," Johnny said fervently. "I was afeard some fool patrol had shot the poor nigger."

Withrow sank down on his heels when he saw how Marse Johnny had taken the news. "He warn't nothin but a fool, Marse Johnny. They ain't a free nigger safe nowheres, right now. He jest got the itch that's in the air."

"Why did you wait to tell me until now?"

Withrow stood up politely and his face went blank and secret. "Lord, Marse Johnny. I come as soon as I hyared."

Johnny knew there was no use asking more, and that Fielding was in Ohio by now to fend for himself. By their telegraph of the spirit they knew more than he would ever know; surrounded by their dark silence, and at such a time, he could not send after Fielding. The only thought he had was how to break the news to Cousin Annie.

But Withrow had brought him something more. He had told Johnny why no one would run away from the farm and only Fielding, unwatched, sleeping on the empty warehouse floor, would go.

There wasn't a free nigger safe in Virginia—not on the roads, not at night. What fear they knew that was not his blew and feathered in Withrow's secret eyes.

They both heard the quick trot and turned to look downriver, as everyone at Beulah did by habit when he heard the sound of someone coming in from outside.

It was Dan Neill in his smart shay, sitting straight in the seat with his stovepipe hat shining in the fall sun, letting a little boy in his proud lap hold the reins of his best trotter. He did not turn in and tie up at the Mansion gate, but brought the trotter straight around the road and up the back creek path as near the office as he could. They could see him jump out and lift the boy down. He turned and tied the chestnut gelding that was his other pride to the hitching post where Johnny's business friends usually came. Johnny could not look at Dan, coming up the path, fleshier now and splendid, without smiling to himself—Dan Neill with a livery business, and thirty niggers of his own, and already a justice of the peace, all on money drawn from Beulah. Johnny couldn't say he hadn't done well with it, as prosperous looking and dangerous as a well-kept shote.

"That will be all, Withrow. Don't tell the others about Fielding," he said for lack of something better to say, knowing there was not a Negro in Beulah who hadn't known it hours before he had. Withrow bowed himself out, first to Marse Johnny and then to Miss Lydia's husband as he came up to the door.

"My, my, what a fine boy," he said politely of the toddling two-year-old who held his father's hand. "My, my." He escaped down the path.

Marriage had made Dan Neill handsome, almost sleek. He had filled out in the face so that his cadaverous weediness was gone. It was as if Liddy's fluttering hands and her nervous twittering, which had once been so gay and now was muted, had gently and subtly fashioned Dan into the outward image of her father that both she and he wanted him to be. He walked relaxed, his clothes fit easily; it had taken two generations of Beulah's women to fit the Irish O'Neills into the mold of their desires. But when Dan walked into Johnny's office and closed the door, he heaved a sigh, as if he had waited a long time to get there, and dived into his well-cut pocket for a twist of tobacco and a knife. The two men were so at home together that neither of them spoke at first. Johnny rummaged for the key to his desk, unlocked it, and brought out a jug. At the same time he stuck a stick of striped red and white candy into his breast pocket.

Dan, satisfied with the feel of his cud in his mouth, turned attention to the pretty child, ruffled and curled, but dusty from the long ride, who was standing in the middle of the floor like a small pup set down in a strange place, not daring to move until he got his bearings.

"Come here, Perry, and talk to your uncle." Johnny held out his hands, palms up, as he would have to an animal to show he meant no harm. The child toddled over and climbed, without a word, into his lap. He reached a hand into Johnny's pocket, brought out the candy, and stuck it into his mouth, never smiling.

Both of the men smiled at each other over his head.

"Swear to God, Johnny, you got a way with the youngins. Miss Liddy says if you iver quit given him presents, she'll know you're in love and goin to get married. You ought to have a passel of your own."

The child had leaned back on Johnny's lap and stared peacefully at his father over the candy.

"The gelding made it in three hours, and I niver brought him out of a slow trot, niver even give him his head. That's stamina, by Gawd." Dan spat at the highly polished spittoon. "Don't you go telling Miss Liddy I let the boy drive. You know how frail she is," he added, with as much pride in Miss Liddy's frailty as he had in the stamina of the gelding.

"What's going on in Canona?" Johnny asked.

"Oh, hell, Johnny. They're acting like a bunch of crazy folks. Everybody's drunk, marchin around. It's a sight. You'd think all the free niggers in the country was goin to swoop down with pikes in the night. They're plumb crazy. They ain't a nigger in sight. A bunch of men was sittin in front of the hotel and a Yankee peddler come by, never hyared yit what was going on. They run him clean out of town and into the river."

Johnny laughed, and then stopped. "It ain't no laughing matter, Dan. What in the hell are we going to do?"

"Nothin. This will pass." Dan sounded so sententious suddenly that Johnny listened, surprised. "They ain't got nothin to do. The ladies and the boys are stirrin up parades and dances for the Companies and God knows what jest fer the excitement."

"Why, Dan, those folks are scared to death. You can smell it."

"Oh, they been scared before."

"I'm glad to hear you say that, Dan." Johnny ran his hand over the child's curls without knowing it, and then gently removed the candy from his mouth. James Peregrine Neill had gone fast asleep in his uncle's lap. "The only thing I fear is that it will be taken advantage of."

"Not with John Letcher for governor."

"John Letcher ain't governor yet and the Eastern politicians can crow awful loud. Men like Ruffin and Wise. It's a hard day for Virginia when men like that are talking the loudest. Ain't we got better sense than to listen? The Mother of Presidents sure ended up with a couple of roosters." He handed Dan a paper from his desk without disturbing the baby.

"Northern fanatics have invaded our Commonwealth . . ." Dan started to read aloud and then threw the paper down. "Dammit. I seen that. That talkative ass Wise can't even call out the militia without it soundin like a cross between a political speech and a damn poem—"

"Somewhere there must be a sane man with the courage to speak, and the power to be heard." Johnny interrupted.

"Let me tell you somethin, Johnny." Dan spat and fell back. "John Wise wants the Dimocrat nomination for president. That's why he's stirrin this fool thing up instead of lettin it be. Playin on fear. Him and them damn nigger-loving flap-jaws in the North."

"I'd hate to be governor at such a time, anyhow," Johnny said soberly to the trees.

"You always did see the other side of the thing. Don't do that, Johnny. It weakens a man."

Johnny didn't answer. He was waiting to see why Dan had driven twenty miles upriver to see him. He knew he wouldn't come straight to the point, but would get up, look out the window, pace around it, good politician.

Dan did, after a minute, get up, set his coat straight, spit the comforting tobacco cud into the cuspidor, take out a red handkerchief to dab the last of the juice from his mouth, and begin.

"Johnny, the country's goin straight to hell." He walked to the window and told it to Beulah. "Now as I see it, the trouble runs deeper than a passel of politicians and hell-far talkers. If they wasn't somethin deeper they wouldn't have nothin to feed on."

Johnny waited. Dan was reading Beulah as Johnny had before him, but what he read was a different thing.

"All over Virginny there are farms like this, Johnny. When you and I were youngins thirty white people lived here and worked. Your paw always said when he was a boy there was even more. Times got bad. It wasn't the niggers that had to move somewheres else to work. Look at thim cabins down there. They was so full of O'Neills you couldn't wade through."

Johnny watched Dan's back. It was the first time he had said "O'Neill" instead of "Neill" in years, and Johnny knew that something had shaken him into telling what was really on his mind.

"All this land, forty niggers to take care of one family of three old women. Even the salt works run by your niggers . . . Goddammit I hate these Southron women. Jest so they got their nests goose-feathered they don't care about nothin."

He turned around, too angry all at once for Johnny to interrupt him, and went to the desk and picked up the tomahawk.

"Goddam," he said to it, "goddam. Listen, twenty miles downriver some of these folks are buildin a right smart town. You-all chasin people away. We're gatherin thim in. Your women come down there aridin high-handed and make my brother-in-law Carver come out and wait on thim in the carriage, when they owe more money than most folks got."

He had gone back to the loud voice of his childhood, forgetting all the buffing that had been done so carefully.

"We ain't goin to have it, Johnny, and we ain't goin to have no fool war to defend the sacred soil of old Virginny. We got better fish to fry. We don't like what you stand fer."

Johnny couldn't move for the child asleep in his lap. Having to sit there made him answer quietly.

"Dan, what we stand for is one thing. What we are is another. You want to be us, God knows why. We don't want to be you. Old Telemachus used to tell me the Indians would eat a little piece of a good warrior they killed so as to get some of his secret strength. You ain't gone far beyond it if you want a war to destroy a passel of land-poor folks ain't got nothing left but their pride."

"We don't want no war, Johnny. You know that, but there's plenty of us wants to git quit of Virginny. We don't want them eastern counties hangin around our necks. By God, we're the rich ones now, *don't you forgit it.*"

The old horn had been blown. Johnny changed the subject.

"It's getting pretty late, Dan. Ain't you going to stay all night?"

Dan sat down again. "Yes, I reckon I kin stand it fer one night. I informed Miss Liddy."

At the mention of her name, the new splendid Dan was in the chair again. "She's mighty frail," he said proudly. "She didn't feel up to the trip."

Johnny laughed at him and Dan knew it.

"Lord God, Dan, it ain't us who'll keep this fool prideful way of living going. It's you! What Pa used to call Kentucky horse politicians and storekeepers. Have you joined a Company yet?"

"No, I cain't see my way to doin that. I don't want to be committed. There's a right smart chance of drinkin and carousin and it upsets Miss Liddy. Besides we are pillars of the Presbyterian Church. We got . . ." He couldn't go on. He began to grin.

"Why, Dan, you sanctimonious bastard. Have a drink. You were talking so damn much I didn't have a chance to offer you one before."

It took the drink to get Dan to tell the news he had come for. Lewis and Sara had come to their door the night before. Lewis said he had been warned out of the county. Sara and the children were with Liddy.

Johnny put down the jug; Dan had not seen him look so hurt. "Why didn't they come here, Dan?"

"There was a passel of vigilantes here when they come by. They didn't dare. Now, Johnny, it ain't nothin to do with you. Times are strange."

"Poor Lewis," Johnny murmured, "couldn't even come home. Hell and damnation to it all!"

"I thought you-all didn't see eye to eye," Dan interrupted.

"Seeing eye to eye ain't got a thing to do with it. Maybe it's because he used to whale the tar out of your damned Irish hide . . ." Johnny retreated into amusement, but his movement had waked the baby and he began to cry.

Both of the men looked at him as if he had suddenly turned into a wild animal. Leah's dog ears had heard and she came rushing into the office and swooped him up.

"He's wet as water, the poor little thing. Dan, I'm mighty glad to see you. Johnny, ain't it early to take a drink?" She was already at the door again when she called back, "You're going to stay all night. It's too late to drive this baby back."

"Yes ma'am," Dan said, as awkward in front of her as he had ever been.

They settled down again when she had gone.

"What I got on my mind is this, Johnny. They's a heap of farmers and a heap of people at the mines, too, don't hanker to trade with the North no more. First place they owe so damn much money to the North that they'll secede for that reason if for no other. I was figurin on raisin some money to start a wholesale warehouse. That's where the money will be. We'll git this river runnin deep enough one of these days to bring coal barges up here. Why, Johnny, it's the thing of the future."

"How are you aiming to make them pay you?"

"Hell, I'm here, ain't I?" He studied Johnny for the next withdrawal, and reached for the jug. "They ain't goin to be no war. Ain't that many damn fools in Virginny, and it will all depend on Virginny."

"We'll have to talk to Ma, Dan, you know that."

"Hell, don't I know it? Three-fourths of Virginny is owned by widdey women, and thim damn fools to the North talkin about wearin bloomers and women's rights. They ain't niver had the net of real women's rights flung over thim, eh, Johnny? Women and niggers, lay there and win."

Johnny had to make Dan wait until he went to change his pants. The baby had wet them. Once alone in his room, he sat, trying to take in the news about Lewis. He sensed, with that sense which makes a man's face go dead with belief, that he would never see Lewis again. Lewis, gangling bitter boy, his shy bitterness turned to God as a man, who could leave his home for a single idea, driven away as a child, but who fought his fights once, and, lately, had begun to turn up in his office when he passed at night, just sitting there, looking exhausted from some struggle within himself, finding Johnny a comfort, but never saying it. Two nights ago he had sat immobile, for so long, looking at the fire and not at Johnny, that he, studying the hollows of Lewis's eyes, his head turned away in profile, thought he was asleep. He had left without saying what he came for. At the door he had muttered, "Thy will, not mine, be done," and had turned to come back and shake Johnny solemnly by the hand. He, used to Lewis's shy gestures, had thought no more about it.

He was not safe, even in his bedroom. His mother raced in, frantic.

"Johnny," she screamed in her high voice she saved, by God's grace, for crises. "Do you know what that fool Lewis has gone and done without a word to his own mother?"

He looked at her as if she were a stranger.

"Did you want him to hang around for a lynching party from a bunch of drunken fools, or to have his house burned with his children in it?" he asked the stranger coolly. "Why in God's name cain't you find some compassion for the man?"

Leah began to cry. "That's the first time you have ever spoken harshly to me, Johnny." Her face was devoid of anything but animal worry—no pity, no sorrow.

He could not touch her for the expected comfort. "Ma," he said instead lightly, "go on down. Marse Perry has given his uncle a wet pair of pants."

Chapter Five

DR. NOAH KREGG drove his gig carefully across the ice of the Gloriana. Down in the river valley the wind was not high and the snow drifted against his face softly, almost too thick for him to see the narrow carriage road which led from Kregg's Crossing through the still whiteness up the hill to the high flat plateau of Albion. He could not even hear his horse's hoofs on the icy road, and could barely make out a difference in the whiteness where twin vapors heaved out of the animal's nose from the climb and the cold.

He tried to keep his impatience and worry from making him use his whip, for fear the horse would slip on the ice; something besides the cloying river valley winter cold made his usually placid face stern and gray, made him take the valuable last minutes to think, think again, impotent and angry, what in the hell a man could do. He forced himself to consider logically, as a man of science, to remember what the old doctor in Lynchburg had taught him when, as a poor member of the Kregg clan, he had gone to learn to be a doctor in his office, because God had meant a poor Kregg to work for his training, not expect some frivolous shower of blessing from his cousins to take him to Edinburgh.

"Concentrate on the organs," the old man had said. "I never saw a woman die there wasn't something pheesically wrong. Pheesically. You leave the other to the ladies' novels."

But he knew it wasn't, in that blind snow, and in that blind despair he had to face at Albion, a thing of the organs.

For three years he had watched while Melinda Kregg wasted

away before his eyes, when they would let him tend her instead of carting her away to some highfalutin foreign doctor who took their money and didn't know the Kreggs—how the pattern of their living and dying went. He forced himself to remember, as if that would help, the pale, graceful young woman whom Crawford had brought back to Albion. The first thing he had noticed about her was that she seldom laughed, and when she did, its gaiety seemed to break through from some secret place hidden inside her. He had seen the first seven years of the marriage, happy enough as marriages went, not warm, but considerate, polite, not tender.

But then, in his own secret heart, Dr. Noah didn't believe much in marriage. He couldn't honestly say he'd seen a great deal come from Kregg marriages anyhow. It was something they had, a family heaviness, like big noses or profligacy that he had seen run through the blood of other families he knew. He could have been describing Albion itself and set down that memory to the permeating influence of the mansion from which he had tended Crawford's parents to their graves at Kregg's Crossing Church.

When the horse pulled the gig up onto the huge plateau, the wind roared and stung. It swept the snow in frail racing veils across the wide lawn, a sea of white, the strong wind clearing glimpses of the black James River far in the distance below Albion's cliffs. The horse faltered with its weight, and absent-mindedly he touched her flank with the whip to urge her on. Through the cruel veils of snow he could see Albion, huge and solid, its thick white columns so anchored they seemed to ignore the driving storm. He brushed his hand across his tear-stung eyes to clear them.

People said that Melinda hadn't ever recovered from the birth of her third child. That August day, three summers before, he had stood beside her great bed after the labor and seen her turn her face away and stare out through the great columns at the sky. Her skin was still glossy with pain, but she had that dim quiet look of hers that dared even pain to make her react. When he tried to show her the healthy red baby girl in his two strong hands, she went on staring.

Dr. Noah could hardly admit it to himself, because of the way he had been brought up, because science fought with the stern

Kregg God planted in his mind, but he had to observe, and he had seen too often that an excess of religion wasn't good for a woman's health. He had seen Melinda Kregg grasp at Crawford's God with a will of iron and lose and lose her strength to its blinding force.

Albion loomed huge above the tiny gig. He heard a door slam. One of the Negroes ran out, his head down against the battling wind, to tether his horse.

Miasma. He glanced again at the thin black snake of the James far below him. Was it true that miasma brought fever, that the land atmosphere could enter the waiting body as the wind was trying to enter him as he waited for the Negro to take his horse? Could the world a woman lived in kill her? He didn't know. He took his black bag from the seat beside him, sick at having to face them, not knowing, stripped by thought of any knowledge of the human mysterious body he might have ever thought he had. He told himself not to be a fool—simple winter fever, call it winter fever. A woman didn't have to die of winter fever.

Inside Albion's black and white marble hall it was warm, protected against the dark, snow-drifting February day. Crawford walked out of the drawing room to meet him, his footsteps echoing through the great space of the hall, and waited without saying a word while he blew the cold from his nose to keep from looking too much at Crawford's face, as frozen as the ice outside.

He could sense the young man struggling to make contact, say anything, and his habitual, "What's the news from downriver?" made Dr. Noah look up at last from the barrier of his handkerchief, bland and smiling, radiating comfort.

"It's going to be all right, Crawford. The convention's still holding out agin secesh. After all, it's six weeks since Christmas when South Carolina went. We'll hold out from both sides, damn them."

Crawford didn't say a word. Dr. Noah faltered on. "If Virginny holds out we can stop the damned thing." He took Crawford's arm and couldn't avoid it any more. "I came as quick as I could."

"Toey says she's some better." Crawford still avoided looking at him. Without speaking again they matched steps up the wide winding staircase. Dr. Noah kept his eyes on the marble head, below them in the stairwell, of one of those statues Crawford and

Melinda had brought back from Europe, as if any amount of naked statues and dim-looking paintings could keep Albion from being Albion, solid, cold Albion, where in all their married life they had hardly made a dent in its rich and bleak splendor. Beyond the open double doors of the drawing room he could see the fine old polished harpsichord with the Lacey name on it, which Melinda preferred to the fine piano Crawford had bought her. When she played it in the evening, her own face was as cool and fragile and thin as the fine notes she flicked from it and sent precisely into the after-supper dead calm. Sometimes she read poetry aloud, preoccupied, and in the last years the Old Testament or Saint Paul, while he sat, family cousin asked to supper once a month, and listened to her, punishing herself with words long beyond her strength, while Crawford kept trying to persuade her to stop and let herself be carried to bed.

Toey must have heard them coming. The quiet, dim Negro woman slipped out of the door of the master chamber and closed it softly behind her.

"I didn't want to talk in front of her," she whispered to Dr. Noah, even in the hall. "She's some better, but she jest wore out. She had the bloody dyree all night. It's quit now." She went on with a rush, warning, "Don' act like you notice nothin like that. She frets about it, don' think it's nice. I done tole her she looks pretty. She's always askin if she looks pretty!" The word was not whispered, but said in an exasperated questioning whine. Toey began to cry.

"Come on, Toey, now quit that. I need you." Dr. Noah patted her arm.

The master chamber at Albion was as impersonal as the rest of the house. Not a piece of furniture had been moved or changed since Crawford's mother's time. The great bed was propped high with pillows for Melinda's heart, and in them she looked dry and weightless; there was some new excitement which made her smile when she saw the two men, but she said nothing.

Beside the bed a little girl played with colored blocks, her pinafore tucked up above her knees, and her soft chestnut curls tangled, neglected by death. She was so absorbed in her game she didn't look up.

"I want to bleed the patient," Dr. Noah told Crawford, ashamed of himself for the act of authority he put on like a coat when he went into a sickroom, but with everything else so tentative, the act itself helped. At least, he'd always hoped so. "You'd better take little Lacey out of here."

"She won't let her go at all, Marse Noah. She jest frets somethin awful," Toey whispered again.

They looked at each other and didn't need to mention it, that part of Melinda's sickness which made her cling to the baby she had rejected.

"Crawford, take her over across the room then."

Awkwardly, Crawford picked up the startled baby. She began to cry, disturbed at her game.

"Keep her still. Let her play with your watch."

Melinda had seen Crawford. "Darling." Her puffed lips, broken out from the fever, cracked into a private smile.

"I'll be right here," Crawford said without looking at her, and began to jog Lacey until she stopped crying and watched him, surprised.

"My dear." Dr. Noah took Melinda's hand to feel her pulse, too fast and weak for him to have to time. By habit, he took out his watch and frowned. "Now my dear, I'm going to bleed you. You'll get relief from the fever. It won't hurt."

"Toey," Melinda whispered, "do I look pretty? Does my hair look pretty?"

"Yes ma'am." Toey sighed. Her brown hand pushed the already dead hair back, hardly touching it as if she knew it hurt Melinda.

Dr. Noah, getting his lancet and uncovering Melinda's arm, watched the woman in the bed. It was curious how the dying—he corrected his mind—the very sick lost personality, became so alike, suppliant, childish, sometimes pleading, but always that physical receding he could never understand, as much as he'd seen it, as if they waited to be called back, hopelessly.

He nodded for Toey to hold the bleeding bowl, and plunged the lancet into the exposed vein of Melinda's arm. Her blood flowed dark into it, lapping the sides of the white bowl as Toey's hands shook.

When he had judged a pint and had seen Melinda's face go paler, the fever flush fading satisfactorily, Dr. Noah applied the tourniquet and nodded as if he were pleased.

Toey took the bowl and poured Miss Melinda's blood into the clean chamber pot. She'd seen so much of it go there it made her cry again, but she kept on kneeling down so that nobody would see her and fuss.

"Darling," she heard Miss Melinda say, "please come here." She sounded better. Toey could see Marse Crawford's fine leather boots, kind of hesitating across the room, the heels not touching the floor.

When Dr. Noah saw the look of pure joy Melinda gave her husband he began to believe in miracles.

"Oh darling." That rapid thin voice like her pulse raced. Crawford seemed hardly to hear her.

"You were never out of my mind. I know you thought about me and it wasn't bad to do that. That's a safe place to be, in a mind. No surprises."

"Miss Melinda, try to sleep." Dr. Noah released the tourniquet for the first time.

Her voice flowed on, weaker. ". . . like holding a baby inside you and never letting it be born. But we had a baby. We had Lacey. Winsome handsome Lacey . . ." She looked at Crawford and closed her eyes.

"You don't say anything. That's because you're a gentleman. That's important." She giggled. "It's a big lie. A big fool lie."

Crawford interrupted her. The man looked awed, afraid of the tenderness.

"Melinda, you *must* prepare to meet your Maker."

Melinda was whispering. When her voice went down Toey got up and ran to the side of the bed, cold with fear.

"Aw, take her hand, please, Marse Crawford." Her begging jarred the room. Crawford didn't move. Toey took the dry hand and pressed it. Melinda's eyelids moved.

"Do you think that He will be a gentleman, too, darling? No wonder the sky is so lonesome-looking."

The room was still. The woman in the bed seemed to sleep. Dr.

Noah pushed Toey's hand aside and grabbed her pulse. It had stopped. It began again.

From the pillows she began again with it. Toey was the only one who bent down to catch what she said.

"Darling, take me out of this hotel soon. I want to go home. Please darling . . ."

She couldn't open her eyes. The diarrhea had begun again, soaking the bed, filling the room with a sweet foul bloody smell.

"Tell Crawford I'm sorry."

The doctor was too intent on her pulse to notice what she said, but Crawford heard it, and glanced at him, startled.

Melinda began to giggle, so faintly that even Toey had to strain to hear her. "I just thought of something. Listen . . ." She giggled again. The fine weak sound died. Toey watched her face flatten as if something had pushed her deeper into the bed, then come forward again, relaxed, white and smooth as wax. Her eyes were open. Toey's unthinking woman's hands came forward, caressing them shut again.

"Oh my God, Marse Crawford, she died laughin," she moaned and went on moaning as she breathed.

Across the room Lacey began to howl, neglected and panicked.

Dr. Noah led Crawford out of the chamber as he always did the husband, as he would have a sleepwalker. "It is the will of God," he told him to break the man's shambling stupor.

"Is it?" Crawford answered bitterly and leaned against the wall to stare at the old fool who could not know that for the last day Melinda had thought that he was Johnny Catlett.

When the snow melted in the western Virginia mountains late in the spring of 1861, the Gauley River rose higher than usual, even for the season. In places it flooded the late May cornfields, but as the Fincastle Greys rode farther up the river, the smaller fields were dry and the spring-pale green fingers of corn thrust up in neat rows in the dark earth.

By its size, Johnny read how far they had traveled east and north into the mountains. At Beulah the early corn had already grown ten inches in the warm rich receptive river valley. As they crossed the ford of Gauley and followed through the hill farms of Nicholas County, it was only six inches, the frail color of the delicate new leaves which made the mountains so young for a few weeks every year. He could not look at a well-planted field without pride; no farmer could. He studied and by habit wished for mild wind, tender sun, and gentle rain to raise the year's young.

A man should not go to war in the spring when every growing thing was so young and needing care. The time to go was the fall of the year when the crops were harvested and men went to fight as they would go to hunt.

Stretched out behind him on the sunny road were the thirty-six men who had joined him. After four days they rode more silently, testing the strength of their horses, the excitement, the hunter's joy gone. Once in a while one of the men broke into song to lure the others. He could hear someone behind him singing softly.

"With a wing wing waddle and a Jack Frost straddle,
To my John Bar battle to my long ways home."

The isolated song, no one joining it, sounded lonely on the narrow road, winding into the indifferent ever-rising mountains. A sweet breeze played in the treetops and made them sigh. Johnny rode with his head down as if he were dozing, to keep young Preston Carver, who rode beside him, from talking.

He heard one of the men call, "Cap'n Johnny!"

Another one said, "Haish! He's dozin."

"My, ain't he a one? He'll make usn a sodjer. He don't give a damn whether he lives or dies."

He could sense adoring eighteen-year-old Preston in his cherry-red uniform the girls designed, and his shoulder curls, turn around and grin with the men.

The new boy asked, low to keep him from hearing, "Who air he?"

"Oh, hell," the man who had been singing told him. "He's a real gintleman from downriver, owns a heap of niggers. Anyhow, hit don't matter, you're in the calvary now, boy."

The boy's joining was the first pure act of war he had seen, and even with the shock of it, Johnny had to smile to himself. They had camped the night before at a farm where a gnarled unsmiling woman let them sleep in the hay-barn so long as they promised not to smoke. They had thought she was alone.

It was hard to find a farm that would take them. Some of the people didn't want the soldiers stealing their food. Not a few had stood at the gates and stared with such hatred in their eyes that Johnny could read their feelings without asking, and rode on.

An old man had called out, "God help ye, mis'able sinners!"

One of the men behind him yelled, "Amen, Brother Ben!"

He had approached the old woman by riding up and asking for drinking water.

"I reckon what you're arter is a place to sleep," she told him calmly, looking straight at him as if she weren't the kind you had to waste time with. "Well, I'm fer ye. I seen ye comin. We don't hanker arter no free niggers burnin up ever'thing. Ye kin have the barn." Then she added, "Don't go tellin thim damned Yankee Bullers up the road. They ain't got no sense nohow."

As Johnny had stood, that night outside the barn, watching and wondering who had planted the straight clean ranks of young corn in fields all around the unpainted board house, he heard a thumping that seemed to come from the direction of the springhouse. She told them she had locked it because she didn't want any of them getting into her milk. He decided it was that stubborn plow horse of Kelly's, as big a fool as he was.

They were mounted early, but not too early to see her set the new milk down by the springhouse door. She still didn't open it.

As they rode away, he looked back. She was taking the lock off. A tall boy ran out and off to the stable, with her after him. The men reined up to watch and laugh. The boy rode out of the stable on a sheepskin saddle, straight past his mother, swerving as she tried to catch the horse. He cleared the snake-fence.

She called after him, "You come right back hyar, Jedediah!"

He was already galloping across the cornfield, riding over the tender corn he had planted so carefully. Johnny watched the horse's hoofs flail it down.

"You bring that thar horse back, Jedediah," the old woman screamed, impotent.

The boy, sixteen, Johnny judged, joined on the end of the troop, seeming to pay no attention to the men's laughter. They rode on out of the sound of the woman's voice.

"My brother's done gone to Grafton. She's about to work me to death. I been locked in the springhouse for three days. Ain't had nothin to eat but milk and it give me the dyree," was all the boy said to Kelly, who had dropped back to ride beside him.

" 'Fore Gawd," he said once they were out of sight of the farm, "hit feels right good to jine the calvary."

Johnny gave the order to halt, the sun at noon. They spread out into a field beside the road to unsaddle their horses and let them graze. He could see Preston Carver coming toward him, eager.

"Preston, you watch these men and see that they're saddled up in half an hour. We want to be in Marlinton before night. I'm going on up to the top and look around."

The boy, his red uniform now covered with dust and dark with sweat at the legs from his horse, saluted smartly and turned back to the men.

" 'Tention!" he yelled.

They had all lain down on the ground and were getting out their tobacco.

"Shut up, Pressy," somebody called. "Quit actin like you got on your big brother's britches."

Preston looked beseechingly around for Johnny, but he had already ridden away up toward the top of the rise. He watched him go, handsome, easy in the saddle, his straight body, his fine horse, his brave ostrich-feather plume casting a running shadow in the road.

Beyond the rise Johnny dismounted and tethered his horse. In front of him the deep valley and the forbidding, evocative range of Alleghenies were blue in the distance. He sank down to rest against a tree, hardly seeing it all any more, away for a moment from the men, thinking of the boy and the trampled corn.

Did a man go to war as to a lover, to a war he didn't believe in and knew they couldn't win, to suicide of an already dying country, broken and old, and young again every year, only to escape his life, or did he go because he no longer cared? Johnny felt unburdened, as if the hope of years, the pain and the yearning, had slipped like an unstrapped load from his back and left him light and empty with grief. Events in the winter piled on events: the election of Lincoln, the mindless anger and fear, the trapped feeling of a surrounded state, the efforts to keep balance, as he knew Virginia could, the final narrow vote that had severed her from the Union, with a waiting South and a waiting North poised on each side of her. Finally there were no more voices of silence, and she had flushed with fear and panic like a grouse, toward the South. He, Captain Johnny, felt swept up as a swimmer by the sudden flood of fear, but still with his head above water, trying as so many had to speak for calm.

At night he faced the new brave brag of the women around him, watching him at the table with awe, to see if he had made up his mind, as he, silent and troubled, still unable to believe the point of balance had been lost, waited to know what he ought to do. Their feminine warlike passion, born of boredom and fed on old fear and new pride, pushed at him.

The letter that Melinda was dead had come in March. After that he drowned in opinion and let himself be carried, doing what unconsciously they wanted him to do, a hollow careless civilized man, showing nothing to their prying eyes after the news.

Although his mother cried and pointed out that no man with over twenty Negroes was expected to go, that Dan wasn't going because he had a family, he could see the steel pride of sacrifice in her eyes behind her sorrow.

On the seventeenth of April, Sara drove up from Canona with the children to go back to the orchard farm for the spring planting. She told them, standing bravely in the dining room, refusing even to join them for supper, that Lewis had given up his preaching and decided he could serve God better in the Union Army. Her mother had bowed her head to the table as if she had been struck down, and Leah had only stared at her until she backed out of the room, and Cousin Amelia watched her hands in her lap, embarrassed.

Johnny jumped up and followed her to the door and took her into his arms to let her cry.

"I cain't understand all this hatred," she kept saying. "I just cain't understand it, though I pray for guidance."

She moved away from him then and, turning in the path, said, "Women are more righteous but they have less mercy than men. The Lord bless and keep you. The Lord make His face to shine upon you and give you peace, Johnny." He had stood, his heart touched for the first time since Melinda's death, until he could no longer hear the clop of her horses in the dark. After he could no longer hear her he went into his office and sat blankly watching one page of a book, too deadened to think any more, wishing to God he could cry.

The sweating mare was drawing flies. Johnny took off his hat to wave them away. When did you let go, when did you let yourself drown in the world, cease to care? He remembered old Telemachus and the nigger-belly catfish. All his life he had been trying to swim away from that great mouth, that hungry jaw, never knowing that he would some day have the energy or even the desire for flight taken from him, and stop struggling, as they said a swimmer did when he was drowning, cease to care with his body.

Thirty-six men. He was not surprised. Even when he had read with humility the broadsheet they had made up in the late night with such spirit, in a language drunk with self-deception, he had known that death never ended any argument, but destroyed the arguers, that men like Dan Neill, new men, selfish healthy men who wanted something, would survive it. He drew the broadsheet from his pocket. His orders had been to pin them up in the towns. He had given the job to young Preston.

MEN OF VIRGINIA! MEN OF FINCASTLE! TO ARMS!

The enemy has invaded your soil and threatens to over-run your country under the pretext of protection. You cannot serve two masters. You have not the right to repudiate allegiance to your own State. Be not seduced by his sophistry or intimidated by his threats. Rise and strike for your fire-sides and altars. Repel the aggressors and preserve your honor and your rights. Rally in every neighborhood with or without arms. Organize and unite with the sons of the soil to defend it. Report yourselves without delay to those nearest to you in military position. Come to the aid of your fathers, brothers, and comrades in arms at this place, who are here for the protection of your mothers, sisters, and wives. Let every man who would uphold his rights turn out with such arms as he may get and drive the invader back.

Johnny grinned. All they'd left out were the cousins and the aunts and there were a hell of a lot more of those in Virginia than there were mothers, wives, and sisters. Spirit had expected thousands. Three hundred men in the whole county had turned up.

Thirty-five men had reported to Johnny, thirty-six now, including the young boy who had escaped from the milkhouse. The rest had something better to do. They straggled behind him, the bachelors, the farmers, the rowdies, the hunters, the kind of men who volunteer—not a shopkeeper among them, except Preston, son of a shopkeeper, unlicked cub, who was still playing a ladies' image of himself as Sir Launcelot of the Kanawha.

Courage and spirit they had, but courage and spirit were not enough. He needed cool intelligence, the kind of man who could count, face crises as what the Yankees called "chores." He had a feeling that not a man on their side in Virginia had had the training for it. He would have exchanged three spirited mares from Beulah just then for one such calm man to help him.

As for arms, they carried squirrel rifles, and enough ammunition for a week's hunting, all the men had ever been used to carrying.

He roused himself and got up slowly, stiff from riding, to go back to his cavalry troop, the Fincastle Greys. They must be "calvary," as the men called it; they had horses at least. Already he was ashamed of his defeated thoughts, but though a man could be made into a soldier, his common sense would keep rising to prick at him, and he knew better than to kick against the pricks.

They found a stable in Marlinton that would take them, and several ladies brought them pies, marching down the single street belligerently defying a good number of their enemies who stood stolid, not saying a word or even seeming to watch them. After the third long day of riding, Johnny slept as if he were dead.

Somebody shook him awake. He thought he was still dreaming when he roused himself to look at Gideon McKarkle, hunkered down beside him.

"I hyared you was hyar and jest reckoned I'd come with ye. Ise on my way to Philippi to jine. Hit might as well commence hyar."

"I was never in my life gladder to see a man." Johnny sat up.

"Oh, quit that, Johnny. Grab that damned fancy hat of yourn. I got a cousin hyar who'll give us some breakfast."

On the way down the board street, their boots ringing in the early deserted morning, Gideon told him.

"Paw tole me to. He said, 'Git up thar, Gideon, and keep thim Feds out of Greenbrar. Jeb won't be no use. I don't want thim comin down hyar with a heap of Ohio free niggers pasturin their damn horses on my farm and layin out to tell me what to do.' "

"Didn't Abby mind?" Johnny asked.

"Naw. She hyared what Paw said."

A man came out of the hotel, glared at them, and turned his back and spat.

"Howdee, Mr. Jordan," Gideon said politely.

The man didn't answer.

"We don't see eye to eye over this question," Gideon explained lightly. "These folks ain't used to niggers and they don't want nary to do with the thing."

"Why I thought these counties voted for secess—"

Gideon laughed so that Mr. Jordan had to look at him. "Over next county they-uns jest wheeled up a barl of brandy and bought the county. Didn't nobody vote but fellows around close to the county seat. Some of the farmers who was for the Union jest stayed home. More'n their barns was worth. Voted!"

At four o'clock on June 2, it began to rain. Johnny's cavalier feather was the first thing to go. It gathered the rain, grew sodden, drooped in his eye. He took off his hat, ripped it out, and threw it in the road. Preston Carver, his fine red uniform now purple from rain, sulking behind because his beloved Captain Johnny was still riding with that strange mountaineer McKarkle, didn't even watch as his horse stepped on it. After the troop had ridden by, the feather lay mashed and half buried in the deep mud of the road.

They rode into Philippi up the narrow Tygart Valley before dark. The rain was heavier. The streets, the yards in front of the houses, the porches, were black with drenched men, huddling against the rain. The mass moved and jostled in the street with no place to go. It was muster day and election day together.

"Lord Gawd, this hyar is a purty mess," McKarkle told Johnny. "Let me take these men on around the river and find thim a place to sleep. You better report to headquarters. And take that poor youngin with ye afore he ketches his deeth of cold."

In the courthouse square, a few boys in the uniform of the young Guard of France were trying in the gloom to teach drill. Some men with brooms, others with branches, some with rifles, were presenting arms awkwardly, with that infinite care of men concentrating on a new thing, to a young cadet from the Virginia Military Institute, who looked about Preston's age.

"Pres—ent ahms!" He called and made Preston's horse skitter. Preston had found something new to envy. The boy could actually give orders.

"Ri—ight tun!" All shapes and sizes of farmers in homespun shuffled around to the right. The boy looked relieved.

"Pressy," Johnny told him, as they guided their horses through the street crowd, "you go on to headquarters."

"I don't know where it is," the boy wailed.

"Where's headquarters?" Johnny caught the eye of a man with a long beard who was fending off the rain, along with most of the rest, with pulls at a jug of warming whisky.

"That thar hotel," he roared, pointing beyond the courthouse square at the drab wooden county hotel, its porches, too, filled with men. "You damned officers kin git in thar. We-uns is catchin our deeth of the rheumatism."

"Press, son, you go on over there and find yourself a place to sleep. I want to ride on up the Grafton Road and take a look."

"Aw, cain't I go with you?" the boy begged.

"You're going to have to larn to obey orders." Johnny smiled, and the boy weaved his horse away through the crowd.

"The goddamned Upshur Calvary got tents," somebody grumbled beside Johnny as he pushed through the mob. "We ain't got nothin."

The mob of men was worse at the covered bridge, where they could find more shelter. Under the bridge roof Johnny had to thread his way through.

"What outfit you from?" a man yelled above the noise echoing inside the bridge.

"Fincastle Greys," Johnny called back.

"I hyar tell." The man pushed his way close enough to grab at Johnny's leg. "Hy, mister, I hyar tell we're all goin to be sent home tomorry. Ain't no guns. What the hell kind of a war is this hyar nohow?"

Several of the men around Johnny made a patch of quiet to listen to the only man who looked as if he might be an officer they had seen in the last hour.

"I reckon you better quit spreading rumors and wait for orders," Johnny called, loud enough for them all to hear.

"He looks like a right peart man," one of them said after him.

"Got a good horse so I reckoned him to be an officer," the man who had caught him answered.

"What hill's this, men?" Johnny called back.

"Up ahead. Talbott Hill," a boy sitting on the fence by the bridge answered.

"Are you a sodjer?" Johnny looked down at him.

"Naw, Maw won't let me. I'm only thirteen. But my brother is," he answered proudly.

At the top of Talbott Hill, Johnny wheeled his horse and sat still, the rain still gentle, but soaking him, and looked down the narrow Tygart Valley.

Somewhere in the past of his mind he heard a phrase. "Why, I will see thee at Philippi then." Then he remembered—Caesar's ghost to Brutus. He could hear his brother Lewis reciting it for his lesson. Tears gathered in Johnny's eyes and dimmed the valley below him more than the rain.

It looked like a sheep-run, the kind of narrow valley shepherds like to herd the sheep through to a high pasture, so they will stay together, jostling and docile. Down in the town below he could see the moving, black crowd of men, from where he sat, like turkeys in a pen.

Directly below, across the river, the Upshur Cavalry had set up their tents in neat rows. It was the only military-looking patch in the drenched valley. A toy sentry walked back and forth. Someone had seen that a long fence rail was put up, and their horses were tethered to it.

Johnny wheeled and rode back down the hill through the deep clinging mud of the road to find McKarkle, just as he inched through to the courthouse.

"Ain't this the damnedest mess?" Gideon said easily. "Cap'n Johnny, I done got the company bivouacked down the road. Leastways I reckon it's called bivouac. Ain't that a hell of a word? We found us a desarted barn. 'Tain't much but it's shelter and fodder ain't nobody tuk yit. You look like a drownded rat. Go on in the hotel." He wheeled and rode beside Johnny, his head down with embarrassment at having spoken so much.

"I'll see to the mare," he muttered when Johnny dismounted and loosed his saddlebags. Johnny stood for a minute on the crowded porch, watching him ride slowly away.

The dark sky and the rain made the hotel too dim inside to see at first. He heard someone holler, "By God, Johnny Catlett. Well, by God. I reckoned you was out West."

Lancelot Stuart grabbed Johnny, making him drop his saddlebags to the floor.

"If I ever seen a man who needed a drink of whisky. Come on."

He let Lancelot lead him to the long crowded bar.

"It's like this, Johnny," Lancelot started in the middle. "I couldn't stay in the Army when it looked like I might have to fight my own people, could I now?"

He poured a drink of whisky down Johnny and guided him to his room. There were only four other men in it.

"You have to be in the Army for a while to know how to look after yourself." He flopped on the bed. "You can share my bed."

"What in the hell's happening here?" Johnny started to strip off his sodden uniform. "First I heard we were to report at Grafton, then Philippi."

"Oh, we skedaddled out of Grafton. Colonel Porterfield rid up there on the cars. He was told he was going to find five thousand troops to defend the railroad. He got off at the depot and there wasn't nobody there at all. I don't know what the hell they expected him to do. Set on the rails and make faces, I reckon.

"He's having a bad time. You seen out there. Ain't six hundred men ready to fight and there must be two thousand in town. If you ain't got your own guns you might as well take your men and skedaddle on back home. The Colonel's trying to get unarmed men out of the town quick as he can before we move."

"I was told there would be guns."

Lancelot laid his head back on the pillow and let his eyes roll up as if he were dying. He recited, "We got a thousand cartridges won't fit nothing and four hundred rusted rifles with the caps too small. Course we could throw rocks. I never seen a Virginny farmer couldn't heave a rock."

The door shook with knocking.

"Git," Lancelot yelled. "We're full up in here."

Major Crawford Kregg, headquarters battalion, strode into the room. He was the only dry man in Philippi. Johnny felt a sickness turn in him when he saw Crawford. His face was thin and dry with suffering; he had aged so that at thirty-five he looked middle-aged, defeated; every move he made was gallant. Johnny, who had thought he could never look at him again, went up and touched his arm.

"Fish?" He made him look at him. He had never seen such bitter hatred in a man's eyes.

Crawford turned his back. "Captain Stuart," he snapped, "we need you. No strategy, no tactics. You're a West Point man. What kind of an army is this?"

He had reached the stage of exhaustion where he didn't wait for an answer. He marched to the window, his boots glistening. "How are we going to make soldiers out of these men?"

"There ain't but one way." Lancelot sat up on the bed and started to pull on his boots.

"How?" Crawford stood straight, studying the mob.

"There ain't but one way to make a soldier—gitting shot at."

Crawford turned and strode past him out of the room.

"Citizen sodjers, oh Lord, what a cross to bear!" Lancelot groaned. "I'll just go in there and listen to a heap of words out of the military manual don't mean nothing."

Johnny sat at the window until the dark had long come. He could hear the rain beating harder and harder on the tin roof. He felt sick from the hatred he had seen, and knew, because Fish was a gentleman, mouth locked against the truth, that he would never exorcise it by speaking. Forces as impersonal as the rain had shaped them, drawn the strings of their manhood as puppets; it occurred to him that Fish's warlike stance, his strut of manhood in the face of death, even that, was like the trained reaction of a dog. He could read the changes in Virginia every time he saw the man. Now Fish was hard, gallant, bitter. He knew that Fish was completely lacking in the recognition of death a man felt from time to time. His training was too complete to let it rise to the surface. Now he could never ask him about Melinda, even as a brother might. In the eyes that had looked at him Johnny was already dead, and all the whys of it lost. He let Melinda creep into his mind and rest there, lingering, until Lance came back.

"Have you had anything to eat, Johnny?" He lit a candle and its pale light flared up, throwing the shadow of the man at the window against the wall and ceiling. "I brung ye something."

Johnny heard the bed creak. "There won't be nothing happenin tonight. We cain't even keep the sentries out. Their ammunition's soaked. Nobody going to move on a night like this."

When Johnny got up from the window, Lance was already asleep.

He went to find his men and see that their quarters in the abandoned barn were at least dry. Gideon and Kelly were making chicken stew.

"We found this hyar couple of chickens, and we found this hyar arn kittle," Gideon explained.

Johnny didn't ask where they'd found it.

When he came back out of the rain into the hotel bar, Preston, now dry and only a little less splendid in red, was talking hard to a VMI cadet. At the end of the bar he saw Crawford, standing alone. He retreated from the noise to his room, tired of the sound of all the voices, tired of the questions.

He couldn't sleep. He lay, watching the reflection of the street flare on the ceiling, even that swimming with rain. Lewis driven to his decision, Dan so sure of his stand, Lance snoring lightly, peaceful in sleep, Crawford never questioning at all—he wondered in the dark if it was only he, and men like him, who were fated to be the know nothings, to question, to see beyond their attitudes, but not to speak.

It rained harder. He thought he had slept. The last sounds of carousing had died; nothing but rain, sweeping, pounding, never-ending rain. He guessed that it was nearly morning and began to drowse again. A light tap began in the corner where the roof had finally begun to leak and the water entered at last. He could not escape the tapping; it forced out thought, the ghosts running and swirling in his sleepless mind, weakened by fatigue, his father's single guffaw seldom heard, Melinda's light imp laughter, honest pure dead sound.

The sound of thunder boomed from Talbott Hill. By the time he sat up, Lance was awake and climbing into his pants. The street flashed awake outside, yelling, running, a howl of men wakened in the rain.

"The Feds are coming!" Lance yelled. "Get your damn pants on."

The cannon boomed again, heavier than the storm. Johnny heard the shell swish in the street. Somebody far away screamed.

He was the last man in the room. He ran to the window. Dark men moved as if the rain itself had become men, moved like slow flood water clogging the street.

As in other moments of his life, he knew complete stillness, the stillness of the woods, of sorrow, of night—just for a moment, acting on him. He knew it had begun and the luxury of questioning was over, thrown away. He had not said a prayer alone since he was a child. He knelt by the window, his hands clutching the window ledge.

"Oh God," he prayed, "forgive us our sins and don't let me have to kill my brother."

After he had gone to try to stop the running retreating mob, there were only the marks of his fingers left white on the dirty sill.

MARY LEE SETTLE grew up in West Virginia and attended Sweetbriar College, which she left in the early years of World War II to enlist in the British Royal Air Force. Her war experiences formed the background for a memoir titled *All the Brave Promises*. After the war she stayed in England and masqueraded for a year as Mrs. Charles Palmer, "etiquette expert" for *Woman's Day*. Since that time she has traveled the world, always bringing far corners deeply into her novels. She is the author of *The Love Eaters, The Clam Shell, The Beulah Quintet*, and a new novel, *Celebration*. In 1978, *Blood Tie* won the National Book Award for Fiction.